HOW I LOSE YOU

www.penguin.co.uk

How I Lose You

KATE McNAUGHTON

Doubleday

LONDON · TORONTO · SYDNEY · AUCKLAND · JOHANNESBURG

TRANSWORLD PUBLISHERS
61–63 Uxbridge Road, London W5 5SA
www.penguin.co.uk

Transworld is part of the Penguin Random House group of companies
whose addresses can be found at global.penguinrandomhouse.com

Penguin
Random House
UK

First published in Great Britain in 2018 by Doubleday
an imprint of Transworld Publishers

A CIP catalogue record for this book
is available from the British Library.

ISBNs 9780857524799 (hb)
9780857524805 (tpb)

Typeset in 11.5/14.5 pt Dante MT Std by Jouve (UK), Milton Keynes
Printed and bound by Clays Ltd, Bungay, Suffolk

Penguin Random House is committed to a sustainable
future for our business, our readers and our planet. This book
is made from Forest Stewardship Council® certified paper.

1 3 5 7 9 10 8 6 4 2

For Sam

THEY WERE BOTH quite drunk.

Well – they were both quite drunk, but he was *more* drunk.

Or rather – she was quite drunk, and he was quite drunk but more so, and also ever so slightly buzzing from the line of coke he had taken to persuade himself that he could still be young and wild.

All of this information would be taken down later, of course, noted and logged and filed and drawn up into medical and legal and tearful explanatory reports, but really, all it was was a detail, a scene-setting perhaps, a mild drunkenness and coked-upness that gave events some context but were hardly the point of them, and certainly – certainly – did not explain anything.

This is how she remembers it.

'Jesus Christ!'

'Whoa there.'

'Jesus fucking Chr— Whoops, sorry.'

'Adam, put that down.'

'But I haven't finished it yet!'

Adam hugged the glass to his chest and eyed her warily. It was a bit rude of him to have walked away like that with one of their host's wine glasses – they should take it back, really, but they were already at the other end of Liverpool Road, and also if they didn't get to Highbury within the next ten minutes they'd miss their train.

She reached towards the glass.

'I can't just leave litter on the side of the street.'

'It doesn't count as litter, some tramp is bound to come and pick it up.'

She moved closer slowly, as though approaching a wild animal. Adam doubled up on himself, the glass pitted into the crook of his stomach. When she took hold of it, he let go gently, slipped an arm around her waist, nuzzled her neck. She kissed him, holding the glass and its stain-red wine away.

'Right. OK. So.'

'Mm?'

'How about we get to the station before we miss our train?'

Adam was heavy in her arms now – he would crumple to the ground if it weren't for her.

'Ugh. OK.'

They set off again. The street was empty, brightly lit: London on a school night. Adam held her close, pulling her into the unsteady sway of his hips. She worried about the time. An old lady crossed the street ahead of them. They should be OK, as long as they kept walking at this pace.

She felt Adam slow, stop against her.

'Ad, seriously, we really are going to miss that train . . .'

'We can't just leave her like that.'

Adam was steady now, suddenly sober, and looking at the old lady with clinical attention. She was in a dressing gown and slippers, Eva realized.

'Oh.'

She was carrying a bundle of something pressed into her belly, and had stopped above a basement flat, clutching the railings with trembling fingers, peering down into the darkness. They walked up to her. She turned towards them amiably.

'What are you two doing out here?'

'Um. Hello. We were just on our way home.'

'You ought to get into the shelter, is where you ought to get to.'

She returned her attention to the basement flat. Adam crouched so he was closer to her level.

'What are you doing out here?'

'I'm looking for Willum, of course.'

'What's your name, Madam?'

'Ivy. What's your name, Sir?'

'I'm called Adam. Where do you live, Ivy?'

'I used to live in London, but they moved us out here when the raids started. I miss Willum.'

Adam was gentle, reassuring – he had this way with people. Bedside manners.

'Where in London, Ivy? Can you tell me the name of your street?'

Ivy was staring at Eva now.

'You really ought to get into the shelter, you know. Especially in your condition.'

Eva looked down at her stomach: flat and, she was fairly sure, not concealing any surprises.

'Ivy? Where in London?'

'Fifteen, Bewdley Street. We've always lived there.'

'Can you check where Bewdley Street is?'

Eva took out her iPhone. She caught sight of the time as she unlocked it: they'd missed the train now.

'You haven't seen Willum, have you? He can't have got very far.'

'Are we close to where you live now, Ivy? Are you cold at all?'

'Oh no. I've never suffered from the cold.'

'OK, so, Bewdley Street is just up there . . .'

'Right, let's check it out. Ivy, we're going to take you home, all right? Have you got your keys with you?'

'Mother gave me my own set!'

'Ad, she can't still be living at the same address as when she was a kid, can she?'

'That might not be her address from when she was a kid – she's probably just confused. Besides, it's that or take her to the police station.'

They walked on either side of Ivy, at her arthritic pace, Adam carrying her bundle for her. Her hands clenched their arms in an old, bony grip. And yet, there was something childlike about her, which made Eva want to swing her in the air like a two-year-old. Eva looked at the clear sky above the immaculate rooftops of Liverpool Road, and wondered if Ivy could see trails of Messerschmitts and V Rockets, smoke gushing out of wounded houses.

When they came to the turn on to Bewdley Street, a dishevelled man burst out in front of them.

'Oh, thank goodness!'

'Hello, dear.'

'Where did you find her? I only just realized she'd gone off.'

'This is . . . ?'

'My mother. Thank you.'

Ivy was still holding on to them, and smiling uncertainly at the man.

Adam looked down at her, up at the man again. Eva felt Ivy's grip grow a little tighter. Adam and the man gave each other a tumbleweed stare.

Eva saw how the man inflated, preparing to take offence, but then something about Adam – an air of authority – made him reconsider. He started to pull things out of his pockets:

'Um – here: Alzheimer's Society membership card. My driver's licence. I doubt Mother has anything on her, but if you like you can come up and—'

The licence had the 15 Bewdley Street address on it.

'No, don't worry, that's fine. We'll leave you to it.'

'She's worried about Willum.'

'Her cat. When she was a child. Poor thing died in the Blitz.'

'Willum?'

'Yes, Mother. Remember, when you were a little girl . . .'

'Well. We'll be getting on.'

'Yes, thank you. Good night.'

'Good night. Good night, Ivy.'

'Good night, dear.'

For a while, they watched the man walk his mother home, and then they turned and went on their way; but Eva could still feel them behind her, going at that frail pace, with Ivy's grip tight on her son's arm.

'Well.'

'Yes. Poor thing.'

'Yes.'

' . . .'

' . . .'

' . . .'

'So we've definitely missed our train now.'

'Shall we get a cab? I don't think I can cope with a night bus right now.'

They sat in silence, looking out of separate windows at the mesmerizing spectacle of shop lights scrolling through the London night. Eva wondered what kind of a life Ivy had led. What kind of life she led now. What was it like, to walk along the quiet streets of Islington, and for your mind to fill them with the sirens and whistle of falling bombs, with burning buildings, and people huddling in thick tweed coats? Eva wished they had asked her what it was that she could see. She wished they had gone into Ivy's world, not pulled her back into theirs: a London of dinner parties and interesting conversations, of money and professional pursuits – the Blitz as far away and unreal as China. Ivy could remember the *Blitz*.

Eva measured out her life in anecdotes, word counts, soundbites. She was a successful journalist. She had even won prizes for her lengthy, discursive articles, the sort of well-researched stuff that is consumed at a leisurely pace over Sunday-morning coffee, opening up unknown and titillatingly shocking worlds to readers stretching their toes under duck-down duvets or summoning up the courage to start the washing-up from last night. Sometimes, over dinner and wine or a pint in the pub, someone would mention to her that they had read something really inter-esting the other day and would regurgitate her own words at her in varying degrees of distortion, and sometimes she might men-tion that she had written the article. But sometimes she would just say nothing, and listen to how her work was being Chinese-whispered into the world.

There was a smudge on the taxi window which blotted out the darker forms outside and turned the lighter ones into abstract, pix-ellated shapes. Flying by in ever-changing geometries, they reminded her of the printing press she had visited on that school trip, reams of paper hurtling through air, letters and typesets and photos so fast you couldn't see them any more, and yet you could identify them, caught in a state between the blur and the defined object. Newspapers surfing the swell between events and their for-getting, clutching at bits of fact and fixing them on the contents of tomorrow's recycling bin. She was the smudge on the window, blurring the world outside into approximate glimpses of itself.

'I'm tired of my job.'

Adam was staring through his window with clenched teeth. He darted a quick look at her before returning his eyes to the road ahead with the grim focus of the terminally car-sick.

'What?'

'I'm tired of my job.'

She looked at him, even though she knew she shouldn't, because this always made him feel pressured to take his eyes off the outside world and look back at her, thus making the nausea worse.

'Where has this come from, all of a sudden?'

'I don't know. Well. Maybe I do know – I think I've been think-ing about it for a while, in a sort of subconscious way. But I suppose I didn't want to—'

'Look, can we talk about this when we get home? I really need to focus on not regurgitating all of that Jack guy's fine wines right now.'

'. . .'

'And stop looking at me, please.' For a moment longer, she kept on looking at him: her man, his face alternately bathed in warm street lamps that brought out the golden highlights in his hair, and in blue-green neons that made him look ill. The chiaroscuro flattered his jawline, still ruggedly sharp after all these years, but also revealed the thinning of his crown. This was a source of some concern: baldness was one of the few things she found physically repellent in a man, along with slender fingers, and nails grown long on the right hand and clipped short on the left for the purpose of playing the guitar. Adam's face was still handsome, though, growing more handsome in fact with the years, more manly – he had features that would age well, even twenty, thirty years from now. Eva anticipated a future of focusing on his clear blue eyes, diverting her gaze from the receding hairline.

Adam tore his eyes off the road to face her, which backlit his nascent tonsure even more.

'What?'

'Nothing.'

She turned obediently to look out of the window once more, as the cab glided to a pause at a red light. Two teenagers were wrapped around each other under the awning of a souvenir shop, their hips pressed up against a windowful of Cutty Sark mugs and masks of famous Englishmen: Tony Blair, Winston Churchill, Prince Charles. The familiar faces gaped at her with dark sockets where their eyes should have been – or rather, where Italian, Japanese, German, Brazilian eyes would one day come to give life to their big noses and plastic grins. She had interviewed Tony Blair once, at the height of the Iraq War, for a feature that had later been greatly praised for its rigour and foresight: she had challenged him relentlessly, accurately predicted much of what the conflict would lead to, had backed him into a corner from whence he would yield the finest, hairline crack of a suggestion that he wasn't quite sure it had been the right decision after all. The truth was, though, that she had been absolutely charmed by him, disarmed by a charisma she had not expected to fall for, and getting a good interview had involved more of a struggle with herself than with the man in front of her. He had written her a brief but friendly note after the feature had come out, and had always acknowledged her when their paths had happened to cross since then, his wry nods in her direction sending an embarrassing tingle through various erogenous zones. She felt it even now, as she stared at his sightless caricature, and shuddered it off.

'You all right?'

'Yeah, I'm fine – just a bit cold.'

Next to Tony, the teenagers' tongues barrelled with the gawky enthusiasm of first love. The cab pulled away, leaving them to their hormonal delights.

When they got home, she was hit with the full force of her drunkenness; she stumbled, weak-kneed, into their bedroom, and flopped on to the bed, hanging her feet over the edge so that her shoes did not dirty the duvet. The bed didn't feel quite like it was moving – more as though it had the potential to move, like a boat anchored in placid waters which you know could swell at any minute.

A shadow fell across her face: Adam standing in the doorway. She couldn't see him, but she could feel that he was laughing at her.

'Shut up.'

'I haven't said anything.'

'I know you're laughing at me.'

Adam laughed.

'I'm not laughing at you.'

'Yes, you are. You always laugh at me when I get a bit tipsy, which frankly—'

'Sorry, what was that? You're slurring your words a bit, I can't quite make out what you're saying.'

'Liar.'

Adam sat on the edge of the bed and cradled one of her feet in his lap. He undid the lace, manoeuvred the shoe off, kissed her besocked toes. He had always had something of a fondness for feet, which was a fetish she absolutely could not understand, especially since she hated her own wide, flat, knobbly ones. But with socks on, hiding the knobbles and hard skin and weird tiny nails, she didn't mind. She poked her big toe towards his crotch, but only succeeded in grazing his belly button.

'Easy, tiger.'

Adam heaved her other foot on to his lap and undid its laces too. He didn't loosen them enough, though, and yanked her shoe too hard as he tried to get it off.

'Ow!'

'Sorry.' He gave the offended foot a tentative rub. It tickled.

'Ha!'

'Sorry.'

Adam gently drew himself out alongside her, one forearm heavy on her belly, his breath hot against her ear.

'What was it you wanted to talk about in the cab?'

She thought about sharing it with him, this feeling of vague dissatisfaction that had been forming in the pit of her belly recently, but she was too tired, too drunk, and the words for whatever it was were too hard to find. Instead, she dragged him into a languid kiss.

Adam pulled softly away, leaving her lips puckered into thin air.

'Hang on a sec.'

He pecked daintily at her cheek, and then was no longer there. The ceiling glowered at her. She grabbed a handful of duvet for comfort; the cover felt reassuringly crisp and clean to the touch. This was one of Adam's most handy quirks: he was one of those people who saw the weekly washing and – this was the real bonus – *ironing* of his bed sheets as a basic necessity, like eating or breathing or going to the toilet. To him, these Sisyphean chores could therefore not be thought of in terms of effort or inconvenience: he would carry them out with brisk efficiency every Saturday, whistling as he did so, as though he actually *enjoyed* the whole process. Eva had quickly become aware of the chasm that lay between them in the early days of their relationship – even as a student, Adam had been a stranger to squalor – when, on the rare nights they spent in her room rather than his, she had observed his confusion as he lifted a dusty book off a shelf or retrieved tea mugs from forgotten corners. Sometimes she secretly missed the cluttered, messy rooms she had kept as her own; but right now, this fresh duvet cover was her only anchor against the threatening chaos.

She heard the splashing of urine in the bathroom. Flush. A tap turned on. Then, predictably, the slip of jeans, T-shirt, boxer shorts sliding off flesh. The tap continued to splutter, the tenor of its splashes changing subtly as the sink began to fill up. Eventually it was cranked off, to be replaced by the more subdued watery sounds of Adam washing his nether regions. She couldn't remember when exactly this habit had started, or, more precisely, when it had become a habit and not a funny quirk that she could tease him about. She also couldn't remember when the last time was that they had fallen into bed together unprepared, unwashed, grubby. Maybe they needed to talk about this.

And in the fug of this late, boozy night, lying in their marital bed, Eva was transported back to an evening years ago, soon after they had moved into the flat. She'd been lying like this back then, exhausted after a day of unpacking, breathing in the fresh smell of their brand-new linen. Adam and Henry had helped the removal men manoeuvre the bed into the room earlier in the day, a task that had proved far more difficult than they had foreseen, because the thing was so solid and heavy and large.

And Adam had walked into the bedroom.

'How'd's it feel, then?'

'Wonderful. It's so *firm*. And so *wide*.' She'd stretched out her arms and legs in all directions to illustrate her point.

'Well, I'm glad to hear it was worth the trouble, because getting it in here nearly broke my back.'

'Oh dear. Does it still hurt?'

'Nah, I think I'm OK now.'

And, to illustrate *his* point, Adam had flung himself into a nosedive. He had landed heavily next to her, and the bed had emitted a loud crack, and suddenly they had both found themselves lying at a thirty-degree angle to the floor.

'Oh fuck. Fuck. Fuck.'

'Oh my God, Adam, you've broken our bed!'

'Fuck.'

Eva had scrambled to her feet to examine the damage.

'Fuck.'

'Oh, actually, I think it's just a screw came loose.'

'Fuck.'

'It's OK, Ad, it looks totally fixable.'

'No, I – can't move. Back.'

'Oh, you're kidding me.'

'No, seriously, I've done my back in.'

She had helped him turn gingerly from his face-down position and get up on to his feet. Adam had stood, slightly bent, wincing with every movement he made, watching her as she had tried to fix the bed.

'I'm not going to be able to do this on my own. I can't lift the frame and screw the legs back on at the same time.'

'Sorry.'

'You really are a ninny.'

'I know.'

'Oh well. Let's leave it till tomorrow. More importantly, what are we going to do about you?'

'Could you fetch me an Ibuprofen? Sorry.'

'Anything for you, my love.'

And so they had spent their first night in their new home sleeping on the sofa bed, Adam flat on his back and waking intermittently with a whimper of pain. Eva remembered feeling oddly comforted by the whole situation, despite being made to share Adam's restlessness: it was as though on this, their first night in the home they had bought together, Fate had thrown them a small test, and they had proved themselves resilient, humorous, loving, in the face of this minor conjugal setback.

Now, the sounds from the bathroom stopped, and there Adam was in the doorway, looking at her again, gloriously naked. She grinned as he started tugging at her belt buckle.

'What are you smirking at?'

She laughed. He laughed too.

'What are you laughing at, eh?'

'Nothing . . . I just love you right now.'

The bed lost its anchor. Adam's overambitious earlier snort of cocaine had left him impotent, but it made the moment sweeter, turned them into partners in the crime of their own ineptitude, Adam flopping around and Eva swaying between bursts of energy and inebriated laziness. Eventually, tiredness got the better of them and, unfinished but content, they drifted off to sleep. Their last words to each other were 'good night'.

She couldn't remember why she had woken up. Was it her mouth, pasty from dehydration, calling for water, or had she perhaps knocked against him in her sleep, or even without knocking against him, sensed his unnerving stillness? From this point on, her memory is strange, disjointed, a jumble of images that are unbearable in their clarity and yet refuse to fit together into a coherent whole.

She lies on her back, still – so very still – and she holds her breath. The silence is unbearable. She has never felt such sheer panic. How can her body be so still, how can he be so still?

Why can't I hear him breathing?

'Adam?'

She can feel centuries of wisdom inside her now, an instinct which she shares with birds and ants and lions and reptilian creatures wading through primaeval muck, with all living beings that are and have been: the sense that, though she has not moved, though she has not yet seen, heard or touched anything, though nothing confirms it . . .

And she cannot move. She cannot disrupt this peaceful stillness, this moment that might still be the two of them lying side by side, warm, comfortable, secure.

'Adam?'

Her voice catches around the word. It doesn't sound like her own.

Her hand reaches out to touch him. His skin is lukewarm, his flesh still giving slightly under pressure but already growing firmer, as though the life has not yet entirely drained out of it, as though maybe she can grab hold of bits of it before they all slip away.

She thinks of how this normally feels, his body baked by their thick duvet like new bread, so hot sometimes she has to move away from it.

And she knows, but doesn't want to know, she can't be sure, can she, without a doctor or something?

'Adam?'

There is a crack in her voice now, a note of hysteria, like the first spluttering drops of a geyser.

Wake up. Turn towards me. You've been doing it for years. You must be able to do it now.

My beautiful, beautiful man. Your hips so slim, I always thought they made you seem a bit fragile. But your arms are strong, especially when they hold me.

How am I going to tell your parents?

She remembers the motions from a first-aid course: feel for the pulse.

I'll have to call them. And what will I say?

Check the mouth for obstructions. Tilt the head back.

And dinner with Bill tomorrow. We'll have to call them to cancel. I'll have to call them. And what will I say?

Pinch the nose.

What will your parents say?

13

But first you have to call an ambulance, before you do anything else you must call an ambulance, if you are on your own you must call an ambulance before you do anything else. Does she scream as she calls the ambulance? She thinks she might. They are so slow at the other end of the line, so calm, asking so many questions.

I'll never see your eyes again.

Am I screaming?

What will I do?

Call the ambulance, then place your mouth over his, sealing it completely, and blow in, two breaths to thirty pumps of the heart, pumping firmly, with both hands pressing down on the middle of the chest.

Who will iron my bed sheets now?

How can you do this to me?

With the first breath she breathes into him, he lets out a low gargling sound, and she pauses in wild hope, but is faced only with stillness, and realizes that it was simply the mechanical rattle of air passing through his voicebox.

I'll never feel your arms hold me again.

How can you do this to me?

You can't do this to me.

Apparently your hair and nails do not immediately stop growing. She looks at them and thinks that they are still alive, and what does this mean?

We made a promise to each other. We got married. You can't do this to me.

How much does she scream? She feels as though she is screaming all the time, but she can't be because she is breathing into him and she can hear his death rattle.

You can't do this. You're my Adam, and when people joked about it, when we joked about it, Adam and Eva, I laughed, but secretly I knew it meant that we had to be together and that we'd always be together, you can't do this to me, how can you do this to me.

My beautiful Adam. You will stay like this, beautiful, thirty-one years old, a man in the prime of his life, while the years make me old and wizened, and what will we do then? We'll be completely unsuited to each other.

You can't do this to me.

Her memory is even more laconic after they arrive. A paramedic takes over the pumping. She sits alone in the living room. There is a policeman. A doctor shakes his head apologetically. Adam is carried down the stairs to the ambulance and she realizes that they will have put him into a bodybag and she doesn't want to see it so she shuts her eyes, but she does it a little too late, or maybe curiosity gets the better of her, and she glimpses the black plastic encasing his unwieldy form, and that image will never leave her now.

And then the phone calls, first to his parents, to hers, then to Carmen, to Henry, then to countless others, the endless phone calls reaching out to an infinite web of people, and those people start arriving, crowding around her, the people and the phone calls, as though she were not now completely alone in the world.

THEY'LL NEVER TELL you this, but life isn't what it seems. Time isn't what it seems. When you lose the man you love, you realize these things.

You'll probably have been thinking that time just moves forward, that your life just moves forward, that we're all like trains chugging along railtracks stretching straight out to the horizon, with no reverse gears, and that our lives are like the landscapes you see going past the windows, one thing after another in ordered hedgerows, events fading into memories once you have gone past them.

When your lover dies, the train stops. And you realize that while it doesn't have a reverse gear, it doesn't have a forward one either. You just thought it did, because the landscape was drifting by so neatly. But now, with your lover dead, time collapses in on itself, the landscape becomes a maelstrom around you, fragments of your life, the memories, the things to come, dipping in and out of view, and you're trying to catch hold of them but they slip out of your grasp. And you're running around this fucking stock-still train, willing it to go backwards, because a few metres up the track your lover is still alive, but that's not an option, and nor is going forwards, so instead there you are on this train with everything that's ever happened to you and everything that ever will flying around the windows, stuck at this moment you'll never get away from, the moment Adam died, the moment your love died, and you realize this is where you'll always be, growing older but still the same, Eva lying in bed touching Adam's near-cold flesh, while outside the sun pretends to rise on another day.

SHE EASES HERSELF out from under the duvet, gently, slowly, inch by inch. She must be careful. She must be quiet.

Though she is not making as much noise as London is. A constant orchestra of sirens, drunken stumblings, and the string of prostitutes along her street, one at each corner, shouting conversations at each other in between customers. They sound feisty, not discontent with their lot. What other lives there are, in this world.

She moved into the flat a month ago, and at first both she and Adam were horrified by the cacophony that seeped through the window at night, the aural spillover from nearby Brick Lane. They have grown used to it now, though; now, she loves the feeling of being in the heart of this busy, dirty city, with its bankers and Bangladeshis and trendy young things. It feels like life. Life. She has a degree, an amazing job, she has Adam, she has a flat in the thrumming centre of London. Her life is beginning; it has begun.

The streets are in full nocturnal swing, but still, if she is too loud, she will wake Adam up: there is a difference between the racket of the outside world and the shifts and bumps of the person you share your bed with. She decides on a swift, clean move: all of this slow progress is getting her nowhere. As discreetly as she can, she heaves herself up, pushing the duvet on to him, swings her legs out, stands. He grunts and moves his head slightly.

Eva walks to the window and peeks out at the prostitute on the other side of the street. She looks bored. All that waiting. And then having to hand your body over to a stranger, which must be boring too, lying there waiting for the guy to finish, while you think about what you are going to buy with the money, perhaps, or other sources of concern. What your friend said to you yesterday. Needing to get that shoe reheeled. Whether start-ups are still a good investment.

She turns back towards the inside of her room. She hasn't got round to buying curtains yet, and the moon is almost full tonight, so that its clear blue light mingles with the street-lamp orange and pours over the bed, over Adam. Half of his chest is uncovered, the duvet rumpled around it, his arm thrown sideways in an elegant arc. His face is free of any of the worry that so easily creeps into it during the day; with this peaceful expression, his tumbling blond locks, he looks like a shepherd about to be ravished by a Greek goddess. This is why Eva got out of bed. She carefully pulls open a desk drawer and takes out her camera.

As she looks at Adam through the viewfinder, studies the angle of his jaw against the pillow, the small shadows he casts on the bed, his place in the composition of the frame, she thinks about how much she loves him, and this moment, this one little moment in their lives, this odd night-time interlude, is when she knows she will spend her life with this man – him, and no one else. She presses the shutter and decides to take another photo with the flash on, just for safety. But the rattle of the film as she winds it on stirs Adam from his slumber, and he opens a wary eye just as she is about to take the second shot. He tries blearily to sit up, arms flailing.

'Hey!'

Eva immortalizes the moment.

'Hey, that's not fair!'

'I'm sorry, you just looked so cute . . .'

She crawls back under the covers next to him, into the warmth. Adam wraps himself around her and goes back to sleep. Eva feels the heat of his body seep into hers, made chilly by her expedition out of the bed, feels him breathe against her, and soon she too is drifting out of consciousness, like a child gently letting itself sink underwater.

PAIN – THERE WAS nothing but pain. Eva wondered how it was possible for her not to have lost her mind yet, when all that surrounded her was pain, when every movement was pain, every thought. When there was nothing left but his absence. When everything that had once been joyful was now a source of searing misery.

She hadn't gone mad, but her head did seem to have blown a few fuses. She would catch herself behaving in some weird, erratic manner, and wonder how long she had been doing that for, already. Like now. She was standing in the middle of the kitchen, looking at the two photos of Adam in bed in her flat in Brick Lane. She had framed them together, a diptych: Adam sleeping peacefully in the gentle light, Adam comically panicked in the glare of the flash. Now she was gripping the frame so hard the blood had drained from her knuckles, and she was stooped like an old lady, peering into the images as though examining them more closely would reveal some vital, previously unnoticed detail. She wasn't crying. She didn't always cry. She did sometimes, of course: collapse into terrifying sobs that felt as though her body was trying to expel its own insides. But mostly, she felt a dry despair, a sort of state of constant windedness before the brutality of Fate.

She would notice she had just been standing there, for ages, probably, and would feel an urgent need to move. Not that the movement would actually change anything about the way she felt, but it still seemed necessary, a flight instinct even though there was nowhere to run to.

She put down the photos and looked desperately around the kitchen for something to do. Every surface was spotless – a pile of immaculate dishes sat in the drying rack: when you were in mourning, it turned out, people came and did your housekeeping for you. It made them feel helpful, presumably. Or perhaps it was a way of affirming that they were still alive: that food was cooked, dishes dirtied and made clean again, again and again, more food and digestion and excretion and dirty dishes, while for Adam the whole cycle had just stopped. Eva busied herself with putting away the clean plates.

That took about a minute, and then there was nothing to do. She looked at the calendar on the wall: 'Henry's Work Party' written on the date before he died. And then there were days that followed that, which he had never seen. And it wasn't even August any more. She took the calendar off its hook and flicked it over to September. And there, at the end of the month, five days marked out: 'ADAM IN BERLIN'.

She hadn't told anyone there – she'd have to call them. Or get her mother to call them. The thought of having to say those words again, to someone who didn't know yet . . . She shuddered, and felt once more the keening surge of his absence. He was gone. He was gone, just like that, and absolutely nothing would bring him back.

She had been struck by this thought for some time, choking up huge gulps of grief like furballs, when her mother came into the kitchen, her arms full of household cleaning products. She put them down hastily and rushed over to Eva, took her in her arms.

'Oh mein Schatz, mein Schatz . . .'

Eva felt the comforting roughness of her mother's wool sweater against her cheek, the lightness of her embrace, the words she was repeating in her ear like a litany:

'Es ist schrecklich, es ist schrecklich, es ist schrecklich . . .'

Eventually her body dried itself out, or got tired of the spasms, or tricked itself into thinking she was still a child that could be comforted by its mother, and the tears stopped. As she pulled away, Eva felt a desperate need for Adam. She needed Adam.

'I – I have to . . .'

'Eva – you are OK?'

'Yes, I – I just need to . . .'

She bolted down the corridor and into their bedroom, quickly closing the door behind her. Drew in a huge sniff of air. It still smelled of him. It still smelled of him.

Yes – their bedroom still carried his scent: in the bed, in his clothes, in the air they had breathed together. She knew that it couldn't last long: already now, it had faded so much. That smell she had so loved – she would lose that too. She thought of the molecules, microscopic bits of him, drifting around her, gently dissipating until they would all be scattered around the globe, or until they had turned into something else, some new matter that could no longer in any way be traced back to Adam. These moments when he still lingered in the room, when she could still pick up one of his T-shirts and inhale him, these were precious. But every time she opened that door and let fresh air in, every time she herself was in here, filling the space with bits of her own body, with her own smell, she was accelerating his disappearance.

Eva lay down on their bed, buried her nose in Adam's pillow, breathed in the place where his head had rested; he was still there, pungent, musty, strong. And in the midst of all this overwhelming pain, for a brief moment, she drew something resembling a small, sad comfort from this fact.

'WAIT.'

Adam grinds to a halt reluctantly, panting into her armpit. She feels woozy. The skyscraper looming over their window glints at her in the morning sun; it is as shiny as a freshly minted coin. She wonders how they can keep such a vast expanse of glass clean, and also whether the office workers sitting up there can see them. They should have pulled the curtains really, but they were too mesmerized by the neon lights of Manhattan last night, the way they made their skin move through hues of red and blue and green as though they were in a scene in a movie. Everything in New York feels like a scene in a movie. Adam pushes surreptitiously.

'Two minutes. Sorry. I just need a quick pause.'

'Pff . . .'

He lets himself bear down on her fully as he settles into the wait, throbbing impatiently. She can't really breathe properly any more, but she likes to feel the mass of him like this – it is comforting, or tender, or something. Eva is looking forward, after this, to having a bubble bath in the decadently huge tub, and then – this will be the best part – donning one of those crisp, white bathrobes. For these alone, it was worth splashing out on a night in a luxury hotel. They are thick and soft and clean, as if they had only just come into existence; it is impossible to imagine how they could have been worn already by other hotel guests, been put through the mundane indignity of a washing machine. They seem so new and innocent. Perhaps this is the real privilege of wealth: the illusion that you are living in a virginal world.

'Two minutes up.'

'Have you actually been timing us?'

22

The expensive white – everything is white in here, white without a speck or a stain on it – the expensive white alarm clock on the bedside table winks a new minute at them.

Eva strokes Adam's back, then lets her hand run further, over the thick, luxurious cotton of their bed sheet. Underneath it, the mattress is exquisitely firm. It is all so – *comfortable*. She shudders internally at the memory of the youth hostel bunk beds they have been laying their bodies on for the past two weeks, springs pushing through rough material, digging into your shoulder blades. If only they could afford to stay in places like this all the time.

They went to visit the Federal Reserve yesterday, down, down, down into the vault to catch a glimpse of gold, lines and lines and stacks and stacks so heavy they had to dig right to the very bedrock of Manhattan Island to lay the stuff to rest. And then you came back out on to Wall Street, passers-by in suits worth more than your annual salary. She wonders what the bankers made of them, scruffy young tourists agape at their mythical city. Whether they noticed them at all.

'Three, now!'

'But I'm so tired . . .'

'I'll soon wake you up.'

It comes out wrong. There is a hardness in Adam's voice that she knows was not intended, makes him sound like a rapist rather than a seducer. She squints over at him. He looks abashed.

'Will you now?'

She grinds against him, and Adam jack-rabbits into action, withdrawing briefly to flip her over and pull her half off the bed, so that now she is draped over it, belly resting in the (white) duck-down duvet, knees on the floor. The (white) carpet, it turns out, is not as soft as it looks – or at least not when you have someone thrusting into you and making your knees scrub into it. She feels a twinge in her tibia where she broke it as a child. It would seem uncharitable to interrupt things now they have just got going again, though – besides which, knees and tibia aside, this feels pretty goo—

The room shudders, as though King Kong has just jumped on to the top of the building, or as though – as though, God, as though there has just been an earthquake, or a bomb has just exploded, or war was declared during their sleep and the first air strike has just begun. She is aware, but in a distant sort of way, because mainly she is just terrified, that the opportunity for a crack about Adam's earth-shattering performance is being lost here. They have somehow both ended up on the floor, in a tangle of limbs and duvet. Adam leaps up and rushes to the window. Eva leaps up, clutches a pillow to her bare breasts, and rushes to the window too.

'Wow.'

'Fuck me.'

Smoke is billowing out from the side of the World Trade Center. It rises in a dark-grey fug which contrasts grimly with the smooth, pale grey of the building. Between the two greys, the angry orange-red of a fire; above them, the clarity of a calm blue sky. The white, the grey, the red, the blue – though the blue will not stay for long – will be the colour scheme by which Eva remembers this day. She watches, riveted, as the fire rages, and in her memory this is when she sees them, though she cannot be sure her chronology isn't a little off, because everything seems to happen so fast, and yet also to last an eternity, on this day. This, as she remembers it, is when: a man and a woman, holding hands, two small black impressionistic blobs of human being plummeting down along the pale-grey tower. The moment goes on for ever – long enough for them to think about the asphalt that awaits them, long enough for them to scream a final 'I love you' at each other. And then they are hidden from view by one of the lower skyscrapers.

Adam, meanwhile, a truly modern man, has turned on the television. This means that he does not see the suicidal couple, which will be a bone of contention later, as he will accuse Eva of having made it up, of not really having witnessed the scene directly – she must have watched them on the TV and turned it into memory, because he didn't see them, and however much she will point out to him that there were those split seconds when he had his back turned to the window, she will never be able to make him admit defeat on this one.

But Eva knows she has seen them and wonders: were they married, a husband and wife who worked in the same office, perhaps even had met in that office, the whole span of their married life framed by the Twin Towers, like bookends? Or were they colleagues who had been too shy to declare their love for one another throughout years of corporate drudgery but who now, in their final moment, had plucked up the courage to come together at last? Can you concentrate on a love story when you are about to die? Perhaps, even, they were total strangers, had never met until this moment when, with the drop outside the only alternative to the fire that was already blistering their skin, they opted for death in the fresh air, and for companionship in that death, their warm palms and interlocked fingers bringing them closer, perhaps, than they had ever been to anybody else, as close as two people could possibly be. After all, we usually die alone.

It will, at any rate, be a source of considerable irritation for Adam to later deny that Eva has witnessed this terrible, beautiful moment.

But she does not know that now.

For now, she watches the smoke rise while Adam switches on the television, and a news reporter, stumbling over his words in a mixture of shock and excitement, blares his commentary into the room. Eva turns towards him and sees, in visual stereo, on the screen before her and, out of the corner of her eye, in the world outside, the second plane. The room shudders again. Or maybe she shudders. Adam is wrapped around her, trembling, protective. On the television, a man in a suit in the bottom left-hand corner of the frame is saying over and over again:

'Holy shit. Holy shit.'

'We need to get out of here.'

They are only a couple of blocks away from the World Trade Center. They are on the thirty-fifth floor of a high-rise building. It is hard to know what is the best thing to do.

'Wait.'

She tries to process something, anything. They are high up. Planes are falling out of the sky. Planes are crashing into tall buildings. There is no shelter in the street. The news reporter talks of terrorism. The news shows people streaming out on to the street. A plane could fall on to the street – couldn't it? Which is safer, street or room? The news reporter says the president is in a school in Florida. What is he doing in a school in Florida?

Nowhere is safe.

'Eva, listen to me. We need to get out of here.'

Perhaps Adam's brain is working, because he seems to know what they should do. Their naked skins are warm against each other, cool where the expensive air of the hotel room caresses them.

Nowhere is safe, but this *feels* safe.

'Yes, let's go.'

They slide off each other, as synchronous as ballet dancers, and bend down to pick up their clothes, which are strewn across the floor in eloquent disarray. A trained detective could reconstitute the scene, from their walking fully clothed into the room to lying naked under the bedcovers, based on the location of Adam's left sock by the bedside table, the angle at which Eva's jeans have crumpled on to the floor. They swoop up pieces of clothing indiscriminately, then Adam hands Eva her knickers, which, inexplicably, he has had to retrieve from quite far under the bed, in exchange for the boxer shorts that she has found intertwined with her bra. He helps her put the bra on; then they are tenderly, silently dressing each other, slipping T-shirts over heads and buttons into buttonholes with the care of a mother dressing a toddler for its first day at school, while, outside of their silence, far, far away from it, the television drones speculations which cannot touch them. Fully clothed now, they hold each other again, Adam whispering in Eva's ear.

'How do you feel?'

'Fucking terrified.'

'Yeah. Me too.'

'I love you.'

'Yeah. Me too.'

They leave the room with the television and lights still on, their toothbrushes still in a glass on the sink, their suitcases still in the wardrobe, for this is how refugees have always left their rooms: still half alive, abandoned possessions waiting obediently for a return that will never come.

They pad along tastefully lit corridors, as peaceful and thickly carpeted as though mayhem had not just broken out in the world outside. Ironic that, on the one occasion they decide to be extravagant and splash out on a room they can't really afford for one night, they should be interrupted by a freakish cataclysm. Though perhaps this means they won't have to pay the bill? Eva steers unthinkingly towards the lifts, but Adam ushers her away – 'No, no, what if something happens?' – and guides her to the stairs.

Thirty-five floors. They patter down, feet echoing on concrete, their breath urgent now, while from the bottom of the stairwell, a long, long way down, a dim clamour speaks of disaster and historic events. The designers of the hotel haven't made such an effort on the stairs, which are pale grey and neon-lit, as though the need to evacuate in an emergency were not worthy of the truly wealthy. A word from her childhood pops into Eva's head: *Flüchtlinge*. Her mother's language is so much more eloquent on this subject: *Flüchtlinge*, 'flightlings', captures the hurriedness of flight far better than the huddled, head-scarved 'refugees' of English. Her mother, the flightling, fighting her way across an inky sea, washing up on a foreign shore with empty pockets, building a new life in a strange land, with nothing to pass on to her daughter from her home but the sounds of her mother tongue. And now, Eva and Adam, flightlings scurrying down a concrete stairwell while the sky falls on to the city.

When they reach the twenty-eighth floor, the fire alarm goes off. Adam and Eva quicken their pace, running down the stairs now, while other shell-shocked guests trickle in and, seeing them, also break into a jog, so that gradually they form a long line like adolescents hurrying to their break down an interminable staircase, sticking in close, diffident clusters for safety. The shriek of the alarm yields to the dull clamour from below as they near the exit, until suddenly they are out on the street, and the alarm inside has become the background noise, the persistent echo of a past life. Frantic hotel staff, the sweat on their faces a sticky contrast to the elegance of their maroon uniforms, run around with clipboards, collaring the guests as they come out. 'It's an evacuation. We have to make sure everyone is accounted for.'

Adam gives their names to a gangly attendant, who solemnly ticks them off the list. Eva remembers him from when they checked in yesterday afternoon: he was clearly as much of a newcomer to this luxury world as they were, the acne scars on his face barely starting to heal, and treated them with a deference none of the other staff had bothered to muster, their more experienced eyes having immediately singled out Adam and Eva as one-night cowboys, with their wide eyes and carefully collected discount coupons. They had liked the guy, and chatted briefly with him about this and that; but now his eyes pass blankly over them, as though their descent down the long, grey stairwell has robbed them of all individuality. 'OK, you're going to have to move on, please. We'll be contacting you as soon as possible if you've left any possessions in your rooms.' Then louder, to the crowd, his American accent reminiscent of thrillers and action movies: 'Move along, please!'

They make their way through the mêlée of the side street and on to the avenue. The place is awash with people. West Broadway swoops right down to the World Trade Center, like a red carpet to a Hollywood star, and so office workers, street sweepers, Starbucks vendors, have all congregated on the sidewalk to gaze at the dark smoke against the clear blue sky. Fire engines stream past them. Perhaps this *is* a fabricated memory, born of hindsight, Eva will be prepared to accept this, but she will still clearly remember the faces of the boys and men hanging on to the fire engines, handsome, intent, noble, set on the destination that will bring death to so many of them. Dotted in between the large red trucks, smaller vans bearing satellite dishes and the logos of prestigious news corporations scuttle towards the scene. On the pavements, a trickle of people pick their way through the crowd of onlookers, turning their backs on the show. They have hunted looks on their faces, and, true children of the melting pot, they are of all colours, ages and creeds. They have been here before, thinks Eva. *Flüchtlinge.* Rwandans, Bosnians, Kurds, Armenians, Liberians, Jews: they have survived because they knew when to run.

But the Americans are not running; they watch in shock, clutching forgotten paper coffee cups, shaking their heads, tears in their eyes. And their stillness is reassuring: perhaps no more planes will fall out of the sky after all.

And in the midst of this horror, this chaos, Eva senses, in a dim, instinctive way, the need to bear witness, made more urgent by the stream of refugees, which is swelling with dirty, bloody, bewildered office workers from the Towers themselves, who are gazed at by the onlookers lining the avenue before being pounced on by a glossily coiffed reporter and her camera crew. As the flow of people increases, those standing still and watching snap out of their daze and join them, swelling their numbers into an anxious, hurrying human river.

Eva turns to Adam.

'Adam.'

'Jesus. I can't believe how many people are jumping from up there.'

'I know. It's awful.'

'They must just not be able to get down. Jesus.'

'I know.'

'Fuck.'

'Adam. I want to go there.'

'Fuck. What?'

'I think we should go down there.'

'What? Why?'

'I don't know. I need to *see*.'

'Really?'

Adam searches her face without a word. He has slight astigmatism, which focuses his eyes into something just short of a squint whenever he is looking at anything intently, and makes him seem inaccessible somehow, as though a thin veil is separating him from the outside world. Eva can see them, his blue eyes, straining to understand her, to get behind her own eyes into what she is thinking. Windows to the soul, they say – but if they are, they are the tinted windows of a black Mercedes, giving only a misleading impression of translucence. And Eva's deep-black eyes, she knows, are more like tinted windows than most. She has no words to explain why she wants to get closer to the Towers.

She looks into Adam's eyes, willing her own to open up to him, hoping that maybe he can read in her what she cannot understand about herself. She wonders what he sees now; what the person he has found in her is really like. She thinks of the people who, still now, are jumping from the tops of the Towers, and the people they hold within them: lovers, parents, siblings, children. It is not just themselves that they are obliterating as they hit the ground, it is those other people as well, the parts of them that no one else knows about, the beauty only they see in them, the jokes only they share, the sins only they have forgiven. With every broken body on the tarmac lie dozens of phantom bodies, splinters of other identities that their owners may not yet even know they have lost.

There is an Adam only she knows: the one that whispers in his sleep when he dreams of teeth and gargoyles and guinea pigs, of soaring waves and tumbles through undergrowth, dreams that make no sense and which he has explained to her, to her only. The Adam who, one day when they were walking down the street, suddenly jumped out in front of a car to push a child out of its way, with no thought for the fact that he was putting himself in the path of several hundred kilos of hurtling metal. Eva can hear them now, the screeching brakes, and her heart in her mouth, and then Adam lying in the gutter propped up on one elbow, his arm wrapped protectively around the quivering boy. He has a genuine, instinctive altruism in him which he would never recognize – just as he would never recognize how judgemental he is, he who likes to think of himself as a fair, open-minded sort of guy, when Eva can clearly see in him the same quickness to jump to conclusions that he abhors in others. What can Adam see in her, she wonders – what darkness she would rather not acknowledge?

'All right.'

He turns and strides off down the avenue, so suddenly that Eva thinks he must be angry with her. When she catches up with him, though, she realizes that she has misinterpreted his brusqueness. Adam is afraid – and, seeing his fear, Eva grows afraid too. She passes her arm through his. 'We'll be fine,' she says, although she's not sure she believes it now.

Though they do not have far to go, the walk down the avenue seems without end: the crowd is shapeless, incoherent, the urgency of some knocking up against the shocked stasis of others, their movements erratic and unpredictable, like the chaotic behaviour of atoms. Every metre of pavement is a struggle to negotiate. As they get closer, a stench of diesel and burning fills the air. There is water everywhere, and the people who walk past them are drenched and splattered with blood and plastery debris. Eva feels Adam's arm grip tighter around her own, stopping her from moving forward.

It's like being inside *Guernica*: the world has collapsed into dissonant angles, fragments that can no longer be made to fit together.

A woman sobbing, hobbling urgently on a broken heel.

A twist of light debris floating by, like the remains of a Chinese lantern.

Two young men, their shirts half ripped off their bodies, carrying a third, inanimate form: rolling head, trailing feet.

A huddle of kindergarten children, screaming at the sky.

Screaming, screaming everywhere.

Running, manic running.

Blood.

She feels she cannot do anything, other than stay still and try to let the situation inhabit her.

Adam, however, is twitchy, eyes darting in all directions, an impulse towards action palpable through his leather jacket. This also she knows about him: his need to *act*.

She sees his gaze alight on something, and turns to see a man staggering towards them, his face covered in a veil of blood. It drips stickily from his chin on to what just an hour ago would have been an immaculately pressed white shirt. A briefcase dangles from his left hand like an afterthought.

The man comes towards them slowly, blinking through the blood slicking into his eyes. He seems unaware that he has hands he could use to wipe it away.

Adam gently takes hold of his forearm.

'I'm – er. A doctor. Well. A medical student. Can I – er. Let me take a look.'

The man stares at Adam without uttering a word. His eyes seem to be looking at them from very far away – another time, perhaps, or a distant, peaceful place. He lets his head be tilted back, the worst of the blood wiped away to reveal skin the same colour as his shirt.

'It's – um. I think it's just a scalp wound. It looks worse than it is – lots of blood because, well, there's a lot of capillaries under there and – um. You need to make sure you keep applying pressure to it . . .'

Adam has removed and bundled up his jumper, and is holding it against the man's head. The man is blinking up at the sky with the mild patience of a child about to receive eye drops. Adam tries to remove the briefcase from his hand.

'Here, if I take this for you then you can . . .'

The man's grip tightens, knuckles whitening under the strain; he pulls the briefcase up to his chest and cradles it carefully. His eyes, though, stay fixed on some point high above them, as though the gods may be about to broadcast a news flash explaining the purpose of this atrocious morning.

His eerie calm, the gentleness with which Adam tends to him, clash absurdly with the hysteria that surrounds them, clusters of people stampeding at every sound and wails that might have come straight from the Underworld, and limping and bleeding and coughing and moaning.

Eva looks towards where people are running away from. She needs to get closer.

'Ad, I'll just go a bit further, OK?'

'Eve, we shouldn't separate. Look at all this, it's chaos.'

'Just to the end of the road. I'll be back in five minutes.'

'I really don't think it's a good idea.'

The man emits a low whimper, and Adam, who is still holding his sweater pressed into his patient's forehead, briefly returns his attention to him.

'Five minutes, Ad.'

Eva starts to walk towards the World Trade Center.

Then a sound like thunder, a rumble that is more felt than heard, that drowns out even the howls of the sirens that have been the soundtrack to their morning. They have time, weirdly, to see the dense white cloud billowing towards them round the side of the building, looking like an avalanche that has been turned at a ninety-degree angle, time for Adam to push his wounded businessman into a crouch and rush to Eva's side, before it hits them and somehow they are lying on the ground. Adam has his arms around her, clinging to her as to a raft, trying, perhaps – ineffectually – to shelter her from the blast. Eva is foetal, her hands cupped around her mouth, and she remembers reading somewhere that this is what you should do in an avalanche, in order to clear enough space in front of your face to be able to breathe – otherwise, the snow drowns you – and she wonders if this is what she has just done, internalizing that piece of information until it became an instinctive reflex. Or did she just raise her hand to her mouth in horror, in an age-old gesture common to Greek tragedies and pillaged medieval villagers and people who witness car accidents? Whichever it was, it has not worked: there is no air around them any more, only dust, and each intake of breath is like daggers, each exhalation a racking cough. Dust is everywhere, there is nothing but the whiteness of dust, the damp sound of dust, the bland smell and taste of dust. And somewhere, behind all that dust, is the pressure of Adam's body. She feels him hacking against her, and for a while it is all they can do to lie there, and this is the moment when, really, she thinks they might die, and she almost envies those who have perished by fire or falling, because at least these are raging deaths, not the slow, painful death of asphyxiation.

Somehow, though, they scramble to their feet, and lean on each other. When their flesh touches – when they clasp each other's hands – they scrape against each other; their skin has turned to grit and dust. And they cannot talk: you need oxygen to talk.

There is a *Flüchtling* in every man. How else do they find their way in this white-out, with shadowy forms crossing their path every now and again only to disappear back into the whiteness, with nothing to tell them what is top or bottom, let alone north or south, or nearer to the World Trade Center or further away from it – how else than by the homing instinct of the *Flüchtlinge,* who always know which way to go through the fires, the bombs, the devastated landscapes, and always know that they must run away as fast as they can if they are to survive? The streams of the displaced, walking along the sides of Congolese roads while rebel trucks drive towards their villages, fleeing the floods of Bangladesh, crossing Poland as the Nazis draw nearer, crossing Poland as the Red Army draws nearer, they have joined them, and soon, or rather not so soon, after a stretch of time that is both an instant and an eternity in the featureless, airless world of dust, they are in New York again, on a sidewalk with scores of other people caked in white, the mass of them moving as one now, in the direction of the *Flüchtlinge*, the direction that takes you – you hope – away from danger.

It takes them so, so long to get off Manhattan; people have been pouring in from all directions, funnelling on to Brooklyn Bridge. And it's when they get there, their lungs thankful for the breezy air above the river, that some instinct or other makes them turn, to take stock of where they have come from, survey the wreckage, and that is when the second tower collapses, frightfully elegant in its verticality, black dust mushrooming into a thin echo of Hiroshima.

GRIEF IS LIKE drowning: there is a mismatch between you and the world around you, a chemical incompatibility. Your body is no longer suited to this climate, with its oxygen and temperate heat.

You find yourself standing in your kitchen trying to boil a kettle, or in your bedroom trying to remember him, or in your leafy, sleepy north London street waiting for the ambulance to arrive that will take his body away, and you are emitting these unearthly wails that do not sound like they could come from a human being, and clutching at the air around you, grabbing at it in fistfuls, trying to pull down the fabric of the universe itself, topple it all on to your head.

It should be possible, with this black hole that is your grief.

But really, the outside world is impermeable to your pain. Your pain stays inside you. And the universe stays where it is. And your neighbours, when they catch a glimpse of you, look away and shake their heads, and thank their lucky stars or Fate or God or an anarchic combination of ungoverned circumstances that such tragedy has not fallen upon their house.

THE DOORBELL RINGS, in exact synchronicity with the silly, two-tone wink of an ICQ message. Eva jumps, uncertain which to deal with first, then looks at the flashing icon: it's Adam. She opens the message.

So I have news!

Hello. What news?

Oh yeah. Hello

How's things going out there?

OK so long story, but I've been doing some work for this guy at the Max Planck Institut here

Things are going good btw

She hears the brief, wet sound of suction in front of her, as though an octopus has just attached itself to her bedroom window. And sure enough, the glass is filled with the squidged-up forms of lips, a nose, half a cheek and, most disgustingly, a grey-red tongue. Eva has never understood why people do this: it is unhygienic, and the glass afterwards is left smudged with sweat and grease. And it creates disturbingly monstrous forms out of familiar faces.

Carmen disengages with a plop and, now almost looking her usual self – her skin is slightly flushed down the side of her face that has been in contact with the window – she grins proudly at Eva, like a golden retriever that has just deposited a particularly large stick at its owner's feet. Eva wrestles the window open. Carmen sticks her head in, still beaming, the sash window hovering menacingly above her, which makes her look like a golden retriever that has unwittingly placed its head inside a guillotine. Carmen is, generally, very reminiscent of a golden retriever – or would be if she did not have quite such formidable brains.

'Is your doorbell bust or something?'

'No, sorry, it's just Adam ICQed me right as you rang.'

'Well, you going to let me in or what?'

'Yeah, hang on, two secs . . .'

2 secs, Carmen here, got to let her in

Carmen has vanished – you might think Eva had imagined her apparition, if it weren't for the greasy trace she has left splurged across the window.

OK

Eva wonders if the rain will wash it away eventually. She doesn't really want to be staring at the world through a smudge of her friend's sebum every time she looks up from her computer.

The doorbell rings again. She runs over.

'Carm in, Carmen.'

'You're taking your time today.'

'Sorry – Adam's got some sort of announcement he wants to make.'

'Oh my God. He's not pregnant, is he?'

'Hi, by the way.'

'Hi. So, go chat to lover boy, I'm bursting for the loo anyway.'

'Mi casa es su casa.'

When she gets back to the computer, Adam's next missive is bleeping on the screen.

And so anyway they've got this research project they really want me to help out on – it wouldn't be a huge amount of work, I can easily fit it around my hospital job – I'd just need to come out to Berlin every few months, isn't that perfect? I was thinking we could even rent a small flat out here, and then have it like a second base to come to – anyway, to be discussed when you're over. Have you booked your tickets yet?

Ah.

Wow, that's great Ad – well done.

It's a while before Adam responds.

Sorry, was making myself a cup of tea. So, when you coming over?

This is tricky. Eva, has, in fact, been trying to answer Adam's question; fragments of messages have, unbeknownst to him, appeared and disappeared on the screen in front of her as she tests out her feelings, cutting and pasting them in and out of one another, attentive to the different ways they resonate depending on how they are agenced together, but never quite sounding right, never quite encapsulating what she really thinks and feels, never quite producing the effect she wants. She doesn't want to disappoint him; she wants him to understand.

Yeah, so about that . . .

Adam, I've been thinking about this, and I'm not sure I'm ready to come to Berlin yet.

Look, I know it's hard for you to understand, but—

Look, I'm not sure I can even explain it to myself, but I don't really want to come to Berlin – I don't know, maybe I'm worried I'll upset my mum.

Look, I think it's great you're so enthusiastic about all this—

Look, I've been thinking about this a lot . . .

Adam, I'm afraid—

OK, so I know this sounds insane, but I'm afraid I might come over and you'll speak better German than me and you'll know the place inside out and—

Eva? You still there?

'So how's the old banana doing?'

Yeah, sorry, Carmen here so hard to focus.

'Good. He's just been offered some sort of research job in Berlin.'

Oh yeah, of course – say hi!

'He says hi.'

She says hi back.

'A job? What, he's going to move out there?'

'No, it's, like, a thing he'd just have to go over for now and again – some sort of research project.'

'Wow. Cool.'

How is she?

'How are you?'

'Hunky-dory.'

Hunky-dory.

'When you going out there by the way?'

'Pff . . . I don't know. I'm not sure I'm going to be able to, after all.'

'What, really?'

'Yeah, it's just – I've got so much on at the moment, and I feel like, you know, I need to get things right otherwise they'll realize they've made a terrible mistake and hand my column over to someone who actually has a clue about journalism.'

'Eva, you're doing fine.'

Hello? I know you two are just nattering away there . . .

'Anyway, if Adam is going to be going there regularly in future, it's no big deal if I don't go over now.'

Yeah, sorry.

'He'll be disappointed, though.'

'Yeah, I know.'

It's cool – I'll leave you to it, got stuff to get on with anyway.

Ping me later re: trip? I'm going to be online all afternoon.

'Hang on two secs.'

Yep, will do.

Love you.

Love you too – well done again.

Thanks.

Carmen is looking at Eva intently, her head slightly cocked to the side.

'What? Why are you looking at me like that?'

'Why don't you want to go to Berlin?'

'I told you, I've just got too much on my plate right now . . .'

'You look stressed out.'

'Yes, well, which proves my point, doesn't it?'

'I mean more stressed out than just work stress. Is everything OK?'

40

Bloody Carmen. Knowing Eva so bloody well. Being able to bloody read her so accurately.

'I'm – I don't know, I feel weird about it.'

' . . . '

'I guess maybe I've always thought the first time I'd go to Berlin it would be with my mother, and I'm not sure I want it to be with Adam instead.'

'Why?'

'Because – I don't know, it's like it's a place that belongs to *my* family, you know? My history. It's got a meaning for us that it doesn't have for him.'

'OK – I guess that sort of makes sense.'

'Please don't tell him I said that, though.'

'I'm sure he'd understand.'

'Well still – don't.'

'OK.'

' . . . '

' . . . '

'By the way, you are cleaning up that smudge on my window when we get back.'

'What smudge?'

'There. Where your *face* was. Man, you have a greasy face.'

'Swarthy roots, what can I say? Do you even own any window-cleaner, Mrs Domestic Goddess?'

'We'll pick some up while we're out.'

'Is Henry joining us, by the way?'

'Oh yeah, he said he should be able to – I'll give him a bell.'

THE DOORBELL RANG. It did this frequently. It did this all the time. People would come in, bearing pots of stew, fresh milk, expressions of concern. They were all so exhausting. Did they not understand that none of them was Adam?

Eva's mother jumped up.

'I go.'

Eva's dad looked up from his paper. How could anyone read a paper, at this time? Even keeping her concentration for the length of a single article was beyond Eva's ability. But then, she supposed, Adam had not been the other half of her parents' life, just a pleasant and reliable son-in-law. It was strange – that they were here for her, really, not for Adam at all, however fond they may have been of him.

She wondered, conversely, what role she would play in Adam's family now. She had grown to feel a part of their loud, expansive tribe, but could she still belong if all that connected her to them was an absence, a memory?

Was her family now reduced back down to this shrunken trio?

She heard a booming voice greeting her mother at the other end of the corridor – even rent asunder by grief, Henry couldn't talk at a normal volume.

'Would you like a cup of tea, Henry?'

'Oh, er, yes, thank you, Mrs Bard. Hello, Mr Bard. Hello, Eva.'

'Hi, Henry.'

Henry, like Eva, carried the marks of Adam's death on his body: he too had stopped eating, and his face looked almost gaunt, the flesh melting from his heavyset frame. He had worn an expression of constant bewilderment since Adam had died, as though he was in the process of working through a particularly knotty philosophical problem. Which, in fact, Eva supposed, they all were; the dispiriting thing was that it did not look like they were about to find any answers. She imagined she probably wore much the same expression as Henry did.

Henry sat down at the table and stared absent-mindedly at the cup of tea Eva's mother had placed in front of him. 'So there's some news from the doctor, I gather?' He didn't like to use the word 'autopsy'.

Eva's father folded up his paper. This was a subject he felt confident talking about: the tale of his investigations and phone calls, the reassuring facts of what had been said to whom when, what bureaucratic obstacles were being put in his way. They were all relieved by it – it was something tangible everyone could focus on together.

'Not a huge amount, I'm afraid. You wouldn't believe the administrative hoops I've had to jump through . . .'

Knives cutting through Adam's flesh. His body on a cold, steel slab. His body in that black bag. His body, in the sense of corpse, not in the sense of 'Ooh, he's got a nice body.'

His – yes, his corpse.

An autopsy, just like on TV. Life had become as unreal and preposterous as TV.

'He still thinks it was most probably a heart attack, but they're still not sure what caused it, or rather, he wouldn't really tell me anything – he said we have to wait for the final results. I'm going to keep pressing him to keep us updated, though. It's unbelievable how long it's all been taking.'

'Yes.'

'Henry, come with me for a sec. I'd like to give you something.'

Everyone looked surprised – it was true Eva spoke little these days. The sound of her voice had a rusty, foreign edge to it, even to her. Henry nodded wordlessly, and they both rose to their feet. Often – well, all the time, really – she felt as though she were floating, as though the world around her had taken on a strange, unreal texture, like a cross between cotton wool and porridge: sounds seemed dampened and distant, and her movements felt slowed, as if she were pushing through something thicker than air, and everything looked hazy. Often she felt as though she were the one who had become a ghost – she, and everyone else around her – and Adam was the only person who was actually made of flesh and blood.

Eva and Henry floated down the corridor and into the bedroom. Henry sat down on the bed and looked around with distant eyes, as though he too were watching the world through a gauze-like veil. Eva closed the door, and felt the strange new breed of intimacy this gesture created between her and her old friend: it wrapped them both in their own sorrow, sent it reverberating around the room with nowhere to escape to.

Henry let his shoulders sag.

'I still can't believe it, Eva.'

'I know.'

'. . .'

'. . .'

'It's just . . . I don't know. Feels like it can't possibly be real.'

'. . .'

'. . .'

Eva let herself slip to the floor, her back against the heavy wood of the wardrobe, the thick carpet dense and comforting beneath her: all the warmth and solidity of home, and yet she felt as if she had been cast out into a windy and unforgiving sea.

Henry looked around at the wardrobe, the carpet, the window.

'It's weird, I look at this room, and I remember – do you remember, when we brought the bed in here?'

'It would be difficult to forget it . . .'

'Yeah. The thing was a fucking nightmare. But, you know – I just remember Adam being so happy that you guys finally had a place of your own, how proud he was that we were having to break our backs hoiking this solid oak bed around . . . It feels like it was just yesterday, and now this . . . It's just so . . . It's so unfair.'

'Yes.'

'It's so unfair.'

'. . .'

'Eva, I . . . There's something I need to talk to you about.'

'Sure . . .'

'I . . . I can't stop thinking that maybe it's because of the coke. That Adam – that he died.'

'But they've already told us it's not – right at the start. They said the quantities they found in his blood were minimal.'

'But what if he – I don't know – had a really low tolerance to it? I mean – a heart attack . . .'

'They've already said that amount of coke wouldn't have affected someone with a healthy heart – that there has to have been something underlying. Besides, it's not like Adam had never taken coke in the past.'

'It's not like he took it every weekend either, though. And it was my fault – I'm the one who took you guys to that party. I'm the one who . . .'

'. . .'

'I mean, I basically just took a line to impress my colleagues. I didn't even feel like it. I was just like, I don't know, oh God these cool young new traders, I don't want them to think I'm some boring, straight-laced old . . .'

'Well, Adam took his own decision to do a line too. Probably for similar reasons.'

'He wouldn't have done it if I hadn't, though.'

'I wouldn't be so sure about that.'

'But I took you guys to the party. What if I hadn't invited you, Eva? He might still be with us now.'

'What if I'd woken up while he was having the heart attack rather than hours after?'

'. . .'

'What if it had happened while he was working, surrounded by colleagues who could have reanimated him right away? What

if he'd had a check-up with a cardiologist that time he did a tri-
athlon and felt a bit weird afterwards? What if his GP had realized
it might be a sign of something serious?'

'. . .'

'There are so many what ifs. We could drive ourselves crazy
with what ifs.'

'I'm sorry, Eve. I'm not trying to make this about me. I just
keep looking back and wishing there was something I could have
done differently, something that would have prevented it . . .'

'I know. So do I.'

'. . .'

'Nothing is your fault, Henry. Nothing is anybody's fault.'

'. . .'

'. . .'

'I talked to our priest about it at the weekend, you know.'

'About the coke thing?'

'No, I . . . I can't really bring myself to even think about that,
to be honest – I just wanted to talk to you about it because . . .
because I don't want you to think I'm shirking my responsibil-
ities. If I've had any part to play in this, I'll . . . I'll face up to it.'

'. . .'

'. . .'

'So what did you talk to your priest about?'

'Just about – well. About Adam being . . . gone.'

'Was he any help?'

'Not really. I just don't understand how God could let something like this happen.'

'But you knew these things happen, Henry. Worse things,
even. Children die.'

'Yes, but – you know. It's easier to accept, when you're talking
in a general sense, that the world has to be like this. That we have
to be tried somehow. But when it actually happens . . . and Adam
was such a good man. A fundamentally good man.'

'Yes.'

'. . .'

'What did your priest say?'

'Well. You know. That God moves in mysterious ways. That I was allowed to be challenged by it, that it's only through being challenged that our faith becomes stronger. And we talked a lot about Adam. About how he had lived a good life, and that its being short didn't take meaning away from that.'

'. . .'

'Eva – can I ask you something? It may be a difficult question – I don't know.'

'Of course.'

'How do you cope with this, not being religious? I don't know how I'd manage if I didn't have my faith to hold on to.'

'But you've just said it challenged your faith.'

'Well, yes – it has. But . . . It's hard to explain. I feel my faith in God has been shaken, but that doubt, those uncertainties, that anger – they're still directed at him. It's like – I don't know, it's like being a teenager and rejecting your parents, rather than being an orphan and not having any parents to reject.'

'It gives you a framework for those emotions.'

'Yes, I suppose so. And I feel less alone with it. I feel like what I'm going through is in a dialogue with someone. Even when God isn't answering me – at least there's someone doing the not-answering.'

'I – I don't know if I can really get my head around what you're describing. I've just never had that sort of belief. I'm not sure I can imagine what it would be like.'

'. . .'

'Do you think Adam is still here, Henry? That you'll meet him again?'

'Yes. Yes, I think I do. I mean, not in a simple way – and I have moments when I question it, when I'm so angry with God I want to reject it all. But yes. I think his soul is still there, somewhere. I can feel his presence . . . Sitting here now, I can feel he's here.'

'So can I. But I'm not sure what I'm feeling is an immortal soul. It could just be our memories, our love for him.'

'You don't believe you will ever meet him again?'

'I just – I can't. I can't make myself believe that. I wish I could.'

'I'm sorry. I didn't mean to upset you.'

'No, it's fine. Everything upsets me these days anyway.'

'. . .'

'Oh. Henry.'

Eva got up, and again the world felt opaque, dense, around her. She opened Adam's half of the wardrobe, where his shirts and suits hung like faint echoes of him.

'I was thinking, looking at you just now . . .'

Henry got up and came to stand beside Eva; they both contemplated these sad, textile relics.

'I was thinking, there's this coat Adam bought . . .'

She pulled it off the rack, her hand faltering slightly under its deadweight.

'It was too big for him, we were going to go and change it – but I think it would probably fit you fine.'

'Oh. Eva. Are you sure? I . . .'

'I think it would be nice for you to have it.'

Henry slipped into the coat, the thick wool seeming to take on a personality of its own with this flesh and bone to fill it out. It fitted him perfectly. On Adam, it had looked faintly ridiculous, as though he had eaten one of the cakes from *Alice in Wonderland* and shrunk a few sizes.

'It looks nice.'

Henry sized himself up in the mirror.

'Thanks, Eve. If you're sure, I . . . This would mean a lot to me.'

Eva felt the tears well up in her eyes and the world drown out around her, and Henry take her in an awkward embrace, his arms made stiff by the dense wool of his fine new coat.

THERE ARE SO many ways to die.

You might miss the lights changing and step out under a revving engine. You might get stabbed in the liver by a maniac, get caught in the crossfire of a shootout, fly through the windscreen of a crashing car, be sitting on an exploding plane. You might stop off for lunch on a whim and get fatal food poisoning from the chicken soup. You might be having a shower and slip and bang your head against the murderous enamel.

There are even, you have discovered, many ways to die in your sleep. You might take an aspirin before going to bed and bleed painlessly, internally, until everything has emptied from your veins. You might have had an aneurysm in your brain waiting to rupture your whole life. You might have mistakenly overdosed on any number of illegal drugs, or deliberately overdosed on any number of legal ones. Yes, you might have wanted to die, without your family or your friends or your wife ever suspecting that you were terribly, terminally desperate. Or you might, as it eventually turned out Adam did, have had a heart that was too large, too thick with muscle fibre, so that eventually your big, big heart just stopped beating. You could, like Adam, have had a mechanical defect that extinguished you, your laugh, your smile, your soul, out of existence. Because life is that fragile, and there are so, so many ways to die.

THEY TUMBLE ON to the train just as its doors are beeping shut, out of breath, clammy from their dash to the platform. Adam heads straight to a free table and creates a mound of backpack, Saturday newspaper, water bottle, snacks, on the seat by the aisle. When he turns towards her, to check she's following him, Eva is filled with wonder: look at him. Look at how beautiful he is. Those wild, golden locks, those vibrant blue eyes, his panting smile at having made the train after all, and them being together on it, and this summery weather – look at him. He waits for her in the aisle, grinning in the midst of these tired commuters, reaching to the seats for support with a grimace of exaggerated surprise as the train lurches forward, and Eva laughs as she is thrown into his arms. She clutches his firm, slender waist and breathes in the wonderful smell of him. He kisses her. Sometimes, when they kiss, she finds herself wishing there was something she could do to get even closer to him, because even when they're kissing, their lips and tongues stay separate from each other, there is still a point where one of them ends and the other begins. Sometimes she wishes she could clamber into him, be a part of him completely.

'Excuse me.'

There is a man behind them with a briefcase and decades of weariness weighing on his shoulders. He looks at them without animosity from within the confines of his suit: he merely needs to get past them, get home, get changed into something more amenable to these sweltering temperatures.

'Sorry!'

Adam clambers over his mountain of stuff into the window

seat, and Eva takes the one opposite him. They reach out with their feet, entwine their legs. Ever since they started going out, they have needed to touch each other – look at him. How could you see Adam, and not want to reach out your hand to run it through his hair, or across his cheek, or down his arm? How could you be sitting across from him in a train carriage and not need to feel your foot nestle into the side of his knee?

They share out bits of newspaper, and before long Adam has fallen asleep and Eva is watching him as his head rolls with the unpredictable movements of the train, his face splattered with shifting light from the sun shining through the trees outside. She wishes she could climb over the table and melt her body into his; she wishes she could see what dreams are prompting the twitches and subtle shifts of expression that pass over his face. She marvels at the density of Adam, that he is a being of flesh and blood in front of her, who she would be able to smell if she leaned forward, whose body heat she can feel under the sole of her bare foot.

Adam slowly stirs awake, and smiles.

'What you looking at?'

'You, you sexy devil.'

Adam yawns and stretches. Eva watches his arm curl out into a tense, straight line, the fibre of muscles flexing underneath his skin, the golden hue his forearms have begun to develop since the sun started to come out.

'Aah. I'm really looking forward to meeting your parents, Eve.'

'Really? Why's that?'

'Dunno – just curious to see the old blocks you've been chipped from, I guess.'

Adam beams, and looks contentedly out of the window, while Eva feels a flush of anxiety surge up within her: what if her dad starts chewing Adam's ear off with a long exposition of the latest negotiations that have been animating the local council? What if her mum is, well, weird? What if Adam sees how limited the horizons of her life have been until she went to university, and is disappointed in her?

'Seriously. I feel I should warn you.'

'About what?'

'Just – my parents. They can be so lame sometimes.'

'Hey, if you want lame, I have lame. My mum goes to flower shows and listens to Phil Collins.'

'Your mum's, like, a barrister! That's pretty cool. And she wears all those Yves Saint Laurent suits.'

'She has one Yves Saint Laurent suit. The rest are all Marks and Spencer's, probably. And come on – Phil Collins. I bet your mum listens to Kraftwerk or something.'

'All I'm saying is I think you need to lower your expectations. And also, for the record, I am nothing like my parents.'

'I bet that's not true.'

'Well, I just mean – if you think they're lame, don't assume I'm lame too.'

'I would never assume that. I think you're amazing.'

'Hold on to that thought.'

Eva's dad is waiting for them in the station car park. He is standing next to the car, and they both look so small: him, the car. He needs a haircut, too: his hair is wispy, flying around in the wind. He exclaims in exaggerated joy when he sees them: 'Aha!' – like bloody Alan Partridge or something – and bustles over, shakes Adam's hand nervously.

'And you must be Adam. Lovely to meet you.'

'Lovely to meet you too, Mr Bard.'

'Hello, darling.'

'Hi, Dad.'

Eva gives him a brief, awkward kiss on the cheek. She can feel her face flush.

'So! Can I take any of that off you, Adam?'

Her father grabs for one of the bags hanging off Adam's arm

and sends the newspaper flying out of his hand. It spreads in mid-air, shedding adverts and supplements. The heavier items fall to the ground, while the lighter ones blow over the car park in erratic gusts.

'Oh dear. Oh sorry. Oh shit.'

'Oh, er – no, well, don't worry . . .'

Adam is frozen to the spot, both arms encumbered by the numerous items he has been carrying, trying to prevent anything else from falling to the ground. Eva sets her bag down on the sections of newspaper closest to them, then starts gathering up the ones that are blowing away. Her dad has rushed after one particularly nimble, single sheet, which flutters along a few extra feet every time he reaches out to grab it. He is half bent over, half tottering along, his expansive arse straining against the seat of his trousers.

'Here, grab these, could you?'

Adam has finally managed to disengage from the plastic bags hanging off his wrists, the rucksack balanced on his shoulder – he thrusts them at Eva, and runs over. His long, slender limbs swing effortlessly through the air: he is like a stag, easily over-taking the slow, boar-like form of her father. Adam swoops in, grabs the guilty piece of paper, says something to Eva's dad, who says something back to him, and they both laugh, and continue to talk and laugh as they walk back towards Eva, but she can't hear what they're saying.

Then they all get into the car, Adam on the back seat next to several stacks and bundles of Labour flyers, posters, leaflets.

'Wow. That's a lot of election material you've got here, Mr Bard.'

'We've got to give it our all, Adam. This really could be our chance to beat the Tories at last.'

'I thought that was already a foregone conclusion?'

'Oh, Blair will win the Commons, of course. I'm talking about the local elections here – this is an old Tory stronghold, but it's just about possible we might manage to change that this time round.'

'Right.'

'You interested in politics, Adam?'

'Yeah, I guess so. I mean – my older brother is quite active in the Labour Party, so, you know, I hear a lot about what's going on from him.'

'Really! Whereabouts is he based?'

'Oh, he's in London – but he'll be standing in South Shropshire.'

'An actual candidate? My, my. Safe Tory seat, though, isn't that? I guess they're giving him a test run to see how it goes?'

'Yes, that's exactly it. He's really passionate about it all. Personally, I read the papers and all that, of course, but I find the international news more interesting than the domestic stuff, you know? But I'm looking forward to voting. It'll be my first time.'

'The first vote I ever cast was for Harold Wilson, back in 1970. Ha! We all thought Labour would sail through . . . But I know what you mean about the allure of international news: I certainly cared a lot more about Vietnam than about stuffy old Edward Heath. Then, as you grow older, you realize that local politics are just as important as national or even international events: it's all part of the same fight. Here, for example, us Labour councillors have been trying to get more affordable housing built in the area we're driving through right now: this is something that would have a real impact on people's lives; just as real as one country declaring war on another. It's just not as sexy as warfare.'

'Well, but – people *die* during a war.'

'You think people don't die from not being able to afford a roof over their head?'

'OK, yes. I see your point.'

'Don't underestimate the power of the local, Adam.'

'He says that, like, all the time. It's one of his pet phrases.'

They are sprawled out on the narrow single bed in Eva's

bedroom – the room she grew up in, its walls still plastered with posters of horses and Kurt Cobain.

'Well, I mean, he's right though, isn't he? Most people's lives are influenced by decisions that are made at a local level, not by these big international conferences or negotiations or whatever.'

'Tell that to the people of Bosnia.'

'Well yes, but – what if you're not in Bosnia? What if you're a Bosnian who's fled to the UK and can't afford to pay for a flat here? What if you end up on the street and die of hypothermia – OK, you haven't been bombed or shot or whatever, but you're still dead.'

'Yeah, sure, no, I mean I've heard this argument a thousand times before . . .'

'I think it's really cool your dad is into all this stuff.'

'It's just – it seems so parochial, most of the time. Like, he'll get so worked up about some detail in a planning permission and go on and on about that for weeks on end, and really then you have to be, like, hey, there are more important things going on in the world than, like, whether the fence is here or fifty centimetres further to the side.'

'Well, I mean, maybe in Bosnia a fence fifty centimetres further to the side is the difference between getting a bullet through your head or not.'

'But that doesn't contradict my point! What I'm saying is, there've got to be ways of having an impact on the world that are – I don't know. More *spectacular* than what my dad does.'

'But – why does it need to be spectacular?'

'OK, maybe spectacular is the wrong word. More – I don't know. More intense, or something. More *alive*. I don't feel like my dad is very alive.'

'He seemed pretty alive to me. And, you know – engaged. Trying to make the world a better place, in his own way. We can't all be Tony Blair.'

'But maybe we should all at least be trying to be Tony Blair?'

'Well, what would Tony Blair do then, though? Without people like your dad to make sure the fences are in the right place?'

'There'll always be people like my dad.'

Downstairs, the front door clicks open.

'Oh. There's my mum.'

'Huh? How do you know?'

'I just heard the front door.'

'Really? I didn't hear a thing.'

These sounds that are so familiar, that have been the rhythm to her childhood and adolescence: she knows each door, its breaks and creaks, she knows how the sounds of footsteps change when they pass from the corridor floorboards to the living-room carpet. She feels like they are all she knows. Adam, at least, grew up within striking distance of Central London, and has that big-city nous about him, that street wisdom. Eva feels sleepy and cossetted, like this room around her: small, reassuring. In lieu of teenage rebellion, she had music magazines and books and those tapes lined up on the shelf, compilations carefully recorded from the radio, with the beginning of the song missing because of the lag before you pressed Record, and the end because they would fade out before they were finished. She picks up one of the tapes: it's covered in bright stickers that she'd had left over from her Panini-collecting days, and, in tag-like lettering: EVA'S BEST SONGS EVA. Adam takes the tape out of her hand and giggles.

'Hey, you need to get together with my mum, you guys have pretty similar taste in music . . .'

'Shut up. That's from when I was, like, twelve or something.'

'Before you'd discovered Nirvana.'

'Exactly.'

'What were you doing on the day Kurt Cobain died?'

'Crying, mainly. I flunked a maths test because of it.'

'Just think. Maybe you could have been a great mathematician if Kurt Cobain hadn't killed himself.'

'I think it would be very unfair on Kurt Cobain to blame my mathematical failings on him.'

'. . .'

'At least he did something spectacular.'

'Why are you so concerned with everything needing to be spectacular today?'

'I don't know. I guess it's being back here, and being hit by how unspectacular my family is . . .'

'Your mum has one of the most spectacular stories I've ever heard!'

'Well – she did initially. She hasn't exactly done anything spectacular with the rest of her life, though.'

'I'm starting to get worried by how much spectacularity you seem to want in people. Spectacularity? Spectacularousness?'

'*You* are spectacular. You are spectacularly handsome, and clever and funny.'

'Are you sure you haven't got your beer goggles on?'

'Quite sure. I wouldn't mind putting some on though, shall we go downstairs and get a drink?'

'Great, I can meet your unspectacular mum.'

Eva's mum is in the kitchen, chopping tomatoes. She briefly acknowledges them when they come in, runs her hands under water, dries them, extends one to Adam.

'Hello, Adam.'

'Hello, Mrs Bard. Nice to meet you.'

'Nice to meet you, too. Hallo, mein Schatz.'

'Hi, Mum.'

Eva always wishes her mother wouldn't be so cool – as in, not cool cool, but chilly cool – when she brings people home. Though at least she isn't as try-hard as her dad. What would be ideal would be something in between both their attitudes, like an average of them.

Though Adam, who is always affable when he meets new people, is undeterred.

'So! Can we help with anything?'

'Oh – yes. Maybe you can chop these?'

She pushes a bag of onions towards Adam. He scans the kitchen, locates a knife and chopping board, and sets to work as though he owns the place. Eva watches their silent backs, and feels half panicky because no one is saying anything, half left out of this quiet culinary companionship.

'So, you have had a good journey here?'

'Oh, yes thanks, Mrs Bard. The train was pretty crowded, but then that's only to be expected.'

'Please. Call me Hanna.'

'Right, yes. Hanna. What should I do next?'

'That is enough, thank you. Maybe you like a cup of tea?'

'I'll make it, Mum.'

'You're sure you don't need any more help?'

'No, I'm fine, thank you. I am just frying these, now.'

Adam sits down at the kitchen table, red circles puffing around his beautiful blue eyes from chopping the onions. Eva laces an arm around him from behind, squeezes him; her mother looks at them and smiles briefly, looks away.

Eva watches her, the familiar profile bent over a frying pan, except then her features become strange, like when you stare at a word on a page for so long that it loses its meaning. She sees only an assemblage of surfaces and lines that do not cohere to form a face, quivering lightly in the heat of the cooking oil. Her mother seems foreign to her, unreachable, while she can feel the warmth of Adam's body in her arms, as known to her as her own flesh.

'So Adam, you are studying medicine, Eva says?'

'Yes, that's right.'

'And you are enjoying it?'

'Yes, it's great. Really fascinating – you know, finding out about the human body, how it works. It's all just mechanics and plumbing, really.'

No further questions. Why does her mum have to be so – *dry*? After all these years in England, you would have thought she could have learnt a few basics of small talk – just throw in a couple more questions, for God's sake, make him feel you're interested in him. But no, she just keeps on frying onions, and she doesn't even seem bothered by it, the silence that is filling out into the room like a toxic cloud. Eva can't think of anything to say. She can see Adam's face furrow as he searches for a line of conversation.

'So, um, Mrs Bard . . .'

'Hanna, please.'

'Right, yes, sorry. Hanna. You – Eva was saying you grew up in Berlin?'

'That's right, yes.'

'Whereabouts, exactly?'

'In Pankow.'

'That's funny, I stayed there the first time I went to Berlin – I've been to the city a few times, actually, I really love it.'

'Yes, it seems a lot of young people want to go there now.'

'Yeah – it must be strange for you, I guess . . .'

Eva's mum shrugs her shoulders.

'Those days are over now, thankfully.'

That cloud of silence again. Eva can see her mother's shoulders tense under the burden of history, and feels a sudden, absurd surge of resentment: why do I have to suffer under this burden too, why can't you just make conversation with my wonderful boyfriend, why do you have to clam up every time this subject is raised? It's in the past now – get over it.

'So yeah, Pankow – I was staying at this guy's flat – it's quite an amazing story actually, I was interrailing with this friend and we met this guy on the night train from Vienna to Berlin and he was, like, oh well I'm going away for a few days so why don't I just give you my keys? – and he actually did, this complete stranger! But yeah, er – anyway. It was a flat near Florastraße, is that anywhere near where you used to live?'

'No, I was more north than this. Further out.'

'Oh. Did you spend any time around Florastraße?'

'Not really. Why?'

'Oh, I was just wondering how much the area I was in had changed since the GDR days – there were a few shops there that looked like they could have been left over from that time . . .'

'Honestly, I don't remember much about Pankow. It was a long time ago. A different world.'

'Right.'

'OK, so. I think we are ready soon. Eva, maybe you can lay the table?'

'Yep, sure.'

They are back in her bedroom, lying squashed up against each other under the duvet that used to conceal the imaginary worlds she would escape to as a child, the feverish investigations of her puberty – this duvet that has seen her body grow from infancy to adulthood. Her parents are still downstairs finishing the clearing-up, and it makes the home Eva grew up in feel so flimsy; how clearly you can hear the clinking of crockery and the rushing of water through partitions and floorboards. What must Adam think of it, having grown up in a huge, beautiful house?

'I really like your parents.'

'Really? I've been feeling so embarrassed by them all day . . .'

'What? Why?'

'I don't know – they're just so – lame . . .'

'No they're not! Your dad's really funny. And I like your mum. She's got this no-bullshit, straight-upness about her, it's really cool.'

'I was worried you might think she was rude. She doesn't always get the whole making-conversation thing.'

'No, I like it! Plus, you can be like that too sometimes, you know.'

'Really?'

'Yes.'

'Jesus.'

'. . .'
'. . .'
'What's that, by the way?'

Adam is looking up at her mum's samizdat. Eva stands up on the bed, shivering as cold air rushes over her skin – God, why can't her parents learn to turn the *heating* on now and again? – and unhooks the frame from the wall.

'Here you go.'

'*Disputatio.* Wow. What is it?'

'It's a samizdat – they were these underground pamphlets in East Germany – well, all over the Soviet zone, really. People would print and distribute them illegally. This one circulated within the community around my grandparents' church. My mother wrote that article there.'

'Seriously?'

'Yeah. Pretty cool, huh?'

' "Was wir nicht wissen sollen." '

'. . .'

She snuggles up to Adam, watching him mouth the German words to himself as she tries to glue as much of herself as possible to him, to draw as much heat as possible off him.

'It's one of the only things she was able to take with her. She gave it to me on my eighteenth birthday.'

'Wow.'

'. . .'

'God, I'm so embarrassed. I feel like I really put my foot in it, asking about Berlin and being like, oh it was so cool, this guy gave me the key to his flat – I mean, being like "Berlin is such a great place to party" when your mum was on the receiving end of its history . . .'

'Don't worry, I don't think you offended her – she just isn't that forthcoming on the subject generally.'

'Still. What a goofbag.'

'Honestly, you weren't a goofbag. I mean, you are a goofbag, generally, but you weren't particularly worse than usual in this specific situation.'

'Ha! How dare you . . .'

They tussle, and Eva can feel the tweak of an erection starting against her leg, and rubs closer to Adam, and then he heaves on top of her, eyes blazing, and she suppresses a giggle because she has just heard the squeak of the stairs as her parents make their way up them, and they both stay like that, Adam and Eva, frozen, eye to eye, as her parents walk past her bedroom door and into the bathroom. There is the sound of brushing of teeth outside, and inside there is muted laughter and gasps, and they're opening up a new chapter in the history of her room and its narrow bed, struggling under the weight of these two almost grown-ups.

YOU THOUGHT HE was your anchor. You thought he would be that firm, still point, whatever howling winds rose up, whatever vicious waves.

You trusted Adam not to die.

But he has cast you adrift, and when you walk the ground seems to slip and duck beneath your feet, and when you sit the whole room tanks like a storm-whipped ferry, and when you talk to people it is as though you are doing it from inside a sound-proof chamber, inches of glass dulling the words coming out of your mouth, and all the time your head feels light, as though it might float off your shoulders and leave your body to crumple into itself. Nothing is certain any more. The trees, the clouds, the cars, the sun, your heart, your lungs, the green fields rustling in the wind, the children howling in playgrounds, the men in sharp dark suits pressing into the Tube, your head, your brain, your mother, your father, Carmen, Henry, the newspapers neatly folded next to cups of frothy coffee, the government, the aeroplanes, the police, the fire brigade, they all might disappear, or break, or collapse under the weight of their own improbable existence. Sometimes, at night, you panic so much that you want to climb out of yourself, and sometimes in the day too, and the only person who could take you in his arms and make you feel better is him, but of course this is not possible, and so you feel worse.

And you drift on and on, a fragile raft in open water, buffeted any which way by a senseless world.

EVA LOOKED OVER at Adam's desk: the majestic computer, the piles of papers, the drawers, the files. The archive of his life.

The time since he had gone had been so busy, such a busy and empty time, full of worried people, and planning the funeral, and the endless wait for the post-mortem, with nothing to do but grieve and organize things. With nothing but his absence, the feeling that she could not reach him, however far she stretched out her hand.

Now he was here, in front of her, in that desk, and she wondered: how much do you want to know?

She wasn't sure. They would never have looked through each other's papers when they were alive. Did death give you the right to intrude on someone's privacy? What was the greater betrayal: prying into the parts of Adam's life that he had kept for himself, or destroying without a glance those last traces of his individuality? Those piles of papers might be hiding the paper trail of an ingenious fraud, a love letter he had left for her in case of his death, the keys to a hidden treasure. What if there was something there that Adam would have absolutely wanted her to see? What if there was something there that he would have absolutely wanted to hide from her?

What if he was not who she thought he was – what if she had never known him?

His massive, oak desk was quietly returning her gaze with the self-satisfied reserve of a pirate's treasure chest. It was diagonally opposite her own – which was a flimsier, cheaper affair altogether, a mere Ikea to his family heirloom – and it nestled against bookshelves that reached right up to the ceiling. This had been their dream, as penniless young professionals: to have a library with towers of books and a general air of turn-of-the-century Vienna. In an ideal scenario, they would each have had their own study, as well – or at least, in her ideal scenario. Adam had laughed at her when she'd suggested it: what was wrong with them sharing a study? She'd have it to herself most of the time anyway, while he was out at work. She had thought of trying to explain to him that it was not so much whether there was someone else in the room with her that made a difference, as the not having a space that was entirely hers; but they couldn't afford it.

Now the room was all hers if she wanted it. All she had to do was clear it of Adam's administrative remains, of that huge desk with its papers and computer. She couldn't get rid of them – she couldn't touch them – and yet she couldn't leave them there, gathering dust like Miss Havisham's wedding dress. To remove those papers, that computer, she would have to decide: to look, or not to look. To let Adam keep his secrets – but there is something so terribly final about the way the dead take their secrets with them. Or to uncover them – but there is something so terrible about uncovering someone else's secrets and not giving them a chance to explain. Perhaps she should remove all of Adam's belongings without looking at them at all, and store them away in a wooden chest, a safe place, leaving them for someone else to discover after her own death. But who would want to discover Adam after she had died, other than the children they had not had the time to have? She was all Adam had left, now that he had deserted her.

So she crossed over the room, from her desk of works in progress to his desk of relics. The land of the living to the land of the dead. She sat down in front of his computer and switched it on, and as it whirred into life, it occurred to her that she had never, not once, sat in this chair where Adam would always sit, looking at what Adam would always see. She noticed that her desk looked tidier from this angle, the more unruly stacks of paper hidden by her computer screen; she noticed that the funny china frog that had been passed down to her from her grandmother was just above where her head would have been, if she had been sitting at her usual place. Damn you, Adam, giggling in secret at the sight of me toiling away with a frog on my head. And now I can't even get my own back on you.

She noticed that on the bookshelf to the left of Adam's desk, where your eyes would naturally wander to, away from the computer screen, was a photo of her. It was the same one as on his desk at work, as she had found out on that awful day when she had gone to clear it out. A porter had carried the cardboard box containing the few sad items with which Adam had tried to cosy up his NHS office. And as they had walked side-by-side down neon-green corridors, Adam's colleagues – uniformed strangers who all, from the cleaners to the consultants, seemed to know who she was – had floated towards them with aggrieved faces before retreating again to their medicinal functions, like Dante's friends in purgatory backing away from an embrace they can no longer give.

The photograph had looked pitiful at the bottom of that box; but here, in the warmth of their beloved library, it was charming and full of life. Even Eva, who didn't like to look at pictures of herself, had to recognize that it was a good photo, the kind that you could gaze upon wistfully on nights when you were separated from your beloved. If she had been the one to die, this would certainly have been one of the photos of her Adam would have most treasured. She looked so tremendously happy in it, presumably because Adam must have said something funny as he pointed the camera at her (typical that he would select a photo in which she was laughing at one of his jokes – here is one thing you loved about me, Adam: that I was such a good audience), and also because she was in New York, with a steamy pavement creating gauze-like swirls around her, and tall, tall, glossy buildings framing the world. Down at the bottom of the avenue, in the background of the picture, one of the Twin Towers was just about visible. We didn't know it then, Adam, but towers crumble, and people die. Or did you know it? Is that why you chose this photo, with its background of ghosts? The dead always seem so much wiser than us, once they are dead.

With the image of her younger self laughing gaily at her, Eva logged on to the computer. She braced herself to delve into Adam's hard drive, his memory.

She would have to go through the whole thing at some point to retrieve his correspondence with banks and internet providers, Christmas card lists, tax returns – for as if the agony of mourning were not enough, the dead must also leave us with an administrative nightmare in their wake – but for now she had one mission only: finding Ulrich's contact details, and then doing something about Adam's email account. It had been nagging at her increasingly over the past two weeks, like a thread left hanging on the hem of someone else's jumper: the idea that Adam's presence on the internet remained unchanged. He still popped up on Facebook, in that daft photo of him at Henry's stag do; in fact his page had become a virtual shrine where people who didn't know him very well could post their condolences. The survival of his profile after death unsettled her, but she also couldn't face deleting it, so she had simply stopped logging on. She had resigned herself to letting it remain on the basis that it seemed to give people some strange outlet for their grief, or shock, or morbid fascination with his death.

But his email account – there was something about its continued existence that was altogether more disturbing; it haunted her. Some people might still be sending messages to his address, not realizing that no one was reading them at the other end. They probably wouldn't even find it odd that they hadn't received a response after a few weeks, because after all we're all very busy and these things back up. To those people, Adam was still alive. They were, without knowing it, communicating with the dead.

She logged on to his email, and the window opened unquestioningly, as though it were Adam himself sitting at the desk, stored passwords and keychains breaking through privacy settings like so many Open Sesames; she was in. It occurred to her that *she* could be a phantom Adam if she so chose, sending out messages in his name, continuing his existence for the people lucky enough not to have yet heard the news. She almost wished she could have done it for his mother, whose grief was more than Eva could bear because it was so horribly like her own. She wished she could do it for Henry, who looked as though the sky had fallen on to his head.

She scanned his inbox: none of the unread messages looked very personal. There were e-shots from cinemas, theatres, wine traders; various medical newsletters; messages that started 'Dear friend' or encouraged him to 'make her scream'. Perhaps this was what it meant to die online: the severing of all human communication, leaving you to be crushed by a deluge of marketing, much like, in the world of flesh and blood, your body was left a prey to maggots and cockroaches.

Eva scrolled on, ticking off the days, going down, down, down, deeper and closer to the date of Adam's death. As she got nearer, the personal emails started to appear, a sparse scattering of them at first, then more and more of them. They were like mirror images of the phone calls she had made that week, an electronic silhouette of people's closeness to Adam: the later, rarer messages sent by the more distant relations, the earliest ones by people closer to him whom she had not yet at that point got round to calling. But she had called all of them; all of these names she recognized, and for each one she could remember how they had picked up the receiver, how the tone of their voice had changed when she told them, how they had looked at her with horror and pity when they met.

And then, most painfully, there were the emails that had been sent to Adam while he was still alive, in between the moment when he had last logged off his account, just before they left for Henry's work thing, and that indeterminate hour, but probably somewhere around four or five a.m., when he had exhaled his last breath. It seemed so unfair that he had not had a chance to see any of these emails, the ones that he would actually still have been able to read.

The earliest of these unread messages, the one that had come closest to having Adam lay his eyes upon it, the one that had come closest to him *alive* – was from her. She had sent it from that computer over there, just as he was shutting his down, and just before she had logged off herself. It was a daft video of Nana Mouskouri performing an old German Schlager song which she knew would make him laugh because they had these jokes together, both about Nana Mouskouri and about old German Schlager music, and this particular video was a real find. No one else would find it as funny as Adam would have done. She didn't think she would ever be able to find it funny any more, now that watching it would always remind her of his not having seen it. Pitiless death, robbing us not just of our loved ones, but of the jokes we share with them.

There was only one name she did not recognize among the people who had corresponded with Adam on the night of his death, and she hated herself for the twinge of jealousy which she felt on reading it. For God's sake – I was never suspicious of you while you were alive, why do I feel this now? But it was such a feminine name: Nadia Kaye. And the email's subject line – PriMed Conf. 2008 – was such a reminder that there were many parts of Adam's life that she was not privy to. It was hard to resist a temptation to assume the worst.

But surely I would be wrong to assume the worst? Nothing could have happened then, I would have noticed, I knew him too well not to have noticed.

Eva's cursor hovered above the email. Was this a Pandora's Box waiting to be opened? Or was the Pandora's Box not opening it, now that she had let doubt creep into her mind? She trusted him. She knew it would be worse to live stupidly in doubt.

She clicked on the email.

Dear Adam,

Great to meet you at the conference, and I hope you had a safe trip home. Sorry for not getting in touch with you sooner, but I have had two angry, flu-ridden teenagers to tend to since getting back, so have had all my time taken up by Mom duties!

I've checked through my records, and the article I mentioned to you was published in the New England Journal of Medicine, not the BMJ – so you were right to be confused!!! Anyway, I have attached a pdf of it as I happen to have it stored on my PC.

Hope it helps, and good luck with your research!!

All the best,

Nadia Kaye

Nadia Kaye, potential conference femme fatale, expired just as quickly as she had been created in Eva's mind, and was reincarnated in the dumpy form of Nadia Kaye, middle-aged Midwestern conference acquaintance. Her excessive use of exclamation marks was a sure indication of her total absence of sexual charm. Sorry about that, Adam – I knew really that it would be something completely innocent. I just had to check because – you wouldn't want me to be walking around not being sure, would you? I just had to check because I'm not myself at the moment – I'm feeling very confused – I don't really know why I do things any more. I hope, if you are still able to see me from somewhere, that you understand. I hope, if you're just a ghost I've created to give an outlet to my grieving, that you understand.

Eva wondered if she should write to Nadia Kaye to say thank

you for your help, but unfortunately Adam will no longer be doing any research, because – because he passed away, for reasons that are not clear yet – because he's dead – because maggots are busy returning his body to the dust from whence it came. She pictured Nadia Kaye in the kitchen of a vast, prefabricated house, wrestling with some improbable kitchen appliance, her husband in the living room, creaking on the sofa as he watched Fox News. Nadia Kaye would be very upset to hear about Adam's death. She would gasp 'How terrible,' and thank her lucky stars for the rude, solid health of her corn fed husband. Nadia Kaye, Eva decided, did not need to know. If Eva did not reply to the email, she would just assume that Adam hadn't got round to it – too busy, too distracted, not polite enough, perhaps. She would remember him – and eventually forget him – as that nice guy she met at some conference or other, and who was working on diabetes. Yes, Eva would let Adam live on for Nadia Kaye – it was comforting to think that that Midwestern home, with its impressively equipped kitchen and its aged sofa, would remain a zone that was free of his death.

So Eva left behind the unread emails, and scrolled down into the realm of Adam's living correspondence. She wasn't doing it to snoop on him – really. She needed to find Ulrich's address, and also she wanted to make sure that there were no people she might have forgotten to contact.

She wondered what it was like to be one of Adam's friends right now – how deep the loss was, how long it would take them to get over it. Because they would get over it, as though it were a hurdle, a mountain peak, an obstacle to be surmounted and on the other side of which was the smooth running track, the open plain again. What place would he occupy in their lives once they were back on that open plain? She wondered what it was like to lose Adam when he was not a part of you, an extension of your being, a loss that could never be got over.

The emails dancing in front of Eva's eyes, each containing a conversation that Adam had had without her knowledge, a relationship that did not involve her, were a comfort to her now, as though their existence were proof that Adam was not just a ghost in her mind, had been his own human being, would continue to be different things to these different people.

At last, she found an email from Ulrich – and then, a few messages down, another name that struck her like a cry from the past, a twinge in an old wound, like the one she still felt in the tibia she had fractured as a child. This she had genuinely not expected. And yet, now that it was there on the screen in front of her, it seemed like she had always known it would be there; like this was what she had been looking for all along. Sender: Lena Bachmann. Subject: Berlin.

She opened Ulrich's email, jotted down his address, returned to Adam's inbox. And now, really, Eva wrestled with herself: should she read what Adam and Lena Bachmann could have had to say to each other? There was no doubt that this was a violation of privacy.

It had been easy to open Nadia Kaye's email. Eva had known, she realized now, that there would be nothing there to rewrite history.

But this. This email felt like Adam's flesh in front of her. As though, by opening it, she would be slicing through his skin, cutting him open just like the doctors who had carried out his post-mortem had. Pulling his innards out into the harshest light – because they needed to, because that was the only way to find out why he had died, to *understand*. How much did she want to understand now? How much more violation could Adam's flesh take?

She couldn't do it – and she was dying to do it in equal measure. Lena Bachmann. Berlin. She had to read it, and she had not to read it.

Eva turned away from the computer and looked at the photo of herself looking back at her.

And she felt a click inside her, as though her brain were shutting down. She told herself that she had to leave Adam his secrets – she couldn't betray his trust. Admin be damned – let these strangers scattered over the world live under the illusion that Adam was still alive. She had to make sure she could never be tempted again to look at what was not meant for her.

But really – really – she didn't want to know.

Lena Bachmann.

She didn't want to know.

She went into the parameters of his email account and fumbled through them until she found the command:

Close down/delete this email account

She clicked on it. A message popped up:

You have 172 unread messages in your inbox. Are you sure you want to delete this account?

She clicked Yes. Another message popped up:

Clicking on OK will delete your account. This action cannot be undone. Are you sure you want to delete your account?

Eva clicked on OK.

EVA FEELS THE sweat streaming off her like rain. She worries she might actually have a wet patch on her arse; it certainly feels like she does. The climb is agony, partly because she is horribly hungover, and partly because she slept so badly last night, her whirring thoughts having joined forces with Carmen's snoring in the bed next to her. She turns to see who's behind her: only Adam, the rest of the group having, it seems, powered on ahead at Henry's surprisingly athletic pace.

'Adam, do I have a wet patch on my arse?'

'Er.'

Adam is struggling to get his words out between pants.

'Doesn't look like it from here.'

'Seriously – tell me if I do. I'm not in the mood for being the butt of any mockery today. As it were.'

'Honestly, I would tell you. You haven't got a wet patch on your arse.'

'OK. Thanks.'

They wend their way up in silence, both intent on keeping their breath for breathing rather than speaking. Eva is very aware of how close Adam is following her, just a few paces behind, and this makes her walk a bit faster – maybe it's because she's worried about a wet patch being detectable at closer range, maybe she wants him to think racing up this hill is an effortless exercise for her, maybe out of some spirit of competition – but always Adam remains close behind her.

The path they are on is made of slippery white gravel – not so much a path, in fact, as a slightly less steeply inclined part of the slope, which otherwise is covered in scraggy bushes and, here and there, the remnants of a stone wall. The slope beneath the path is sheer but not cliff-like, and looks as though falling down it would have none of the magnificence of plummeting off a rock face, while still being potentially fatal: it would be a scratchy, undignified death, as you bounced down off patches of scrub. Going along a particularly steep section, Eva slips and has to right herself by grabbing a nearby bush; she has avoided an embarrassing end, but gouged a hole in her hand. Adam rushes towards her, or rushes as much as he can without slipping down the mountainside himself. He takes her hand in his and winces.

'Bleargh. Sorry – can't look.' Adam pushes her hand away and stares into the middle distance. He looks a bit green.

'What's the matter?'

'Blood – not a massive fan. I'll be fine.'

'You're studying to be a *doctor*, for Christ's sake.'

'I know. I'll get over it. We just haven't been doing that much practical stuff yet – haven't had a chance to – you know – immunize myself against it.'

'Well, let's hope you get over it before you have to operate on anybody.'

'I'm not planning on becoming a surgeon.'

'Oh, that's all right then.'

' . . .'

'Fuck, this hurts.'

'OK, OK, hang on a minute.'

Adam sits down on the path and fumbles around in his backpack – he always takes a backpack with him on every walk they go on, and Eva has been wondering what he can be putting in it to make it look so full. Now, here is part of the answer, at least: Adam pulls out a large first-aid kit, opens it up, takes out stuff.

'OK, come here.'

Eva sits down next to him.

'Give me your hand.'

'You sure you can handle this, cowboy?'

'Ha ha ha. Just thank your lucky stars I'm here to stop you from getting septicaemia.'

'You can't get septicaemia from a bush, can you?'

'You never know.'

Adam, his face set into a grim and frankly rather odd expression, swabs at the cut in Eva's hand with an antiseptic wipe. It stings.

'Ow.'

'Sorry, got to clean it out properly.'

Once he has finished rooting around inside her wound, he gets out a roll of gauze and wraps it around her hand. He is gentle, focused. Eva likes the feel of his light touch on her wrist, the softness of the bandage after the stinging alcohol; it is like being a child again, being cared for. And there is something intimate about the contact of hands, like when someone reads your palm, as if your fingers are trying to communicate with each other. Adam secures the bandage neatly and grins at her.

'Expertly done, Doctor Adam.'

'Hey, you may laugh, but it usually takes years of medical training to do that properly.'

'You wouldn't have any water in that big bag of yours, would you?'

Adam pulls out a large bottle of water from his backpack.

'Oh cheers, you lifesaver.'

Eva hadn't realized how parched she was. The water has the sweet, cool taste it only has when you are very thirsty indeed.

'What do you think those old bits of wall were for?'

'Terraces. Henry was saying earlier on there used to be quite a lot of vineyards around here.'

'Oh right. Yeah, I guess it's the right weather for it, isn't it. I wonder why they're not growing anything any more.'

'Don't know – Henry marched off before I could ask him. I guess we should try and catch up, if you're feeling OK now?'

'Yes, I think I should manage. I did only scratch my hand, you know.'

'Er, yeah, sorry, I didn't mean—'

Eva laughs, a bit worried that she came out blunter than she'd intended just then.

'Hey, don't worry, it was sweet of you to ask. Come on, let's go.'

And off they trudge again, though at a slower pace this time, their breathing less frantic now. He's a funny guy, old Adam: fancy studying medicine if you can't stand the sight of blood. And yet it suits him somehow that he would battle with himself to do something that will help other people. He's kind of geeky at first sight, but really tough when you get to know him – tough with a sense of knowing what he wants to do, of always being really certain of what the right thing to do is. Whereas Eva never really knows what to do, and finds the right thing very difficult to identify most of the time. Like what the right thing to do is right now. That is very hard to identify indeed.

'Hey, Adam?'

'Yeah?'

'Nothing.'

'What?'

'Nothing.'

'Yes, something, you were going to ask me something.'

The gravel of the path is white, so white in this hot sun that it hurts your eyes. It slithers and scrapes under their feet as they walk on in silence. Adam is good at choosing his silences – at knowing when to stop probing, so you volunteer information of your own accord. He will make a good doctor, if he gets over the whole blood thing.

'It's nothing really. Just boy trouble.'

'Oh.'

' . . . '

'Do you want to talk about it?'

'I don't know. I don't know if there's much point.'

'Is this about that guy from *Varsity*?'

'Mm-hm.'

'Right.'

Adam is good at choosing his silences – at knowing when to stop talking so you feel the weight of what is left unsaid.

'What's that supposed to mean?'

'What?'

'That "Right"?'

'Um. I don't know. Nothing.'

'Uh-huh.'

Adam removes his baseball cap and passes a hand through sweat-drenched hair, which makes it spike on end like an expensive haircut. Underneath his high-tech walking gear, he could be a young shepherd from an ancient Greek myth: he has the effortless grace and golden locks that goddesses fall in love with.

'But – you are going out with him, then?'

'I don't really know, to be honest.'

'What do you mean?'

'I don't know whether we are going out or not.'

'How can you not be sure whether you're going out with someone?'

'I don't know, Adam. It's complicated.'

She feels irritated with Adam for implying, by the edge of disbelief in his voice, his slightly raised eyebrow, that surely things should be simpler. Things are never simple, she wants to scream at him. But she can't put her finger on why exactly.

'Eva?'

'. . .'

'Eva?'

'. . .'

'Hey.'

'Hm?'

'Hello, you still there? Complicated how?'

'Just – complicated.'

'Well, let me know once you've worked it out.'

'Why, you interested in the vacancy?'

Eva wonders where that came from, and whether she was being aggressive or flirtatious just then. She turns to check Adam's reaction: he is crimson and avoiding her gaze. She has clearly embarrassed herself. They plod on in silence.

A few steps ahead of them, the path turns, stops rising, and levels out on to a grassy plateau; they stop to take a last look at the valley below. It is a strange landscape, this: you could be forgiven for thinking it mundane as you make your way through scrubby woods, and then suddenly you come to a more exposed bit of slope from which the view tumbles down to a limpid river, to rise again on the other side in a lush canopy of pine trees topped off by bleached, wind-sculpted rock formations.

Down in the valley, you can see the village they are staying in, and a corner of their swimming pool, a vibrant, artificial diamond of blue in the middle of pale stone walls and red-tiled roofs. Well – their swimming pool. They have made it theirs, through long evenings of lounging around it with cocktails in their hands, of pushing each other in fully clothed when they are least expecting it. But really, of course, it is Henry's parents' swimming pool, tastefully sculpted out of the same limestone as the mountain itself, and paid for with last year's bonus, as Henry's father made sure to let them know. They all met them, the parents, when they convened at Henry's place in Highgate to pick up the keys and the car to drive down, and it was the first time Eva had seen such a huge house in London, such money. Henry's dad had seemed angry the whole time, for no particular reason, and his mother was elegant, glacial. Eva wonders how they can have produced such a benign person as their son – or if Henry will eventually turn into them, like the ugly duckling becomes a swan.

Speaking of the devil, Henry is ambling towards them, looking inexplicably undisturbed by the heat, as though he were a kindly bear built to live on these woody slopes.

'Ah, there you chaps are! We were worried you might have fallen down the mountainside.'

'Where is everybody?'

'They're in a *ferme auberge* just down that path there; we thought a cooling pint might be in order. Not a bad view, eh?'

Henry stands next to them on a small ledge overlooking the valley.

'Didn't you say those terraces used to be for vines, Henry?'

'I did indeed. Whole region used to be covered in them.'

'Why don't they make wine here any more?'

'First World War. All the young men from around here were sent off to the trenches and hardly any came back. Apparently this whole area used to be farmland until that happened.'

'What – even that wood we just walked through?'

'I'm not sure – I think so, though. Weird thought, isn't it?'

They watch the dry landscape in silence for a while.

'Anyway, shall we go and get that beer? I'm bloody parched, I am.'

Beer turns to wine, which turns to the merry group tumbling back down the rocky paths with jubilant abandon, which turns to more wine by the side of or indeed even in the pool, which turns to a lengthy, talkative dinner, of those that are the lifeblood of friendship. By the end of the evening, only Henry, Adam, Carmen and Eva are left reclining on the plump sofas of the tastefully rustic living room; they are always the last four standing, united by a common conviction that any social event only really comes into its own at its tail end, when less hardy guests retire, and only the true, most dedicated revellers remain to practise the fine art of late-night conversation, tongues loosened by alcohol and fatigue.

Eva is watching Henry watching Carmen. Those two. When it isn't one, it's the other. Ever since they met, across a brain-damaging number of sambuca shots on the final leg of the freshers' pub crawl, they have been playing a game of emotional

cat and mouse with each other, in which each one suffers bru-
tally intense periods of pining for the other – but never both at
the same time. Never before has Eva seen Cupid so contrary. A
few weeks ago, she was listening to Carmen bemoan her undying
love for Henry, who, having pursued her in vain for the whole of
Michaelmas term, returned from the Christmas break mysteri-
ously cool towards her. Then, just before they came here, Carmen
met some philosophy student from the year above, and now he is
all she can talk about. Which of course, muses Eva, means the
balance of unrequited love was just about due to swing back to
Henry's side. He hasn't taken his eyes off Carmen for at least five
consecutive minutes now.

'How's your cut?'

'Hm?'

Adam has just made a trip to the munificent parental drinks
cabinet, and is handing her a glass of something golden.

'Oh. That.'

She looks at her bandaged palm.

'Does it feel sore at all?'

She squeezes her hand.

'Maybe a tiny bit.'

'Maybe we should disinfect it again. Just to be on the safe side.
I've got some disinfectant in my room, if you want.'

'Yeah, that's not a bad idea.'

Eva looks at Adam, expecting him to go and fetch said disinfectant for her, but he doesn't move, and is looking at her as
though he expects *her* to do something. Only when her eyes flit
to Henry and Carmen, deep in conversation on the sofa, does she
realize what he is up to.

'Oh right. Yeah, great. Let's go, then.'

'Ow.'

'Sorry.'

Adam holds her hand as though it were a delicate bird. His is lean and knotty, a wiry hand: it looks older than the rest of him, more mature.

'You have very beautiful hands.'

'Oh. Thanks.' He stops swabbing briefly and looks at them. 'So do you.'

'No, I don't. I've always hated my hands.'

'They're nice. Slender.' He puts a plaster on her palm.

'Cheers, big ears.'

She reclines on the bed, propping herself up on her elbows. Adam busies himself with putting things back into his first-aid kit. Every item inside it has a designated place, slips into a pocket or is held fast by a strip of elastic; he returns plasters, swabs, blister pads, disinfectant, with elaborate care, but just as he is trying to close the kit, tugs too hard on the zip and sends it flying across the room.

'Shit!' he exclaims, louder than the situation really warrants, and scrambles to the ground, where a small number of blister pads lie strewn, the only casualties of this otherwise perfectly belted-in set of medical supplies.

Eva wonders why it would never occur to her to bring blister pads on a holiday that is clearly going to involve a large amount of walking, and why, conversely, Adam is so meticulous. She thinks about asking him, but he looks like he might not appreciate the interruption.

So she stays silent, and thinks about the day.

Adam, first-aid kit packed, zipped and returned to its rightful drawer at last, sits back on the bed, his hand resting right next to her knee. He is silent too. Outside, the racket of crickets reminds Eva of the dry landscape surrounding Henry's house.

Adam opens his mouth to say something, but she has already started her sentence:

'I keep thinking about what Henry said.'

'What did Henry say?'

'You know, when he was talking about all the young men here being wiped out during the First World War.'

She wants to cry. Thinking about the trenches always brings a tear to her eye. This is ridiculous.

'Eva, are you OK?'

'. . .'

'Eva?'

Adam makes an awkward movement, perhaps to put his arm around her.

'I'm fine, sorry. I always get sentimental about the First World War, can you believe it? I guess it's all that schmaltz we get fed about the Somme and VE Day . . . Sorry, it's so ridiculous.'

'I don't think it's ridiculous.'

Adam is looking at her seriously, with none of the cleverer-than-thou one-liners that she might have been composing in his place. They talk for some time about that sad, lost generation, those dulce et decorum est, the horrors of war that are so far away now, almost indecently far away, for can it be right for flowers to bloom out of furrows that were once soaked with blood? Adam thinks so, has the quiet conviction that death must yield to life, but Eva wants those butchered youths to rage against their ungrateful successors, hiss into the air like poison gas, haunt the world with the futility of their patriotic sacrifice. They talk of the unreality of a world in which death can come so easily, where standing too tall can earn you a bullet through the ear, the terrible finality of it.

'Of course, it's thanks to agriculture dying out in places like this that half our parents were able to recolonize the South of France. No rural exodus, no second homes for the English. Essentially, Wilfred Owen's loss is the modern investment banker's gain.'

'Speak for yourself. My parents haven't colonized anybody.'

'Well, neither have mine. Though I suppose you have the added dimension of being a Hun, and you're right, they haven't done so well on the property front either then or now.'

'Well, my mother certainly didn't.'

'No.'

'. . .'

'But – I mean – your grandparents must have had a house, or a flat or something, right?'

'I don't know. I don't know if people were even allowed to own their homes in the GDR. But if they did, I guess it will have just been given to some other family after they died.'

'But what about all their stuff?'

'I imagine they got rid of it. They were hardly going to forward it on to someone who'd escaped the regime.'

'Who's "they", though?'

'I don't know – the authorities? The Stasi?'

'. . .'

'. . .'

'It just seems so extraordinary that there can be nothing left of them, that they weren't able to somehow put anything into safe-keeping for your mum . . .'

'Yeah, I know.'

'. . .'

'Sorry, I'm not picking very cheerful topics of conversation this evening, am I?'

'Oh God, don't worry. I'm just thinking about what it must be like for your mum, having something like that to deal with.'

'Well – it's been tough on her, I think. But also, you know – she has a life in England now. A family, a house. I don't think it's something that's with her all the time.'

'She's rebuilt herself.'

'Yes.'

'. . .'

'Do you think we'll ever end up like this, Ad?'

'Like what?'

'Like our parents. With all this money. All these houses. I just can't imagine it, somehow.'

'Well. I doubt I'll ever have as much money as Henry's parents.'

'No – but Henry probably will.'

'You're right – that is hard to imagine. Well, hard in one way, easy in another: I can imagine Henry *having* the money, I just can't imagine him *doing* whatever it would take to get it.'

'I can't imagine any of us doing whatever it takes to make money. Being grown-ups.'

'Well – we kind of are grown-up, technically. Aren't we?'

'It certainly doesn't feel like we are.'

'I guess we're lucky it doesn't.'

And so, well beyond the small hours, they reflect on the good fortune of being born into an era of unprecedented European peace, on the sufferings of their forefathers, on their privileges of youth, of comfort, and of education.

It is only when she is tiptoeing down the corridor to her own bedroom, having pulled the door to behind her with a discreet creak, that Eva thinks about the way Adam was sitting on that bed, far closer to her than was really necessary, and the way he almost touched her when she was upset, but didn't dare, and how he had been about to say something before she spoke first, something that was painful and terrifying and vital to say, and realizes that maybe she failed to pick up on some signals there. She feels a shiver run over her skin and her stomach leap up to her throat, like when a car drives too fast over the brow of a hill, but it's too late to turn back, she's missed her chance, and so she creeps into her room, where Carmen lies on her back, hands folded across her stomach like an Etruscan statue, and one foot poking out from under the duvet into the breeze of cricket song carried in through the open window.

YOU ARE LIKE an animal being hit by a stun gun, your long, bony limbs scrabbling on the mossy ground as you try to get up again, but then they hit you with another shot, and another, and another, and every time you manage to raise your body a few centimetres off the ground it's the same, they just keep on coming, but although you are being stunned over and over again, over and over, you can't just let yourself sink down into the forest bed either, let the cool breeze stroke your silky fur and the night descend, you have to keep fighting to get up, because that is what life does, it goes on, one day after the next, waking up and drinking and pissing and even eating, despite the fact that for a while you really didn't eat, but then even that had to stop, you had to start eating again because your body just kept trying to get back on its feet, and so yes, eating, and, therefore, as a consequence, shitting, and going to sleep, and before you know it you're waking up into another day, days and days and days, and though these days all merge into one because there is little to distinguish one from the next, still they manage to take on a kind of long, slow momentum, which in your stunned state you can't really grasp the nature of, but you sense that it is pulling you away from where you want to be, which is by Adam's side, and all you can do is keep struggling to stand up, and look around manically with the huge, soft-brown eyes of the hunted beast, your ears twitching at every sound, poised for a final blow that never comes.

FIRST, THEY GO for a walk around Richmond Park. It's sort of on the way from the station, apparently, and according to Adam they should enjoy some peace and quiet while they can, before tackling his family. He actually uses the word 'tackle', as though they were a rugby squad: charging, muscular flesh that needs knocking over.

When they reach the gate, the park stretches out in front of them in a slow, descending ripple, dapples of intense greens and golds and browns right out to the horizon.

'My goodness. It's huge.'

Adam laughs.

'*My goodness*? Since when do you say "my goodness"?'

'Oh. I think I might be semantically prepping to meet your family. Can't be bursting out in "fucking hell"s in front of your mum, can I?'

'Don't worry, it would take more than that to shock my mum. To be honest, she'd probably be more taken aback to hear "my goodness", like I'm bringing back a girlfriend from the 1950s or something . . .'

'Ha ha ha. Anyway. Bloody great big park you've got on your doorstep.'

'Have you never been to Richmond Park before?'

'No – why, should I have?'

'No, I guess not, it's just – I don't know, funny to think that someone could never have been to Richmond Park. I mean, it's like – Richmond Park.'

'Uh-huh.'

Eva decides not to explain to Adam that London is not

self-evident to people who have grown up outside of it. That she is starting to feel somewhat familiar with some parts of it now that she has to traverse it on her way to and from uni, but that on the whole it remains sprawling and unknown. That before she started university, London to her was Piccadilly Circus and Shaftesbury Avenue and Greenwich and Hyde Park and the British Museum, a handful of places vibrantly remembered from school trips, and nothing in between.

They walk down soft, earthy paths, winding in and out of clusters of trees and clearings. Adam's hand is firm and warm around hers, and from time to time he leans over to kiss her cheek or temple, gentle kisses for this gentle autumn day, and from time to time she unhooks her hand from his and laces it around his waist, and he puts his arm around her shoulder, and she rests her head in the crook of his neck – though they cannot hold this uncomfortable position and keep walking for long. Or sometimes she will slip a hand under his T-shirt to feel his soft, surprisingly hot skin, as if to remind herself that this is what lies beneath.

There seems to be almost no one else around, just the leaves murmuring in the wind, the occasional burst of birdsong. Then they emerge into another clearing.

'Look!!!'

Eva points in astonishment.

Adam nuzzles her ear, whispers, 'Gorgeous, aren't they?'

On the other side of the clearing, no more than a dozen metres away from them, a cluster of deer nibble at the trees and grass. A couple of them turn to watch Adam and Eva, who have frozen where they are; the others twitch their ears at them, registering their presence without concern. They are magnificent creatures, tall, strong, and a rich, ochry brown. Several of them are sporting small antlers, which they occasionally wave around with a circular movement of their heads, as though testing their wind resistance.

'Wow. They're so . . . tame.'

'Well, I mean, you know, they're pretty used to people wandering around.'

'What, you mean you've seen them before?'

'Oh yeah, of course. The park is full of deer. Didn't you know?'

'Um. No.'

'Ah.'

'Is it something I should know?'

'I don't know. I mean, I guess it's what most people think of, if you say "Richmond Park". "Deer." But I mean, yeah, you've never been to Richmond Park.'

'. . .'

'It used to be the royal hunting grounds, that's why there's so many. I guess – possibly it even still *is* a royal hunting ground? But no, they couldn't go hunting in public parks, could they?'

'Also wouldn't the deer be more worried about us if they were used to being hunted?'

'Yeah, you're right. It can't be any more. Pretty sure it used to be, though. Anyway, we can ask my mum.'

They start walking again, and as they get closer to the deer each head rises in turn, fixing them with a long-lashed gaze until they have walked past. There is no fear in their looks, but a tensing in their massive hind legs suggests that they are ready to spring off if necessary, a cautious instinct handed down to them over the centuries from those forefathers who did know the baying of hounds, the cracking of shotguns.

'Huh. Where is everybody?'

They have stepped through a triple-locked front door into a large, expansive house, a thickly carpeted entrance from which Eva can glimpse an equally thickly carpeted living room, and stairs rising to another floor. Books line the walls, and every piece of furniture looks antique, weathered.

A tall, graceful woman appears from behind a door to their left, from which wafts the rich scent of roast chicken and potatoes, the steam of bubbling pans.

'Hey, where is everybody?'

'Hello, darling. And you must be Eva. Lovely to meet you. I'm Harriet.'

Adam's mother gives her son a warm, brisk kiss, then grasps Eva's shoulder and kisses her on both cheeks. She does it so confidently that she manages to avoid the moment being awkward, even though Eva had already started to panic about what the correct way to greet her might be.

'The boys are all outside, Dad's gone to pick up some more wine for lunch, we were a bit short. Would you like something to drink? Tea? Beer?'

'Oh, er – a cup of tea would be lovely, thank you.'

'I'll grab a beer, yeah.'

Damn. Eva regrets not having said beer, it might have helped calm her nerves a bit. She wasn't at all worried about meeting Adam's family, but something about his mother – how ridiculously *elegant* she is – and this huge, tasteful Edwardian house, have made her feel extremely self-conscious all of a sudden.

'Um. Can I – maybe help with anything?'

'Oh no – it's all pretty much ready to go. You two go out and say hello to the boys, I'll put the kettle on.'

They walk through the kitchen, the mouth-watering Sunday-roast preparations, Adam pulling a beer out of the fridge on the way with well-versed movements, and out into the garden.

Three faces turn towards them as they step out of the kitchen door, and Eva feels an uncanny flutter in the pit of her stomach; they are like variations on a theme: the golden hair, clear blue eyes and aquiline nose of Adam pulled into ever-so-slightly-different angles and relationships, the same yet not the same. They have been slouching on garden chairs around a table adorned with half-drunk bottles of beer, but they stand now, long limbs and flexing young muscles, to greet their guest.

'So, this is Eva. Eva: Matt, Luke and Bennie.'

Adam points them out in quick succession before falling into a complicated sequence of firm clasping of hands, manly hugs and resonant pats on backs. Each of them also shakes Eva's hand, beaming at her affably, though does she detect a wryness at the corner of their lips, a mischievous curiosity in what their brother has brought home? Matt, the eldest, now has his arm around Adam's neck as though he is about to snap it.

'So you're the special girl who's patient enough to put up with this reprobate, eh? How much have you paid her, Ad?'

He ruffles Adam's hair, or perhaps knuckles his skull, it is hard to tell, then grabs hold of his beer.

'Well, come on then, let's crack this open. You got one, Eva, or did it not occur to Adam to offer you anything?'

'Oh, er – no, actually, but—'

'Please excuse my brother. If I hadn't seen him grow up here with my very eyes, I would think he had been raised by wolves. Would you like one?'

'No, thanks. Actually, I think your mother is making me a cup of tea . . .'

'Ah, you're in good hands, then. In that case: cheers, guys!'

There is something about Matt's suave deference, the smoothness with which he turns from smiling at her as though they are accomplices to clinking bottles with his brothers, presenting her with his back in polite dismissal, that Eva finds skin-pricklingly irritating – and then she remembers, of course, he is the politician one, a rising star within New Labour, there have even been whispers of him standing in a safe Tory seat at the next election, get him broken in. He is a taller, even thinner version of Adam; his bony figure and long limbs, which are now gripping his brother's shoulder, look a bit creepy.

They clink bottles of beer and one-up each other with ridiculous toasts, most of them in-jokes that she cannot begin to unravel, and some of them jibes directed at Adam and his supposed inability to nab a girl, what is it he's done to convince this charming one to come to Sunday lunch with the family, jibes which she imagines are meant to be complimentary but in fact make her feel cut off, on her own in the face of a solid wall of brotherhood.

She looks at these strange, not-quite-iterations of her boyfriend: Luke, the second-oldest, is a more muscular version, not as tall as Matt but better proportioned, the most rugged and masculine of the lot. In contrast to Matt's constantly turned-on charm, he has an easy confidence, doesn't need to push himself to the forefront in order for his presence to be noticeable. And Bennie, the baby brother, who is still in school, is like an illustration of harmony out of a Renaissance painter's manual, the family features assembled into the most pleasing composition possible, a cherubic face and graceful body that already hints at the strong man ahead, though of course, being sixteen, he does not realize all of this, merely jostles a little awkwardly against his big brothers and gazes at them in adoration.

And Adam, Adam is slighter and more earnest, and he is hers, she realizes with a small thrill; even if they haven't been going out for that long, this meeting of the family is a consecration of that, and while he may have grown up with these boys, while they may share uncannily similar features and much of the same genetic material, still there is a place for her in his life, a different one.

And it makes sense of Adam, somehow, of the even keel of his character, that he has these loving, shoving mirror images of himself to ground him, to remind him of what he is and what he is not, in the ways they are alike and the ways they are different, that he has had them to define himself with and against since the day he was born.

Eva wonders what it feels like, to have siblings, what other person she would be if she had grown up with three boisterous brothers at her side.

Adam ducks out of the jostling and comes over to her, laces his arms around her waist.

'You all right? Shall I go see if my mum's done making that cup of tea?'

'It's fine, I'll go – I'm feeling unhelpful enough as it is, I don't want your mum to think I can't even fetch my own tea.'

'No need to feel unhelpful, honestly she'll have had everything planned out since this morning, there's usually no room for outside intervention.'

'Oh, really? That sounds like a spoilt child's excuse for not helping with any of the housework to me . . .'

'Hey! I'm very good with the washing-up, I'll have you know . . .'

Unfortunately, Adam's brothers overhear this, and it opens up a rich new vein of mockery. Eva slides out of his embrace and walks over to the kitchen.

Adam's mother is standing at the sink, rubber-gloved hands poised in mid-air around a foamy pan, gazing fondly out of the window at her boys.

'Must have been quite a handful, raising that lot.'

She turns with a smile.

'You can say that again. I kept hoping we'd have a daughter, balance things out a bit, but no, just me and five men around the house.'

She says it proudly, as though it is actually an achievement that her womb will only bear male children.

'You'd like your tea, I suppose? It should be nicely stewed by now. Pot's over there, and there's milk in the fridge.'

Eva pours herself a steaming cup from an enormous teapot. She baulks at the weight of it, and wonders where they can have got hold of such a thing, it must be twice the size of her parents'

teapot at home – but then, of course, this is a family of six, twice
the size of her own, life on a different scale altogether.

Adam's mother chuckles fondly, and Eva turns towards her;
she gestures outside with her chin, her hands now busily scrub-
bing the contents of the sink. Eva goes over to stand next to her,
and sees that the boys have fallen into a full-blown tussle, a heap
of pushing arms and legs and laughing faces on the grass, like
young stags testing their antlers.

'It's – er . . . nice they still play with each other.'

'Yes, it is. Though they're not usually quite this excitable. I
think they may be trying to impress you, Eva my dear.'

'. . .'

'Though you strike me as someone who is not that easy to
impress.'

Adam's mother smiles conspiratorially.

Eva blushes, and wonders how she can have given off that
impression.

'Um . . . You're really sure you don't need a hand with
anything?'

'Oh no, honestly, it's all pretty much ready to go. You go outside and enjoy your tea – though if you could herd the boys
towards the dining room in about twenty minutes' time, that
would be much appreciated.'

Eventually they are halfway through Sunday lunch, Eva having
ushered in the boys at the required time and Adam's dad having
returned from his errand, a pleasant, quietly witty man. There is
an open lovingness about Adam's parents which seems to radiate
over their sons, and provokes in Eva an unsettling feeling of
inadequacy. They are all so confident, so worldly, so *English*,
stretching their legs out in front of their chairs with the easy
comfort of gentlemen in a London club. Eva dreads to think what
they would make of her small, provincial family, of her odd, German mother and her nervous father, and it makes her

tongue-tied – which hardly matters anyway, since most of the meal so far has been taken up with Matt relaying juicy political gossip and discussing his electioneering prospects, a topic she has little to contribute to. Or, in fact, she reflects, she has much to contribute to, since her father has been a lifelong and very active member of their local Labour Party, but this again seems so laughably provincial that the mere idea of bringing it up makes her cringe.

She feels so – so *unimpressive*. So not-cosmopolitan, not-tuned-in, so *ordinary*. Like a mongrel thrown in with the pure-breds.

Then the father asks Matt about some other young New Labour hotshot who is also being considered for the seat he might stand in, and Matt responds with expert evasiveness, something about not having the exact facts on where things are with that, and lets the topic slip into thin air by turning to Eva with a look of oily curiosity.

'So, Eva – sorry, I didn't mean to monopolize the conversation like that, just lots to fill everyone in on, as you can hear. But we're all here to meet *you*. Why don't you tell us a bit about yourself?'

With six near-identical pairs of blue eyes directed at her, Eva feels a paralysing flush creep up her stammering throat.

'Oh. Er. I mean . . . I don't know. There isn't much to tell, really.'

'Oh, come on, it sounds like you've got a far more interesting family than us lot. Adam was saying you're half German?'

'Oh, um – yes, my mother is from Berlin. East Berlin, in fact. But, I mean, yeah, she came over to Britain in the seventies. I mean, she escaped from East Germany, and ended up here eventually.'

'Escaped? What, like, you mean, she got out clandestinely?'

Bennie's eyes have widened into a goggle, and something about his intonation in asking this question, the excitement, the disbelief, the fascination, snaps Eva's timidity in two. She looks around at the attentive faces, and realizes she has a story, an exceptional one: a story that makes her special. She sees Adam look at her, the pride and love in his eyes.

'Yes – it's a pretty unbelievable story, actually . . .'

'How did she get out?'

'She had help from a friend of the family, a guy in West Germany. He'd arranged for a boat to come and pick her up, in the Baltic Sea – she went up to the coast on some kind of trip with the Communist youth organization, so that was her cover. And then the plan was that someone would come and pick her up in the night with this sort of dinghy – obviously you couldn't get an actual boat so near to the coast without attracting attention – and then they would go out to the middle of the sea, cross over the territorial waters, and there would be a boat waiting to take her to the nearest port, in Denmark.'

'Jesus.'

'You make it sound like it didn't go to plan, though?'

'It didn't. Or at least, not exactly. The pick-up went OK, but it was really stormy that night, and they couldn't just decide to push it back a couple of days, it was then or never, so they had to set out into the rain and these huge crashing waves and – well, they got lost, basically. They ended up going around for much longer than had been planned, without having much of an idea of what direction they were heading in, and then at some point, thank God, they see some lights in the distance and start signalling at them frantically – they're almost out of diesel at this point too – and the boat comes towards them and they realize it's not their guys, it's the East German coast guard . . .'

'No!'

'Yes. And so they turn their lights off and huddle down – luckily it's a pitch-black night and in the storm they're almost invisible, and more importantly inaudible – and they manage to slowly putter away and the searchlights miss them by inches, and basically by some miracle they get away from them, and by an even greater miracle they manage to find the right boat just as they really are about to run out of fuel.'

'Wow.'

'Yes, they were very lucky. My mother messed up the nerves in her left hand, because of the cold, she kept taking her glove off so she could manipulate the compass more easily, and now she can't really feel anything in that hand, but that's pretty much it.'

'Wow.'

'And presumably she wasn't able to return to East Germany until the Wall came down?'

'Oh – she's never been back. Her parents died not that long afterwards, and, well, I suppose she felt there was nothing to go back for.'

'My goodness.'

A silence descends over the table – what misfortune, how lucky we are. Eva can feel Bennie's bright eyes on her – he still has some of the child's absolute involvement in the story he is being told – and Adam's too, how much he admires her, how pleased he is to be able to show her off to his family. Eva basks in the glow of mystery and suffering conferred on her by her mother's epic saga, is starting to rack her brain for more juicy details she could share, when Matt raises his glass.

'Well – thank God people no longer have to do such things to escape oppression, eh. Here's to the end of history.'

Bennie redirects his wide eyes to his brother.

'What do you mean, the end of history?'

'It's a book, you numbskull, look it up. I thought you were meant to be getting a proper education. Get thee to a library, and be thankful we no longer live with a battery of nuclear warheads pointing at our precious home.'

Eva smiles at Bennie.

'Don't worry, I don't think history is quite over yet – there's still enough wrong with our world to keep us busy for a while . . .'

'Well quite, and that's why people like me are going into

politics. But for someone like your mother, it must have been a relief, to see that destructive ideology die the death.'

'I think she'd disagree with you, actually. She's very critical of the system as it is now. And she would tell you that there were a lot of things that were good about the GDR, that worked better than our society does now.'

'Like what? I mean, why did she go to all those risks to get out, if she thought it was so great?'

'Perhaps – I don't know. Perhaps she didn't realize what would be waiting for her on the other side. Didn't realize until she got to the West that the East did some things better. Like having a sense of community, of communal purpose.'

'Unless you didn't happen to agree with that communal purpose and got sent to Siberia.'

'I'm just saying it's a bit more complicated than that.'

Suddenly, Eva doesn't want to spin a tale any more – doesn't want to turn her grandparents and mother into characters in the simplistic narrative that Matt has dreamt up. She feels ashamed of her earlier expansiveness, her thrill at having an audience, at being able to give them what they want, a scene out of a spy movie. When actually, it is real.

Luckily, Matt has launched into an exegesis of Fukuyama's theses for Bennie's sake, and nobody seems to expect her to contribute to the conversation any more.

It is real. When her mother has told her about it, there has been no excitement at the suspense, no boastfulness about the danger. Only the memory of those terrifying, huge waves, an unimaginable cold, and water, so much water, rain and sea and darkness and water, every minute lasting an hour, and the horror of discovering that what you thought was your rescue is a certain ticket to solitary confinement. Eva reddens with the shame of it, tries to focus instead on Adam as he basks in the glow of his warm, caring tribe.

And she realizes that this is one of the things she loves about him, this confidence in his own origins, in a world that wants to do him good – and that this confidence is strong enough for her to share it too, to wrap it around her like a new skin.

'IT'S SO WEIRD – it's a bit like being on holiday – all of this.'
'What do you mean?'

'All this – people coming round. Coming round and just sitting around. And endless cups of tea. We all just sit around, making cups of tea.'

'You know, Eva, you can say if it's too much. If you need to be alone. People would understand.'

'No, that wasn't what I meant. I just – I'm just observing. It's just strange. It's like the world has ground to a halt, the way it does when there's a Tube strike, or when it snows.'

'Except we haven't all used it as an excuse to go down to the pub.'

Carmen shot Henry a glance that Eva felt propel her into a bygone era: the twinkle in her eye, the mischief curling the corner of her lip . . . It was as though the old Carmen was back, as though the intervening years of death and destruction were briefly being lifted.

'I mean . . . We could, though.'

'We could what?'

'We could go down the pub.'

Henry bristled with Englishness.

'But – I mean – Carm. I don't think Eva . . .'

'It's fine. Carmen's right. Adam would much rather we went and had a pint in his honour rather than sitting around here moping.'

'Well – I mean – if you're sure . . .'

'Come on, Hennes, you know it makes sense. Besides, you're always boasting about your Irish roots – don't your people celebrate their dead by getting wasted?'

'Oh – we're getting wasted now, are we?'

'Let's start with a pint and take it from there.'

It was such an exquisitely painful, joyful moment. The bustle of the three friends as they pushed their chairs back, cleared the table, picked up their coats. The rustle of arms being slipped into sleeves, the tying of shoelaces. It was like countless moments at university, or on London evenings after that, when Adam had been with them. It was as though performing the actions they had shared with him might bring him back, or at least pushed them a little closer to him. For the first time since his death, Eva could feel the joy of who he was, of who he had been, even though she could also feel how much this joy would make his absence all the sharper once it had run its brief course. She smiled at Henry and Carmen.

'Dude. It's a while since I've seen you give us one of those.'

A smile. She was smiling. Even though Adam was dead. Her facial muscles felt slightly strained, unused to the once-familiar motion, like an athlete back out on the running track after recovering from an injury.

And then the old twinge, after all, tears streaming down to her upturned lips.

'Oh God, now I'm crying . . . But I wanted to say . . .'

She spluttered, and both Henry and Carmen started to half-cry, half-laugh as well.

'Sorry, I didn't mean to set you off . . . No, I wanted to say, this is good. I think Adam would approve. And I can, you know . . .'

It took her a few more incoherent gargles to get the words out.

' . . . this is bringing him back to me a lot more than . . . I don't know. It's like he's with us, in spirit.'

'Yes.'

'Yes, I feel that too.'

' . . .'

' . . .'

' . . .'

'Right then, let's do it. Lamb?'

'Lamb.'

As they took some final moments to dab their eyes dry, Eva's father returned to the flat and walked into the kitchen.

'Ah. Carmen, Henry. Hello.'

'Hi, Jim.'

'Hello.'

'Can I get anyone a cup of tea?'

'Thanks, Dad, we were actually about to go out.'

'Oh really? Good. Where to?'

'To the pub.'

'Right. Well, yes, why not.'

'We won't be long though.'

'Oh no, take as long as you like. Your mother should be back soon too, she and I can take care of dinner.'

'Right.'

'Sorry to hear about your job, Henry.'

'Oh. Yes. Thank you, Mr Bard. Well, you know – it's just . . . the way things go, I suppose.'

'Hm. Yes. Well, I'm sure you'll have no trouble finding something else.'

'Let's hope so . . .'

'Why? What happened to your job?'

'You haven't been watching the news much lately, have you, Eva?'

'Um. No . . .'

'I'll explain once we get to the pub. Come on.'

'Right-o. Yes. Off you go, then.'

'Right, yes.'

'Bye, Jim.'

'Bye, Mr Bard.'

'Bye, Carmen. Bye, Henry. Bye, love.'

They filed out of the flat under her father's watchful eye, like teenagers, like kids, like people from before the time Adam died.

'**R**IGHT, SO. EVA, gin and tonic, I assume?'
'Oh, it's all right, Henry, I'll get this.'

'No, no, no, really, this one is definitely on me. I have a couple of announcements to make, you see.'

'Oh. Well. OK, then. Yes, G&T.'

'Carm?'

'I'll have an Old Bombardier please, Henry.'

'Adam?'

'Um. Pint of lager. Any.'

'Right-o.'

Henry manages to carve himself a passage through the Friday-evening pub crowd, mainly by throwing his weight around.

'Helps to be a rugby player at times like these, doesn't it?'

'It certainly does. Yet another area where a public-school education gives you an unfair advantage over the rest of us.'

'What's all this about announcements? Either of you know what he's on about?'

'I have no idea.'

'Let's just hope he's not about to tell us he's got that ghastly woman pregnant or something.'

'Oh my God. I hadn't even thought of that. It can't be that, surely?'

'I'd have thought Henry had enough sense of propriety not to let that happen accidentally.'

'Let's hope so.'

'Imagine. We'd be saddled with her for *life*.'

'*He*'d be saddled with her for life.'

'Oh, please let it not be that.'

'I know we've been over this a million times already, but what *does* he see in her?'

'Right, I might just leave you two to bitch away for a while and help Henry carry those pints.'

'Oh, like you've never said a bad word about her.'

'Just wish me luck getting through the crowd. I never did have the right frame for rugby.'

'Yes, I've always wondered why Eva went for such a puny type as you.'

'Charming.'

'It's his mind, Carmen. Adam has a very attractive mind.'

'Hey, I didn't say bitch about *me*.'

'Ad, I hate to break it to you, but that would kill off about fifty per cent of the conversations Eva and I have together.'

'Besides, you seemed to be saying you disapprove of us bitching about Georgie? I mean, we've got to talk about *someone* . . .'

'OK, fine. I'm going to help Henry.'

Adam's technique for negotiating a London crowd is to slide between the cracks; it's a talent as well, to reach your goal through unobtrusiveness. Soon, he too has disappeared into the mass.

Eva looks at the bodies, packed together like T-shirts in an overfilled suitcase. Or Semtex. She tries to get an estimate of numbers: fifty, maybe, between here and the bar. There were three more suicide bombings today in Baghdad. Forty-three dead. She thinks of the Admiral Duncan, and feels a fleeting surge of adrenalin that is half panic, half something else. Excitement? Why else do people watch disaster movies, thrillers, the nine o-clock news?

'You guys are lucky, you know, Eva.'

'Hm?'

'Just – that you and Adam have such a good relationship. There aren't that many of those around.'

'No, you're right. Although I think it's mainly me who's lucky to have Adam.'

'He's lucky to have you too. You're both lucky.'

'Hm. Anyway. To return to the topic of the heinous Georgie . . .'

'Ugh.'

'Come on, Carm. Don't you think you should speak to Henry?'

'What, about how heinous Georgie is?'

'Well – yeah.'

'Are you serious?'

'I think *Henry's* serious. Don't you?'

'Well – yes, I think he probably is – but, I mean, we can't exactly butt in and tell him to split up with her, can we?'

'Do you think she'll make him happy?'

'. . .'

'. . .'

'Good question. I don't know.'

'If we think she won't make him happy, don't we have a duty to intervene?'

'Well – I don't know. I don't feel I can judge whether she'll make him happy or not. I mean, he has chosen to go out with her.'

'. . .'

'Eva, if you feel so certain about it, why don't *you* talk to him?'

'Because – I mean, come on . . .'

'Come on what?'

'Come on, you're the one who has this – *thing* with him . . .'

Carmen laughs, head thrown back, throat open.

'What *thing* do I have with Henry?'

'You know what I mean.'

'We're friends. Close friends.'

'He'd be much happier with you than with Georgie.'

'How can you possibly know that?'

'. . .'

'And who says I would want to be with Henry, anyway?'

'Oh come on, don't tell me you've never thought about it.'

'Here they are.'

Henry sloshes beer over the table as he plonks the pints down; Adam promptly but carefully deposits his drinks and mops up the spillage with a napkin he must have taken from the bar with precisely this eventuality in mind. Henry, oblivious, stretches out in his chair.

'So.'

'So yes. Henry. What's all this news you've got?'

'Well.'

'. . .'

'Come on, Henry, we're all on tenterhooks here.'

'I feel I should warn you, Carmen, that you're not going to like it.'

'Why am I not going to like it?'

'Because I have been offered a new job.'

'Doing what – designing weapons to kill Iraqi children?'

'Not quite, but I fear bad enough in your eyes – I've been offered a position as senior analyst at Lehman Brothers.'

'Oh. Right.'

'I told you you wouldn't like it.'

'I don't not like it! You're putting words into my mouth.'

'Only because I know you so well.'

Henry's take-it-or-leave-it bluster is betrayed by the genuine anxiety in his eyes as he looks at Carmen; he really is worried about what she'll think, isn't he?

Adam makes a valiant attempt to lighten the atmosphere.

'Well, congrats, Henry old banana – cheers!'

'Cheers! Yes, congrats, Henry.'

'Cheers. Congratulations.'

'Cheers.'

'OK, so please do not interpret this as me criticizing your choice, because I'm not. But – you're becoming an investment banker, right? Aren't you kind of lacking in mathematical knowledge for that?'

'No, all I'll have to do is read the papers – at my level you're looking at the bigger picture. The grunt work is for the junior analysts.'

'Aren't you a bit young to be senior?'

'Well. OK. A few strings were pulled. But you know, Carm, I actually have quite good analytical skills – they put me through a battery of tests and my results were more than decent.'

'Of course, I don't doubt that. Well, well done. I mean, it's great.'

'I'm certainly excited about the fat wad of cash that's going to be landing in my account every month, let me tell you. But yes, it's going to be a really fascinating job. I mean, I know you disapprove, Carm, but these guys really are at the centre of things, you know? You're having a real impact on the world, working for a company like that.'

Poor Henry. They've had enough impassioned arguments over the evils – or not – of the financial sector for him to know that his best friends aren't going to share his enthusiasm for his chosen career path. And he really is so enthusiastic, bubbling with excitement at the life to come! Eva has often wondered why Henry doesn't just fraternize with his own kind, who would share his world view unquestioningly. He is the most tolerant of them all, really, and the bravest, nurturing his closest friendships with people who disagree with pretty much everything he stands for. If Carmen and he ever do manage to get it together, they'll certainly be in for some lively debates over their cornflakes every morning.

'Well. That's really great.'

'Yes, I'm very happy. I mean, you know, my job at the moment is perfectly fine, but I was starting to worry I'd never be able to buy a house at this rate . . .'

'Henry! We're not even thirty, for Christ's sake.'

'Still, you know, you want to be thinking about these things. Englishman's castle and all that. So anyway, I was going to have a little drinks party to celebrate, next Friday, if you guys are around.'

'Adam's in Berlin then, aren't you?'

'I'm afraid I am.'

'I'll come along, though. Though I won't be able to stay too late, I'm catching an early flight the next day.'

'Oh, really? Where are you off to?'

'Iraq, actually.'

'Jesus! Seriously?'

'Yes.'

'I can't believe you just drop that into the conversation like you're off for a weekend in Mallorca or something.'

'Oh my God, I would definitely tell you if I was going to Mallorca – that would be a far more traumatic experience.'

'Seriously, though, Eve, you're actually going to Iraq?'

'Guys, I am a journalist, you know, it's kind of part of the job description . . .'

'Aren't you worried?'

'From what I've heard, you're not really allowed to do very much, to be honest, the military is very careful about what they allow you to see. So don't worry, I'll probably be stuck in my hotel room most of the time.'

'Adam, aren't you worried about this?'

'Well, I mean, yeah, of course, but Eva's right, it is her job . . .'

'Hm. Well, be careful though.'

'I'll send you guys a postcard. So, anyway, Friday night then, Henry. I will make sure I get my packing done early, and I will be there.'

'OK, well, good. Carmen, you around?'

'I am indeed. But Henry, what was the other announcement you had to make?'

'Ah. Yes. Well, it's not entirely unrelated to these house-buying considerations, actually.'

'What – you've found a house already?'

'No, no, no! Georgie and I are engaged.'

If any of Adam, Eva or Carmen had been taking a sip from

their drinks at this point, they would have spluttered them right back up. Luckily, Henry seems to interpret their reaction as mere surprise.

'Wow!'

'Wow.'

'Well.'

'Wow.'

'Well. Congratulations again, Henry!'

'Yes, congratulations.'

'Yeah, congrats.'

'Well. That was quick, Hennes! How long is it you guys have been going out?'

'I proposed on our nine-month anniversary. Georgie's the kind of girl who wants a ring on her finger, you know . . .'

'Yes, I can imagine.'

'Wow.'

'Well. Amazing.'

'So how did you propose?'

'Oh, nothing very original, I'm afraid – took the train up to Chichester on the Thursday, under cover of a work trip, to ask for her father's permission, took her over to Paris on the Friday, and fine wine and dined her in that restaurant halfway up the Eiffel Tower on the Saturday – I'd prepped them to bring us some champagne and oysters as soon as we arrived, dropped down on one knee, and there you have it.'

'I didn't know anyone still asked for the father's permission.'

'Well, I like to do things the proper way, you know.'

'Georgie must have been thrilled.'

'Well, at least she said yes, thankfully for me.'

'Well. I think we should have a toast.'

Adam raises his half-empty pint; Carmen follows suit, her features set into a poker face; Eva lifts up the remains of her G&T, which she has almost entirely downed in the last two minutes; they clink against Henry's sturdy Guinness.

'Cheers.'
'To love, my friends!'
'To love indeed.'
'To love!'
'To love . . .'

SOMETIMES YOU SEE something funny, and you know that Adam would have found it funny too, so you start to tell him about it in your mind, but then the laughter changes in your throat, it sort of gurgles out and into choking instead, and then crying, and you feel like you have become this sort of terrible machine, something resembling a meat grinder or pasta maker, where whatever you put into it comes out in tears.

Laughter has become impossible, or rather not impossible, because actually you do laugh, but laughter has become the prelude to weeping, a burst of emotion that can only lead you back to grief, which is where all your emotions take you now, joy, frustration, anger, fear, elation, anxiety, delight at spotting a bird hopping on your windowsill before it rises up into the sky, awe at the sight of snow weighing down the slender branch of an elm tree, relief when the Tube train starts moving again, rage at the inflexibility of a computer system that seems to not want to let you cancel your joint bank account, they are all, it turns out, mere preludes to grief, grief is the highest trump card, you know now, when all other possible feelings have been exhausted, it is grief that will remain.

THE PHONE RANG.
'Hello?'
'Eva.'
'Oh. Hi.'
'How are you doing?'
'Well. You know.'
'. . .'
'Sorry.'
'Don't be silly. Of course it's hard. I know it's still hard.'
'. . .'
'I know it is, Eva.'
'. . .'
'Eva?'
'. . .'
'. . .'
'Yes . . .'
'Maybe this isn't a good time.'
'No, it's fine. How are things?'
'Oh, you know. Ticking over. More or less. I'm not entirely convinced we'll still be here in a year's time, but for now most of the leaks in the boat seem to have been stopped.'
'Uh-huh.'
'We miss you, though.'
'Why, is there a me-shaped leak?'
'Oh come on, that wasn't what I meant – I mean – obviously – not that you're not indispensable – well, I suppose there is a you-shaped leak but, you know, we can find other ways to plug it. Bit of a square-peg-in-a-round-hole situation, obviously, but that

can be dealt with. We want you to take your time – all the time you need.'

'Bill, what are you trying to say? I can't work out whether you're being passive-aggressive or just rambling.'

'I know, neither can I most of the time. That's what decades of married life do to a man.'

'. . .'

'Sorry.'

'Don't apologize, you're still allowed to crack a joke. But listen . . . I don't think I'm ready to go back to work yet. I'm sorry. I know it seems like it's been a while, but . . .'

She wanted to scream that she wasn't ill. She didn't just have some condition that you recovered from, moving on, rebuilding your life, as though it were just a Lego set and not a miasma of relentless pain. People didn't seem to understand that, while for them there may be days and weeks and months going by, time wasn't working like that for her any more. She was trying to swim upstream. Because there was the point in time where Adam died, and before that there was the time when he was still alive, and maybe if she kicked her feet hard enough she could make it back there, against the current. Even if she was only treading water for now, in a large pool that was just the time after his death, not this or that many days or weeks or months after, it made no difference, and why couldn't people understand that?

'Look, Eva, I wouldn't blame you if you never went back to work. It's just I've got the bloody Board on my back and you know what shareholders are like – they're less capable of human sympathy than Stalin circa 1937.'

'Why do they care about me, though? It's not like I can turn the internet off, or do whatever else it would take to save their paper.'

'No. But you are a marketable name, and in this time of crisis that is something they can cling on to. Which, my dear, leads me to the crux of the matter: you cannot write at the moment, which

I personally find entirely understandable. But the Board is in a flap and wants your name back in our opinion pages. So . . . I have suggested we reprint some of your old articles. A sort of Eva Bard retrospective. Highlights from our sharpest commentator on international relations in the Age of Terror. Or something like that. What do you think of that bloody stroke of genius, eh?'

'Bill, I've only been a journalist for about five years.'

'Eight, I think you'll find. I checked.'

'Whatever. Well. Anyway. If you think it'll keep the Board happy, I don't mind you reprinting my old articles. Go ahead.'

'Well, I was wondering if you would mind giving me a bit of a hand with selecting them?'

'Bill. The longest I can focus on anything these days is about three minutes. I don't think you quite understand what state my mind is in at the moment. Think of me as someone with very severe brain damage.'

' . . . '

'Bill? Are you still there?'

'It will come back, you know, Eva. You'll start being able to think again. Or, I mean – to think about other things.'

'But I don't even want to think about other things – I just – it just doesn't interest me any more . . .'

' . . . '

'It's weird, you know. I was thinking – ha! OK, so maybe I am doing a bit of thinking now and again – But anyway, I was think-ing, it's so weird, there's been this huge financial crisis going on, I mean potentially the actual death knell of capitalism, and I just really don't give a shit. I can't get myself to take the slightest inter-est in it.

'You will, Eva. Eventually. And it won't be a bad thing – it won't mean you're forgetting Adam, or not doing him justice in some way.'

'Won't it, though? I think that would be exactly what it would mean.'

'. . .'

'You know, I was already having doubts about my job before he died. The evening before. I wanted to talk to him about it. I tried to, in fact, but we were in a cab and he gets carsick if he can't concentrate on the road.'

'. . .'

'Got carsick. Used to get carsick.'

'. . .'

'I was feeling – I don't know. Tired of it all. Like what use is it really, what we do?'

'Eva, how can you say that? We tell people what's going on in the world. We make it a little less ignorant, with every article we publish.'

'Do we, though? Don't we just tell the stories people want to hear? What about all the ones we don't tell?'

'Surely that's no argument not to tell the stories we do tell?'

'. . .'

'. . .'

'I wanted to talk to him about it, but he was too carsick and then I couldn't be bothered to try and explain once we'd got home. I thought I'd just wait till tomorrow.'

'. . .'

'. . .'

'I'm sorry, Eva.'

'. . .'

'Adam was very proud of your work, you know. He didn't think you were wasting your time.'

'. . .'

'Eva?'

'Yes. Yes, I know.'

'. . .'

'Yes.'

'And I'm very proud of your work, too. I'm rather proud of myself, in fact, for having spotted you.'

'Now you're just trying to flatter me . . .'

'No, really, Eva. I remember being so bowled over by that material you brought back from 9/11 . . .'

'Well – it wasn't exactly hard to come back from 9/11 with good material . . .'

'But you jumped in there, Eva – you went straight to the action. It was journalistic instinct at its purest – and the detail with which you managed to register what was happening, despite being in so much danger yourself . . . It's a rare talent. I remember thinking, goodness, we have a natural-born frontline reporter here, and all you'd been assigned to before that seemed to have been reporting on local magistrates' courts and various pointless press conferences . . .'

'Yes, I was grateful to you for pulling me out of the hellhole of general reporting.'

'I asked Adam about it once, you know. About what it had been like for him, you wanting to rush to the Twin Towers like that.'

'And – what did he say?'

'That he was terrified – rightly so, obviously. But that he could see it was something you needed to do – that something was driving you to go there. A need to bear witness, he said.'

'Hm. He's probably right about that. Was – was right.'

' . . .'

'You know, that's another thing about him being gone. When I think about that day – I mean, it was one of the most horrific – one of those experiences that you'll always carry with you. That no one else will really ever be able to imagine, to understand, if they weren't there. But we were there, together. We could understand what it had been like, really been like. But now he's gone, I have no one I can share that with any more.'

' . . .'

'We disagreed about some of it too, you know. Some of what happened. It used to infuriate me. But now I miss even that – that sense that my memory of the day could be questioned, could be up for debate – that it was fluid in some way. Now it's fixed – I'm left with only my version, the story I've told myself about it.'

'...'

'...'

'I'm sorry, Eva – so sorry. I don't know what else to say.'
'I know. It's fine.'

'...'

'...'

'But try. Do it for me. Take a quick look at those old articles of yours, pick a few out. See if you can fire up your deadly synapses again.'

'...'

'Come on. It won't take you that long, and it'll do you good. You'll see.'

Eva wondered why everybody was so fucking keen on things that did her good these days. Have some of this nice pot roast, it'll do you good. Let's go for a walk, it'll do you good. Have a good cry, that'll do you good. Why don't we go and watch a comedy show? It might do you good, you know. It was as though there was an unofficial period during which everybody was agreed that they had to indulge her grief, and they had now moved on to the buck-up-girl-sort-yourself-out-chin-up-and-all-that phase. There was nothing she cared about less in the world than a fatuous pile of her old articles. Adam was never coming back, and five months, five years, five decades from now, that was never going to change.

'All right.'

'That's the spirit! I'll have a shufti through them too and we can compare notes. Maybe have a coffee in a couple of weeks' time?'

'Uh-huh.'

'...'

'...'

'We all miss you, you know, Eva. Board or not.'

117

'. . .'

'. . .'

'Uh-huh.'

'Anyway, I'd better leave you to it. Take good care of yourself, Eva.'

She hung up, noticing as she did so that this was rather out of character. She used to be someone who could never say goodbye: always the last to leave a party because she couldn't bear to work her way through a crowded room bidding farewell, always repeating niceties on the telephone until the line went dead at the other end. Now, it seemed, she was one of those people who cut others off mid-sentence. Interesting. She was frequently noticing, these days, small shifts in her behaviour which she assumed dated back to Adam's death. She had few feelings about this beyond a mild sense of curiosity and, occasionally, a distant concern that his death might be turning her into a different person. What if she were no longer recognizable to a hypothetical Adam returned from the grave? Would she still be able to do his memory justice if she was forgetting who she had been when he was alive?

Eva stared at her spent phone for a while, then at the kitchen around her. She heard the clatter of post through the letterbox, and went to take a look. There were two envelopes on the doormat: a bank statement, addressed only to her, where once it would have carried both their names. And a theatre brochure, addressed only to Adam. Eva burst into tears.

Some time later – minutes, hours, she wasn't sure – she was rummaging around their filing cabinet, trying to find the folder in which to place the bank statement. Another new character trait: she had never, in the past, been the kind of person to immediately file anything. That was Adam's field of expertise. Perhaps he was, ghoul-like, taking over her body. You're welcome, Adam. I'll gladly live for us both. It is, in fact, the only reason I continue to live.

Adam's superior administrative skills had also meant that he

118

had taken charge, over the years, of setting aside Eva's press cuttings. Oh, what the hell, she thought. I might as well take a look. She set aside the piece she had written about the Congo, her first Iraq trip, her indictment of the international humanitarian aid system. Tony Blair, of course. 9/11, of course. She stumbled on an article she had forgotten, about a kid in East London who had started a community initiative to foster contacts between recently arrived immigrants and their wary native neighbours. The terrorist interview. Each article brought back memories, not of the places and people it was about, but of the stage in her and Adam's relationship when she had written it. She remembered the steamy hotel in Kinshasa from which she would try hopelessly to get a Skype connection to talk to him; how angry he'd been with her for going on that trip. She remembered the excitement and outrage they had both felt about the aid piece, which they had essentially written together after Adam's disillusioning elective in Sudan: he had been shocked by the disorganization and arrogance of the people working for the small NGO he had flown out with, and Eva's further research had revealed an opaque, self-serving system of dubious benefit to the poor people it was supposed to be rescuing. It reminded Eva of one of her later articles, about the rise of Al-Qaeda-inspired terrorism in Kenya as a result of the Sudanese conflict. It would be interesting to put these two stories side by side, perhaps under the title 'The myriad ways in which East Africa continues to be fucked over, from colonialism to the present day'.

This chain of thought startled her: she was thinking like she used to. Making connections. And she remembered how much she used to *care* about all the violence she had seen in the world, how much she had wanted to understand it. How meeting the young man – still so young, younger than she was – who had wanted to shatter his own body into thousands of tiny pieces in the name of Allah, who had wanted to shatter other bodies into thousands of tiny pieces in the name of Allah, as many of them as possible, what an uncanny moment that had been, how she had looked into his eyes, and listened to what he had said, and felt at once like she understood him completely, the fire, the rage, the willingness to die for something so much bigger than yourself, but also could never understand him. How she had once wanted to make sense of all this, connect all these dots – Al-Qaeda, Iraq, the West, the Congo, the South, the East, Afghanistan, the CIA, the Soviets, Bosnia, Chechnya, the blood and the blood and the blood – and how, after having seen so many bodies torn apart, so many glazed eyes and strewn limbs and flies crawling through open mouths, how one quiet body in a cosy bed in North London had made all of that seem futile, had taken the sting out of all this pain and injustice.

Eva couldn't find the article about Kenya, so she opened an earlier drawer (Adam ordered them by five-year periods, into which all sorts of different documents – medical records, letters, tax returns – were placed, as though he was modelling his life on the economic history of the USSR) – and gasped as she caught sight of a folder entitled 'Berlin'.

For a while, she just gazed at the tag, 'BERLIN', written in Adam's meticulous handwriting – too meticulous for a doctor. She could see the strokes of his pen, imagine his fingers guiding it carefully, attentively, remember the care and attention with which these same fingers would trace a stroke down the inside of her arm. Then she slipped her own fingers, gently, into the opening of the folder, and took out a slim wad of papers of different shapes and sizes. A few flyers for concerts and bars – 'La Femme im Club Bassy', 'BAIZ BLEIBT', 'Walacatha' – and she felt a pang of anger towards Adam that she didn't know what they all stood for, and whether he had been there, and now she couldn't just ask him about it. A beer mat inscribed with 'Berliner Pilsner'. A couple of theatre programmes: 'Volksbühne', 'Schaubühne'. A world that was Adam's, and that she knew nothing about. And a slip of paper, on which he had written a name and address – Ulrich's name and address. He would have written those words down years ago, when he first started looking for a room in Berlin. And then Ulrich had become a part of his life, and she had never even met the guy. She ran her fingers over the slip of paper, over the strokes of Adam's pen.

And then that name again, that name she had been trying to ignore ever since she'd looked through his emails, but which she realized now had been lying in wait for her all along, in some dark corner of her brain.

Lena Bachmann.

And the name screamed at her and made her doubt and made her pulse race and the world shift into an ever so slightly softer focus before her eyes, and maybe start to move a little, and she had to put a hand out to steady herself.

What had this life been, this other life of his?

What was this city, that was hers and not hers?

She had to know.

She rang Bill.

'Eva.'

'Bill. I'll email you the articles I've selected tomorrow, OK? And then you can have the final decision on what goes in, I don't want to have to deal with it. I'm going to go away for a while.'

'Blimey. That's a bit of a turnaround.'

'I'm going to Berlin.'

'And why ever not? Eva, I'm on a Tube, about to go underground – look forward to the email. And auf Wiedersehen.'

Eva laughed, giddy with fear. 'Auf Wieder—'

But they had been cut off.

'OH FOR FUCK'S SAKE.'

' . . . '

' . . . '

'*What?*'

'You're doing it again.'

'I'm doing *what* again?'

'You know.'

'I really don't!'

How has it got to this stage? She's sure they didn't argue like this a few months ago. She's sure a few months ago he made her feel good about her globetrotting lifestyle, like it was actually something that was quite sexy about her. Why do they always argue now? How do you get to this stage?

'You're trying to make me feel guilty.'

'For fuck's sake, Eva, what have I done?'

'You know. You're giving me that look.'

'What fucking look?!'

'You don't want me to go, do you?'

' . . . '

'You know how important this is to me, and you don't want me to go.'

'I'm just worried about you.'

'Bullshit.'

'How can you say that?'

'I don't remember you being this worried when I went off to Iraq.'

'That was – different.'

'I know it was bloody different! You know what the difference was? Iraq was at *war*. Congo: not at war. At least, not in the part I'm going to. So I don't know why you're suddenly getting so concerned about my safety, after happily waving me off to total shitholes for years.'

'How can you say that? You know I've always worried about you when you've gone off to those places – I just didn't want to be holding you back.'

'So why are you trying to hold me back now?'

That wasn't what she meant. It's a terrible thing to say. Of course Adam isn't holding her back, has never held her back; on the contrary, he's been pushing her forward, supporting her, giving her a strength she would never have had alone. The problem, when you are in the middle of an argument with someone you love, is that you have a range of choices of things to say, things that might be true, hurtful, unfair, honest, downright lies, caring, nasty, vindictive, generous, or any combination of those things, and usually you go for exactly the wrong one. And then, once the words are said, they are out there, in the open air, inscribed on the register of all the things you have ever said to each other, and there is no getting away from them any more.

'Is that really how you feel about me – that I'm holding you back?'

Adam's mood has shifted, from conciliatory to cold, hard-eyed, wounded.

'Of course it isn't. You know it isn't.'

'. . .'

'I'm sorry. I shouldn't have said that. It just came out.'

'But you said it.'

'I know. I'm sorry.'

Then, the challenge is also that you don't have to choose your words just once, get them out and live with whatever they have created – there are always more things you could say, more potentially disastrous options, and once you've started on a conversation like this you have to just keep on going until you have

123

dug deep enough into each other's insides to reach some kind of conclusion, or stalemate, or exhaustion.

'Adam. There's something you're not telling me. I know you always worry about me, but come on, you wouldn't be like this about me going if there wasn't something else. What is it?'

Adam looks at her inscrutably. The problem with these kinds of arguments is that the person you love also has a huge panoply of words to choose from, and they all have consequences of their own. It's all this reacting to each other's words that is the problem.

'Adam – I can't know where to start if you won't tell me what you're thinking.'

His voice answers with a hard edge that scares her:

'I don't know what I'm thinking.'

' . . .'

'But – you must feel this too – that things haven't been going well between us for the past few months.'

She has been feeling it, of course – has often been railing against him internally, has even daydreamed of what a life without him might be like – but it's worrying, and unexpected, for it to be brought up by him. And how strange, that there is no particular incident at the root of all this, or at least none that she can pinpoint, that they just seem to have slipped into this state of natural irritation, as though it is just life itself that has been eroding their love, just the passing of time.

She doesn't answer for now, lets Adam slowly come out with the words, form sentences, watches his moves before making hers, like a poker player.

'And – I don't know. I guess I feel strange about you going when things are so fragile between us. I've always felt in the past, when you've gone on these trips, that whatever happens, at least I don't have any doubts about – well, I don't know, about where we stand in relation to each other. Right now – I don't know.'

'Right now you don't know what?'

They used to joke about divorce. When you marry someone,

you develop this gallows humour, in the euphoria of this big adventure you've embarked on together: oh my God, I'm going to have to divorce you if you put this knife in the dishwasher again! You didn't ring the plumber? You forgot? That's grounds for divorce, you know. Divorce like a bogeyman, something to give you the thrill of a scare, because you sort of believe in it even though you don't really. A joke word. And now neither of them wants to say the joke word, because the joke doesn't sound so funny any more.

'I don't know – I don't know if you're going to be with me, if you go away. Before, I always knew that you would be thinking of me, loving me, missing me, wherever you were – that I'd be a part of your life, even if we weren't together. Now – now I'm not sure I will be. And I'm not sure you'll be a part of my life.'

'. . .'

'I think – to be honest, it'll be a relief not to have you around to argue with all the time.'

'. . .'

'Isn't that terrible?'

There's a catch in his voice when he says this, and she knows he means it as a reaching out to her, but she can't help but let anger dictate her reaction. Our stupid pride. Our stupid, self-defensive reflexes.

'If it's going to be such a fucking relief not to have me around, why are you trying to stop me from going?'

'Because I don't want to feel that way about you. And I don't want you to be feeling that way about me. To be relieved that I'm not there.'

'Who fucking said I'd be relieved not to have you around?'

He's right. She definitely will, in a way, be relieved not to have him around. How have they come to this?

'I think you will be. Would be. At least a part of you would.'

'. . .'

'. . .'

'And what's – I mean, where's the evidence for this? What makes you think that's what I'm thinking?'

He almost whispers it, as though it is a dangerous thing to bring up, as though he is uttering one of God's secret, forbidden names:

'The Holden Prize party. You'd rather not have had me there. When you were talking to all those people, you'd rather I hadn't been there.'

'When I was talking to all those people? Which people?'

'That Tom guy, for example.'

' . . .'

'I think you're looking forward to being with him in the Congo. To not having me around.'

'Who the fuck cares about Tom?'

This is disingenuous. She totally fancies Tom. It would be hard for Adam not to have noticed, given it's the first time she's fancied someone else – in a serious way – since she and Adam have been together. Tom, with his inky-black hair and astonishing green eyes, his sardonic sense of humour, his pumped-up war photographer's frame, so imposing next to Adam's slender figure.

Her heart goes out to Adam; all he needs is some reassurance. But she worries it would sound untrue, because it kind of would be, in a way, even though of course she still loves him and wants to be with him and knows that Tom is basically a bit of a tool, it's just he is also very sexy, right now, at this moment in time, after months of marital attrition, Tom is definitely a sexy proposition, but also an irrelevant one, and Eva is worried that Adam might not understand all the subtleties of this. She can't risk sounding insincere, and also, by the way, she is pretty pissed off about all these accusations, when she has always been faithful to Adam, and wasn't planning on doing anything with Tom even if, admittedly, she isn't completely immune to his charms.

'I don't give a shit about Tom, OK? He's a self-satisfied womanizer. I can't think of anyone I'd less like to have an affair with.'

'I don't believe you.'

'Christ. Then what the hell am I meant to say?'

' . . .'

' . . .'

' . . .'

'I'm not going to bloody Congo to bloody shag Tom.

' . . .'

'Jesus. I can't believe we're even having this conversation. I mean, if anyone has the right to ask questions, it's me, anyway.'

'What the hell is that supposed to mean?!'

'You're the one who's got a whole other life going on in Berlin.'

'What the—? I'm there, like, for a week every three months or something. And it's not like I haven't asked you a million times to come over with me.'

'Still.'

'Still what?'

' . . .'

'What?!'

'What about that Lena woman?'

'Who?'

'Lena Bachmann.'

'What about her? She's just a friend.'

'I thought she was just a colleague.'

'She's not a doctor. Just someone I know in Berlin.'

'You told me she was a doctor.'

'Well, you must have misunderstood me.'

'You told me she was a fellow doctor you'd met at a medical conference.'

'Well, I mean . . . She's not. She's just a woman I know in Berlin. I've met people in Berlin and struck up acquaintances with them, sorry.'

'That's not how you told me you met her.'

'As I said, you must have got the wrong end of the stick.'

'It was pretty clear, the way I remember the conversation.'

'Well, I don't remember it, so how am I supposed to answer that accusation?'

'Ah, so I'm accusing you now, am I?'

'Aren't you?'

'What am I accusing you of, exactly?'

'I don't know, you tell me.'

'No, really, you tell me – I'm interested to hear what you think I think is going on between you and this Lena character.'

'OK, this is just absurd. We are ending this conversation right now.'

'Right. Interesting.'

'For the record, though, I can't believe you're trying to put this stuff on me.'

'What stuff?'

'I'm not even going to dignify that with an answer.'

CARMEN TUGGED NERVOUSLY at the sleeve of her sweater: she would pinch a bit of it at the wrist, and twist it until it was double-wrapped around her fingers, then let it go again. With every repetition, the fabric stretched a little more irreversibly, its deformation setting like drying cement. Georgie was eyeing Carmen's hands with fascination, wincing with every twist: in truth, the sweater looked expensive, not something to be destroyed so thoughtlessly. Carmen didn't even seem aware that she was doing it.

They were waiting for Henry to come back with the drinks, and as always happened when Georgie was left without him, they were all struggling to think of what to say next.

Both Eva and Carmen had put their hands to their wallets when Henry had offered to go and get the first round, uncertain of how dire his situation had become. He'd waved them away blusterously.

'Oh come on, I can still stretch to a round at your leaving drinks, Eva.'

But Georgie had winced at that as well. She had deep bags under her eyes, which her make-up could only do so much to conceal. Carmen's eyes, in contrast, had more like faint rings around them, the colour of a week-old bruise, and they had a tendency to dart around frantically when she wasn't being careful.

How broken they had all become.

It was Georgie who finally thought of something to say.

'So, you're leaving tomorrow then, Eva?'

'Yes.'

' . . . '

' . . . '

'It's very brave of you.'

'Brave?'

'Yes – to . . . just go off like that. To somewhere where you don't know anybody. After . . . all that's happened.'

'Well. I don't know. It feels like the right thing to do, somehow.'

'You're not worried you'll feel lonely?'

'I'm lonely as it is, Georgie. Unfortunately.'

Eva surprised herself by the frankness of her response – she was hardly used to having heart-to-hearts with Georgie, of all people. And Georgie surprised her with her reaction, a slow, sad nod of understanding, an undisguised display of feeling that was quite out of character. Carmen had noticed it too, and was examining Georgie with curiosity.

Then Henry returned with the drinks, and ideas of things to talk about. Though he looked worried too, his face drawn and weathered in a way it never used to be, he still retained his usual bonhomie. The only time Eva had seen him lose it, really, was in the weeks immediately following Adam's death. And then, either because it was such an essential part of his character, or because it had been so successfully drilled into him by his polite English upbringing, it had slowly returned, and even now, in spite of the circumstances, it endured.

Carmen and Henry were now verbally sparring with each other about something or other, which usually would have made Georgie nervous, but she didn't seem to be noticing it: she was looking intently at Eva, somewhat unnervingly. Then she leaned over towards her.

'Why – I'm sorry, obviously you don't have to answer this if you feel I'm being indiscreet – but why *are* you going?'

Eva was disarmed.

'Um. Well. No, I mean, it's fine, you're not being indiscreet at all. I suppose – Berlin was such an important part of Adam's life, you know, he absolutely loved it there, was fascinated by it. And I never got to share that with him – through my own fault, by the

130

way, it just never seemed the right time to go, and well . . . You never know how much time you have, do you?'

Georgie gave another of her weirdly wise, sympathetic nods.

'And so. Well. It feels important to see that now, to understand what it was that he loved so much. It feels – this is probably going to sound really insane – but it feels like a way of keeping him alive, or, I don't know, the memory of him alive. That probably doesn't make any sense . . .'

'No, it does. It does.'

Georgie stared mournfully at her untouched vodka-tonic, ran a perfectly manicured finger along the side of the beer mat underneath it. She seemed to be wandering off into some worrisome train of thought.

And Eva wondered what an honest response to her question would have been. Why *was* she going to Berlin? There were so many factors, too much complexity to come up with an answer even for herself, let alone for Georgie. She thought of Adam, the shine he used to have in his eyes when he came back from one of his trips there, and how she used to deliberately ignore it, how she wouldn't let him take her there, and how guilty she felt about that now. And she thought of her mother's voice on the telephone when she had called to announce her departure, the barely concealed fear as she tried to dissuade Eva from going, claiming it would be too much for her right now, grieving alone in a foreign land, and the resignation that replaced this fear when she understood that Eva was not going to be talked out of it, and anyway Berlin was hardly entirely foreign, the place half her family was from, and at this Eva felt a twinge of excitement, of curiosity, and this too she felt guilty about, because it was exactly that excitement that Adam had wanted to share with her. And also she felt guilty about the name hovering in the back of her mind, Lena Bachmann, and the accusation of Adam it implied, and was this trip, were all these supposed other reasons for going, just excuses for a green-eyed poke around in Adam's affairs?

Georgie cleared her throat awkwardly.

'Eva . . .'

'Yes?'

'Can I ask you something? I mean . . .'

'. . .'

'I . . . how are you going to live? You haven't been working for so long now – where are you going to get the *money* from?'

She said it with such urgency, such passion. Of course. Because what else could be on Georgie's mind right now than the *money*, where the *money* would come from?

'Oh, er . . .'

'I'm sorry. I'm being horribly indiscreet again. You don't have to answer if you don't want to, of course.'

'No, no, it's fine . . . Actually, money is the least of my problems – I have quite a few savings, and, well, Adam, being Adam, had taken out life insurance, so I'm kind of fine for a while . . .'

'Oh. Oh good. It's good at least that you don't have to worry about that.'

Eva wondered if that was a flicker of envy she'd just seen in Georgie's eye, just before it darted over to Henry.

Henry beamed at his wife.

'All well, my love?'

Georgie smiled wanly.

'And you, Eva? Feeling ready for the Krauts?'

'Yeah. Yeah, I am, I think.'

'Well, *prost* to that, I say.'

'*Prost.*'

'. . .'

'. . .'

'You're very jovial this evening, Hennes.'

'Oh, well. You know. No point in moping about, is there?'

'No, I suppose not.'

Now that it was just Eva and Henry doing the talking,

Carmen and Georgie had sunk back into oddly similar positions, eyes lowered, discreetly wringing hands.

'Any news on the job front?'

'Oh, it's an unmitigated disaster. The whole system has seized up – basically, no one's hiring any more, and as you can imagine there are thousands of people like me vying for any opening that does come up . . . No, the golden age of finance is over, I'm afraid. I'm thinking of trying something completely different, actually.'

'Meaning?'

'I'm not sure yet – there's this fast track teacher training pro gramme they might be opening up, apparently, or maybe I'll look into getting a job in the charity sector . . . Give a little back to the community, you know?'

'And that's all doable, financially?'

'Well, depends on how you look at it, doesn't it, George?'

Henry gave Georgie's back a rueful pat. She looked broken, Henry radiated buoyant good humour. Perhaps adversity was what he needed: after all, Henry came from a line of men born with silver spoons in their mouths, who only really came into their own once they had been thrust into the malarial swamps of the Raj.

'What Henry means is that it's doable if we sell the house.'

'Oh.'

'. . .'

'Hang on – which house?'

'Oh, the cottage definitely has to go. But, I mean, we're barely ever there anyway, are we, darling?'

Georgie nodded slowly, bravely, as though giving the go-ahead for an axe-man to hack through her neck.

'The real question is what we do with our house here. We may need to downsize, I'm trying to work it all out at the moment. Basically, in the manner of all the rest of this bloody crisis, our entire assets rely on lines of credit that all lead back to my now non-existent annual bonus.'

'. . .'

'But, you know. It's only stuff, at the end of the day.'

Perhaps it was mourning for Adam that had made Henry so resilient – or refocused on what he viewed as important in life. And yet, Eva was surprised to find she couldn't hold it against Georgie that she was so distressed by this turn of events – after all, her pain was real, whatever the cause. She too had had the foundations of her world pulled out from underneath her. She was losing her home, her nest, the kingdom which she had built up for herself, and without which she was turning into a quivering, lost little girl, a far cry from the harpy Eva and Carmen used to mock.

How broken they had all become.

'Isn't it weird . . .'

'. . .'

'. . .'

'. . .'

'Hm? Eva? You were starting to say something?'

'Just . . . That it's so weird . . . how Adam doesn't know about any of this. That – I mean, that all of this stuff has happened since he died, this huge crisis, everyone talking about the world never being the same again, wondering if this is the end of capitalism . . . And there was nothing of that before. It's like he was living in a different world.'

Eva wasn't explaining it very well. Henry was looking at her quizzically, Georgie was looking away – reverting to her usual form of seeming a bit embarrassed when Adam was mentioned, as though it had been poor form of him to have died so young. Only Carmen was nodding at her slowly, understandingly.

'Yeah. It's weird.'

Eva thought of what it was she did mean: that Adam seemed like an innocent, a bit naïve, almost, placed at an unfair disadvantage by his ignorance of current events, like medieval people not realizing that the Earth revolves around the Sun, or that bloodletting is not, on the whole, very good for you. That time, or history, was still letting them in on what happened next, whereas he would never know. And it gave the thought of him a kind of extra evanescence, the milky-white sheen of the innocent, the pure, the ghosts who no longer have to dirty their hands with this messy business we call living.

'OK, SO – NO, move that way a bit, there's a road over there.'

'This way?'

'Yeah.'

Adam takes a few steps to the left.

'Yeah, OK, that's good, I think we're good.'

'Right.'

Adam holds up her coat as wide as he can. Eva does a final check: he is more or less blocking the view from the road – otherwise, it's empty fields behind her, a grey barn in front of her. It'll do. She makes sure the bag is within easy reach, then starts undoing her shoe laces. She is wearing trainers, jeans, a loose T-shirt and two sweaters of increasing thickness: the comfortable, easily modulable outfit she favours for long-haul flights. Adam wolf-whistles as she slips off her trousers.

'That is *not* helpful.'

'Sorry.'

'Can you double-check there's no one coming? I need to change my bra, too.'

Adam glances over his shoulder.

'The coast is clear.'

She rapidly unclasps it, slips it off, dives into the overnight bag Adam packed for both of them, pulls out her frilly, special-occasions one, and just as she is straightening up, bare-breasted in the countryside chill, the barn door swings open, releasing a tangy whiff of warm, grassy excrement, a chorus of grunts and shuffling, and a lanky, prepubescent boy. Finding himself nose-to-nose with Eva, he stops, stammers.

'Uh. Uh. Sorry, sorry . . .'

For a few seconds he seems unable to move, then his eyes flicker down to her breasts and he quickly turns away, busies himself with closing the door behind him. He walks away from them, a painful-looking red spreading up from his throat.

Adam bursts out laughing.

'Well, someone will be having some colourful dreams tonight . . .'

'Shh! Oh my God, how embarrassing . . . Poor kid.'

'Poor kid? You've just made his day.'

'Stop giggling and do up my dress, will you?'

'I can't wait to tell Henry and Carm about this . . .'

'Right, let's go, I'll switch shoes in the car, I won't be able to get through this mud in my heels. Oh my God, the shame.'

They pick their way across soft clumps of upchurned earth back to the rental car, Adam looking at once ridiculous and it has to be said quite sexy in his waistcoat and cravat, Eva's movements restricted now by her tight dress, so that she has to be careful not to lose her balance as she skips over the larger puddles of mud.

The drive takes them through a picture-perfect English countryside, narrow lanes lined with high hedges and the occasional glimpse, past a gate or a turn in the road, of fields rushing downhill and rolling up again, dotted with cloud-like sheep or naughty-looking ponies. And all so green, green, green and pleasant. Yesterday she was in a world of yellow dust, asphyxiated bushes stretching claw-like twigs to the sky.

'You OK?'

'Mm-hm.'

'Tired? You must be tired.'

'I feel all right, actually. Apart from I wish I'd had a chance to have a shower. Do I look manky?'

'You look great. That dress is fantastic.'

'Thank you.'

'You're sure you're OK for us to go straight there, though? I don't think anyone would notice if we took a quick break, gave you a chance to, I don't know, register the transition . . .'

'No, don't be silly, we'll be late if we do that.'

'Well, sod it, we'll be five minutes late then, what's the big deal?'

'Adam, you of all people cannot afford to be late.'

'Well, I mean, OK, but . . .'

'Honestly. It's fine. I had time to mull over things on the plane, anyway.'

'Right.'

'   . . .   '

'   . . .   '

'That boy, though . . . the one who came out of the barn . . .'

'Our goggle-eyed friend?'

'Yeah.'

'What about him?'

'He – he kind of reminded me of. You know. The kid. The kid I saw.'

'   . . .   '

'   . . .   '

Maybe she is just seeing his face everywhere. Or maybe there was something similar about them both, a certain swing in their limbs, or maybe it is something common to all boys that age, the unease of manoeuvring a body grown long and unwieldy overnight.

'You're sure you don't want us to stop and talk about it?'

'No, really, it's fine. Besides, we're almost there.'

And indeed, after another few hedgerowed curves, they come to the church, a beautiful, modest English country church, grey stone walls weathered by centuries of rain and frost, into which is being ushered a swarm of morning suits and fascinators.

'Shit. I should have brought a hat.'

'OK, so hang on, they said there'd be somewhere to park on the left-hand side of the church. Oh, look, that man is waving at me, it must be over there.'

'I am literally the only girl here without a hat.'

'I'm sure that can't be true.'

'Look around you!'

A riot of feathers, flowers, ribbons, precariously perched on blindingly glossy coiffures, bob along from the car park to the church.

'Look, Carmen isn't wearing a hat.'

Eva leaps out of the car.

'We are literally the only girls here without hats!'

'Oh hey. You guys actually made it in time.'

'O ye of little faith.'

'Where's Adam?'

'Just over there – he's parking the car.'

'Ah, OK. And you – all good? You must be destroyed.'

'Nah, I'm all right.'

'How was Iraq?'

'Hm. Yeah. I'll tell you about it later, it's not exactly festive material. But, you know, fine. I mean I'm fine.'

'OK . . .'

'Hey Carm!'

'Hi Ad. You got the rings?'

Adam taps his breast pocket.

'Right, well. We'd better get you into position, hadn't we?'

No sooner are they in the church than Henry appears, booming greetings at all who cross his path, before whisking Adam off to the altar. Carmen and Eva watch from the back of the church as Henry points things out to Adam, demonstrates taking a few steps forward, kneeling, turning. Adam nods seriously.

'Henry looks happy, doesn't he?'

It's true, he does. He stands tall and straight, clapping a sturdy hand on Adam's shoulder when he wants to show him where to move to, breaking now and again into a confident, excited smile.

'Yeah, he does.'

Adam is the one who looks nervous, following Henry's every

word and move, as though to miss a single one of them might spell disaster.

'Shall we sit down? I think Henry's reserved some seats for us at the front.'

'Yeah . . . But . . . I mean . . . Carm?'

Carmen turns round, her willowy body twisting with feline elegance under her long blue dress. She looks inquisitively at Eva.

'You're – I mean – you're OK?'

Carmen smiles.

'Yeah, of course I am.'

They make their way to their seats at the front.

'It is weird, though, isn't it?'

'What is?'

'I mean – all this. That it's happening. Actually happening.'

'It'll be you and Adam next, Eva. You'll see.'

Eventually the church fills up, the chatter settles, organ music bursts out around them, and Georgie appears on her father's arm, beautifully wrapped up in intricate layers of white silk and lace, like an expensive Christmas present, and looking on the brink of tears until her eyes meet Henry's beaming gaze and she does actually start to cry, but also to smile, and, awful as the woman is, even Eva has to recognize there's something quite sweet about the moment, that this is love, after all. She glances over at Carmen, who also has a tear in her eye, but it seems a happy tear, a tear caused by the obvious emotiveness of the situation, rather than by anything else.

The service drags on rather interminably under the leadership of an uncharismatic priest, and Eva finds it hard to focus, finds her mind wandering back after all to the past week, the earth and sand colours, ochres and varying shades of yellow, the persistent smell of burning, an acrid stench of rubber and gasoline that follows you everywhere you go, lodges in the back of your nose, and she can smell it again now just thinking about it, and the ceaseless noise, dry rat-a-tats and bangs of uncertain provenance. And above all, how eerily life goes on in a warzone; people still need to do their shopping and send their kids to school, it turns out, even with snipers guiding their crosshairs on to their heads.

Only Adam awakens her interest: how awkwardly he moves in his stiff, rented tailcoat, how he fumbles when he has to hand over the rings and almost drops one on the floor, and it all seems like such a game, like they're kids playing with a plastic tea set, but no, think of the legal ramifications of that ring slipped over that finger, of those words 'I do.' They are all so grown-up, all of a sudden. And she supposes Carmen is right, she and Adam probably will go through the whole rigmarole themselves in not too long, because that's what people do, isn't it? Even in a warzone, that's what people do, they are just a bit more likely to be interrupted by a suicide bomber or a stray missile.

At the reception, Adam and Eva find themselves separated from Carmen, Adam's role as best man having earned them pole position right next to the table where Henry and Georgie are sitting with their families, while Carmen has been relegated to a more backwatery section of the room – which shouldn't really be much of a surprise, given that Henry is unlikely to have had much say in the seating plan.

The guests try to identify their seats, squinting at the placeholders. So many people, each with their own name, their own piece of cardboard telling them where they need to be. Eva watches Henry embrace old ladies, slap young men's backs. So many people. So many parts of her friend's life she was not aware of. The room is like a map of Henry's relationships, each person a fragment of his life, his past, his personality – shards of his exploded self.

So why is Carmen on the outer reaches? Why is Georgie at the centre?

'Do you remember the first time we met Georgie?'

'Hm? I don't know. When was the first time we met her?'

'Seriously? You don't remember? It was that evening we were meant to be going to the Ivy . . .'

'We've never been to the Ivy, have we?'

'No, precisely. We didn't go. Henry had messed up the reservation somehow – I think he'd booked it for a different month or something. We ended up just going for a curry instead.'

'Oh, hang on, yes, this is ringing bells . . .'

'I can't believe I'm having to remind you of this! It was meant to be, like, our big introduction to Henry's new girlfriend.'

'Yeah, no, I can remember us standing outside the Ivy and trying to decide where to go instead . . .'

'And Georgie was so *angry*. That was my very first impression of her. So pissed off with Henry for having got the booking mixed up. And he was being so – so *meek*, so conciliatory. I was really shocked. That she would be so mean to him, in front of his best friends. And then she was so snooty about us going for a curry instead.'

'Well, she was probably really nervous about meeting us all. You know what she's like – it will have been really important to her for our first evening together to be in a fancy restaurant. She was probably just thrown by everything not going to plan.'

'But that was also what I found so weird about her – I was like, if you love Henry, surely you can't get upset about something like that? Booking for the wrong month is such a quintessentially Henry thing to do . . .'

'Ha ha, that's very true . . .'

'She felt like such an intrusion. I was like, if you weren't here, the four of us would just happily go for a curry together, not have to spend hundreds of pounds on dinner, and that would be that.'

'Well, that was probably why she was so nervous – she could probably tell that you thought she was intruding.'

'She gave me this look at the beginning, when it was becoming clear what had gone wrong – like she was trying to get me to join her in being angry with Henry. A kind of "We're both women having to put up with these idiotic men" kind of look. She was probably pissed off I didn't back her up.'

'You're sure you didn't give her an "I am Eva having to put up with an idiotic Georgie" kind of look?'

'Hmph.'

They fall silent as their table fills, and the starters arrive: *foie gras poêlé* for well over two hundred guests. There was a time, not so long ago, when their dinners were just pasta with bacon and tomato sauce and Cheddar cheese grated on top, and sitting on the floor and cutlery that didn't match. They blame it on Georgie, that everything has turned into a performance, but the fact is they're all slowly accumulating table sets and heavy cookbooks, and talking about mortgages instead of love, meaning, the fire in their bellies.

Eventually, Eva falls into conversation with the man next to her – Bertie? – and he turns out to be a nice enough fellow, a bit shy and stammery, but surprisingly knowledgeable about the history of the Middle East: he fell in love with archaeology as a boy, on a school trip to Petra, would have loved to become an archaeologist, in fact, but what can you do, there's absolutely no money in it. But he still goes on digs when he can, and charts with concern the destruction of various precious finds through conflict or natural disaster, from the shores of the Mediterranean to the mountains of Afghanistan. It is a sorry world we live in, when the last traces of ancient civilizations can be destroyed before our very eyes.

The guy sitting opposite them overhears their conversation.

'Did I hear you say you'd been to Iraq?'

'Oh. Yes. I've just got back, in fact.'

'Ah, well you need to tell old Eddie here all about it.'

'Oh, really?'

'Eddie!'

The Eddie in question – smooth, amiable – turns towards them.

'Hm?'

'This young lady here – I'm sorry, what was your name?'

'Eva. Young man.'

'Eva here has just returned from a tour of duty in Iraq.'

'Oh – you're in the army?'

'God, no! I'm a journalist.'

'Maybe she can report back on how your investments are doing, Eddie-o.'

'Investments?'

'Oh, I work for a fund that invests in the security industry. Benno here is being a little facetious.'

'Security, huh? Which fund?'

'Oh, you probably won't have heard of us, we're a very small outfit.'

'Try me.'

'We're called Coutts Withers Jones.'

'So by security you mean arms manufacturers.'

'Well – among other things, yes.'

'Well then, I can report back that your investments do an excellent job of pulverizing twelve-year-old boys at fifty feet.'

'Hey, steady on.'

'Riiiiiiiight . . . Moving on swiftly . . .'

Eddie, who hasn't reacted while everyone around him tries frantically to pedal the conversation back to safer waters, holds Eva in a level gaze.

'It's hardly that simple, you know.'

'Isn't it?'

Then Henry and Georgina appear at their sides, and all eyes turn jovially to the married couple. Henry is beaming, his chest as puffed as a peacock's.

'Everyone happy here?'

'Oh, absolutely, old chap.'

Georgina smiles absently at them, like a queen with affairs of state on her mind, and scans the room with eagle eyes. Behind them, Eva catches a glimpse of both of their sets of parents, deep in conversation, the fathers nodding seriously at each other, the mothers tapping one another's arms affectionately with their long, immaculate nails.

Henry and Georgina are off again, Georgie having signalled with the most discreet of nods that there is something they need to attend to on the other side of the room, and Henry having immediately picked up on it, playing his role to perfection. The rest of the table falls back into chatter, carefully avoiding Eva and her talk of pulverized children, so that she is free to just speak to Adam instead.

'Well, you rattled them a bit.'

'What was I supposed to say? That guy's the one who brought the subject up. I mean, I've just come back from *Iraq*, what the hell do they think is going on out there?'

'Yeah. I know.'

'Anyway. Let's not talk about it now.'

'Right.'

' . . . '

' . . . '

They watch the bridal pair make their way through the many tables, clinking glasses and exchanging pleasantries. Eva tries to pull her mind back to the present occasion.

'He's really in his element, isn't he? Henry, I mean.'

'Yeah. So's Georgie.'

'Well, apart from the fact there's enough tension coming off her to power the National Grid for the evening.'

'Ha ha – that's true. But she's loving it, Eve, look at her. This is her thing, being the host of an enormous party. She's loving the tension.'

'And the *at*tention.'

'Isn't that the whole point of getting married?'

'What, so you can get some attention?'

'So you can be the *centre* of attention.'

'I thought it was about declaring your love for one another.'

'Well, that too. And look at them – they're quite cute together, really.'

'Hm.'

'It – it makes sense, doesn't it? For Henry. He's – I don't know. He's marrying into his kind.'

'That's weird – that's exactly what I was thinking. I was looking at his parents and Georgie's just now and thinking, they're all the *same*.'

'His tribe.'

'Yes. Maybe none of us realized that Henry had a tribe. That this is where he belongs.'

'Yes. It's weird, isn't it? It all just seems to make sense. Like everything is in its place. In a way that I don't think the same event with Henry and Carmen would have made sense.'

'Really? Do you really think that?'

'Sort of. I mean – I don't know. Who knows. I'd probably be saying the exact opposite if we were watching Henry and Carmen get married.'

'Adam, I think you maybe need to stop talking about a putative marriage between Henry and Carmen. I'm worried you'll get everyone mixed up in your speech.'

'Oh God! My speech. I'd actually managed to forget to stress about it!'

'Sorry . . .'

'No, it's good you've reminded me. I should really nip out and have a last-minute practice, if that's OK? Will you be all right on your own with the arms dealers for a bit?'

'I'll be fine.'

Adam slips away, and Eva finds her gaze drifting over to Carmen, who is talking animatedly to the guy sitting next to her. There is a slight mania to her gestures, an abruptness to them, that makes Eva tense with worry, but then she notices something about the position of the guy talking to Carmen, how he is leaning in towards her, and she realizes that actually this animation probably doesn't seem frantic to him, it probably just seems attractive. And there is something magnetic about Carmen right now, the elegant curve of her neck as she cocks her head to listen to him speak, the wide open flash of her smile, and it's true what Adam said, you can't really imagine her being up there in Georgie's place, marshalling events according to some carefully laid-out life plan, because Carmen is too – she's too *free*, that's what it is, her supple gestures, her quick eyes, there is too much freedom in there.

She notices Eva looking at her, and comes over.

'Nice-looking guy you were chatting to there.'

'Oh, he's actually surprisingly interesting. I mean – for a friend of Georgie's. Or sort of friend; actually I think he's just a colleague. Which maybe explains why he's not unbearable, if she doesn't know him that well.'

'She probably befriended him specifically so she could seat him next to you at this dinner. Say what you will about Georgie, I think she'd actually be a pretty good matchmaker.'

'Yes, she's got that slightly maniacal matronly thing going on, hasn't she?'

'I was talking to Adam earlier about the first time we met her, do you remember?'

'Oh Jesus – the Great Ivy Fuck-Up? How could I forget? She was such a *dick* to Henry. *Whoops*. Probably shouldn't have said that quite that loud . . .'

'Yeah, no, she was though.'

'But it's weird, I've been thinking this evening – it's so weird, it's like – these are his *people* . . .'

'Ha! That's exactly what Adam and I were saying. That it's like this is Henry's tribe. How he looks like he – I don't know, like he belongs.'

'So – maybe Georgie's not so bad after all.'

'I just – it's so weird that we're not all at a table together. The four of us. That you've been relegated all the way out there.'

'Ach, come on, Eve – it's not that bad. I'm used to it.'

'Used to what?'

'Being on the outside looking in.'

'Now you're just being melodramatic.'

'OK, maybe I am a bit. But anyway. At least I got to chat to an eligible bachelor. Your table seems a bit duff, huh?'

'Oh no, there's a couple of nice enough people. I just managed to alienate everyone by giving an honest response to a question about what life is like in Iraq these days.'

'Oh.'

'Yeah. Turns out it's not acceptable material for a wedding reception.'

'Was it that bad?'

'What, Iraq or my faux pas? Well, both were, to be honest . . .'

'I meant Iraq, you ninny. You have that distant look on your face where I can tell you've seen something horrible.'

'No, there . . . there was this kid. In a village we went through – just a kid, twelve or something – anyway we were just driving through and stopped off to buy something to drink, and he was helping out in this little shop. Just a nice kid, trying to persuade us to take him with us back to the UK, told us he supported Arsenal . . . And later on we drove back through the village and the shop was just rubble, and all that was left of him was half a leg, I recognized it because it still had his shoe on it, I'd noticed the shoes when we were talking to him, they were kind of swanky, I'd wondered where he'd got such nice shoes from . . .'

'Jesus.'

'Yeah. Sorry – I shouldn't be bringing this stuff up now.'

'No, Jesus. I mean, you've only just got back . . .'

'It's just – somehow this one has affected me more than things like this usually do. I normally manage to keep this – I don't know – self-preserving distance, I suppose you might call it. Even on 9/11 – it was like there was this internal switch inside of me that flipped and gave me this weird . . . detachment, I suppose. I remember being freaked out by it, but also thinking this is what is making me able to look at all this, and it's important for someone to look and tell everyone else what's going on.

'. . .'

'But with this kid . . . suddenly it just seems so pointless. Who's going to take an interest in one more dead boy in Iraq? There's nothing left but the fact that it's awful – an awful death of a sweet, perfectly normal boy.'

'Yes. It is awful.'

'. . .'

'. . .'

'Sorry. I shouldn't be talking about this on Henry's big day. And I'm fine, really. It's just . . . that poor kid.'

'Yes.'

'. . .'

'. . .'

Then Adam is walking up to the mic, and though Eva can tell that he is nervous, he does an excellent job of the speech, pitching it at exactly the right level of innuendo to make the whole room chuckle, hinting at grittier details for those in the know, but also delivering, at the end, a genuinely heartfelt tribute to Henry and Georgina, and to their love for each other. Carmen and she both have a tear in their eye by the end of it, and they smile at each other, and indeed it does feel like everything is as it should be, like everyone is in their place, and Eva smiles at Adam as he returns to *his* place by her side, and feels the reassuring weight of his hand stroking her back, and though she cannot quite stop thinking of the boy and his shoe, she feels too that this is where she belongs, this is her luck, and she manages to feel grateful for it.

YOU THINK OF the pale faces of the dead, the numerous dead from so many ages, pushing out of sandstone in church crypts or flaking away in the pale paint of a mural, and of the arrogance of the living who look at them and think how quaint, they knew nothing of penicillin or the workings of an aeroplane.

And how Adam has joined their ranks now, how already your present would be unrecognizable to him, plummeting stock markets and yet on the other hand the new hopefulness of Yes We Can, and you in the midst of this, strangely detached, browbeaten by grief, looking at his smiling blue eyes in a photograph and seeing in them only their ignorance of what is to come, of the knowledge that is now your burden.

And yet you also wonder what knowledge those eyes hold that you yourself are ignorant of, just like the angular figures of an Egyptian fresco hide within them the secret of how the pyramids were built, and it seems to you that the dead, and Adam, are another people entirely, at once innocent and knowing, as opposed to the living, who are knowing and innocent.

There is a tree outside your window, with browning, yellow, atrophied leaves, and when the wind blows they tumble in a dry pitter-patter reminiscent of rainfall, and you think this might be the sound that the dead make as their souls touch lightly on the earth and become one with it again, turning their backs on the progress of temporal events, taking their secrets with them. It is as sad as the sight of those leaves lying on the ground, still golden for now, but already starting to dissolve into a mushy decay.

EVA SIGHED AS, for the third time in the past half-hour, she tried to put something into the pouch on the seat in front of her, only to find that there wasn't one there. Bloody Ryanair.

She rearranged her travel gear on the tiny tray in front of her: a giant, milky coffee, an empty bottle of San Pellegrino, a blister pack of Nurofen, a pointless book – she had lost the ability to read since Adam died. Lost the ability to read, but not, oddly, the compulsion to buy books. It would catch her out when she was on autopilot, like today in the Stansted WHSmith, the old thrum of excitement at the pristine covers, the promise of stories and secrets and revelations within – but now, whenever she sat down and tried to focus her mind on actual words on a page, that terrible night was all her imagination could escape to. Adam's story had eclipsed all others.

If only she had somewhere she could put that bloody book. It was good to focus on small irritations. They were like a mosquito bite distracting you from the cancer that was eating you up inside. This plane was like a skin around her, covered in mosquito bites – the non-existent pouches, the way your knees rubbed into the seat in front of you, the incessant announcements on the tannoy, the cheap nylon of the air hostesses' blouses – and she the tumour within, dark and festering.

A steward passed and whisked away her empty bottle, imperious, not deigning to ask for her permission, nor acknowledging the invasive brush of his hand against hers. Close on his heels, a second steward pushing a refreshment trolley tried to hustle a drink at her. They smiled so sweetly when they wanted to sell you something. Her throat was tickling, but she didn't want to give Ryanair any more money, so she sent him on his way. She was going to Berlin, cramped, thirsty, a mild, modern-day martyr. In other ages, there would have been more dignity to a trip like this, this pilgrimage of a widow in her husband's footsteps: she should have been a wealthy heiress with a stately entourage and three extra carriages to carry her library, or a peasant woman making the epic journey by foot, using her last few pennies on the crossing from Dover and then begging her way across the continent. The modern experience was so cheap, with its creaking plastic seats and canned air filled with coffee breath.

She hated this bitterness, that sometimes it was the only way to stave off despair. She tried looking out of the window.

The sky beneath them was dappled with soft clumps of cloud. They looked close enough to reach out to; far, far below lay the sea. It was a standard aeroplane view; familiar yet incomprehensible, this being above the clouds, encased in a heaving mass of metal. This was one of the things that she and Adam had shared: a childish excitement at the wonder of it, a gleeful enjoyment of the paraphernalia of flight. She remembered how acutely, how strangely they had felt it on their way back from New York, a guilty relief after the nervousness of days spent waiting for normal traffic to resume, with the images of those planes and those towers on a loop in the very air that they breathed. When they had at last found themselves in the boarding lounge at JFK, oppressed by the tense jaws and jiggling knees of their fellow travellers, Adam had put his arm around Eva.

'Are you feeling nervous?'

'Yes.'

'We'll be fine.'

'I know.'

'I mean, statistically . . .'

'I know. But still.'

'Yes. I know.'

They had all filed on to the plane like a funeral procession, the boarding bridge tight around them, had settled meekly into their seats. Hers was by a window, and Eva had looked out on to the damp, grey, solid world outside, unable not to wonder whether this was to be her final, fiery journey. Then the take-off, the tension of waiting to see whether they would suddenly tilt into an unnatural turn, whether anyone would stab an air hostess in the jugular – and, once they were up and away from the city, the feeling of exhilaration, of having dodged death once more. With what excitement and relief they had explored their onboard entertainment options and greeted the arrival of their first meal tray! They had tugged the covers off their aluminium platters in perfect unison, compared with interest Adam's chicken tikka to Eva's baked salmon, while several tons of metal and gasoline hurled them through the air, so precariously safe. Ryanair was more honest than your BAs, your Virgin Atlantics: there was no glitz here to distract you from the creaking and heaving, the superhuman effort that was necessary to save you a few hours' travel time.

No, this plastic mode of transport was not doing her journey justice – and yet, perhaps it was. Why kid yourself with illusions of elegance – a high-altitude glass of champagne, a seat you could actually relax in – when all you were was human wreckage, of love deprived, returning to the home you had never set eyes upon?

IT IS STARTING TO acquire the patina of familiarity: a certain clunking of the wheels around this bend, the houses along the railtracks which she can pick out from each other now, the seat she prefers to occupy if she can: facing forwards, of course, on the right, just back from the window, but this is better than the next seat down, which is next to a tiny end of window not big enough to look through properly. There is a window problem, as far as the design of this train is concerned. Who would have thought life would become so suburban so quickly?

A short, sharp uphill walk which is never as bad as you anticipate it's going to be, and then she's home – *home*. She feels the now familiar proprietorial thrill as she steps through the front door: these wooden floors, this charming fireplace – there's no denying it's a nice flat they've got themselves here. Why then this faint feeling of dismay that tinges her homecoming?

She goes straight into the bedroom, puts her bag on the floor, and surveys her kingdom. The bed is pristinely made, ironed covers, proudly solid. It is a good bed. An expensive bed. She notices that, in the far corner of the room, her mother's samizdat is hanging, newly framed. Bugger. She's been saying for the past two weeks that she'll go and buy a frame for it, and now Adam's gone ahead and done it for her. Eva feels the righteous anger of the slovenly, who would get around to doing the dishes eventually, if only they were given the time. She moves closer and inspects the frame: at least Adam, who is not to be trusted in matters aesthetic, has had the wisdom to go to John Lewis, and it is tasteful if not particularly exciting. Now she resents herself for getting annoyed with him, feels a surge of tenderness towards this man, her husband, but a boy still, really, who takes such good care.

She looks at the words inside the frame, streaky ink on rough grey paper, the edges damaged by water, calling for freedom, democracy. Her mother's pseudonym in block letters at the bottom of the page: 'LUTHER', in reference to the ninety-five theses hammered to a church door in rebellion against Catholic tyranny. A long, noble history of resistance to oppression.

Adam is clattering and sizzling in the kitchen, while Eva sits down on the bed and stares out of the window at the knobbles on the tree outside. She is worried about this interview next week. It's flattering, of course, but being asked to dress down the prime minister feels like punching above her weight, and reawakens her sense of being an emperor in new clothes, her success owed only to flukes and bluster. She is no Luther, that much she knows. She doesn't have her mother's toughness, her courage, her moral integrity. Eva is soft, having grown up in more pampered circumstances, is weak, having never been tried.

She doesn't have the clout to take on Tony Blair, and she wishes she could be alone to think about it, but she lives with Adam now, and she wonders when married people find time for privacy, for making sure they are still who they think they are.

Adam pops his head round the door.

'Everything OK?'

She smiles.

'Yes. Sorry, I'll come through and give you a hand in a minute. I was just catching my breath.'

He comes over to her and kisses her fully, tenderly on the lips.

'Don't worry, I'm perfectly happy out there. Take your time.'

Perhaps this is the time you get for yourself, stolen moments in an adjacent room, with the sound of the other present but removed, a reassuring disturbance. Perhaps this is the exiguous space her inner world will have to inhabit from now on, the price to pay for having a pair of arms around you every night. And yet she loves him. Does Adam have these thoughts? Is he enjoying his brief solitude in the kitchen now, savouring his stolen moment of contemplation before she walks in to break it?

For the sake of something to do, she bends forward and starts to remove a shoe. But no. Midway, she realizes this is no time for practical, quotidian gestures: this is her time for self-reflection. She reclines back on the bed, one leg still crossed over the other, laces dangling, and looks up at the ceiling, at the desultory light-bulb that hangs in the middle of it. She really must pick up that lampshade. But for now, she must think about Iraq.

She was there several months ago, in the buzz and heat of the green zone, and the trip was made surreal by the fact that they were in the middle of completing the purchase of the flat, so that her time was divided between face-to-face interviews with obfus-cating American officers and satellite phone conversations with Adam and her bank manager. Talking to Adam in particular had unsettled and calmed her all at once: being transported to a cosy nook of middle-class London, when all around her were distant explosions and adrenalin-crazed journalists. At times, she had felt as though she were losing herself, who she was, her mortgage and stylish wardrobe and BFI membership in London seeming impossible in this world of dust and ammunition. At times, Adam's voice on the end of the crackly line had felt like the only thing that connected her to her supposedly normal life.

She needs to use this trip to get under Blair's skin, find an anec-dote that will unsettle his smarmy rhetoric.

A tinkling crash from the kitchen and a muffled string of expletives chase away whatever brainwave she may possibly have been about to have. She allows herself a moment of petulant exasperation at Adam, even though she knows it is unfair since it is hardly his fault that she isn't feeling very inspired this evening. Then she finishes removing her shoes – the pull of the laces, the tug off her heels are such strangely comforting movements – and goes through to the kitchen.

'Don't come in, you haven't got shoes on!'

'Oh. Right.'

She stands in the doorway, watching her husband gingerly picking tiny pieces of ceramic up off the floor, cradling them in his palm. A pan of Bolognese sauce is spluttering vigorously on the hob behind him. He turns from his crouching position and looks up at Eva with the expression of a guilt-ridden dog.

'I'm really sorry.'

'What is it you've broken?'

Eva takes a cautious, tiptoeing step into the kitchen – and then she sees: a small, curved piece of incredibly fine porcelain, a delicate pattern of intertwined violets.

'Oh, Adam.'

'I'm sorry. I'm really, really sorry.'

Eva picks up the fragment and sits down at the dining table, staring at it blankly.

A louder-than-usual hiss from the Bolognese makes Adam twist up and round, lithe as a cat. He gives it a frantic stir, then returns to picking through the wreckage.

'We might be able to stick it back together . . .'

'Don't be ridiculous. Look, it's smashed to smithereens.'

The venom in her voice makes Adam flinch.

'I'm sorry, I – I don't know how it happened, I was emptying the dishwasher and I must have put it down too close to the edge of the sideboard or something and . . . I'm really sorry.'

She follows the line of a twisting violet, and thinks of how she never really liked the pattern, too floral for her taste, but nevertheless, aside from the samizdat, this was the only thing she had, the only family belonging her mother was able to take with her when she fled East Germany, and an afterthought at that, a tea cup hastily slipped into a pocket in the rush of escape.

She imagines – has often imagined – her mother huddling into a thick coat in the dead of night, taking one last glance around the family home she will never see again, and suddenly thinking

I must take something with me, some keepsake, something tangible into which I can pour my past. Her eyes roving around the room and alighting on the tea set, and, of course, what would make more sense than to take one cup from this complete set to treasure with the knowledge that identical ones are sitting on a shelf back home, to leave this shelf to display the incompleteness of her absence?

And this incongruously fragile thing somehow survived the perilous journey, this precious heirloom that was then handed down to her, Eva, the only object connecting her back to her grandparents, and now this oaf has gone and broken it by being his usual clumsy self. The frustration, the anger, well up in her eyes, and soon to her own surprise she is sobbing loudly, like an aggrieved toddler.

Adam, who has been guiltily stirring the spaghetti sauce, comes over to her, tries to take her in his arms, but she shrugs him off sharply.

'Why – why couldn't you be more *careful*?'

'I'm sorry, Eve. I really am.'

' . . . '

' . . . '

'It was all I had *left*.'

'I know.'

' . . . '

'I'll try to stick it back together again. It might be possible.'

'It won't be, Adam – look at it.'

The edge of the piece is thin as a razor blade. She could crush it into dust, this sole remaining possession of her lost family.

'I'm sorry.'

Adam stands by her awkwardly, head hung in shame, not daring to touch her. Eva sniffs, the tears running down her cheeks silently now, as silent as her dead grandparents, as silent as her mother when her painful history is evoked.

'I'll clear the rest up.'

She picks up the other fragments with care, marvelling at their fragility, then fetches the dustpan and brush to sweep up the remains too small to be worth saving. Adam, after hesitating for a while, has returned to the Bolognese, which after all will not be stopped from burning just because there is some kind of crisis going on. Her fury at him has descended to mere irritation now, and is secondary anyway to the sadness of having lost a precious object, the symbol of so many memories.

She disposes of the debris in the bin, setting aside only the biggest shards, which perhaps something can be done with, while Adam busies himself over the linguine. Once she has finished cleaning up, she stands by him, watching the water boil.

He kisses her on the cheek, tentatively.

'I'm sorry.'

'I know you are.'

'Sit down, it's almost done.'

She walks over to the dining table, takes a seat by the fireplace, looking out on to the garden and the kitchen. Autumn has set in, and the evenings are getting darker now, but it is still light enough outside to see how the leaves on the big hazelnut tree are losing the intensity of their green, how the roses have faded. She spots some movement in the grass, and sits up straighter.

'Adam!'

In a corner of the garden, a fox is rummaging around in what is left of the barbecue they had at the weekend. He is quite big, and his fur is full and glossy – he is a healthy, suburban fox, a different breed from the mangy creatures she used to come across going back to her place in Brick Lane. Eva wonders if living here will have the same sleekening effect on her. Adam, who was in the middle of bringing their food over, tiptoes cautiously for the rest of the journey, sets the steaming plates down on the table, and stands by her, his arm on her shoulder. The fox must have sensed his movement, because it looks up at them and stares for a while with its yellow, pensive eyes. Then with cool, unhurried movements, it picks up the remains of a lamb chop and trots off across the garden, its bushy tail bouncing along comically behind it. Adam laughs gleefully. Eva smiles sadly, ruffles his hair, and meets Adam's eyes again for the first time that evening. He is sad too.

'I know I've broken something that can't be repaired. But I'll try and make it better – somehow.'

'It's all right, Ad – it's only a thing. It just makes me sad, you know?'

'I know.'

'Come on, let's have some dinner.'

It smells rich and delicious – Adam is rightfully proud of his family recipe for spaghetti Bolognese. She feels a surge of love for her husband, who is so sorry for what he has done, who knows why it has upset her so much. She feels the warmth of this kitchen, of this food, of this evening they will spend doing something unexciting and domestic, of this haven they have made their home. She thinks, as she smiles at this man proudly wrapping a slop of pasta around his fork, that really love is a strange and wonderful thing.

EVERYTHING WAS WRITTEN in German, everywhere. Easyjet boasted about its *billige Flüge*, free copies of the *Berliner Zeitung* were dotted every few metres along the corridor, you picked up your *Gepäck* from here, followed that sign to the *Autovermietung* from Hertz. Eva inhaled, drank in, caressed the words with her eyes. They felt so – *familiar*. In other airports she had landed in, she was always overwhelmed at first by the opacity of whatever foreign language or script had taken over the familiar logos and predictable signs. But here, it was as though they resonated with a part of her that had been lying dormant for years. The words unlocked meanings with the immediacy of a mother tongue, and yet engulfed her in their otherness. She felt this other Eva inside of her, this German Eva, stirring, filling out, awakened by these words like a cactus flowering after a few drops of rainfall in the desert; she felt she could be allowed to grow vigorous, occupy all the space in this body which was, after all, hers as well.

Perhaps it wasn't even a bad idea: to this German Eva, the loss of Adam might feel more remote, less acutely a part of her. His death, and their whole relationship, had happened in another language: even though Adam had, from time to time, tried to get Eva to speak German with him, Eva had always refused. Back then, she had been worried that they might find he spoke the language better than she did. She realized now, as she felt the letters and sounds around her nestle comfortably into her understanding, that this was a ridiculous fear. But perhaps there had been something else in there as well. Perhaps she had felt that she needed to keep some part of her away from him – had

161

she foreseen, perhaps, that losing him would destroy her so completely that she needed to keep one half of herself out of reach?

She waited at the *Kofferlaufband* for her *Gepäck* to arrive. The suitcases trundled by, each one bearing its tiny, hidden world, and she felt the ground go soft underneath her when she read, on the name tag of one of them, the words: 'LENA BACHMANN'. Her breath caught in her throat, her heart started pounding, and she turned, absurdly, to check whether there was a mysterious woman standing next to her, ready to extend a leather-gloved hand and grab the case. There was none, though, just a weary-looking teenager, and anyway when Eva looked at the label again, the letters had resolved themselves into a different name altogether, Lena Bachmann disappearing into thin air, a mere trick of her mind. Eva saw her own case moving towards her, focused on that: getting into position and taking hold of it, its handle cool and hard beneath her fingers. It swung lightly into the air, a reminder of how few belongings she had brought with her, tugging pleasurably at her arm as it arced around her, its feather weight drawing her into this new place.

As she turned to leave, the man next to her heaved his suitcase off a little too enthusiastically, and knocked into her.

'Oh! Entschuldigung!'

'Kein Problem, kein Problem.'

'Hab ich Ihnen Weh getan?'

'Nee, wirklich – nix passiert.'

'Na dann. Schönen Tag noch.'

'Gleichfalls.'

Eva had turned her back on him before she realized she had just had her first conversation in her mother tongue in twenty years – and the guy hadn't even seemed to notice that she might not be from around here. She tingled with the thrill of it.

Walking to the sliding doors of the Arrivals terminal awakened a familiar fantasy: on countless arrivals in airports the world over, she would imagine that there was someone waiting for her on the other side, some long-lost friend or dark handsome stranger. As the doors parted to let her through, she would scrutinize the faces in the waiting crowd, searching for a flicker of recognition, a friendly smile – and, advancing into the battery of flickers and smiles aimed all around her but not at her, closing in on hugs and kisses and yelps of joy and then walking clean past them, she would feel a delicious thrill of solitude. She would walk briskly away from the reunited lovers, the happy families, the polite business greetings, and revel in the sense of her own freedom.

Once, a long time ago, she had shared this fantasy with Adam, and on a handful of occasions after that he had surprised her by standing there waiting for her on her return to London. The first time he had done it, she remembered, was when she had returned from the Congo. They had had terrible conversations throughout that trip, a string of near arguments intercut by crappy hotel internet connections, progressively aggravated by the exhaustion Eva was feeling as her journey drew to a close, and no doubt also by Adam feeling bored and alone in London, and worried about her, and also worried about – well, yes, that whole situation. It was only in recent weeks that it had occurred to Eva what those trips must have felt like to him. That the sense she would get of being uprooted, violently thrown into a different reality, the shock of readjustment that would accompany her return every time – that he must have experienced a mirror image of these feelings, that the dislocation could not have been one-sided. Why had they never talked about it? Eva would have the conversation with Adam in her head. She spent a lot of time in internal dialogue with Adam these days. It seemed the only thing to do, but also a travesty of his memory, since how could it be fair to turn Adam purely into a creation of her mind?

When Eva had arrived at Heathrow that time, even more exhausted than the night before and still bristling from their last terse exchange, the unexpected sight of him waiting for her had made her angry, as though he had come purely to rob her of her freedom, to put his stamp on her; though she had also felt some relief that she would be driven home rather than having to fight her way back on the Tube.

The next time he had done it, though, a couple of years later, she had had enough lonely returns to be caught completely off guard again, and this time she had been overjoyed to see him, having spent the whole flight back daydreaming about nestling into his arms. She remembered scanning the crowd, caught in a paradoxical space between her fantasy of finding a friendly face and her certainty that none would be there – and then, against all odds, meeting Adam's eyes, seeing the delighted smile on his lips at having been a step ahead of her.

Now, she strode through the exit at Berlin Schönefeld, and cast her eyes over the small huddle of welcomers. Her heart sank, leapt, stopped, shattered in her ribcage as she saw, there, behind the fat man in the flak jacket, Adam looking at her with his familiar smirk. By the time she had taken her next step, though, he was gone, leaving in his stead a youngish man with only the most passing of resemblances to him. These tricks of the light – of her eyes, of her mind – wearied Eva. They were like scenes from a second-rate Hollywood melodrama – and yet so real, so anguishing to experience. The world seemed a more protean place, now that she had a mind so desperately in need of a change to the laws of physics, so hungry for a resurrection. She understood those old myths so much better now: how Orpheus's love for Eurydice could have been strong enough to overpower even Hades, how you could feel a love so deep it would be conceivable for it to overcome death itself. And so hers did, casting projections of his face on to the canvases of other people's bodies wherever she went.

In her anger, that first time that Adam had come to meet her at the airport, she had felt tempted to walk right past him, to turn her back on his attempt at a reconciliation. Now, turning her back on this Adam who wasn't Adam, she felt guilty that his expectant ghost would be left hanging behind her, as dismayed and hurt as the live Adam would have been if she had walked past him all those years ago. Like Orpheus, she could feel the weight of her loved one walking behind her; like him, she wanted, with a strength of want that could have toppled mountains or turned cities to dust, to turn round and set eyes on her beloved brought back from the dead. But Eva was wiser than Orpheus, knew that the only way to keep Adam behind her was to point her eyes straight ahead. So that was what she did, and she wondered whether anyone here could see the evanescent figure that was trailing her.

She took the slip of paper with Ulrich's address on it out of her pocket and glanced at Adam's handwriting, drawing comfort from the familiar scrawl. Then, before she knew it, she was out of the terminal. Cool, German air rushed into her lungs, and she fancied it still bore the scent of the Siberian pines it was born in before rushing over the Urals and the Central European Plain. She looked up at the dull grey sky and the tired grass beyond the car park: so this is the heart of Europe.

She paused, not knowing where to go from here. She felt on the threshold of something, as though each step she took might either send her plummeting off a rock face, or lead her into the splendour of a hidden valley. She had never before felt so completely alone. She had always travelled with other people before she started working, and on her numerous trips as a journalist had always had Adam and the foreign news desk within a text's or a phone call's reach. How much she had shared with Adam – how many small, quotidian details, about being on a train or in a café or across from a man who looked like the fat, Afghan version of Henry – how many texts and emails and insignificant chatter, the stuff of life. Now she had to make those comments to him in her mind, like a madwoman.

A yellow sign saying 'S-Bahn' pointed her along a grim strip of asphalt, which small handfuls of people were trudging up and down. They were all young, many in couples or groups of friends, or alone but with an air of excitement and confidence in their own good fortune. Eva followed them along, aware of the loud rattle of her four-wheel suitcase in the midst of all these backpackers.

The walk led to the S-Bahn station, a drab clutter of news-agents and wurst stalls in a tunnel underneath the rail tracks. Eva floundered as she tried to work out which platform to go to, until she noticed that one of them said the train would go via Alexanderplatz, the only name she recognized and which she knew was in the centre of town. She walked up to the platform, and was struck once again by the ease with which she navigated this place that was at once so foreign and so familiar. Where other tourists were squinting at the incomprehensible timetables and ticket machines, she breezily studied her options, finally selecting a monthly travel ticket: after all, she was here indefi-nitely, wasn't she?

She boarded the train, a boxy, plasticky thing with plenty of room for bikes and hardly any passengers – so unlike the cramped London Tube. It set off, whizzing alongside a road through a flat landscape of houses and barren fields. This is the heart of Europe: this dreary plain, these faceless suburbs, these semi-industrial com-plexes. This is Prussia, those feathered warriors. This is East Germany, that grey utopia.

At a station called Betriebsbahnhof Schöneweide, an enor-mous dog stepped on to the train, followed by a man who was presumably its owner. The dog looked like an Alsatian, but was about the size of a Great Dane. Its massive head wore a meek expression, two kindly eyes looking out over a muzzle that could easily chew your arm off. The man had a similar air: grizzled, handsome, a twinkle in his eye. They sat down in the square of seats next to Eva's, the man with his nose in a book, the dog on its haunches and sniffing the air with relaxed curiosity.

Then the train hit the city. After Treptower Park, it soared over the Spree, revealing a majestic vista of industrial riverside buildings, a white statue of two wrestling stick men with their feet in the water, and, in the distance, the futuristic shape of the Fernsehturm. River vistas were Eva's favourite in all the cities she visited: they all had similar perspectives, a certain grandiose sweep, and yet they were all so unique to the place they were in, a quintessence of it. Nowhere was the perfection of Paris more evident than when you drove along the *berges* of the Seine; nowhere did the City of London boast its opulence more proudly than seen from one of the bridges straddling the Thames. Berlin looked huge and eclectic glimpsed during this brief crossing: a jumble of high rises, wastelands, giant neon adverts and artworks. Then the train dived back into the city: grey buildings, graffiti, patches of land where nothing was.

Just before Ostkreuz, the train paused in an urban void. Grey cement façades, a slip road rising slightly alongside the railway: it was like a place you had always expected but never known, familiar in its strangeness. It might have been what you'd be met with if you sat on a Tube train till Stanmore, Walthamstow, Cockfosters: the bare necessities of a city – walls, roofs, transport routes, and a lifeline connecting it to the pulsating centre. But here she was almost at the centre already, just three stops away from Alexanderplatz. As though Berlin were just an assemblage of liminal spaces, concentric circles of excentricities.

At the station, a young woman got on, and sat down opposite the man with the dog. The dog, by this point, had lain down behind his master's seat, just by the entrance doors to the carriage, so that each new traveller was greeted by a nodding Cerberus. Now, though, as the train pulled out and rattled between rows of square windows and tiny balconies, it rose with a languid huff and turned its huge body towards the girl. She looked like a student, early twenties probably, casually pretty, her attention plunged into a book which was removing her far, far away from this train, this day, this particular set of contingencies in the time–space continuum. The dog stood contemplating her with interest, then started inching towards her. It was like watching a car crash in slow motion, as the formidable beast closed in gently on this rose petal. Only when it nuzzled its way into her lap did the girl lift her eyes from her book and register her admirer. He looked up at her with sad brown eyes. Outside the window, the buildings shooting by were gradually gaining colour and character – perhaps this city did have a centre after all. The girl, after a few moments of shock at having such a behemoth put its head between her legs, smiled kindly and patted it. The morning sun cast a golden light on orange, yellow, glowing warm buildings.

The dog's owner, who had been following the whole scene out of the corner of his eye, clicked his tongue, and the beast promptly retreated to lie at his heels. He smiled charmingly at the girl. The train was pulling out of Warschauer Straße now, hurtling through a no-man's-land beneath the rest of the city. Scores of other railway tracks stretched out to the left of it, while on the right Eva caught sight of a lonely football cage, its wire meshing absurdly or artistically dotted with green plastic buckets. Over on the other side of the river, a giant prefabricated purple box sat surrounded by tractors and piles of mud, sporting a neon sign that seemed to have no one to flash at but her. The grizzly man had started chatting to the pretty girl. Eva envied them the ease of the meeting, the warmth of the smiles, their artifice-less good looks. The older man was probably a bit of a rogue, a charmer who had done this a thousand times before and was only really capable of returning the fidelity of his dog. The girl was probably young and innocent enough to have her heart broken. But oh to be that young and innocent, to have your heart broken by a rakish older man!

Eva's eyes met those of the dog, gazing up at her with the mournful compassion of the mutually excluded. But though she would gladly have run her hand over its soft, silky crown, the animal stayed put, welded now to the patch of floor by its master's feet.

She turned again to the city flashing by outside her window: it was tower blocks in the best Soviet style now, huge buildings that looked as though they had been fashioned out of cardboard. Adam had told her about them, how there was an avenue here that could have been Moscow, and how he loved to cycle along it. She imagined him now, zipping alongside her train on a ghost bicycle, the wind in his hair. She wondered if her mother had cycled along it too, as a girl, on a more old-fashioned bike, when the buildings were being put up, perhaps. The tower blocks ran dully in front of her eyes. If Communism had won the battle, would the stuccoed façades of Chelsea have seemed as mistaken in their delusions of grandeur as these drab buildings did now? If her mother hadn't left East Germany, would these cold tower blocks have looked like home to Eva?

But, already, these remnants of a glorious workers' past were being replaced by enormous holes in the ground and semi-constructed buildings, the triumphs of capitalism gradually taking over Alexanderplatz. Adam had told her about this, too. Where East German families would once have sauntered over a vast expanse of concrete of a Sunday afternoon, the gut of a future shopping mall was exposed for all to see, all concrete girders and steel rods reaching for the sky, soon to welcome those same families – a little older now, frazzled around the edges, world-weary after so many regime changes – into a warm, stultifying circus of special offers and elevator music. Eva tried to imagine where the giant bust of Lenin that once adorned the square would have stood; but there was no room left for him now, amid the shops and the advertising panels.

When the train doors opened at Alexanderplatz, the man and dog and the girl got off, with an offer of coffee proffered and accepted. Eva followed them: she needed to change trains here to go to Ulrich's. She watched them disappear down an escalator, and felt a pang of jealousy: she had never gone off for coffee with a strange man like this – she and Adam had been so young when they got together. And now that she could, she didn't want to. Had Adam seen pretty girls on the Berlin S-Bahn and wished he could have invited them for a coffee, wished that he hadn't pledged his best years to her, Eva? Had he walked around Alexanderplatz thinking about her, or about something completely different – somebody completely different?

She took the slip of paper with Ulrich's address on it out of her pocket and stared at Adam's handwriting, as though that was going to give her any answers. And she thought about the other slip of paper she had stowed away in her luggage, the other address, also found at the bottom of that cardboard box: Lena Bachmann, Finsterstraße 45. She made her way down into the belly of the U-Bahn station, and wondered what it was she was looking for here, exactly.

THIS IS A MEMORY that has no beginning. It starts in medias res, or rather does not start, or end, but hovers in her mind like a multitude of photographs strewn across a carpet, images side by side and on top of each other, fragments of time freed of the links of cause and effect.

She sees her father ushering her into the living room, whispering a 'Quiet, darling' of uncommon gravity.

She sees so many pictures on the TV screen. A young man with slick, jet-black hair, eyes gleaming under a battery of photographers' flashes, smiles straight into the camera; he is so completely, perfectly happy that Eva feels she might burst with joy. She falls in love for the first time in her life; his bright, clever eyes, his long nose and cheekbones will remain with her for much of her adolescence.

She sees the crowd around him, hundreds, thousands of people, as far as the eye can see, sitting with their feet dangling in mid-air over lurid graffiti, arms around each other, singing, grinning into the wind.

She hears a litany of words that mean nothing to her then: Bornholmer Straße, Schabowski, Checkpoint Charlie, Gorbachev, Honecker, Kohl, Friedrichstraße, die Mauer, die Mauer.

She sees a woman in a glowing department store thrust a handful of banknotes into a journalist's face, talking enthusiastically as she gestures around her towards an escalator, a shoe shop, a promotional offer for Christmas tree decorations.

She sees a pickaxe pounding at the Wall, which splinters with surprising ease, revealing dusty grey cement under the bright paint. Hands claw at it, frittering it away, and though she is only ten, Eva can see the avidity, the anger, the joy that these fingers express.

She feels hungry, because it is past her dinnertime, and no one seems to want to unglue themselves from the television to make something to eat.

She sees a weary official blink up at a crowd of journalists and mumble a few words which set off a frenzy in the room, questions shouted over each other at this little stammering man.

She sees a soldier with his rifle hanging limply by his side.

She sees a crowd flood past a raised barrier.

And next to her sits her mother, watching the television, silent and perfectly still, two streams of tears on her cheeks flowing as steadily as the thousands of people pouring through concrete gaps into the promise of West Berlin.

STILL IN THE BLEARINESS of half-sleep, Eva reaches out and runs her hand over the empty mattress beside her.

She wonders first where Adam is, then where she is.

On the other side of the wall, there is a mechanical sound, the clicks of plastic against plastic and whirrs which she eventually identifies as paper being pushed out of a printer, just as she identifies the room around her as being her bedroom in her parents' house, remembers that this is where she is.

Which does not answer the question of Adam's whereabouts.

She gets out of bed, slips on her dressing gown and goes out into the corridor. She says his name as she pushes open the door to her father's study.

'Ad . . . ?'

Sudden, shuffly noises. Adam, lit only by a desk lamp and a rim of light from the printer, is staring at her with widened eyes.

'Ah. Hi.'

'Are you OK?'

'Ah, yes, fine – sorry, you just surprised me there, I thought I was the only person awake in the house.'

The soft, blue glow of the printer is strangely alluring – Eva steps towards it like an absent-minded moth, makes to pick up the papers it has spooled out, but Adam grabs them first and holds them face down against his crotch, as though to protect his modesty.

'What on Earth are you doing?'

'I just needed to photocopy something for this conference . . .'

'What, in the middle of the night?'

'I know, I just woke up and I kept thinking about it and worrying that if I didn't do it right away I'd forget . . .'

'You're such a weirdo.'

'Yeah. Sorry, I didn't think I'd wake you up. I hope I haven't disturbed your parents.'

'They'll be fine, I don't think they can hear it from their room.'

'Oh good. Anyway. All done now.'

He slips past her out of the room, papers in hand, and vanishes back into their bedroom, so that for a moment it seems to Eva like she might have dreamt the whole thing, she is so barely awake and the night-time stillness is so deep. But then she does hear the sounds of zipping and rustling paper behind her bedroom door, and she notices that Adam has left the printer on, which is unlike him, and the desk lamp too, and she goes over to turn them off.

And on her father's desk is the picture of her mother with her parents, which is odd because usually it sits on the bookshelf in the living room – perhaps her dad has decided to keep it closer, this picture of his wife from a time long before he knew her.

She picks it up, and looks at it: her mother, aged what, sixteen or something, her long hair tumbling in wild locks around her, looking proudly, almost defiantly into the camera, with her father and mother on either side of her, both stiff and smiling uncertainly, awkward about posing for the picture, perhaps, or else with other things on their minds. They are standing in front of a gate, behind which can be glimpsed the church Eva's grandfather had just taken over. Grandfather. How strange that this photograph provides the only faces Eva can put to those names, grandfather, grandmother, Opa, Oma, condemning them to a life in her mind as two slightly uncomfortable ageing people, an image which sits dissonantly with the thrilling, subversive adventures she simultaneously imagines them having had. How strange that this photograph and the samizdat are all that is left of her mother's family ever since Adam broke the Meissen tea cup that was their only other remaining possession.

The whole house is quiet now, as though time has been removed from it.

Eva puts the photograph back down on her father's desk, switches off the printer and lamp, and feels her way back to the bedroom in darkness, her fingers touching tentatively on walls and doorframes, until they have found their way back to the warmth of their duvet and Adam's smooth skin.

THERE IS A PERSON you knew once, in all of his beauty and tenderness and infuriatingness and joy, in all of his countless dimensions, and then there is the moment of his death like poison ivy around your memory of him. You try to get it out of the way, but it won't budge.

He lies there, dying all over again, every time you speak to him.

And you see that death is above all a distance, an unbridgeable chasm between you, the mysterious stillness of his body so radically different from the time and movement that continue to run through your flesh, and time and movement run through your brain too, neurons firing and synapses crackling into questions and doubts: who is this person I thought I knew so well, who I thought was a part of me? Who is he when now he is a strange corpse, mute, entirely closed to me? Did we ever understand each other, touch each other, talk to each other? Did we ever look into each other's eyes and see in there a fire that was like our own, recognize somebody who was not completely a stranger?

THIS CORRIDOR IS EXACTLY as she would have expected it. Long. Smooth. Antiseptic. She takes her time walking down it, because the longer she spends doing that, the less soon she will be inside the room. The décor is ominously placid: pastel colours, Italian landscapes, still lives. So conspicuously gentle. Here and there, a poster with health advice delivered in the simplest possible terms. She feels oppression in these signs of benevolence, the threat of the institution. No one should have to be here. She hurries along the corridor.

Carmen turns as she walks in, with a wan smile that suits the setting. The glint in her eye is absolutely the same as it has always been. Eva sits on the chair by the bed, lays the flowers on the trolley by Carmen's head. Another still life: grapes, a box of chocolates, today's *Guardian*, a plastic glass and water jug hazy from years of repeated sterilization, a battered copy of *The Spy Who Came in from the Cold*. Flowers.

'Actually, I'd better put these in water, hadn't I.'

Eva rises, weirdly self-conscious of her movements, which only makes them more jittery. She grabs the flowers too tightly and skits over to the sink in the corner of the room, while Carmen watches her in silence.

'Hm. I don't suppose they've given you a vase? You'd think they'd provide vases.'

She puts the plug in and stares at the sink as it slowly fills with water. She can see her reflection in the tap, and wonders how many faces have been mirrored here, what shades of insanity have contemplated their distorted features in the gleaming metal. She is postponing the moment of having to return to

177

Carmen. She removes the wrapper from the flowers, crumples it up – so loud – and throws it in the bin, puts their stalks in the water. They hang a little limply over the edge of the sink, each one so lonely and fragile now that it is not held close to its companions by an elastic band. She returns to the bedside, sits down, looks at Carmen.

'They called me the hyacinth girl.'

'They're daffodils, actually.'

' . . . '

' . . . '

' . . . '

'God, I'm sorry, Carm, I haven't even said hello. Hello.'

'Hi.'

' . . . '

' . . . '

'How are you feeling?'

'Tired. I think they're drugging me.'

'Well – they probably are. I don't know. Well, I mean, they almost certainly are.'

'Bastards.'

' . . . '

' . . . '

Eva looks at her friend: the white hospital gown, the frantic darting of her eyes.

A different person.

She thought they knew each other, she thought they shared all their secrets, the fears and joys buried deepest within them.

How long has Carmen been hiding this darkness, this terrifying landscape of conspiracies?

'Do you want to talk about it?'

'About what?'

'About what happened.'

' . . . '

'Remember, Carm? You were on London Bridge.'

'. . .'
'. . .'
'A crowd flowed over London Bridge, so many . . .'
'I had not thought death had undone so many.'

A SINGLE MATTRESS on the floor, one pillow, the duvet encased in a cover that had faded over the years. A clear desk and a non-ergonomic chair (surely that must have killed Adam's back?). A clothes rack lined with hangers, just the basic skeletal structure, in the corner of the room. One of those canvas clothes-storage units you got for about twenty quid in Ikea. It looked like a monk's cell.

Ulrich appeared with a towel.

'I give you a – er – Handtuch.'

'A towel. Thanks.'

'No problem. So. Probably you want to rest a bit?'

'Well – I'll unpack at least, yes.'

'No stress, take your time. When you want, I can show you around the Kiez – the neighbourhood.'

'Thanks, that would be great.'

'Ach so – also, I wanted to show you this.'

He pulled a box out from underneath the canvas thingy.

'Some papers of Adam. I have not looked at them, but maybe there are some things in here you want to keep.'

'Oh. Thank you, Ulrich.'

'So. I am in my room. When you want to go out, just say.'

'Yes, thanks.'

Ulrich wasn't how she'd imagined him: he was tall, massive, like a bear. His movements were slow and gentle, but you could tell, if you looked at the bulk of his biceps pushing out at his T-shirt, that he had force to unleash. He seemed to find it perfectly natural for Eva to be staying with him, and she wondered if this was just because he was used to renting his spare room out, or because through Adam he felt he knew her already. What had she imagined he would be like, actually? Eva wasn't sure. Perhaps she hadn't imagined anything: Ulrich had been a name she had heard Adam mention hundreds of times, but had never tried to flesh out in her mind. She'd never, really, tried to flesh out any part of his life here in her mind.

And now, in this large, sparsely furnished room, she tried to imagine that life. Adam arriving, like she just had, putting his suitcase down, reclaiming a space that would have grown familiar to him. It was strange to picture him, so house-proud back in London, living in these spartan conditions. She looked at the mattress, tried to imagine him wrapped up in that single duvet, and suddenly she could see him, how sweet he looked when he was asleep, with his hair mussed up and a quizzical furrow to his brow. The clarity of the memory pushed a surprised sigh out of her: such images came less frequently to her now, and she sometimes worried that he'd been erased from her brain. The only problem with them was that they made her feel his absence all over again. But then, wasn't that why she'd come to Berlin: to recapture the fading memory of him, and therefore also of her loss?

If only one could come without the other.

She opened up the box that Ulrich had pulled out for her, flicked through the first few sheets of paper: medical-research stuff. Wedged at the front, a few photos stuck on to pieces of card: one of her at home – she remembered that day, just a regular lazy Saturday, reading the paper at the kitchen table and the sun pouring through the bay windows so beautifully that Adam had wanted to immortalize the moment. A photo of the two of them on their honeymoon – God, they looked so young. And a photo of the two of them with Henry and Carmen at uni, lounging outside on a sunny day. God, they looked like children. The photos had Blu-tack marks on their backs – Adam must have put them up on the walls during his stays here. She peered into the box: sure enough, there was a packet of Blu-tack at the bottom of it. She smiled: good old, ever-organized Adam.

She stuck the photos up on the wall above the mattress, then started to unpack. Sliding a stack of T-shirts on to one of the canvas shelves, she had an uneasy sense of Adam making the same gesture, as though the room itself had a memory that it was projecting on to her, or as though a loophole in time had been opened up and she and an Adam from years ago were standing simultaneously on the same spot. As though she and Adam were the same body.

It had scared her sometimes: how much she needed him, as though they really did share one body. How sometimes, when she was far from home, away on assignment, seeing so many other lives, so many other ways of living, she would feel that she was only one of a thousand different possible Evas, a mere fragment of a fractured self, and it was only the way Adam would talk to her as though he knew who she was that gave her some reassurance. If she allowed herself the thought experiment, after they'd had a row or something, of imagining a split-up, a life without him, she couldn't imagine who she would *be*. It was the same terrifying panic as she felt now, allowing herself to face up to her thoughts on Lena Bachmann. Would she uncover something here that might force her to retell the story of her relationship, of who she was, of who he had been?

And yet. It seemed laughable, this idea of Adam having had an *affair*. If you put it like that.

And yet. Why had he stopped, at some point – a point that had arrived slowly, unidentifiably over the years, like a slow-growing tumour, but then settled down to stay – why had he stopped asking Eva to come to Berlin with him? Because of another woman, another life in which he was another Adam?

And yet. Of course Adam was Adam. Of course there was nothing to worry about. Of course this presence she could feel sharing her movements, stacking clothes carefully on top of each other, smoothing them out, was the same man she had known, would always know. And would find again here, maybe.

'REMIND ME AGAIN why we decided to do this, when neither you nor I have the first clue about DIY?'

'Because, Herr Doktor, it's meant we were able to buy a much nicer place than we could have afforded if we'd gone for anything we could actually live in.'

'Could you hand me that tray with the white stuff?'

'This looks really liquidy.'

'Really?'

'Yeah.'

'Let's see.'

'Ad, can't you come down off the stepladder? I'm worried if I hand it to you up there you'll pour it all over me.'

'I don't want to come all the way down off the stepladder!'

'Come halfway down, then.'

'OK, I'll come halfway down.'

Eva hands Adam the tray of white – what is it? Plaster? Polyfilla? She's never quite sure what the difference is.

'Hm, it is quite liquidy. I definitely used the amounts they put in the instructions, though.'

'Still. I really don't think it'll work like that. It'll just drip down all over the wall.'

'Hm. Maybe you're right. Maybe we should bung a bit more powder in.'

'And from the way you're handing the tray back to me, I'm guessing you mean I should bung a bit more powder in?'

'I'm on the stepladder!'

'Right.'

Eva mixes more of the stuff – plaster, Polyfilla, whatever – in. It solidifies into curd.

'Shit, I think I've overdone it now.'

'Well, just chuck some more water in.'

'This could go on for ever.'

Luckily, there is a sink in the kitchen: one lonely sink waiting patiently to be joined by white goods, cupboards, a sideboard. And a kettle, on the floor. And a Stella Artois fridge Henry stole from his rugby club, also on the floor. The floor is the only place anything can be on, as there is nothing else in the kitchen. Eva loves it. This is how you build a life together: from the ground up.

'OK, I think I've got it.'

'Let's have a look?'

'. . .'

'Yep, that seems OK. Right.'

Adam totters back up to the top of the stepladder.

'Hang on, Ad. Aren't you meant to sand the wall down first? I'm pretty sure your dad said something to that effect.'

'Oh. Really?'

'I think so.'

'It can't actually make that much of a difference, surely?'

'Well – I don't know.'

'Maybe I'd better check the book. Could you pass me the book?'

'Yep.'

Eva hands him *The DIY Bible.*

'. . .'

'. . .'

'Hm. You are supposed to sand the wall down first. Well spotted. Do we have any sandpaper left?'

'I think I've still got some in the bedroom. Hang on a sec.'

Eva walks down the short corridor. Kitchen and dining area; living room and study on the right; bathroom on the left. Bedroom. If they have kids, they can always convert the study into another bedroom. In a few weeks, they will have turned this into a home; in a few years, this place will be as familiar to her as her own skin. And now, it is so gloriously, so excitingly new.

There is sandpaper in the bedroom. There is no bed in it yet. Just think – their bedroom, and they've never even slept in it. Their kitchen, and they've never even cooked in it. Just think how much cooking and sleeping they will have done in this place in a few years' time.

'Here you go.'

'Right. Thanks.'

Eva leafs through *The DIY Bible*. There's a section about how to make your own spice rack. She's never thought of that. It would be nice to have their own spice rack.

'How about making a spice rack?'

'We've got one already. It's going to the left of the sink.'

'Oh.'

'God. I hate sanding.'

'Really? I quite enjoy it.'

'I fucking hate it.'

'Do you want me to take over? I really don't mind it that much.'

'No. We said I'd do the kitchen.'

'Suit yourself.'

'Don't you have a job to do, anyway?'

'I'm taking a break, Stakhanov.'

'Can that break involve making a cup of tea?'

'That's not unheard of, in a break.'

'No – in fact it's quite the done thing in some parts.'

'Would you like one?'

'Oh, well. If you insist.'

'Builder's, or Earl Grey?'

'Builder's. *Obviously.*'

It's so much fun, boiling a kettle up on the floor. It feels like such an adventure.

Eva studies the fireplace. It's gorgeous – Edwardian. The tiles are delicately painted with some kind of flower or bramble. All of them original. Some of them are cracked, which she loves. A home should feel weathered, like it has a history. The grate is black with ancient soot.

'I love the fireplaces.'

'I know, they're amazing, aren't they? Though I think my favourite is the stained glass. I just can't get over it. Look at this one, this bluebird: isn't it beautiful?'

'Ad, please stop waving at the window, I'd rather you didn't break your neck right now. But yes, it is amazing.'

'Our house.'

'Our flat.'

'Our flat.'

'Well – the bank's flat.'

'The bank's flat. Amazing.'

'Here's your tea.'

'Thanks. Oh – well, wait, maybe I'll come down for it. Just let me finish this last bit.'

'. . .'

'. . .'

'Do you realize we're married?'

'I know – it's crazy, isn't it?'

'And we've, like, got our own place?'

'It's just – it's amazing.'

'I'm so happy.'

'So am I.'

And with that, Adam comes down off the stepladder at last.

WHAT IS THE meaning of a life so short?
What is the meaning of a life that has left nothing behind, that barely had time to touch the world before disappearing again?

You think of the plans left unfinished, the projects begun that will never be completed, the paths opened up only to be met by a dead end.

And you wonder was it worth it, the being born and all the learning and growing, all that effort laid to waste by so early a death? Was it worth loving someone just to be left with such a painful, profound absence? You might live another span of Adam's life, another two even, perhaps, though of course perhaps not, and would that give your existence more weight, would that give it more meaning?

Or are we all just as insignificant as each other, whether we die in childhood or youth or old age, brief interludes of life in the long eternity of our inexistence, and if that is the case, really, what is the point of it all?

EVERYONE IS LEAVING to move on to the next pub, but Eva still has an almost-full pint, and also can't find her scarf, so she gets down underneath the table, and after some rummaging finds it trampled underneath Jimmy or whatever his name was's chair. It is dusty and one end of it is covered in something sticky. Fucking hell.

A guy appears at the table with a full pint of lager in his hand.

'Hey, where is everyone?'

'They've moved on to the Mitre.'

'Fucking hell. I've only just managed to get myself a fucking pint.'

'I know, it's ridiculous. I'd only just started mine as well.'

'. . .'

'. . .'

The guy plonks himself down in the seat next to hers.

'Oh well. I was kind of hating it anyway, weren't you? Shall we just have our drinks in peace?'

'Um. Yeah. Cool.'

'So how come you didn't go to the Mitre with the others, then?'

'I couldn't find my scarf. I've got it now though. But it's got this weird shit on it . . .'

'Eurgh. Gross. What is that stuff?'

'I think it might be a sort of concentrate formed through centuries of spilled beer.'

'Probably contains molecules from a pint once drunk by Byron. You should frame it.'

'Hm. I suppose that's some consolation.'

'What's your name, by the way? I'm Adam.'

'Eva.'

A pause.

'It really is Eva.'

'Ha! That's funny.'

The pub, after heaving with students and their loud, nervous chatter, has reverted to a certain degree of calm, although it is still quite packed. Its clientele consists mainly of middle-aged men. There are angry sounds emanating from a back room; a darts contest seems to have got out of hand.

'This isn't quite how I imagined the Garden of Eden.'

'No, me neither. I don't feel particularly prelapsarian, either.'

A hefty man in a pink waistcoat walks past their table, lets out a low belch.

'Join the club. I think you might have already eaten the apple, or whatever it is you're meant to do.'

'I don't think it actually is specified that it's an apple. Technically, it's the fruit of the tree of knowledge of good and evil.'

'How's your knowledge of good and evil feeling?'

'Fairly tuned. I spotted a lot of twats this evening.'

The door to the pub opens and a hubbub of freshers swarms in, drowning out the older men and their darts-based bickering. Suddenly every seat, every inch of floor is filled again, and a deafening racket of barking voices and nervous laughter enfolds them.

'Fuck.'

'I think we've just fallen from grace.'

'Yep.'

'Shall we go on somewhere else?'

'Isn't everywhere going to be like this tonight?'

'I know a cool little café just round the corner, I think they're open late. Unless you'd rather go to the Mitre?'

'I am definitely not going to the Mitre. Come on then, let's see your cool little café.'

Adam stands up to put his coat on. To the left of him, a guy with floppy hair and a weak chin is hollering at another in a cut-glass accent.

'Chap! Chap! What you having?'

The guy who is being addressed as 'Chap' – tall, dark, well-dressed – turns to the girl next to him and shrugs his shoulders in what is presumably meant to be a disarming manner.

'Everyone at school called me "Chap".'

Who are these people, and what has given them this astonishing self-confidence? To the right of Adam, a gawky boy – this one really is a boy – is trying to wrestle his way to the bar. He lacks the assertiveness to get very far. He has a kind face, and would seem quite sweet if it weren't for the fact that he is laughing so sycophantically at the inane comments of the two posh boys.

'Shall we go then?'

Well. This Adam guy, at least, seems normal. A little try-hard with his 'I know a cool café' stuff, but not in a desperate way – and he's someone, well – you feel you can *talk* to. This was how she had imagined university: full of people you could *talk* to.

'Yes, let's get out of this hell-hole.'

They prise their way through nervous boys and overdressed girls, trying not to get doused in beer spill, and then they are out of there. Eva takes a deep breath of cool, crisp air – a welcome change from the smoky fug inside.

'It's this way.'

'How come you know your way around here so well already?'

'Oh, my brother studied here, I've been up a couple of times.'

The screeching sounds of drunken students still reaches them from the other end of the street. They set off in the opposite direction, and soon turn into a small, quiet alley. Cambridge is blue at night; the cold light makes the stone walls and cobblestones glisten, as though they have just been rained upon. Adam walks briskly and in silence, as if she's not there. He has lost the affable air he was sporting in the pub, and now looks serious, determined.

Eva likes it, this lack of conversation – it's a relief after the constant effort of the past two days.

Adam turns to her.

'God, it's nice not to talk for a bit, isn't it?'

'I was just thinking that.'

They let each other toy with their private thoughts, listening to the beat of their footsteps in this quiet darkness, taking in the venerable façades that contemplate them from the height of their centuries. On one street, there is a Sainsbury's sitting opposite the gate of one of the colleges, sort of tastefully camouflaged within an old-looking structure, but a Sainsbury's nonetheless, which feels disappointing, gives the whole place a Disneyland feel, as though the colleges have been built by Americans to make the supermarkets more attractive, rather than the other way round.

Still, good to know that there is a Sainsbury's here.

Then down a street that is all back ends of shops and featureless expanses of cement, past a couple of pubs hiding away from the hordes of freshers, and here they are in the café, which mainly reminds Eva of the inside of a Little Chef.

'Hm. Nice.'

'It's all right, isn't it? What do you want?'

'Um – I'll have some wine, I think. Hang on, I'll give you some cash.'

'It's OK, I'll get it.'

She watches Adam walk over to the counter. It occurs to her that the others will all think they're getting off with each other, but then she remembers the others probably won't have noticed she's gone, apart from Carmen who definitely will, but won't go spreading rumours anyway. Not that she cares. The point is, she can feel the strictures of how this will be perceived from the outside, and it is a drag, a boring, predictable drag. She likes this guy, why shouldn't they hang out together?

Adam looks over from the queue and smiles at her. It is a kind smile, which makes him seem older than he is. Underneath his adolescent body – slim, nervy, too eager to please – he has this quiet self-assuredness. It is as though, Eva realizes, Adam actually knows who he is. With him looking at her now, she wonders if he is planning on pulling her. She hopes not. It would be a shame to ruin a delicate affinity by jumping into a predictable fumble. How Eva longs for the world, her life, not to be what you might expect! How handsome Adam is, with his aquiline features and shock of blond hair, and a certain fineness in his limbs which makes him look as though he might disappear. Actually, handsome isn't the word. Nor is cute, nor good-looking. He is beautiful, like a painting or a statue. A beautiful boy. She hopes he doesn't stick his tongue down her throat.

The other people in the café all look relaxed; they chat without trying to impress each other or establish a position in the pecking order. There can't be any freshers among them. Eva has a sudden, vertiginous sensation that she will never be like them; but she doesn't want Adam, who is walking back over to her, to think she is crazy, so she bites back the angst and smiles at him.

He sets two steaming mugs down on the table.

'Sorry – they don't serve alcohol. I assumed a hot chocolate was OK . . .'

'Wow, no – now you've given me that, I realize it's exactly what I've been wanting all along.'

'Yes, that's exactly how I feel. Thank Christ we're not in the Mitre.'

'I'll drink to that.'

They both set to their hot chocolates, hands wrapped around them like bunnies' paws.

'Nice café. I like the, er, atmosphere. Restful.'

'Yeah, sorry, I was just thinking it's not as nice as I thought it would be. It's a bit tacky, isn't it?'

'No, I mean, it's fine. I mean, I probably wouldn't want to come and spend every evening here, but, you know, it's a nice break from fresher's week.'

'I guess it seemed cooler to me when I was, like, fifteen and visiting my big brother.'

Is he a tiny bit disappointed? She's been sort of assuming that he's just this effortlessly confident guy, but there's a flicker of discomfort in him all of a sudden, a loss of bravado now that his great little find has turned out to be not quite so great after all. She feels bad – she didn't mean to put him down. She hasn't put him down. She wonders if he thinks she's full of astonishing self-confidence.

'So, have you met anyone interesting this evening? Present company excluded, obviously. I'm sure no one can beat my knowledge of quite nice cafés that seem really cool when you're fifteen.'

'Not really. I got stranded at a table with that Alex guy from the year above and a bunch of people whose sole topic of conversation was Britpop.'

'Oh dear.'

'I mean – I like Britpop, you know, but I never realized people could find so much to say about it.'

'Sounds pretty similar to the guys I ended up talking to.'

'It's kind of a bit of a let-down, isn't it?'

'What is?'

'I mean – I thought we were meant to be the finest young minds in the country – I was kind of expecting to be meeting people here you could talk to about other things than *Top of the Pops*.'

'Such as?'

'I don't know – surely we should all be having impassioned debates about philosophy or politics or something? Not just getting wasted.'

'Well – it's only our first week here – I'm sure the philosophical debates will start at some stage.'

'It's just – I was so looking forward to going to university at last, I was expecting it to be so exciting . . .'

'And reality isn't living up to your expectations?'

'I don't know. Maybe I'm judging this place too fast. And I have met one really cool girl – Carmen. We're on the same staircase. She's kind of . . . Just really easy to talk to, you know?'

'Isn't that just a way of saying that you get on well?'

'I suppose so. But she seems to be like that with everyone, whereas . . .'

Hm. Maybe she shouldn't be telling this guy how intimidating she finds it all. Don't want to sound like a loser.

'I know, it's kind of exhausting, all this having to be really chirpy with every new person you come across. But, you know – we'll all get to know each other soon enough.'

'That's very level-headed of you.'

'I don't know – I just look at the guys in the year above us, and they're all so comfortable here, it's as though they've been here for ever. It was certainly like that for my brother. Why wouldn't it be the same for us?'

'I was thinking the exact opposite: I was looking at the guys in the year above us and thinking I can't see how I'll ever be like them.'

Adam smiles.

'I'm pretty sure you're going to end up being proven wrong.'

'Yes, I suppose you're right. Or I hope so, anyway. Though I hope I don't end up like that Alex character.'

'God, me too. What a creep.'

' . . .'

'I do know what you mean, though. I had a kind of weird moment when my mum dropped me off here – this kind of sudden panic, like I was a kid being dropped off for his first day at kindergarten or something. Ridiculous.'

'Maybe it's knowing that we're embarking on a new chapter of our lives – and a really important one. I mean, university, that's meant to really define you, isn't it? To be the best years of your life or whatever. But right now we're on the threshold of that, and it's kind of daunting.'

'Yeah, maybe. I think in my case it wasn't helped by the fact that my mum insisted on driving me up here. I'd have been fine if I'd just come up on the train, I reckon. And I mean, she's really busy at the moment, and I was like, "Mum, I can just take the train, it's really fine," but she was like, "No, no, no, I have to take you, I'm not going to let my boy head off to university all alone," and I mean, she's really not like that usually, I mean I've been going away on holiday with friends and stuff like that for years and she never stresses about it. But, yeah – somehow the fact that she dropped me off here, and looking at my stuff sitting in this empty college room . . . It felt like, Oh shit, oh shit, this is actually real. And to make things worse, she actually took this guy who's in the room next to me to one side – this guy called Henry, he's really hilarious actually, you'll have to meet him – and gave him this speech about how he had to look out for me and she could tell he was a reliable young man who wouldn't let her down, and I mean, luckily Henry isn't a dick, basically, so he just laughed it off when he told me about it and was like, "Yeah, my mum's really crazy sometimes too," but imagine if she'd said all that to someone who wasn't so cool? I'd be the laughing stock of the college by now.'

'I'm sure there's quite a few people with similar tales – I mean, you've got to see it from their point of view as well, it can't be that easy for our parents to watch us all fly the nest.'

'Yeah, I guess you're right. How about you – how's your mum reacting to losing her little girl?'

'Oh. Kind of – normally, I think. No outbreaks to any fellow students, at least. Though I mean – my mum left home in pretty crazy circumstances, so it would be weird if she were freaked out by me just going to university.'

'Why – what happened when your mum left home?'

'OK, "left home" isn't quite the right way of putting it. She's from East Germany originally, and she fled to the West when she was, like, nineteen.'

'*Seriously?*'

'Yep.'

'How – I mean – what happened?'

'She, like, went up to the Baltic Sea and this friend from West Berlin came to get her with a kind of dinghy thing and then took her to a boat.'

'Wow.'

'Yeah, I know, It's kind of a crazy story.'

'And – I mean – why did she want to leave East Germany, was there a particular reason or was she just, like, I don't know, I need to get out of here?'

'No, there was a reason – or at least, it was kind of a precaution, I guess. Her parents had just been put in prison, and I think she felt it would be safer for her to leave – or at least, that her life would be easier if she left.'

'Wow. Jesus. And what had your grandparents done?'

'I don't know exactly, to be honest. I mean, they were involved in groups opposing the regime. They were quite religious – well, I mean, my grandfather was a pastor, in fact – and, you know, that wasn't very popular with the East German government. As far as I know, all they did was take part in discussion groups at their church, that sort of thing – but it seems that was enough for the Stasi to take an interest in them. They'd been making their lives difficult for a while – by doing stuff like stopping my mum from going to uni, for example – but then, yeah, suddenly they got thrown in prison and she doesn't really know why. Or I guess she knows part of it, maybe, but not everything.'

'Wow.'

'Yeah.'

'And – what happened to your grandparents, then? How long were they in jail for? I guess you weren't able to see them until the Wall came down?'

'They died long before I was born, unfortunately. In prison, in fact.'

'Oh Jesus. I'm sorry.'

'No, it's fine, I mean – I never knew them.'

'Oh my God. That's awful.'

'Yeah, sorry, bit of a conversation-stopper . . .'

'No! I mean, as long as you're comfortable talking about it . . .'

'Oh, sure, don't worry – there's not much more to say, really. My mum made a life for herself in England, I guess. Though she's never managed to lose her German accent . . .'

'Did she not talk to you in German, then?'

'Oh sure, yes. She spoke German to me when I was a kid.'

'Na das ist aber toll! '

'Ha! You speak German?'

'Ja! Wir können miteinander Deutsch reden, wenn du willst. '

'Um. I don't really speak it any more, to be honest.'

'Really? How come?'

'Um. I don't know – I kind of stopped after primary school – I think I felt like it would make me look uncool or something. Or maybe I was worried I wouldn't fit in. The World War Two jokes get kind of tired after a while.'

'Hm, yeah, I can imagine. Shame, though.'

'Yeah. You're so stupid when you're a teenager, aren't you?'

'We still are teenagers, aren't we?'

'Hm. Yeah, I guess we are. Anyway. You speak German, then?'

'Yes, I did it for A level. It was my favourite subject, in fact. And I've spent a fair bit of time in Berlin too.'

'Oh, really? How come?'

'Oh, I just love it. I went there on a school trip in the early nineties, just after the Wall came down, and it was just mind-blowing. This one half of the city that still had a foot in the Communist era, and all these ruins . . . I was too young to really explore the party scene back then, unfortunately, but still you could feel that there was this incredible, anarchic freedom . . .'

'. . .'

'I guess you must have seen a different side of it, though, if your mum is from East Berlin.'

'Oh – I've never been, actually.'

'Really? How come?'

'I don't know, I guess – my mum has never wanted to. I mean, I guess she doesn't have particularly good memories of it. And she has no family left there, anyway.'

'Really? No siblings or aunts and uncles or anything?'

'No, she was an only child, and her parents didn't have any siblings either.'

'And you've never wanted to go back?'

'It's funny you use the phrase "going back" – I've never been there in the first place . . .'

'But still. It's where your family's from.'

'Well – half of it, yes.'

'You've never been curious to see what it's like out there?'

'I don't know, I – Not really, to be honest. I mean – it's not that all of that isn't important to me. I definitely feel it's part of who I am: I grew up speaking German, or when I was a kid at least, and my mum would read me these German stories and everything . . . And I think there are definitely a lot of things she taught me, a lot of values that probably have to do with her growing up under Communism, so I guess that's always something I've felt is a part of me. But, I don't know. I feel like all of the stuff I'd be interested in seeing, like East Berlin as it was when she was growing up, that's all in the past now. I'm not sure what I'd be looking for if I did go to Berlin.'

'Well – there are still a lot of traces of the past there.'

'But, you know – if my mum doesn't want to go, doesn't want to help me decipher those traces . . .'

'She really doesn't want to go back?'

'I don't know. I mean, to be honest, it's not something we've really discussed much. I just kind of know she doesn't want to.'

'Right, sure – I understand.'

'. . .'

'Well, if you ever do decide to go to Berlin, I'd be happy to give you some tips.'

'Thanks, good to know – I'll bear it in mind.'

ONCE SHE HAD unpacked, Eva went to the toilet. She had to stop herself from knocking on Ulrich's door and asking for his permission – she lived here now, or would for a while, at least. She needed to behave as though she were at home.

The bathroom, like her bedroom, was sparse and white, the only indications of life a towel draped over the radiator, a bar of soap on the sink and a tube of shower gel on the side of the bath. There was a cupboard hanging over the sink, which Eva peeked into: it was packed full of male grooming products, packets of plasters, medicines. There was a shaving brush, which bristled at being exposed to the light: it must have been resting slightly against the door that Eva had just opened. She felt herself flush at having intruded on Ulrich's intimacy in this way, and closed the cupboard again.

In contrast to the bathroom, the kitchen was narrow and cluttered, and consisted mainly of inventively repurposed objects: four Moët & Chandon cases provided the struts for a shelf, a fruit crate pinned to the wall with an extra board nailed into it became a spice rack. One shelf had a line of jam jars glued to the bottom of it by their tops; they contained sugar, coffee, loose-leaf tea. Eva gave one of them a twist, and it unscrewed free. Ingenious. There was an old dresser with chipped paint and no glass where glass should have been. Eva put her hand through the non-existent pane and touched the plates and bowls inside. She thought of the tasteful, carefully selected furniture of her and Adam's home back in London; it was a nice kitchen they'd created for themselves. But this had a certain ramshackle charm to it too. They were both nice kitchens. She wondered if Adam had liked it.

She ran herself a glass of water, still not feeling quite comfortable with the idea that she could do this without checking with Ulrich first. She needed to be like Adam, at home in this foreign kitchen. He would have turned the tap on with the familiarity of habit, would have known how long you needed to wait till the water was properly cold, perhaps would have cast a glance at the unwashed chopping board on the side and shaken his head in affectionate despair at Ulrich's messiness. Perhaps would have washed the chopping board. She hadn't thought about this before: Adam sharing a domestic existence with this burly German man.

'Everything is OK?'

Ulrich was standing in the doorway, like an oak tree: solid, firmly rooted, imperturbable.

'Oh. Yes. Sorry. I was just getting a glass of water.'

'No problem, take whatever you want. Maybe you like a coffee?'

'Oh thanks, that would be great.'

She stepped aside to let Ulrich manoeuvre his body into the room. The space was too narrow to allow for more than a couple of centimetres as he went past her, and she caught a whiff of the aftershave she had just seen in his bathroom cabinet.

He unscrewed the jam jar that contained coffee; his hands were enormous and chiselled, as though they had been sculpted out of granite. They looked like hands that could till a field, or lash a sail to a mast.

'Actually, you know what? Sorry, I won't have one after all – I've drunk far too many coffees today already. But have you got some herbal tea, maybe?'

'Sure. Or I could make you a hot chocolate, also?'

'Oh. Wow. Yes, a hot chocolate would be lovely.'

Ulrich smiled.

'Adam was used to say, my hot chocolate was the best he ever tasted.'

'Ah. Well. In that case, I definitely want hot chocolate.'

'WHERE DO THESE GO?'
        'Well – I mean – I don't know any better than you, do I?'
'Well, where *should* they go?'
'Where do you think?'
'I don't know. That's why I'm asking you.'
'OK. How about in there?'
'Oh. Actually, I was thinking of keeping that cupboard for things like flour and stuff . . .'
'Ah. Right. Fine.'
'It's just because it's high up, you see, mice wouldn't be able to get to it, I think we should keep it for foodstuffs.'
'Yes. I hadn't thought of that.'
'I mean, we'll put everything in jars anyway, obviously.'
'Oh Adam. What would I do without you?'
'What?'
'No, you just – it's good you think about all these things, because they would never occur to me.'
'Well, you know, it's our place. I want it to be nice.'
'Yes, so do I – I'd just be terrible at actually making it nice in any practical way.'
'You make it nice by being here.'
'Flatterer!'
'So where should we put these?'
'I don't know. Down there?'
'Oh, no, remember, that one's for . . .'
'You're just trying to wind me up, aren't you?'
'No, I'm not! I'm just trying to have us decide together.'
It is sometimes hard to tell whether Adam is teasing or not. In

this case, Eva decides, following close examination of his guile-less expression: no.

'OK. Why don't you tell me what you were thinking?'

'Well. I mean, I'm open to all suggestions really, but I was wondering about either there, in the cupboard two across from the sink, or in the commode.'

'. . .'

'You don't seem convinced.'

'No, I just – I mean, both those options seem fine to me.'

'Are you laughing at me?'

'No, no, of course I'm not . . .'

'You are! You're smirking.'

'I just – sorry . . .'

'What's so hilarious?'

'It's just – I literally cannot see what the difference is between putting them in the cupboard or in the other thing.'

'The commode?'

'. . .'

'What?!'

'Oh Adam, I mean, who actually says "commode"?'

'It *is* a commode! That's what it is!'

'You've got to admit, it's a pretty funny word.'

'OK, "commode" is a pretty funny word. Still, you'll be happy when you've got a well-furnished kitchen to swan around in.'

'I will indeed. Especially with such a well-furnished man inside it.'

'Flatterer.'

'Aren't those a bit heavy, by the way?'

'Yeah, they are actually.'

'Shouldn't you put them down?'

'Yes, but where though?'

'OK, I vote for the commode.'

'You're not just saying that because you like saying the word "commode"?'

'You're the one who keeps saying "commode"! No, I just think it's the right place for them.'

'OK.'

While Adam shifts objects around from one oaken shelf to another, Eva creeps up behind him and slips her arms around his waist.

'You know, I really don't know what I'd do without you.'

'Mm.'

'Mm.'

'Right, enough of that, I've got a commode to sort out.'

'What's that noise, by the way?'

'What noise?'

'That ringing noise.'

'Oh. It must be our landline.'

'I didn't even know we had a landline.'

'I got it installed yesterday. It's on that little ledge by the front door.'

'What would I do without you?'

Eva sets off in search of the phone. It's an old model with a cord which she recognizes from Adam's room when they were at university. It feels strange to have to stand in one place to have a conversation on it.

'Hello?'

'Hi, Eva.'

'Henry! How come you're calling on this number? How come you even have this number?'

'Oh, er, I don't know – why, what number am I calling on?'

'Our brand-new landline – it's really weird, it's one of those old phones with a cord where you can't wander around while you're talking, it's really making me realize how—'

'Um. Eva.'

'Er, yes? Is everything OK, Henry?'

'Not really. I mean, I'm fine – I'm absolutely fine. But . . .'

' . . .'

'Something's happened to Carmen.'

SMOKE FILLED THE bar, curling around tables and stools like a lazy ferret. She wasn't sure how they'd found a way of escaping the smoking ban, which surely was meant to apply across the whole EU – or maybe they just ignored it. Eva liked it: it felt like going back in time, to the smoky pubs they used to hang out in as students, or when she was living near Brick Lane.

'Adam liked this place a lot. He said it reminded him of being younger.'

'Yes, I can see why. It reminds me of the places we used to go to when we first lived in London. I think it's the smokiness that makes it feel that way.'

'Funny. This is what Adam said, also.'

'Oh dear – I didn't realize we'd got to the stage of having the same thoughts as each other . . .'

'It is quite beautiful, I think. To know another person so well.'

'Hm.'

A nice thing about Ulrich was that he didn't mind sitting in silence. In this stillness, side by side, watching life unravel in the bar, Eva could almost convince herself she could feel Adam sitting here with them – not right next to them, but at another table perhaps, one a little behind them, that was just out of sight.

Her eyes strayed to Ulrich's hands: they were broad, weathered. Nails clipped short. Hands that told a story. What had these hands done? Repaired bicycles, shaken Adam's hand, made hot chocolate. Put up shelves. She wondered how many women had felt those hands run over their bodies.

But enough about the hands. Eva wanted to concentrate on the traces of Adam, on her memories, which felt so changeable and fading. Sometimes she would be walking around the city, or talking to Ulrich, and it was all so new that her life in London, with Adam, would seem unreal, a life that belonged to another person.

And yet, she wasn't another person. She mustn't let the days pull her further away from him. Mustn't let life take over. Perhaps she should wall herself up somewhere.

'So you and Adam would come here often, then?'

Ulrich smiled – a fond smile, a smile full of memories.

'Yes – it was something like our – Stammkneipe.'

'Your local.'

'Yes.'

Eva tried to imagine, over her shoulder, out of view, Adam nursing a beer, breathing in the smoke, living his other life.

'Actually, I think Adam liked this place so much because the first time he came here, there was – how do you say it? Krawall – this – a crazy thing. A big battle with the police. There was this guy from an anti-fascist group, he came here, and then some cops came in and tried to arrest him.'

'What had he done?'

'I don't know – somehow they were after him, and they knew he had come here. But so, there were some other people in the bar, they tried to stop the police from arresting him. And then more police arrived, then more people started opposing them. Eventually there were five police vans outside, and almost everyone in the bar was fighting with them.'

'Wow. It sounds like a proper riot.'

'Krawall. Yes.'

'How did Adam react?'

'Ha! Actually, I had to stop him from getting involved. It was the first evening we went out together, the first time he was renting my room. Suddenly I saw on his face that he wanted to jump in – you know, when you can see that someone has this – in their expression?'

'A look in their eye?'

'Yes, maybe.'

'But a look like what?'

'Like suddenly – first he was looking quite shocked, maybe scared even. And then he changed – like he became a cat who has seen a mouse, who wants to . . .'

'Pounce?'

'Yes. And I thought, Oh Gott, this English man, I don't want him to spend his first night in Berlin in a police cell because of me. He was so excited, but he would not have been excited by a stay with the Berliner Polizei.'

'Bloodlust.'

'Ja, genau. So I stopped him from going, I took him outside, and we watched the fight from a distance. At one point three policemen carried out one woman, she was screaming like crazy, I never heard such a scream. Some neighbours came down out of their flats to see what was happening. Adam wanted to go and help her, too, but I again stopped him.'

'Well. Thank you. It sounds like you did a good job of keeping my husband in one piece.'

'It was funny, because afterwards I thought, boah, this guy is a bit crazy, maybe I don't want him living in my flat if he is so violent – but I never again saw him act like this.'

'I never saw him act like that. Ever.'

'He did not tell you about this?'

'He did – about all the police coming into the bar, the fight. He didn't tell me that he had tried to jump in.'

'Maybe he did not even remember – maybe he had this moment of rage, of bloodlust like you say, and then forgot.'

'Or maybe he was embarrassed to tell me – Adam wouldn't have felt very proud to have reacted like that.'

Or, who knew – maybe Adam hadn't felt ashamed at all. Maybe he did have this rage inside him. Eva had a rage of her own that she seldom showed to the world: a rage at life, for being so mundane, a rage at death for having robbed her, a rage that things couldn't be different, that you couldn't make them be different. She imagined Adam standing up behind her, stretching his lithe body, testing the suppleness of his joints, throwing some punches into the air, left, right, left, right, limbering up for the struggle.

And if he had been different to what she knew in this respect, what else about his life here might be unknown to her? Had he sat in this café with Lena Bachmann, leaning towards her with an earnest, steady gaze, just like Ulrich was leaning towards Eva now?

'Still until now, I cannot believe he is . . . Gone.'

'I know. I often can't, either.'

'I miss him a lot. He was a good friend.'

'Yes.'

'. . .'

'I'm sorry I didn't call you before the funeral. I just – I don't know. I wasn't thinking straight. Or maybe I didn't realize that he really had a life here. Friends.'

'It's OK. Of course, this was a difficult time for you.'

'Still. I should have thought of it. You should have been there. I'm sorry.'

'Don't worry. I just wanted you to know, I miss him.'

'Thank you.'

Eva felt as though Adam's presence behind her was expanding, his ghost turning into a force field that filled the space behind her back, filled the whole bar except for the area that was within her field of vision. As though Adam was everywhere except in front of her. In front of her was Ulrich.

'So – where are you from, Ulrich? I'm sorry, I've hardly asked you anything about yourself.'

'From Berlin.'

'Oh really? Which part?'

'From Marzahn.'

'Is that East or West?'

'East. Very East.'

'My mother is from East Berlin too.'

'Yes. Adam told me.'

Ulrich took a sip from his beer. His hand rugged and thick-knuckled around the glass. Had that hand torn pieces of concrete from the Wall, swung a hammer against it, thrown a victorious fist into the air? She thought of Adam's hands, so slight in comparison. Of Adam now, a thin, ghostly presence – Ulrich a mass of solid, warm flesh. She closed her eyes and took a deep breath of smoke-filled air, and was grateful that no one chose to interrupt the silence in her head.

THE TRUTH IS, you are afraid of dying. Ever since it happened, you have been aware of the fragility of life, of the many angles from which its end can come, and you have feared for the wholeness of your body, you have feared that it might be your own death lurking in that shadow, in the squeal of an oncoming car or the twinge of pain in your chest.

Every day, you fear death may come.

It felt at first like this had to happen, since you couldn't possibly live with this pain, this grief, and being incapable of living, surely you must die.

But you realize now, this is not the same as wanting to die.

You realize now that you have been selfish all along.

The truth is, you do not want to follow Adam into death.

You are not like one of those tragic medieval lovers, or like those elderly couples people speak so fondly of: she just wasted away after her husband passed, they went within months of each other, they simply couldn't live without each other.

You have so much life left inside you.

You loved him, you did – but not enough to die. This is where your ways must part.

So where does this leave love? Love, which bridges the gap between selves, but has not convinced you to plunge a dagger into your battered heart and thus stay true?

ADAM IS ON the loo when the doorbell rings.
'Hey Eve, doorbell, did you hear?!'

Why Adam thinks she would hear him hollering and not the doorbell, Eva is not quite sure. Nor is she quite sure what it is he does in the bathroom exactly that keeps him there for so long. She has noticed that the amount of time he spends in there has gradually increased over the years, along exponential lines: inching slowly upwards while they were boyfriend and girlfriend, and, over the three years they have been married, positively skyrocketing. And she, the goofball, smiles fondly about it all – it's amazing how being in love makes you see something endearing even in your partner's oddest habits.

She opens the door, collects a package from a sweaty DHL man, hollers at Adam as she walks down the corridor.

'It's a package for you from a – er – Ms Lena Bachmann.'

'Oh great, thanks.'

'Looks exciting. Nice and thick.'

'Just boring medical stuff, I'm afraid. Woman I met at a conference last April.'

'Shall I put it on your desk?'

'Yeah, that would be great, thanks. Be out in a minute.'

This is what married couples do: holler conversations through bathroom doors. It makes Eva feel safe and warm inside.

When she puts the package down on his desk, how could she not notice that the list of attendees of the April conference is lying just there, with the names of the people Adam met carefully highlighted according to some sort of colour code? How could she not notice, without even needing to turn anything over, that the page she is looking at includes the names from A to C, and that there is no Lena Bachmann among those names?

Though she thinks nothing of it, of course.

SHE DECIDED TO walk it. There was no reason not to. It was bitterly cold, a real continental wintry cold which made you realize how far you were from the sea and its pacifying effect: how, in contrast, the water lapping at London's toes shielded it from bitter Januaries. But Eva was equipped now with various pelts: fur boots, thick woollen jumper, leather coat, fur hat – in extreme weather conditions, it turned out that nature provided the best arsenal for survival. And, once you had found a way to encase your body heat, it was a glorious, sunny day; a day for walking, enjoying the light and the sense of aliveness you got from seeing your breath crystallize into icy clouds in front of you.

And then there was Berlin, stretching out beneath her feet with its cobblestoned streets, its disjoints, its invisible stories. When Ulrich was with her, he would point them out to her, the layers of history: a Soviet block here, a Nazi building there, streets that had welcomed a debauched demi-monde since the 1920s, how you could still see the traces of all that had come before if you knew how to look. And when she was on her own, she would marvel at its fragmentary nature, how incohesive the whole place was, with turn-of-the-century apartment buildings interrupted by blocks of 1960s cement or brand-new glassy towers or simply nothing, and she would wonder where to look for the traces that concerned her, the traces of Adam, the traces of her mother.

Well, she was doing it now.

She was like the Man with a Movie Camera, an eye floating through space, recording everything that lay before it with equanimity. She went past a café called Babel, a huge expanse of drinking space, furnished with a haphazard but tasteful selection of 1970s East German furniture: PVC, plywood, lime greens and dirty beiges conjured up the spirit of a discarded regime. The people reclining on the harried sofas, however, were fully of their time, sporting asymmetrical haircuts, smartphones, and doctored H&M clothing. As she peered inside, like Tiny Tim looking in on the good cheer he will never know, a young man walked over to his boyfriend and planted a big kiss on his lips.

Kastanienallee sloped downhill now, and the flurry of cafés gave way to residential buildings on the left, a straggly park on the right. She'd noticed, taking the U-Bahn here, that Pankow lay not much further up north, and Eva wondered if her mother had grown up in similar buildings, played in a similar park. This one looked sullen and uninviting, as though it had sprung on to the street by accident and now found itself obliged to stay there, constrained by some obscure bureaucratic regulation. She hardly needed to, but Eva checked the address she had found in Adam's contacts list: Finsterstraße 45. Here was the street.

She wished she had an excuse for getting lost, for delaying the moment when she would find herself face to face with the truth. She decided to walk as slowly as possible. Eva wondered why she couldn't have more dignity, why she couldn't walk upright with tears streaming down her face for all to see, instead of scuttling along, doubled over her grief as though it were a fragile load she had to shield from the elements. It was her lack of anger, that was why: it would be easier to stand tall in the face of some different kind of wrong – some betrayal. Perhaps that was the reason she wanted to meet Lena Bachmann – Lena. If she and Adam had had an affair, she might be able to feel angry with him. Angry that he had left her. Angry that he had moved so far away from her that she couldn't even close her eyes and see his face any more, and yet the pain was still there, the grief, swelling and receding like waves, but never leaving her alone. Angry at Adam for this most complete desertion.

Well, yes. But that was a bit unfair on him. Maybe she could get angry with Lena instead. She imagined her – a pretty, confident woman – opening her door to find herself confronted with this deranged English widow bringing news of the demise of her lover. She imagined breaking down, and Lena comforting her. She imagined Lena breaking down, telling her between heart-rending sobs that Adam was the only man she had ever loved, that her life was meaningless now with the knowledge that he was gone; and they would share their grief and memories of him, two rivals united by their common loss. She imagined Lena opening the door, and there being a five-year-old boy in the kitchen behind her, quietly doing his homework, the son of Adam. Or she would walk in and kill Lena Bachmann. Or Lena Bachmann wouldn't be there, her husband would, and he would be like a carbon copy of Adam, and Eva would walk in and make love to him.

Number 100. She was getting closer. Finsterstraße was two long lines of blocks of flats, pale, impersonal. She came to one building that was shabbier than the rest, and noticed its dents and chips, how in places it looked as if an iron hand had ripped fistfuls out of the façade. Adam had told her about the bullet holes: how so many buildings still bore the mark of the street fighting that had raged through the city in the final throes of the Second World War. There hadn't been as many as Eva had expected, several years of renovations having made a decent stab at erasing the past.

This was a concrete façade, so the holes were deeper, like flesh wounds. The front door to the building was open; Eva went in, and saw that the walls in the inner courtyard were also riddled with pockmarks. They rose up in elegant arcs towards the windows above, like flower stalks. Eva tried to imagine the scene: the Russian soldiers down here, gunning at every opening, the Germans taking potshots at them from their higher vantage points. They would be boys, fervent and Aryan, dying splendidly for a revolting idea they would never grow old enough to understand. Afterwards, as the walls stood smoking from the shock of the bullets, the Russians who had survived would go up into the flats and rape the women. Eva listened carefully to the silence of this residential street, trying to find the echo of all this violence; she heard a bicycle creak past outside the building, and a baby crying in one of the flats. Wrong place, wrong time – those people were here sixty-five years too early. You draw your lot in life, and then that's it.

She stepped out on to Finsterstraße again. She felt ready for Lena now, whatever her story might be. She walked away from the bullet holes, past newer façades that no longer remembered the screams of the dying. When she came to number 45, where the building should have stood, there was a little wasteland: a few heaps of rubble and some dry bushes attempting to grow in between them. Numbers 43 and 47 stood firmly around it, as though they had both had a limb shorn off but were trying to put a brave face on the whole affair. In a corner of the patch of land, behind the rusty wire that fenced it off from the street, a single daffodil blew mournfully in the wind.

'A CROWD FLOWED over London Bridge, so many . . .'
'I had not thought death had undone so many.
Why are you quoting *The Waste Land* at me, Carmen?'
'I can't discuss that right now.'
'. . .'
'. . .'
'Oh, here, I brought you this, too.'
'I don't like it.'
'What are you talking about? You've always loved this stuff.'
'That's a lie.'
'It's Fruit and Nut. It's your favourite.'
'You're talking to me like I've got Alzheimer's.'
'Sorry.'
'. . .'
'. . .'
'Jerusalem Athens Alexandria'
'. . .'
'Vienna London'
'You've lost me, Carmen.'
'Unreal.'
'. . .'
'You know London.'
'Yes, I do. I also know Jerusalem, Athens and Vienna. I've never been to Alexandria though.'
'You're talking to me like I'm mad.'
'Well . . .'
'Well?'

'You *are* kind of mad. I mean, it'll get better – but right now you're quite mad.'

'How do you know it will get better?'

'That's what the doctors say.'

'So we can't be sure.'

'You've got to get better, Carmen – you can't just leave us to soldier on without you.'

'You'll manage.'

'We won't.'

'People do.'

' . . . '

'I feel like my brain is trapped inside my skull.'

'I think that's where it's meant to be.'

'Unreal.'

' . . . '

' . . . '

'Carm – can I ask you a question?'

'Of course you can.'

'Does the name Lena Bachmann mean anything to you?'

'Huh?'

'Lena Bachmann? Adam might have mentioned her. Ring any bells?'

'I don't think so. Why?'

'I don't know – no reason.'

'There's no such thing as no reason.'

' . . . '

'I mean, my memory is not very reliable at the moment. I'll probably have forgotten this conversation by tomorrow.'

'Yes, I know.'

'Is that why you've asked me?'

'Ha! I hadn't thought about it, but maybe.'

'You have a shifty look about you, Eva.'

'So do you.'

' . . . '

'. . .'

'It's such – an effort, isn't it?'

'What?'

'Life – it's so tiring.'

'Don't talk like that, Carm.'

'Why?'

'Because you scare me.'

'Why?'

'Because . . .'

'You're afraid to tell me.'

'Yes.'

'I don't like Fruit and Nut. Never have, never will.'

'That's not true.'

'What's not true?'

'That you don't like Fruit and Nut. You've always bought a bar before you go on any train journey, for as long as I can remember.'

'Maybe I was deceiving myself.'

'What if you're deceiving yourself now?'

'Good question.'

'You wouldn't be Carmen if you didn't like Fruit and Nut. It's one of your most distinctive features.'

'Maybe I'm not me, then.'

'Yes you are. You are most definitely you.'

'How do you know, though? How do you know who I am?'

'I don't know, I just – do.'

'How do you know who you are?'

'Er . . .'

'. . .'

'. . .'

'Eva?'

'Yes?'

'How does anyone ever know anything?'

'Good question.'

EVA WALKED ON to the end of Finsterstraße and tried to get her bearings. None of the street names she could see meant anything to her, but then, above some rooftops, she spotted the tip of the Fernsehturm. Alexanderplatz. One place she knew, at least, in this city full of unknown people, unknown streets. She couldn't believe her mother hadn't told her more about her home. How much of our lives we keep to ourselves; how secret our pasts. Would her mother have stood here and seen familiar buildings? Would Adam have hopped confidently on to a tram without needing to check where he was going? It was an attractive proposition: to think that she was inside their mental images. But although she hadn't been here very long, she understood already that it couldn't possibly be true: Berlin was changing too fast, with its building sites on every street corner, its general air of upheaval. What could be left of the city Adam had first discovered twenty years ago? What could be left of the city her mother had been exiled from over thirty years ago? Words, names, which meant nothing to her, and to them would have conjured up places they would no longer recognize. Why had she come here?

For Lena Bachmann, partly. And she realized that what she felt now, walking away from the hole between two buildings that should have been her rival's home, what she felt now was relief. She had tried to find Lena Bachmann, and failed. She would need to look harder, of course, but for now, she had been granted a stay of execution.

For now, she didn't need to know.

So she might as well ignore her.

Eva turned on to a street that looked like it led towards

Alexanderplatz. The light was going now, going fast, and the street was eerily empty. She jumped when a man came round a corner in front of her, shoulders hunched against the cold. She felt her heart rate shoot up.

She wondered how she could have become so fearful. Or perhaps she wondered how she had managed to be so fearless in the past. She had wandered alone through blacked-out African cities, listened to rockets being fired outside her hotel window, always trusting that the world would send her back to Adam in one piece, always dismissing his concerns for her. And now, now that she had come home to where half her family was from, a home that happened to be one of the safest and most affluent cities in the world, she was afraid of walking down a poorly lit street for ten minutes. Perhaps she had needed Adam to worry about her so she could feel brave.

This route had been a poor choice: it was lined on one side by the high, forbidding arches of the S-Bahn, and on the other by some kind of commercial park, all low, square buildings and neon brand names fizzing in the rain. Had Adam ever seen this side of Berlin: its cheap, miserable, in-between zones, not devastated enough to be cool wastelands, performing some kind of obscure function in keeping the more attractive parts of the city afloat? Could her mother imagine that this, too, was the face of her childhood home? How isolated we are by the limits of our experience – by the tiny, incidental meanings that attach to tiny, incidental things and together form what we call our lives. She could have been walking in Adam's footsteps exactly, and still come no closer to seeing Berlin with his eyes. If you were to take a map and trace her itinerary along these streets, and then add to it all of the routes that Adam had taken during his time here, and then all of the ways her mother had been as a girl – still those three sets of lines would never intersect, the three cities never merge into one, separated not just by time, but also by the thin layers of skin that divide one body from another.

Eva lost all fear as she walked past the drab buildings of the commercial site: they were too mundane to be anything other than the backdrop to a slightly miserable, lonely walk home. Soon she would be back at the flat, and Ulrich would make her one of his amazing hot chocolates. No grandiose horrors could happen here. Horrors never happened where a Hollywood script would have you expect them: they hid in your bed, and were barely distinguishable from everyday events because they were so real.

ADAM APPEARS, CARRYING a thick plastic tray, which looks like it has been in use since the 1950s. Eva makes to get up and help him offload its contents, but is once more thwarted by the fact that the table and chairs are a single unit, solidly welded to the floor: it's almost impossible to get back up once you have sat down. He puts down two uninspiring mugs and an enormous fruit scone before conscientiously returning the tray to the entrance. He moves so comfortably in this world of pale, aseptic surfaces, all blues and lime greens and dirty whites, and it strikes Eva that of course this *is* his world: the old man with the drip drinking tea at the next table, the hush of suffering, the inconsiderate laughter of a group of medical students stuffing down sandwiches. And out there, Carmen.

Adam expertly manoeuvres himself into the tight space between the chair and the table.

'How can you stand working in this kind of place?'

'Says the frontline reporter.'

'I'm not a frontline reporter.'

'These scones are the best in the country, by the way.'

'How do you know?'

'We have the same caterers. I'd rather work in an NHS hospital than on the streets of Basra.'

'I wasn't sent to Basra. I just – it's so *lifeless* here. It's as though fighting disease means you have to fight life itself.'

'Well. Sometimes that is exactly what you have to do.'

'. . .'

'They're just knocking her out for now. They have to bring her down.'

'But she'll get better?'

'I don't know.'

'. . .'

'I mean, it's not my field, obviously – Oh. Here's Henry.'

Eva turns round. Henry is walking towards them through the plastic cafeteria. He stares at them but doesn't see them, his eyes guiding him to his goal while his mind stays behind, in that room. When she and Adam left, Henry had just taken Carmen's hand, and was gently stroking her forearm. It made Eva realize how little physical contact the two of them normally had: compulsory kisses and hugs in greeting, and even those were avoided wherever possible. Now Henry's movements were so tender, and Carmen seemed, through her chemical fug, to find comfort in them. Eva knows that that is what is on his mind now: his hand touching hers. The picture is so strong that everyone else in the cafeteria seems to be able to sense it. The infirm, the dying, they sneak glances at Henry as he goes past them.

He is walking incredibly slowly. His imposing frame seems to have shrunk, become brittle somehow, in the space of the last twenty-four hours. Adam and Eva watch him dumbly as he makes his way towards them, tries to squeeze himself on to the bench next to Eva, gets wedged awkwardly underneath the table, buttocks still in mid-air, then, with considerable effort, disengages himself from the demonic thing. Eva can think of few circumstances in which this bout of slapstick would not send the three of them off into howls of laughter; but how could anyone laugh at the sight of Henry's grief? Even the medical students across the room have had the delicacy to shut up. Adam slides a chair over from another table.

'Thanks, Ad.'

'Let me go fetch you something, Henry – what do you want? Tea? A cake or something? A scone?'

'I don't think I can eat anything right now.'

'Tea, then?'

'I don't know . . .'

'Tea. I'll get you some tea.'

And Adam is off again. Henry has his eyes fixed somewhere in the centre of the table, most probably on the smudge of butter left on it by its previous occupants; then he raises his gaze slowly until it meets Eva's.

'What the hell is going on, Eva?'

'I don't know, Henry – I . . . I don't understand.'

'What's happening to her?'

'I don't know.'

Henry's eyes wander back to the smudge.

'Did anything – did anything happen just now – after we left you alone with her?'

Henry shakes his head, still in slow motion, as though it is a huge weight he is carrying on his shoulders. Carmen's head – what a weight it must be to her right now.

'No. I think she's going to be out for a while, with all those drugs they've given her. But – but . . . I felt like she knew I was there, somehow. Do you think I'm being ridiculous?'

'God – Henry. No. Of course not. And I'm sure you're right. I'm sure she knew you were there.'

'What if she doesn't go back to normal, Eva? What if we've lost her?'

'We haven't lost her. I'm sure . . .'

'We can't know that.'

'No. You're right.'

'We actually can't be sure. We really can't.'

'I know.'

Adam is back with a mug of brown, milky tea. It has stains running down one side of it, which might be from this brew, or from some more ancient one, or from the accumulation of generations. How many teabags has that mug held, how many cancerous, HIV-positive, heart-attacked hands have sought solace by wrapping around its warmth? Poor Henry. Poor Carmen. Poor all of them.

Adam gives Henry's shoulder a consoling grip before sitting down next to him. Nobody speaks. Eva thinks of Carmen. The first time they met, over mugs of tea not unlike the one Henry is holding now, at the freshers' welcome thing in the library common room. That time they went to have lunch at the tapas place near Carmen's flat, and emerged again twelve hours and five bottles of rioja later, filled with the glory of friendship, and wine, and conversation. That time they went travelling around Italy together, no boys allowed, because the boys in question, who are now sitting opposite Eva in this dreary hospital canteen, had, each in their own way, trampled on their hearts. It was a trip of magnificent ruins, the paintings of Fra Angelico, succulent food, and ceaseless analysis of Henry and Adam. Does Henry know how much they have discussed him? He must know.

'I just – I just don't understand.'

'I don't know if there is anything to understand, Henry. This kind of stuff just – happens sometimes.'

'But – Carmen? She's, like, one of the strongest personalities I've ever met. She's fucking fearless.'

'I think weirdly it's often people like that who end up developing this sort of thing.'

'What sort of thing, though? What's wrong with her, Ad?'

'I mean – I don't really know. Some of what you've been describing, it sounds a bit like a schizophrenic episode, or bipolar disorder or something like that.'

'Jesus.'

'But, I mean, it's really not a field I know very much about.'

'. . .'

'But, I mean – based on what you were saying. Well. I don't know.'

'It was crazy, guys. Really crazy. I've never heard someone come out with such crazy stuff before.'

Poor Henry. Getting that phone call. Carmen in a panic, telling him she's in danger, terrified, and he rushes off, terrified as

226

well because of course he believes it must be true, something about a gang and they almost trapped her on London Bridge, and now she's hiding down on the bank of the Thames, she's managed to clamber down, but they're still after her, she thinks they might be closing in, how the hell did she even get down there, and Henry rushes over, ploughs his way through the maddening throng of commuters, terrified because for all he knows he's about to jump into a mass of knife-wielding youths and he's never been a particularly brave guy, but for Carmen, of course, he'll do it. He'll risk his life for Carmen, Eva thinks, and it hits her what an extraordinary thing that is, how rare.

'It was awful, guys. Awful.'

And then to find that there are no enemies without – that, worse, Carmen is in danger from her own self. To have to listen to her senseless explanation, to witness the madness and start to doubt that you are the one who is sane, so convinced is she of her self-constructed hell, to have to be the person who calls the ambulance, who gets those people to come and get her, who gets those people to pump her full of the drugs that are keeping her a flicker of consciousness away from a coma. Henry, who is still clutching his tea but has not yet drunk a sip of it, looks about him wildly. Looks without seeing. What are his eyes taking away from these faded monochromes, the lime-green trays, the yellowing tables? What would Carmen see in them? Messages scrawled into the plastic, threatening signs, hidden cameras monitoring her from behind a drinks dispenser. People who are not what they seem. The world is a blank screen, and on to it we project our fears, hopes, expectations.

'It was – it was all so real to her, you know? She was so convinced of what she was saying, and I didn't want to disagree with her in case it made her stop talking to me, but then I didn't want to encourage her, either . . .'

'Tell us again what she was saying, Henry.'

Tell us again. How many times have they said those words to each other, and to Carmen, over the years? Tell us again about that time you put on the swimming costume you hadn't tried on before buying it, remind us what his exact words were, remember when we were in that dive bar on Greek Street and . . . The cues to hilarious uproar, fond memories, gentle mockery; a litany of old friendship. And now Adam's 'tell us again', asking Henry for an altogether more sombre memory; asking not so they can join in laughing reminiscence, but so Henry can get it off his chest, so they can try, the three of them, to *understand*. So that maybe, in the retelling, Henry will mention a detail he missed the previous time round, and which will suddenly make everything clear. How Carmen cupped her hand around his ear and whispered into it, because she was worried they might be being listened to, that her phone was bugged, or maybe the walls around them, or something. So she and Henry sat down on a low wall overlooking the Thames and, as the suits continued to march into the City above them, she whispered her fears into him.

'So it started with that weird Russian oligarch man she works for – what's his name again?'

'Maïakowski. Yes.'

'And that was what she'd spoken to you about on the phone as well, right?'

'Yes – well, she implied it. She wouldn't actually say his name because she was worried someone might be listening in. But when I saw her, she said that the people who were after her had been sent by him.'

'I thought she'd never met Maïakowski?'

'That's what I thought, too.'

'No, she did, quite recently though. I mean, I don't think anything major happened – the partner introduced her to him soon after they made her an associate. She thought he was a creep.'

'I'm not surprised.'

'But I don't think it's really Maïakowski that's bothering her. She seemed more to think that he was some kind of stooge, putting his wealth at the service of whoever wants to harm her. She didn't really seem to know who it is who's actually behind it all – it was all just "they" want to do this or that, "they've" been watching me. And when I asked her who "they" were, she just shook her head. I didn't know what to do. I – I mean, I was worried if I said outright how crazy she sounded, she'd start thinking I was one of "them". And . . .'

'. . .'

'And, this is hard to explain, but it was so *real* to her, I started to wonder if *I* was the one who was crazy. She was so convinced of what she was saying, it was like we were these two realities facing each other, and I wasn't sure mine was more persuasive than hers.'

'. . .'

'. . .'

'And – what was the poetry stuff? When I was in there, she started reciting all these T. S. Eliot lines to me . . .'

'Yes. So then she starts going on about how that idiot she was going out with last year, you know . . .'

'Russ.'

Henry knows he's called Russ. Whatever.

'Russ, yeah. How Russ gave her this poetry anthology, and she read it the other day and realized it contained loads of messages for her, which only she could understand.'

'So, this is the bit that I don't get: they were all really famous poems. Surely Carmen can't think that Wordsworth is sending her messages from beyond the grave?'

'I mean, given the rest of what she was saying, that wouldn't be impossible. But no – the point is that Russ selected the poems, it was an anthology he'd put together for her. So she thinks he's sending her messages through which poems he's chosen.'

'So "they" is Russ?'

'No, again, he seemed to be part of a wider plan. And then the rest was less specific: I can't take the Tube because the people on

it are all hired extras who are watching me; there are people out
to kill me, even the guy in the local cornershop has started to
behave really weirdly towards me . . . Kind of classic paranoid
stuff. I mean there were moments when I thought she was having me on, what she was saying sounded like it was taken straight
out of some crappy Hollywood film.'

Henry's mobile starts ringing.

'Oh. It's Georgie. I'd better take this. She's tried to ring me several times this morning already.'

Henry has splashed tea all over the table putting his mug
down, and pushes his chair away a little too sharply as he gets up.

'Sorry, guys. Hi, darling. Sorry I couldn't ring you back earlier . . .'

They can hear Georgie shouting angrily at the other end of the
line. Henry walks away from them, his big frame stooped as
though he is himself one of the maimed and diseased that haunt
this cafeteria. It's unlikely that there's much room in Georgie's
world for the clinically insane, even though – or perhaps because –
she comes from a family where respectable in-breeding has
produced several crackpots per generation. But you probably
don't talk about it; and you almost certainly don't go and spend
the day in hospital for the sake of a crackpot who is neither kith
nor kin, a mere friend.

Henry comes back towards them.

'Hold on, darling, I'm just picking up my briefcase.'

Mobile crooked on his shoulder, he makes a dumb show of
gestures and facial expressions: I have to go, we'll talk soon.
Adam and Eva nod a mute goodbye, and watch their friend walk
away from them, from Carmen, back to his wife – back to the life
he has inexplicably chosen for himself.

SHE LOVED THAT sound, the announcement of company: the key in the lock, the front door clicking open. The muffle of Ulrich taking his shoes off in the corridor. He knocked on her door.

'Eva?'

'Yes? Come in.'

'You are not busy?'

His body filled the doorframe.

'No, not particularly – what's up?'

'So. I want to show you something.'

He walked over to her. He was holding an envelope of photos in his hand, slightly outstretched in front of him, like an offering.

'I just went to get these, they are from an old film I still had in my camera. There are photos of Adam here.'

Eva's heart starts pounding – she feels afraid, as though something is about to be revealed. She stands, takes the envelope out of Ulrich's hand, opens it. He shifts so that he is standing next to her, bending his head down over her shoulder to look at the photos too. She can feel the warmth coming off his body so close to hers, or at least she imagines she can feel it.

There are lines and lines of windows in a concrete façade. There is the angular top of a tower block against a vibrant blue sky. There are Adam and Ulrich smiling at the camera, their arms around each other's shoulders, in front of the entrance to a building. There is Ulrich on his own, serious this time, in front of the same entrance.

'Where is this?'

'Marzahn, where I grew up. Adam wanted to go there. Maybe

you know, it was the biggest of the Neubausiedlungen in the GDR – where they built all these Plattenbauten, these big buildings that were built by the Communists.'

Concrete slabs everywhere. A vast esplanade with a few stunted trees, but mainly pavement, gravel, a wet sandpit. A bright-green structure that looks like a giant spider web: hooked legs digging into the ground, a thick black net stretched between them. In the next photos, Adam is standing in the centre of the net, arms raised, roaring.

Then he falls, and the camera captures him in mid-air, his look of surprise, the wince as he hits the net, the tangle of arms and legs. Eva laughs, and Ulrich does too, and then they look at each other and they laugh harder, and at some point both of their gulps of laughter turn into sobs, until Eva is just weeping gently, and Ulrich is choking his tears up, his body doubled over, spasming, as though he is trying to throw up his grief.

At first Eva holds the photos out in front of her to avoid them getting wet, then she puts them down, Adam's grinning face beaming up at her from the spider net, and extends a tentative hand to Ulrich's arm. Her fingers meet the stone-hard line of his biceps and rest on it gently in an awkward and quintessentially English gesture. She is like a starch-collared butler being presented with a crying child, petting it nervously while murmuring 'There, there.'

Eva sniffs away her own tears and picks up the photos again. Ulrich's tears are silent now, and he pulls a tissue out of his pocket to wipe them away.

'And so – this is where you grew up?'

He nods.

Eva looks at the angular, boxy buildings, the mournful bursts of brown bushes or grass trying to make a place for themselves in between these slabs of cement.

'It's funny, you know – to look at these photos and think I could have grown up somewhere like this too. If my mother had stayed in Berlin, I mean. It's so different from the place I grew up.'

'What was it like? The place you grew up?'

'Oh, sort of – so provincial. Small town. Neither countryside nor big city, and therefore also with neither the advantages of one nor the other.'

'Then maybe it is not so different from growing up in Marzahn. It was like a village – everything was there: my school, the shop, the Sportshalle – most of the time we did not leave these few buildings. Every day, walk to school, and on the way back we played in the playground.'

'Ah, well it was very different for me, then: I had to be driven everywhere. That's what I mean by our town only having disadvantages: it was big enough that you couldn't just walk everywhere, but not so big that it had anything exciting going on in it.'

'Ha. We could not have been driven everywhere, not many people had cars. Actually, probably that was why we could walk everywhere on our own as kids, because there was so little traffic. Today you could not do it – too dangerous. We were very free, I think.'

'It's funny to hear you say that. That you were more free in East Germany.'

'Well. As a child.'

'I really feel it, you know – that this could have been my life. I could have grown up somewhere like this too, if my mum hadn't left. It's like you had this parallel childhood that could have been mine. Like, I can picture myself as a little girl, sitting in our living room watching *Neighbours*, and it's like with just a click of a finger I could have been running around the Plattenbau of Marzahn with you.'

'Do you think you would be a very different person?'

'I don't know – what do you think?'

'I think probably yes.'

'I feel like that little girl is in me, though – the little girl running around Marzahn. The person I would have been if my mother had stayed here.'

'The East German Eva.'

'Yes. She's in here somewhere.'

'But how your mother would have met your father?'

'Well fine, yes, there would be a few details to work out in this parallel world . . . But still, it's like I look at these photos and they awaken a memory in me that I don't actually have. A memory of a life that could have been.'

'Probably it would be very different from what you imagine. Such a life.'

'But I do have this memory. This phantom memory. Does that sound crazy?'

'No. But memories cannot really be trusted, even when we are remembering things that did happen to us, so . . .'

'That's funny, that's the kind of thing Adam used to say.'

'Oh yes?'

A photo of Adam in front of the tower block, long lines running up towards the sky.

'Yes, we used to have this argument about what we'd both seen on 9/11. We were in New York – I guess he probably told you about it. And he said it wasn't possible I'd seen some of the things I'd said I'd seen. The people falling. The second tower coming down. He couldn't remember all those things. Whereas I have such a clear picture of them. He said I must have created those memories for myself from things I'd read or seen afterwards. But he wouldn't accept that maybe his own memories were flawed, that he might have forgotten some of the things we'd seen. It used to drive me mad.'

'Probably all memories lie a bit. Probably it is not possible to have a true image of the past.'

'Exactly! I'm sure we were both a bit wrong, that's what I would say to him. Which also, of course, meant that we were both a bit right. In particular, that I was also a bit right.'

'Maybe he did not want to have seen these things, but you did? Like now you want to see yourself in Marzahn, even though you know you were never there.'

'Now you sound like you're siding with Adam and just saying I made everything up . . .'

'No, I am saying we remember the past the way we need to remember it. The way we need to see it, to make sense of our lives in the present.'

YOU LIVE. YOU live, and live, and live.

And every breath that fills your lungs, every beat of your heart, every flicker of excitement you feel at the sight of something new, is a betrayal of Adam, who cannot breathe, whose heart was broken and stopped, who knows no novelty any more.

You inch onwards through life limpingly, treacherously, guiltily, and you wish it didn't, but it makes you resentful of him, that he has burdened you with this guilt, and you wish he would stop, with his lack of fault and his alabaster corpse peacefully lying there, dead and not caring, not needing to care, but of course it's the guilt talking, you know that really, the guilt of the survivor, and so, because really, what else can you do, on you live, guilty and alive, guilty because alive – guilty but alive.

THEY HAVE ESCAPED to Richmond Park. It's hardly the ideal day for it: the weather has been unpredictable all morning, the sun ducking behind clouds and back again, short bursts of drizzly showers interrupting you when you least expect it. But they needed to get out, away from the mournful poses of Adam's family gathered round the kitchen table, which, frankly, Eva was finding a little over the top – it's not like anyone has died, after all.

'Do you remember, we came here before I met your family for the first time?'

'Oh yes, we did, didn't we?'

'You were so surprised that I'd never heard of Richmond Park, like I was saying I'd never heard of the Great Wall of China.'

'You'd never heard of Richmond Park?'

'No! Oh my God, let's not have the same conversation again. I'd only been to London twice in my life before I went to university, why would I have heard of Richmond Park?'

'I don't know. I suppose it's the kind of place you just assume people know of.'

'I felt so – clueless, so provincial . . . I was so nervous about meeting your family, too. Like you were this cool, big-city boy and I was the country mouse . . .'

'You can't possibly have thought I was cool! I am so not cool.'

'You seemed cool to me.'

'Well, *you* seemed cool to me. You *were* much cooler than I was. I was just a geeky boy – I couldn't believe my luck when we got together.'

'Seriously, do you not remember me being a nervous wreck back then?'

'Absolutely not. You hid it very well, if you were.'

Adam puts his arm around her, and they stop for a moment to cuddle. Eva buries her nose in his neck, smells the warmth of his skin mingling with the earthy scent of the path, the fresh, wet wood of the trees lining it. There is a melancholy to the moment, because of Bennie of course, but a sweetness to that melancholy, to the fact that they are sharing it with each other. It feels like the closing of a parenthesis, of this period when they were pulling apart and then slowly, warily, since she got back from the Congo, started moving closer again. She's glad that they have this intimacy back now, this willingness to support each other – that she can stand next to Adam right now, and be of some support.

'I remember being so struck by Bennie that day, too. Do you remember? All your brothers were sitting outside in the garden when we arrived at the house.'

'I don't know – maybe, yeah, vaguely . . .'

'I remember being struck by how – sort of *radiant* Bennie was. Like he was this angel.'

'We all thought he was an angel.'

Bennie, the baby of the family, has fallen into disgrace. He started university this year and has, in the few months since then, it seems, managed to build up a small drug-dealing empire. He has now been sent home while the university decides whether to deal with the matter themselves or take it to the police, and the Lorvener family has rallied to come up with a line of defence, and also to try and understand this new development in the character of their cherished youngest son and brother. Bennie has responded by switching off his usual charm and growing broody and monosyllabic.

'He will be fine, you know. I mean, even if they do press charges, with your mother's connections there's no way he'll get into any real trouble. And even if he gets sent down, he'll get a place at another university. You'll all be laughing at this in a couple of years' time, honestly.'

'I know. I know he'll be fine. That's not what I'm worried about.'

They have resumed walking down the tree-lined avenue, green buds pushing out of the bare branches above them.

'I'm worried – I'm worried that he's not *himself.* I mean, what the fuck? Playing at being this gangster, putting his education on the line just so he can make some money he doesn't even need – and look at him now, he's behaving like a total jerk. Where's my little brother gone?'

'He's just afraid. Of what might happen to him.'

'That's no excuse to lash out at Mum the way he did this morning, though. It's like he's a different person – how can you change so much in just a few months at university?'

'Maybe it's not that he's changed, though. Maybe it's just that you've found out about an aspect of his life that you shouldn't have found out about.'

'Come on, Eve, he's dealing drugs, for God's sake! He deserves to get into trouble for it.'

'Sure, I'm not disagreeing with that – but what I'm saying is, he also could have got away with it and still be your sweet baby brother when he's around you and it would all have been fine.'

'. . .'

'We all behave slightly differently in different contexts – it doesn't mean we're not who we claim to be. And come on, he wasn't off killing people or beating them up or anything. Dealing a bit of dope when you're eighteen doesn't necessarily mean you're going to turn into some kind of criminal mastermind.'

'So – what? You're saying it would be better if he hadn't been found out? For us as his family not to know about it?'

'Wouldn't it be? What have you gained from it, really, apart from a legal headache and everyone feeling really disappointed with him? Whereas if you didn't know anything, he'd probably grow out of it as soon as he got a proper job, and you'd all still have your happy family dynamic.'

'But – wouldn't it be a lie? Wouldn't we not know who he really was?'

'Do we ever know who anyone really is? Do you know what's going on in Carmen's head, for example? I mean, would you have been able to predict when we were at university that she'd lose her grip on reality?'

'No – but that's not who she is. When she has these – phases. It's not her.'

'Isn't it? Who is it, then?'

'...'

'Or, I mean, come on, Ad, do your parents know every single thing about what you get up to? You take drugs yourself.'

'Only, like, once in a blue moon at a party – and it's hardly the same as *dealing* them . . .'

'Imagine if you took a dodgy pill, though, and ended up in hospital and your mum had to come and pick you up – wouldn't the same thing happen to you as is happening to Bennie now? Perfect Doctor Adam is revealed to have a drug problem? When actually it's quite a small, irrelevant part of who you are?'

'Hm.'

'All I'm saying is the fact that people have their secrets doesn't necessarily mean that they're being bad or dishonest.'

Adam gives Eva an anxious, searching look, walks on in thoughtful silence. Then he turns back to her.

'So – you're saying that you'd rather not know? If there was something – some information that someone close to you was hiding from you. Something important. You'd rather not know about it?'

'I mean – it would depend what the information was.'

'According to what criteria, though?'

'I guess – I mean, I guess depending on how the information affected me, and how directly. Whether the knowing or not knowing would be harmful to me. Or not.'

'So if finding out might be hurtful to you, you'd rather not know?'

'Adam, is this some roundabout way of trying to tell me you're having an affair?'

Adam looks aghast, and Eva realizes, of course: their reconciliation is still fragile, she shouldn't imperil it by being too robust.

'No! Jesus! Of course not!'

'Joke! Joke! I'm sorry. I was just being facetious.'

'Jesus . . .'

'No, I mean – look, of course it's complicated. Including the present situation. Maybe it is good all of this has come to light – maybe Bennie was on a dangerous path and this is allowing you all to intervene, to avoid him losing his way. But maybe also everything would have been fine if he hadn't been found out, and you'd still have your baby brother.'

'. . .'

'I guess what I'm saying is, he still is your baby brother. His having this one thing you didn't know about doesn't have to change that.'

'. . .'

'And people have secrets. It's OK. Or sometimes it's OK. For people to keep some things to themselves. As long as it doesn't hurt others.'

'Define "hurt".'

'Ah, well. That, of course, is a whole other, thorny matter. But, I mean – don't we all know? Deep down? When something should be revealed, and when it shouldn't?'

That anxious look from Adam again, and Eva wonders if it is her secrets he has been talking about all along, if it is her integrity he's worried about.

'Ad, are you asking me if there's something I'm hiding from you? Because, really, I was just talking about—'

'No, I know – really, I know. That wasn't what I meant at all.'

'Oh. Good.'

'I get what you're saying. I think.'

'. . .'

'Yeah. I think I get it.'

THE LIGHT DIFFUSED gently over the dawn-time buildings, pulling them into the day with its glow. They have spent the night talking, unexpectedly: they were just going to go for a nightcap, but the words dragged on, words and words and words deep into the night, words that made them forget the passing of time apart from when it meant the bar they were in had to close and they would move on to another, and another, and another, until now, at the time when other people are emerging from the depths of rest, they are walking around Berlin, closing their eyes to feel the sun bathe their faces over pink and orange and gold façades, closing their eyes to feel the warmth of the moment, the presence of the other at their side.

Eva felt an urge to take Ulrich's hand in hers: it seemed the natural thing to do, when you were walking through the dawn of a city, the only two souls out on the streets. She wanted to feel the swing of that hand in hers. She wanted, absurdly, to lift it to her lips and kiss it.

She had wanted to kiss Adam's hand that morning, after the ambulance had arrived to take him away. She had taken hold of it, but it was so cold already that she had recoiled from it, could not bring herself to let her lips touch it.

She tries to pull herself into the moment; to be here, now. She looks at the long shadow thrown by the trees, crooked where they wrap down from the pavement on to the street, at the bicycles and pot plants and empty clothes racks on the balconies above them. She listens to the birds announcing the new day, to Ulrich's footsteps as he walks along beside her. She tries to be

here, and when her mind makes to go back to the past, she tries
to stop at last night, last week, rather than last year, last decade.
She tries to rewrite history.

They turn on to Bernauerstraße, and Ulrich points dismiss-
ively at the ground.

'Die Mauer.'

Two lines of bricks run along the side of the pavement, tracing
where the Wall used to be. You wouldn't even necessarily notice
them without someone to point them out to you. But if you
do, you suddenly understand certain things about the space of
the city around you. Like why over there, on the other side of
the street, stand ugly specimens of fifties and sixties social housing blocks; why here, just on the other side of the phantom Wall,
is a stretch of urban bracken. Over there, the working classes
and Turkish *Gastarbeiter* of West Berlin in their rooms with a
view on to, here, the death strip, with its bright searchlights and
snarling dogs.

Up ahead of them, a large band of revellers stumble down the
street, their loud drunken chatter piercing the silence. They cross
over from East to West without seeing the trace under their feet,
without sensing the density of the barrier that once stood here,
hearing the grunts of the watchdogs. Eva thinks of the wall she
has seen in Palestine, how grey and impenetrable it seems, how
impossible to imagine that it might one day be removed. That it
might one day be nothing more than a faint mark in the pavement, easily overlooked.

And then they turn into a side street, and because Eva is scanning the ground for more signs of the city's divide, she notices
other marks in the pavement.

'What are those?'

In front of a stately front door, a cluster of gold squares has
been worked in between the cobblestones.

'Stolpersteine. You have not seen these before?'

'No. What did you say they were called?'

'Stolpersteine. Er – how you say? When you walk and you fall over?'

'To trip? Stumble. Stumblestones.'

'They are for Jewish people who were deported. They have the name of the people who used to live in the house. You really have not seen these before? They are everywhere in Berlin.'

'No. Or I guess I'd never noticed them.'

Eva walks up to them and reads:

HIER WOHNTE
HERTA ABRAHAM
GEB. MICHAELS
JG. 1895
DEPORTIERT 1942
THERESIENSTADT
ERMORDERT IN
AUSCHWITZ

HIER WOHNTE
RICHARD ABRAHAM
JG. 1895
DEPORTIERT 1942
THERESIENSTADT
ERMORDERT IN
AUSCHWITZ

HIER WOHNTE
RUTH NELLY
ABRAHAM
JG. 1934
DEPORTIERT 1942
THERESIENSTADT
ERMORDERT IN
AUSCHWITZ

'My God.'

'Yes. There are a lot of these around here. It used to be the Jewish quarter.'

'. . .'

'. . .'

'1934 to 1942. So young.'

How can one city have seen so much suffering? Traces upon traces of the dead and oppressed, pale traces which in their insufficiency drive home how justice will never be done to them, how the present with all its forgetting will always be cruelly indifferent. And yet these pale traces will remain, hammered as they are into the very fabric of Berlin, trodden upon and ignored, but ultimately still *there*, still under our feet.

They walk on in silence for a long while, lost in thoughts of the past.

'I would like to show you my Berlin.'

'Your Berlin?'

'A piece of my Berlin. Would you like to see it?'

'Yes.'

They turn off into another side street. Eva wondered what her London would be: the street she and Adam had lived on; Carmen's flat; a few pubs. The various routes she had cycled to the office, to the Maudsley Hospital. You owned a city out of habit, and suddenly London felt like it was very far away; suddenly, it felt as though she might never have owned London at all. It was reassuring that Ulrich, at least, had his Berlin.

'I lived here, just after the *Wende*.'

'Really?'

'Yes. In this building.'

They stopped. Ulrich studied the façade briefly, then pointed towards a row of windows, which were all indistinguishable from each other in the cold, grey concrete.

'I was living in that flat. I moved in with a group of friends when I was a student. There were many empty flats here, so if you could find a way of getting in you could live there.'

245

'What, so you were squatting?'

He nods absent-mindedly. How little she knows about his life. About these memories that are him, that she has never heard – and which she might come to know, through confidences, childhood tales, but which will remain, nevertheless, a part of him – which will remain, nevertheless, foreign to her. She doesn't know which window he means, and anyway, they all look the same.

'Which window was it?'

'That one – look.'

He stands behind her, lifting her hand in his to point at it.

'One, two, three up; one, two from the left.'

She looks at the window. They start walking again.

'Now all the buildings are – saniert.'

'Renovated?'

'Yes. Renovated. But then, here it was really fucked up. A lot of empty buildings, a lot of squats. A lot of illegal bars, they were very cool. Here . . .'

He points at a glossy building, glass and steel glinting at them in the sunlight.

'This has not been here before. When I lived here, it was a ruin, the building had been bombed in the Second World War. There was only one floor left, and also you could go down into the basement. So some guys made the basement into a bar, and I came here a lot.'

' . . .'

'We all felt so free. We were in the middle of these ruins, and we could do anything.'

'I envy you that, you know. That you were a teenager here, at such an exciting time. In the middle of this insane upheaval. And that you were in East Germany as a kid – you've seen so much *change*. I feel like the world I grew up in was just so cosy and boring and monotonous . . .'

'Yes, I feel lucky: the Wall fell at just the right time for my generation – we were young enough to adapt to the new system, but old enough to remember the old one and see what was good about it as well as what was bad. And, after all, it was all the destruction that came before that made Berlin such a fantastic place in the nineties. We were partying on bombsites.'

'Did you think about that, back then?'

'Not really. Or maybe, yes. Probably we thought we were aware, but were not really, you know? We didn't think about the little Ruth Nelly Abraham, or at least not when we were partying.'

'How could you? I mean, it's a lot of history to take in all at once. You were living through a historical moment yourselves.'

'We are always living through historical moments.'

Eva looked up again at the shiny new building that had replaced the ruin of Ulrich's youth.

'Still. I wish I could have seen Berlin as you've seen it, all these transformations it's been through.'

Across the road from the stainless steel was a small patch of bare land, a mixture of earth and gravel and grass and bushes that seemed to be waiting for something.

'This is what it was like. A lot more of Berlin was like this.'

' . . . '

'I remember, I showed Adam this place too, but then this new building was not finished, and most of the houses on the street were not renovated yet. It has changed so much, in just a few years.'

'Yes.'

'He liked the building site – it was huge, with enormous cranes, and the structure was there, but just long steel – er – Stänge – nothing else. It looked like a ruin, too, a futuristic ruin. We bought some beers from the Späti and watched the workers build it. Adam was fascinated.'

'Yes, he told me about the building sites, that it was one of the things he loved about Berlin.'

'It was something we all loved. We maybe did not realize, I think, that one day these building sites would turn into this.'

'You'd rather have kept the ruins?'

Ulrich shrugged.

'I know that is not possible. But I miss the ruins. They made you feel more free than all this money.'

'WAIT, NO, HANG ON, run that by me again – what has the loft extension got to do with anything?'

'The point is, the loft extension should, they reckon, increase the value of the house enough that they can remortgage part of it and use that as a deposit.'

'And why Spain?'

'They like it there. And apparently it's really easy to get a mortgage for places in Spain at the moment.'

'Do you think it's a good idea?'

Adam shrugs.

'I don't really see what harm it can do. I think it would be good for them to have a new project with my dad retiring next year. Plus we'd get free holidays in Spain out of it.'

'That's a good point.'

'And anyway, it's their money.'

'True also.'

'Do you want another drink? I was thinking of trying out that Sazerac recipe Henry was talking about.'

'Hit me with it.'

Adam starts examining the drinks cabinet. Eva stretches out on the sofa, considers turning on the TV, decides not to. She has been feeling so – so *content* recently. Their flat is done at last, her job is going really well, Adam's job is going really well, and they are happy and relaxed and comfortable together. There is something a little unsettling about this degree of contentedness, this lack of obstacles to overcome – it's like they've been struggling up a steep slope for years, and now the open plateau stretches out before them, the going so easy. They have to readjust their limbs to not needing to climb any more.

'Eve?'

'Huh?'

Adam laughs.

'Did you not hear me just then?'

'Huh? No, sorry, I was lost in thought – did you say something?'

'I asked you what's on your plate this week?'

'Oh. Um. Bill wants me to file that story about Kamran Sheikh.'

'You haven't written that up already?'

'No. I'm going to try and talk to some more of his former classmates – I still feel like there's something I'm not managing to get to the bottom of.'

'In what sense?'

'Just: what is it that makes him capable of committing such a barbaric act – how can anyone bring themselves to slit someone's throat, in the name of anything?'

'Well, he's probably a psychopath or something.'

'I don't think he is, Adam. I think he's just a guy like you and me. There actually isn't very much evidence that these guys are psychotic, or mentally ill in any other way.'

'They must be.'

'But they're not.'

'So what's your explanation, then?'

'I don't know – that's the problem. But I think . . . I think he starts from a point that we would all recognize. That there is injustice and violence in the world, and a lot of it is directed against Muslims.'

'So, what – the answer to that violence is to slit someone's throat? I mean, come on, it's revolting. And imagine doing that – you have to actually look the guy in the eye before you kill him.'

'But isn't the real problem that we so often *don't* have to look people in the eye before we kill them? That war is becoming like a video game, where a guy can sit in a military base in Texas and fire missiles at Iraqi families, where people dying are referred to as "collateral damage"?'

'That doesn't make cutting someone's head off any less horrible.'

'No, and I'm as revolted by it as you are – but my point is that I feel like they're two sides of the same coin, and not just because of the issues involved, but because of the way they operate. Terrorism is all about making the violent acts you commit as visible, as spectacular as possible, while our armies make their violence as concealed, as sanitized as possible. And not just our armies – our economies, our businesses. What about the kids who die sewing clothes for us in Bangladesh, or mining cobalt in the Congo so we can power our PlayStations?'

'As I said, none of this makes beheading someone any less repulsive.'

'I know, I agree! But I think the repulsion is the point. The repulsion is the only thing that will shake us out of our sense of security.'

'So this guy is a monster out of tactical considerations?'

'Well – no, not just. I mean, those tactical considerations are there, but you still have to make yourself be capable of killing someone. No, I think – it's a way of defining yourself, I think. In a complex, confusing, unjust world. It gives you easy answers. And it gives your life meaning, to be fighting on the right side.'

' . . .'

'I mean, he was so convinced, Adam – it made him convincing, too. The power of what he believed, when you were talking to him . . .'

'That's exactly what Henry said about Carmen when she was psychotic.'

'But this was different – nothing of what he said sounded crazy. He'd just drawn the wrong conclusions.'

'Hm.'

'It's like – I think it's an identity thing. All these guys like him

I've spoken to, they're all second- or third-generation immigrants. And it's like this is a way of defining who they are.'

'You're a second-generation immigrant, and you're not even interested in where you come from.'

'But I'm less obviously an immigrant, and for the record, I am interested, I just . . . Anyway. My point is, these are young guys who feel they don't belong anywhere, and being in a group fighting the jihad gives them a sense of belonging. Maybe.'

Adam falls silent, distracted by his cocktail mixing. Eva's mind stays with that young, angry man, his passion and fury, and the way he looked at her as though she was lost.

Adam hands Eva a heavy tumbler.

'Ooh, this looks nice.'

'Well, try it first – it's an untested recipe . . .'

Adam sits down, and Eva tries to think about a way to explain to him what she means about the conundrum that is Kamran Sheikh, but she can't seem to formulate it, and also it is hard to get Adam to understand the complexities of human nature sometimes. Because he is such a decent man – has lived his whole life sheltered from anything that might inflect his decency – he does not understand the darkness of other people.

And then the strangest thing happens: sitting there lost in thought, Adam raises his hand to his lips in exactly the same pensive automatic gesture as the one Kamran had, when she was asking him a question he needed to think about before answering, and she remembers how disturbed she was by that gesture, and realizes now that the reason for this was that it made Kamran remind her of Adam, and, now, Adam remind her of Kamran. And she wonders what genetic mystery can be at the source of this uncanny mirroring.

It makes Adam seem as remote from her now as Kamran was across that prison table.

Eva searches for something to say, something that can reconnect her to Adam, to his voice, to the reality of him sitting there, being who he is.

'Oh Ad – did you take down my mum's samizdat from the bedroom wall?'

'Yes – I thought it could do with reframing.'

'Ah. Right.'

'. . .'

'You know, looking at that – it makes what I do seem so futile.'

'How do you mean?'

'I mean – you know, my mother was putting her life on the line. Or, at the very least, her freedom. What she was writing – it *mattered*.'

'What you write now matters.'

'Not in the same way. Or at least, not at the same cost to me.'

'. . .'

'I mean, we can't know, can we? How we would react in that situation. Whether we'd have the courage to do something like write pamphlets that could get us thrown in jail, or bumped off.'

'No. But that's not the situation we live in.'

'Isn't it, though? Isn't there enough injustice in this world that we could be risking our lives to right it?'

'You do risk your life. You fly out to warzones.'

'But there's very little risk, really. In the places I go to. It's the soft version of warzones, nowhere near the front line.'

'. . .'

'I mean, my mother lost everything. She came here with nothing to her name but a pamphlet and a tea cup.'

'. . .'

'. . .'

'It's weird, you know, Eva.'

'What is?'

'It doesn't make sense. That your mother wasn't able to retrieve anything from your grandparents.'

'What do you mean?'

'Just that. She must have been able to get someone to send her something.'

'She couldn't communicate with them, it was too dangerous. And then they died . . .'

'But she must have been able to communicate with them. There were ways. I've talked to Ulrich about this. Even if you were worried about them being intercepted, you could find ways of getting letters through. And nobody was living in isolation – there will have been friends, parishioners she could have contacted . . .'

'Well, so – what are you saying?'

'I don't know, really. Just that it can't have been impossible for your mother to communicate with *anyone* from back home after she left. Ulrich was telling me about this cousin of his—'

'Jesus, have you told this Ulrich guy my whole life story?'

'What? No. We were just talking generally . . . Is that your phone?'

'Oh. Yes.'

'It's all right, I'll get it.'

As Adam walks away, it strikes Eva that he doesn't ask her to come to Berlin with him any more. He stopped, she can't pinpoint when exactly, probably worn out by her constant fudging of the issue, and she feels disappointed that he doesn't still ask, even though she knows her answer would probably still be the same.

'Here you go. It's Carmen.'

'Thanks. Hey there.'

'Hi, Eva.'

'What's up?'

'Ah.'

Carmen catches her breath, can't quite get the words out.

'Hey Carm, you OK?'

'Yeah, I'm, er . . . Well no, not really.'

'Shit. What's the matter?'

Adam raises an inquisitive eyebrow. She gives him a 'not good' look.

'Carm? Can you talk?'

'Yeah, I mean – I'm fine really, I just – I just had this weird . . .
I'm not having a breakdown, though. I just had this – anxiety
attack.'

'What happened?'

'I don't need to go back to hospital, though. Really.'

'What happened, Carm?'

'I – I was in the kitchen and I was going to make some dinner
and . . .'

The words come out with difficulty, fighting as they must
with tears and breaths and gulps.

'And I took out this chopping knife and put it on the table
while I went to get some vegetables out of the fridge, and then
when I turned round again, I don't know . . .'

'. . .'

'It was . . . It was like I could see the knife, this huge chopping
knife, and I could see the potential it had to slash through my
throat, I don't mean that I actually wanted to do it, I really didn't,
that's why I was so scared, but I could see that that knife had the
capacity for me to pick it up and plunge it into me, like it was
something contained within it. And I couldn't bear to look at it
because it was like I could feel the hint of it across my throat, the
shadow of it. So I just left the house. I had to leave the house.'

'Where are you now?'

'Just – walking. I'm close to my place.'

'Do you want me to come get you?'

'No, I'm fine, but – could I come over to yours? I just need to be
with people, I think.'

'Of course. You're sure you don't need fetching, though?'

'No, no, honestly. I'll come over now though.'

'OK. Call back if you need anything.'

'I'll be fine. Thanks.'

Adam sits down on the couch, wraps his arms tight around Eva.

'What's happened?'

'She's had, like, a kind of freak-out.'

'Oh shit.'

'I mean, I don't think – I don't think it's, like, a psychotic episode again. It sounded more like a panic attack. She, like – got freaked out by this knife, like it might hurt her.'

'Hm. That sounds a bit psychotic to me.'

'I don't know, she seemed to me – to realize it wasn't actually a real danger though, that the fear was coming from her.'

'She's coming over now?'

'Yes.'

' . . . '

'In fact, I imagine she won't have eaten – the knife was because she was about to make dinner. I might go and see if there's anything we can give her when she gets here.'

In the kitchen, Eva pulls out each sharp knife from the block of wood they are stabbed into and studies their stainless steel blades. It is true, of course, that they have that violence contained within them. She takes out a tea towel and wraps the knives inside it, as though sheathing the blades in cotton will dull them, as though hiding them from view will reduce their power. Then she puts them in a drawer. She surveys the kitchen, looking for anything sharp, pointed, potentially harmful. There is nothing – just smooth, wooden surfaces, rounded edges. But she can't stop thinking of the knives in the drawer, how Adam sharpens them regularly – he finds it soothing, he says – and how their razor edges could cut through flesh like butter.

'HELLO?'
'Hey, Carm – it's me.'

'Eva! Hi.'

'Is this a good time? You sound like you're somewhere where things are going on.'

'No, it's just I'm on Green Lanes – hang on, let me duck into a side street so I can hear you better . . . So – how's things?'

'Um. Yeah. Good, I guess.'

'What have you been up to this week?'

'Well . . . What's that noise?'

'Ugh. Somebody's just started drilling a hole in the road . . . Hey, why don't I go home and call you back, that OK? It'll only take about fifteen minutes.'

'Sure – take your time, I'm not going anywhere.'

Eva thought about what she'd been up to. Wandering the city in this strange state of unexpected respite: her failure to find Lena Bachmann had given her licence to ignore her doubts about Adam for a while, but slowly they had begun creeping up on her again, and she knew she couldn't postpone her search indefinitely. She looked around her room: the chalk-white walls, the sparse furnishings. It all seemed so foreign: this history-weary city, this shadowy woman she was looking for, the Adam who had known this woman. The future felt so foreign: if she found her, what new territory would Lena Bachmann reveal, what new Adam? Eva just needed to hear a familiar voice, someone who rooted her in her home and her past.

But in the meantime, she might as well do what she should have done the minute the address had turned out to lead nowhere.

She switched her computer on, and it sang a major chord at the world. Lena Bachmann was in there. We were all in there, ones and zeroes multiplying exponentially, expanding into the vastness of cyberspace. We all left traces – an IP address, an old email account, our names at the bottom of a forum thread. You could find anyone on the internet if you looked hard enough.

She typed 'Lena Bachmann' into Google. There was a solicitor of that name in Munich, whose brilliant career in the field of corporate tax law filled most of the search results on the first page. Eva clicked on her bio page on the Allen & Overy website: born in 1986. A little young, surely? She would still have been in school when Adam started his trips to Berlin, and it said here that she had gone to school in Düsseldorf. It seemed strange that someone of so few years could be so well versed in the art of fiscal evasion – surely it should be the province of middle-aged fat cats, men with bald pates and weasel eyes. Lena Bachmann stared back at her, stern, beautiful, fully conversant with the niceties of the *Handelsgesetzbuch*. This was not Lena Bachmann.

She typed in 'Lena Bachmann Berlin'. Eva had a feeling she was still here; she belonged here, in Adam's memories of this place, of that time. There were several hits: one who was in a band; one who ran a beauty salon; one who worked for some historical research institute; one who was a social worker and had taken part in a Franco-German youth project the previous year; one who posted a lot on various political forums, and who could have been any of the others. None of them had a helpful bio like Lena Bachmann from Munich did; in fact, not one of them had a photo of herself online – Germans being, on the whole, as Ulrich had explained to her, more protective of their privacy than people of many other nationalities due to their decades of experience of police states. But they did all have contact details of some kind, apart from the social worker, who could presumably be tracked down via the Franco-German youth project. Eva wondered if she should just pick up the phone, start ringing them. But she didn't like the idea of doing it blind like that, of ringing Lena Bachmanns who weren't the real Lena Bachmann. She had imagined herself walking up to her front door and announcing herself, and Lena knowing immediately who she was, why she had come there. She had imagined the look they would exchange, full of knowledge, of unspoken understanding. She didn't want to bring these strangers into the story, these homonymous impostors.

She logged on to Facebook; even people who weren't on Facebook were on it, in the background of a friend's photo or mentioned on someone's wall. Of these Lena Bachmanns, only the manicurist and the musician had their own profile – as did Lena Bachmann in Munich, looking a picture of health in all her photos. Eva knew that the Lena Bachmann she needed probably wasn't on Facebook at all, as Adam wasn't friends with her; but his profile was the key to tracking her down.

She hasn't looked at it in so long – hasn't wanted to, it's too weird, this continued virtual existence of his. The traces we leave, the ones and zeroes that still belong to him; when the flesh is dead, when the spirit is gone, what happens to our electronic souls? She can't delete it, and she can't look at it. But it is the way to Lena Bachmann.

Eva opened Adam's Facebook profile. Seeing a photo of him was still a shock: to be reminded that he had actually existed, that he had actually ceased to exist. In a ribbon at the top of the page were the photos she knew off by heart: she had been around when most of them were taken, had taken quite a few of them herself, and had looked through them to exhaustion as she was preparing the funeral. In the stultifying, long weeks just after Adam was buried, it had been one of her few activities. Now, these photos felt like a way back into the past, but a past that had become unreal, like childhood or adolescence. Had she ever, really, been that person smiling next to her handsome husband? Had Adam ever been anything other than a gaping absence? She clicked on the thumbnail of one of the photos from their last holiday in Henry's house, one of the ones she knew best: Adam and Henry beamed at the camera – at her – holding a huge carp which Henry had managed to wrestle out of the river at the bottom of the village. The carp's eye also seemed to be looking into the lens, as though it too were posing for the photo and had leapt back into life once the shutter had clicked. Although she had looked at the picture hundreds of times, there was something different now about Adam and Henry's expressions. She had always thought of this as one of the happiest shots, a perfect reminder of sun and holidays and friendship – but in their previously radiant faces she now detected a hint of doubt, an anxiety around their eyes. As though there could never be such a thing as simply being happy. You took a photo of someone and you thought that you were immortalizing them, fixing them in that state for good; but the faces that looked back at you changed. You couldn't just pin people down like a collection of butterflies.

She clicked on Adam's friends list. It was a jumble of different eras and areas of his life: people from college – including some pretty obscure ones – medical professionals from all over the world, guys from his running club, school friends, friends of hers, of Henry's, of Carmen's, in that way that social networks real and virtual have of branching out into each other. And random people, connections picked up along life's haphazard way, some of them names she didn't even recognize. She scrolled through them all, stopping off methodically at each German-sounding name. Anko Barnheim, Anna Blau, Stefan Deutsch were all members of the ICHS, which organized the big conference Adam went to every year – medics. Irrelevant. Plus they all seemed to live in Oldenburg.

Facebook pinged a notification at her: Ulrich had invited her to some sort of event, a demonstration to save the Berlin Wall. Why did the Berlin Wall need saving? She didn't have time to worry about that right now. She clicked on 'Maybe' and went back to the friends list.

There was a Barbara Friedrich who lived in Berlin and who, judging from her photos, might be a primary school teacher. She was a possibility. A Fritz Heinecker who lived in London – maybe? And then she had it: Magda Herzfeld, Wissenschaftlerin an der Humboldt-Universität zu Berlin, Institut für Geschichtswissenschaften. The same institute as Historical Research Lena Bachmann. That had to be the one. For the sake of doing things conscientiously, Eva looked through the rest of the Germanic names, but she knew she had her – and sure enough, none of the remaining ones seemed in any way relevant. She googled the Institut für Geschichtswissenschaften at Humboldt University and noted down the telephone number for Frau Professor Bachmann. She would call and make an appointment as soon as she'd finished talking to Carmen.

And she wondered if she should tell her friend about Lena Bachmann after all.

She had burdened herself with conjectures and imaginings and invented dialogues and accusations and Adam and Lena and Adam and Lena, and maybe it would be good to get all this out of her head and into her friend's ear, get some outside perspective?

But it would involve so many explanations. The hints of something amiss unnoticed, that had only fallen into place after Adam's death. The address that had led nowhere, Eva gratefully hanging on to this as an excuse not to find out just yet, perhaps even hoping she might never find out, was never meant to know after all. And now, so easily found, a correct address from which there was no escape.

And anyway. This was a thing between her and Adam, an issue they had to sort out between themselves. She couldn't bring Carmen into this. There was no room, even for as close a friend as her, inside this intimate sphere of hunches and low, soft, jealous undertones. The only person who did have a place here, maybe, was Lena Bachmann herself.

'Hey.'

'Hey – that better?'

'Yes, much better.'

'So.'

'So.'

'What's up?'

'Oh – not much, really. I just wanted to hear your voice. I've been feeling a bit homesick this week, I guess.'

'Well – home is but an Easyjet flight away . . .'

'Oh no, it's not that bad. Hearing your dulcet tones will do the trick.'

'So you're still enjoying yourself out there?'

'I don't know if "enjoying" is quite the right word, but I feel – yeah, I don't know, I feel it was a good thing to come here.'

'Good how?'

'Well, you know – to see the places Adam went, there's something – something comforting about it, I guess. And it's funny, lately I've been feeling – I don't know, it's like there's this part of me that's kind of waking up. I mean, you know, with the whole fact my family is from here, it's like I'll see parts of East Berlin, what they're like, or meet people who come from there, and it'll make sense of some small thing about the way I was brought up, or how my mum behaves or something.'

'Like – what sort of stuff, exactly?'

'Like – I don't know, this is a really obvious one, but people here have a reputation for having a Berliner Schnauze – a "Berlin muzzle". Meaning they have this sort of really abrupt way of communicating with you, like when you first get here and get on a bus or try to buy a stamp or something, it feels like people are being really aggressive, but actually they're not, it's not rude, it's just the way they communicate. You're not expected to get tangled up in politeness like you are in England – I feel like my mum has a bit of that Schnauze sometimes.'

'Hm. Interesting.'

'Yeah. Anyway, you really should come over, you'll see what I mean, I think.'

'Yes, Henry and I have been trying to work out dates.'

Eva hears the click of Ulrich coming through the front door like an electric current through her body, and hears his deep, enthralling voice:

'Hallo!'

'Hang on, Carm – Hi there!'

'Hey, Eva?'

'Yes?'

'Did you see I have sent you an invitation to a demonstration they are planning for the Berlin Wall in— Oh, sorry. I knock again later.'

Ulrich had pushed his head through the door and, seeing Eva on the phone, pulled it out again clumsily, drawing a giggle out of her.

'No, no, it's fine! Sorry, Carm.'

'What was that?'

'Oh, nothing, just – Ulrich – you know, the guy I'm staying with – just saw I was on the phone and it made him stumble in an amusing manner.'

'Oh. Right.'

Eva will not tell Carmen, either, about the way her heart lifts whenever Ulrich appears, about how she can't stop looking at him, about how much time they are spending together, how much they talk. She won't admit it to Carmen, because she is barely admitting it to herself.

'Anyway, yes. How are you doing, Carm?'

'Hm. Not great, to be honest.'

'Oh. Shit. What's going on?'

'Well, nothing's happened, particularly, I just – kind of had a depressing session with my psychiatrist this week. I've not been reacting that well to the latest cocktail of drugs he's been giving me, and he didn't seem very optimistic about the chances of us finding something else that would work . . .'

'What does "not reacting that well" mean?'

263

'I've been OK mentally – I mean, I still feel like this stuff is semi-lobotomizing me, but, you know, they haven't been worse than any of the other drugs on that front – they've just been making me feel really physically ill, like nauseous, and then I don't sleep well because I'm feeling so shit . . .'

'Have you stopped taking them, then?'

'He's put me on a new cocktail. I guess we'll just have to see how that goes.'

'Well – it often takes a while to find the right mix of drugs, right?'

'Yes, but – I sort of feel, like, the way he was talking, he was trying to prepare me for the eventuality of it not working.'

Carmen's voice is so small at the end of the line, tinny and frail, and it makes Eva feel like there is an unbearable distance between them, not the actual distance that separates them, which is there too, of course, miles and miles of it, but rather a more profound, essential distance between their beings, paradoxically made more acute by the fact that she has Carmen's voice almost inside her ear, her thin, small voice.

'I – I thought you were – better.'

' . . .'

'I mean – after Adam died. You coped so well.'

'That was different. Don't take this the wrong way, but it was somehow – I don't know, something normal. I mean, it was awful. But it was also – one of those things that happen, you know? An awful thing, and it hurts, and you have this unbearable grief, but so did you, so did Henry. We were all sharing that grief. I had the same feelings as you, the same thoughts as you – or, not the same, of course, you were his wife, but, you know . . . The grief, it was a normal emotion to be feeling. And maybe it helped me that I wanted to be strong for you, too. I wanted to be able to help you.'

' . . .'

'Whereas, with this – I don't know if I can win against my own demons, Eva.'

'. . .'

'Sometimes I feel like I'm gone. Like I'm not going to come back. Like there was me, but that person's gone, and I don't even know who this person here is. I'm thinking these thoughts, but I don't know whose thoughts they even are.'

'You're still you. You're Carmen. We all go through rough patches sometimes.'

'I feel like my soul has been plucked out of me.'

'We're here to help you, Carm. Whenever you need it, you just have to call me, or call Henry. You know.'

'. . .'

'What?'

'I just think sometimes you're on your own, you know?'

'You're not on your own.'

'You can't get inside my head, Eva. Thankfully for you.'

'. . .'

'I can't even seem to get inside my head. It's like I'm looking at this person and I don't even know who this person is, and this person is me. And if the drugs can't fix it, that'll be what I'm stuck with.'

'I really think you need to try and not worry about that until you've actually tried all the options.'

'I know, it's just – for some reason it suddenly struck me this week that it's possible there might not be a solution. That this might be it. And that got me thinking, I mean, you know, that would mean I can't have a job any more, or at least certainly not a job as a lawyer, nobody's going to employ someone who has a psychotic episode every two years . . .'

'Well look, I mean, seriously – I really would try not to focus on that bridge until you get to it. If and when.'

'Yes, I know. I just – for some reason I hadn't actually thought about the fact that this could be a possible outcome, and it's scared the shit out of me. It's like I can see all of these roads stretching out ahead of me, and each one has a sign on it with the combination of drugs I have to take to lead a normal life, except for one shitty dirt track that is just like "No drugs and a future of constantly recurring psychosis", and all these barriers are coming down at the start of the roads with the drugs and soon the only one that'll still be open to me is the dirt track . . .'

'Look, I can understand, it must be terrifying for that to be a prospect you might have to deal with. But you're not there yet. If you'd told me two years ago what my life would look like now, I would have thought I'd never be able to survive what was coming. But, I don't know – somehow I'm still alive, somehow I have survived it. People do. We survive the worst stuff life throws at us. But I would never have believed that if you'd told me back then, and I'm certainly glad I didn't know in advance what I was going to have to deal with.'

'. . .'

'If your body wants to live, it'll get you through more shades of hell than you ever dreamt you could get through.'

'But it's my mind that's diseased, Eva.'

'What, you think I didn't go crazy after Adam died?'

'I'm sure you went crazy. But you didn't go psycho-crazy. You didn't catapult yourself into a reality that doesn't exist.'

Eva wonders: what is this story I have created about Lena Bachmann? Am I perhaps raving, creating alternate worlds that bear no connection to reality?

'Look, I don't know – all I'm trying to say is, try not to think about it, because that will not help you in any way.'

'. . .'

'But if you have to think about it, remember how extraordinarily capable of survival we human beings are.'

EVA ARRIVED EARLY at Humboldt University, with twenty minutes to kill before her appointment. She hovered uncertainly in front of the gates: there was no point going in before Lena Bachmann was expecting her.

And how strange, to have an appointment with the woman your husband may have been having an affair with, to have booked it into your diary like a visit to the dentist.

The whole situation was absurd. What on Earth was Eva doing, turning up in this woman's office in the role of the potentially wronged wife? She hadn't told Lena Bachmann who she was, other than the broadly true fact of her being a British journalist, and now the concealment seemed like a terrible idea, the set-up for a showdown worthy of a soap opera finale. What was she going to do – burst in there exclaiming, 'I am the wife of Adam Lorvener!'? She was behaving like a madwoman.

She took a deep breath and turned back towards Alexanderplatz. The Fernsehturm rose up beyond the stately buildings of Unter den Linden. It looked like something out of a cartoon or a sci-fi film, or a hastily assembled prop for a school play: a giant glitter ball with a huge barbershop red and white spiral stuck on top of it. Cut out against the vibrant blue sky, it couldn't possibly be real.

She wondered what Lena Bachmann's story was: what side of the divide she had grown up on, whether as a child she had been brought up to view the Fernsehturm with awe or derision. Eva had spent so much time imagining what Adam's mystery woman might be like, filling in the gaps with projections and absurd conjectures, that she had forgotten that she didn't actually know the first thing about who she really was – that Lena Bachmann, for all the time they had spent together in her mind, was a stranger to her. She walked away from the gate: it wasn't time yet.

Next to the university stood what looked like a small classical temple. Eva walked between the thick, massive pillars on the porch and into the building.

A sandstone-lined room with a domed skylight in the centre of the roof. Underneath it, bathed in a shower of sunlight, was a large bronze statue of a woman cradling a man in her arms. The space was heavy with silence.

Eva walked up to the statue. In front of it, the ground bore the inscription: 'Den Opfern von Krieg und Gewaltherrschaft' – 'To the Victims of War and Tyranny.'

The woman was vast and hunched, wrapped in swathes of cloth, a headscarf around her head, clogs on her feet; her body was wrapped around the man, who was bony and naked. The eternal baboushka and the body of Christ, Mother Earth and her wayward child, Humanity, the Pietà, the Mother mourning her dead Son. The woman was all curves, in contrast to the man, whose long, angular limbs, bent into something like a foetal position, only accentuated how far he was from the rounded forms of infancy. And yet she cradled him, her son, her son killed by violence, her son grown out of his warm, soft baby cheeks and into the hard lines of adulthood, of the horrors men can inflict on each other. She cradled him, this creature whom she had given birth to only for him to go forth into death.

And the statue seemed at once to be speaking for all of the dead sons and all of the mothers, the hordes and hordes of them that the twentieth century had gnashed in its jaws, and also to be speaking for this one mother and her only dead son, for the uniqueness of each loss.

And Eva felt quiet tears run down her cheeks as she cried for her own loss, which was as great as all these other losses, because each loss was as great as the next in this multitudinous sea of losses.

She turned around and saw other faces looking up at the statue, tourists from all over the world, each lost in the solemn recognition of a universal pain.

And, realizing she was now five minutes late for her appointment, she hurried out, wiping her cheeks dry, and over into the university, up a grand staircase clad with red marble, through corridors lined with portraits of great German men, and then through more tired corridors lined with neon strip lights and notices to students.

Then a door with a nameplate: Lena Bachmann. She knocked before she could give herself time to think about it.

'Come in!'

She had a deep voice and quite a strong German accent. Eva pushed open the door to find herself facing a woman who was quite a bit older than her. Considerably older than her. Fifteen, maybe even twenty years. An attractive older woman, quietly at ease in her own body. Whatever faces, hair colours, sizes and shapes she had given Lena Bachmann, Eva had always assumed that she was roughly the same age as her and Adam.

'Eva Bard?'

'Yes.'

'Nice to meet you.'

She shook Eva's hand, a warm, firm grip.

'Would you like some coffee?'

'Yes, that would be lovely.'

'Sit down, if you want. I come right away.'

Lena Bachmann disappeared. Eva cast a glance out of the window. Small clumps of people sat, bathed in a mellow sun, on the steps of the opera across the avenue. Its rippling façade, echoing the pillars of other eras, the wide sweep of its steps, the self-conscious grandeur of its lines and curves, seemed laden with the memory of countless other buildings with similarly majestic façades and steps and lines and curves, the people sitting on the steps now part of a grand coterie of people sitting on steps in front of pantheons and theatres and cathedrals and train stations and operas, throughout human time and still now, in other places, and this seemed extraordinary to Eva, that she too had sat on the steps of theatres waiting for her friends, and that she shared this gesture with people in Ancient Rome and Alexandria and some sort of futuristic Beijing.

'Please, sit down.'

Lena Bachmann was back, two cups of coffee in her hands, nodding at the chair in front of her desk.

'I am sorry, we only have instant here.'

'Oh, no problem. Thank you.'

They took their places on either side of the desk, as though Eva were a student there to negotiate a bad mark on her coursework.

'So.'

'So.'

'You have said you are a journalist . . . ?'

'Yes, but – actually that's not why I'm here . . .'

'Oh?'

'I'm – you know my husband. Adam Lorvener?'

'Adam – ach so. Yes, of course, I know him.'

Before she knew it, tears had welled up in Eva's eyes. Just like that. Out of nowhere. She hadn't cried like this for a while – but it was having to say those words again, to someone else who knew Adam, really knew him, cared for him. Lena Bachmann looked at her perplexedly.

'I'm sorry. I've come because Adam is dead and—'

She was interrupted by another surge of tears; Lena Bachmann did look thrown off balance now. It was a look Eva had got used to seeing, that unique brand of shock and incomprehension.

'Mein Gott.'

' . . . '

'I am very shocked to hear this.'

'I'm sorry, I should have let you know, but I didn't know how to contact you.'

Lena Bachmann lowered her head and muttered to herself: 'Der Armer.' It was a moment of pure, private grief that seemed to encompass her memory of Adam, her sorrow at his loss, her dismay at the cruelty of Fate.

'What happened?'

'He died in his sleep. It turned out he had a heart condition that nobody had noticed – a thickening of the heart muscle. It's very rare, and it doesn't have any symptoms until the heart just stops beating. You know when sportsmen drop down dead in the middle of a race or a football match, you must have heard of cases like that? That's often what the problem was.'

She didn't get upset saying this – it was a speech she had down pat now, and besides, it was easier to focus on the technicalities, the rational explanation, than to talk about the loss, the terrible mystery of death.

'Mein Gott.'

'. . .'

'I am so sorry to hear this. It must be very hard for you. Adam was a wonderful young man.'

'Yes.'

'Thank you for telling me.'

'No, it's – there's nothing to thank me for. I'm sorry to be bringing such bad news.'

'I'm sorry you have lost your husband. Terrible. And I'm sorry for Adam. It is not right to die so young.'

'No.'

'. . .'

'. . .'

'What are you doing in Berlin?'

'This is going to sound a bit mad . . . I didn't really know what to do after he'd died, and I knew that he loved it so much here . . . so I decided to come. I suppose I felt like it would be a way of – of – I don't know. Of getting closer to him.'

'I understand.'

'Really? I won't mind if you tell me I'm completely bonkers.'

'Bonkers?'

'Oh, er – crazy. I won't mind if you think I'm crazy.'

'I am a historian – I spend most of my time trying to understand people who we cannot talk to directly any more.'

'A ghost-hunter like me.'

'Yes, maybe.'

'I found an address for you – in Adam's things. But when I went, there was nothing there. Finsterstraße, I think it was.'

'Ah, yes. My old flat. The building has been knocked down. They want to build some luxury apartments there.'

'But then I found you online.'

'. . .'

'I – I'm not quite sure how to say this. I have a reason for coming to see you – for looking for you. A – a question, I suppose. There were things – a few years ago, we – Adam and I – we weren't getting on so well. And there were some things – I thought maybe he might be having an affair here. Maybe – well. I wondered if he might be having an affair with you. I mean, I didn't even think about it at the time, I think I only half believed it anyway – but I – I don't know. After his death, it just became important for me to know – to know what your relationship was. It bothers me that there's something so important about him that I don't know, now that he's dead.'

'You thought he is having an affair with me? Did Adam tell you this?'

'No. No, he didn't at all. He wasn't honest with me about who you were, so I thought . . . I'm sorry.'

'It is me who is sorry. I hope this has not made you suffer more. So Adam did not tell you anything about what we did together when he was in Berlin?'

'Um. No.'

'Ah. Then maybe I should explain.'

'...'

'...'

Say something. Jesus.

'...'

'...'

A trio of Italians pushes past them, laden with Primark and Selfridges bags: two to each hand, thick, shiny cardboard and flimsy brown paper bulging with promise. It's a good distraction from not having anything to say. The width of each person plus purchases considerably exceeds that of the Tube aisle, so that much shuffling and acrobatics are required for them to pass. But still, before too long they have squeezed on their way, leaving a ponderous silence in their wake.

'I wonder if Peter Atwood will be there.'

'I would have thought that went without saying.'

'Not necessarily – he sometimes likes to not turn up to these things just to make it clear how far above the rat race he is.'

She can feel Adam shift in disinterest next to her – her and her hack's gossip – judging her for not having anything more interesting to talk about. She only brought it up to make conversation. She doesn't give a rat's arse about Peter Atwood.

'Are you hoping he'll get to see you in all your prize-winning glory?'

'I haven't won the prize. I'm only shortlisted.'

'You'll win the prize.'

He says it with such dismissive certainty. She wants to talk about how much she hopes she will get it, how afraid she is she won't – she's had nothing else on her mind since she heard about the shortlist. But she doesn't want to bore Adam with self-centred career talk. When did he stop being able to listen to her? How have they reached a stage of needing to make conversation with each other?

'. . .'

'. . .'

Perhaps she doesn't listen to Adam. But he hardly says anything any more. She would listen if he did.

'. . .'

'. . .'

Perhaps she doesn't listen.

She thinks about the novel in her bag, and wishes she could take it out and occupy the time with reading. She wishes there wasn't this expectation that you will chat to your travelling companion on the Tube. It's perfectly normal for her to read when Adam is around in other circumstances – in the living room, or in bed. But to do it now would be to admit that they have nothing to say to each other. She feels panic rise inside her, and panics even more as she realizes that it is the same panic you feel when sitting next to a tricky conversational partner at a dinner party: the tremendous anxiety of not knowing what to say to a stranger. Have she and Adam become strangers to each other?

She sneaks a glance at him. He looks tired, bored, stern. She has never before felt so strongly that she has no idea what he is thinking. She wonders if she still finds him handsome.

He is handsome, obviously. But does she still find him attractive?

'. . .'

'. . .'

Then, mercifully, they are at Piccadilly Circus, joining the mass jostling to position itself at their carriage exit. As they stand there waiting for the train to roll into the station, the warm, impatient bodies hemming them in on all sides, Adam puts his hand on her waist and leans in behind her.

'You're going to get it because you deserve it. You know that, don't you?'

She looks round at him, meets a warm, loving gaze. Suddenly she remembers why she married this kind, wonderful man. He kisses her. The train pulls into the platform and disgorges them, along with countless others, into the London evening.

'What was it – 326, right?'

'No, 316, I think. Hang on, let me have a look.'

She pulls the invitation out of her bag, feels a tingle of thrill at once more catching a glimpse of her name, handwritten, on the stiff, thick card.

'316.'

'Well, here we are, then.'

They look at the weighty oaken door, which speaks of pipe-smoking gentlemen and discreet porters. When they push it open, it does, in fact, reveal a porter.

'May I take your coat, Madam? Sir?'

They exchange a glance, two imposters in this stuffy, outdated world – it reminds her of being students, giggling at having to wear gowns at formal hall. The porter looks at them as though he is used to this kind of reaction, and takes their coats with quiet deference.

A few steps down a corridor rich with wood panelling and burgundy paint, and they walk into the hall. The luxuriant thrum of the chattering classes swells over them, wraps them in a cloud of gossip and guffaws and snide asides. Eva immediately finds herself scanning the room for allies, enemies, people with power – plotting a route through the gathering, friends to retreat to, targets to accost. She feels the thrill of the cocktail-party chase, made more acute by the knowledge that, as a shortlistee for the prestigious Holden Prize, she herself is one of the hot tickets this evening. She feels Adam tense beside her – he hates these things, the overwhelming numbers, the way people are always looking over your shoulder to check if there is someone more useful to talk to. She needs to find someone to park him with – Jonathan must be in here somewhere.

'Eva! My money's on you, old bean.'

'Oh God, I waste enough of your money as it is, Bill . . .'

'Nonsense! No one deserves this more than you. Listen, I can't stop to chat, I have to go and schmooze old Tim Peters before he gets so sozzled he'll forget our conversation, but I'm keeping my fingers crossed for you, OK? Catch you later.'

'See you later, Bill. Let's dive in, shall we?'

Adam looks exhausted, and faintly green.

'Are you all right? You don't look too good.'

'I'm fine – just completely whacked. Sorry if I'm not at my sparkliest this evening – I might have to retreat to a corner while you go ahead and work the room, I'm afraid.'

'Well – it's not that I particularly want to, but I am going to have to do a bit of hobnobbing . . .'

'I know, I know. It's your job. I don't mind at all.'

'Really? You're sure?'

'I'm sure. Let's go and find Jonathan, he must be in here somewhere – he and I can settle down with a beer while you dazzle everyone with your wit.'

'Well. Let's go and get a drink, at least.'

They dive into the sea of hacks, snake their way between nattering clusters, dodge past trays of canapés. Eager eyes search for Eva's, keen to show by congratulating her that they have a personal connection to one of the star guests – but she ignores them, glowering as she carves a route through the crowd in front of Adam. This evening of all evenings – this evening that could mean so much for her career – why does he have to act like a deadweight dragging her down, why can't he make an effort?

Jonathan is leaning against a table in a corner of the hall, strategically positioned within striking distance of the bar, and close to a couple of chairs on which it might be acceptable, later, to sit down. He is chatting to a lithe young man with long, beautiful eyelashes.

'My darlings! I was starting to worry you might miss all the champagne.'

He speaks in the catty, whispering monotone he reserves for glamorous social events, to mark himself out from the effusive, try-hard crowd. Usually Eva likes being taken into this conspiracy, but this evening she resents it by association with Adam.

Jonathan slides over to the bar and returns with two flutes of champagne.

'Tuck into these. This is Patrick. Patrick, these are Adam and Eva. Yes, those really are their names.'

Patrick nods at them, a strange, silent boy. His eyes gleam with intelligence under those butterfly lashes

Someone taps on Eva's shoulder. She turns to find herself facing Marie Szpozinski.

'Eva, hi. Marie Szpozinski.'

'Yes.'

Obviously she is Marie Szpozinski.

'I don't want to interrupt you and your friends, but I just wanted to congratulate you on your nomination. I absolutely *adored* the Kamran Sheikh piece.'

'Thank you.'

'We should have coffee some time.'

She slips a business card into Eva's hand; Eva wonders where she pulled it out from.

'Oh. Wait, let me give you mine . . .'

Champagne glass in one hand and Marie Szpozinski's business card in the other, Eva flails around for a split second.

'Don't worry. I'll only lose it. Just give me a call next week. And enjoy the evening.'

Eva turns back to her drinking companions. Jonathan is raising an eyebrow at her; Patrick watches inscrutably. Adam gives her a proud but wan smile.

'Patrick, darling, I spot Roger over there. If you want to talk to him this evening, I would do it sooner rather than later.'

Patrick nods, and slips off in Roger's direction. Eva wonders what his voice sounds like, and whether he will actually try it out on Roger or just stand there watching him mutely. She feels an absurd pang of envy. Oh, to be a beautiful young man trying to get a foothold on Fleet Street, to have fluttering eyelashes and a career ahead of you! What if she doesn't win the prize?

'So, Eva, my dear, how are you finding the giddy heights of journalistic stardom?'

'Everyone keeps staring at me.'

'That is only to be expected.'

'I don't know – it's a bit creepy.'

'Well, of course, most of them are eaten away with envy.'

'Or shock. Disbelief.'

'No, just good old green-eyed envy.'

'You deserve this, Eva – you really do.'

'Ah, Eva. Behold your supportive husband. How did you manage to find him? Though I have to say, Adam, you look dreadful tonight.'

'Oh. And I thought I could always rely on you, at least, to succumb to my charm . . .'

'Well, I do, my darling, of course I do, but really, you do look very tired. Eva, what have you been doing to him? Have you earned your success by drinking a pint of his blood every evening?'

'Jonathan. You always portray me as such a harpy.'

'Only because I'm jealous, darling. Jealousy and envy – they surround you tonight. But at least neither Adam nor I begrudge you your prize.'

'Nomination. But yes, you're probably the only two people here that can be said of.'

'And Patrick. Patrick is not envious of you.'

'Why not?'

'Because he is convinced it's only a matter of time before he is in your shoes.'

'And do you think he's right to be? Is he any good? He's very beautiful.'

'He is very beautiful. You and I need a top-up.'

Jonathan whisks her glass off her and slices off between two tailcoats. She got through that quickly. Adam's glass is still three-quarters full.

'You got through that quickly.'

'I know. I must be nervous.'

'Sorry. That sounded like I was getting at you. It wasn't meant as a criticism, I just—'

'I didn't take it as a criticism.'

'I didn't mean   '

'Really. It's fine. I didn't take it like that.'

'It sounded like one, though.'

'It's fine. Really.'

'I don't even know why I said it. Stupid.'

'I knew what you meant.'

This is good. Apologizing fills the space between them while they wait for Jonathan to come back. He returns with brimming flutes.

'So, Adam, aside from playing the sacrificial victim to your monstrous wife, what have you been up to recently?'

'Oh, you know – the usual grind . . .'

'Adam's too modest to boast about this, but he's been doing pretty well recently too: his team have been awarded a research grant by the Wellcome Trust.'

'Adam! I raise my glass to you. Still looking into your old fatties, I presume?'

'Yep. Though I'd watch my words if I were you, Jonathan, with the amount of booze you drink, it's not inconceivable you might contract diabetes at some stage.'

'Well, I've never denied my own decadence. Though it would be a little galling to be lumped in with the overweight masses – I have, at least, always been careful about my waistline.'

'Well, you know, cream cakes aren't the only things that contain sugar. In fact, most of the stuff we eat and drink nowadays does. And then there's the fact that everyone sits in offices all day and drives everywhere. Processed food, sedentary lifestyles – you might say diabetes is the symptom of everything that's wrong with the way we live now.'

'A decadent disease for a decadent people.'

Around them, the room is a blaze of evening gowns offset against dark, well-cut suits; glass chinks sweetly against glass, and every now and then a snippet of Fleet Street gossip drifts past their ears, as tantalizing and insubstantial as popcorn.

'Actually, this might interest you, Jonathan: part of the study is looking into how far treatment outcomes are influenced by patients' relationships with their doctors.'

'I didn't realize patients were supposed to have relationships with their doctors.'

'Meaning . . .'

'Now I know it's acceptable, I might have to rebook an appointment with my new cardiologist.'

'Meaning . . .'

'Though I wonder what an affair with a cardiologist would be like – do you think their knowledge of the heart's innermost workings makes them more or less amenable to its flutterings?'

'Most of the cardiologists I know are total players, I'm afraid.'

'Heartless specialists of the heart.'

'I'm afraid so. Anyway. We're leaving the Lotharios out of this study, but what we are interested in is how the way patients relate to their doctors influences what they tell them, how they manage their disease.'

'Are the fatties lying about how many Mars bars they've had for breakfast?'

'For example. But it goes further than that: often people won't report how many hypos they're having because they think it's their fault. They're embarrassed that the doctor will think they haven't been taking their readings properly or have been miscalculating how much insulin to take. Even though, more often

280

than not, it's simply due to the nature of the medication, which requires a hell of a lot of fine-tuning before you get it right. It's fascinating. Why don't our patients just tell us the truth? It's not like I have a go at them when they do tell me what they're really up to, even the worst stuff . . .'

'But they feel guilty. And they view you as their judge. You are the confessors of the twenty-first century, Adam.'

'But we're talking about people's lives and deaths, here. Their not being honest with me about how many hypos they're having, or what their eating habits are, can have a real impact on how long they live. It could be the difference between them living to see their grandchildren or not. And yet they would rather sacrifice this for the sake of not looking silly in the eyes of a man they see for half an hour once every six months.'

'People have always died for honour. Walked to their deaths out of embarrassment.'

'I told you you'd find it interesting.'

'I do. I need to think about it some more. Diabetes as a symbol of the decline of Western civilization. A disease born of our over-saturated, consumption-driven economics; the doctor as high priest of our rudderless society – as the final, ineffectual representative of some remnant of morality. I could probably eke an essay out of it.'

Adam has revived; gone is the dark grey under his eyes, the hint of pale green in his cheeks. He is rosy and attractive, frothy with champagne. It saddens Eva that it should take contact with a cynical old queen to bring this out in him; there was definitely a time, not that long ago, when she could animate him in this way. But he doesn't tell her about these interesting thoughts he has; not any more than she tells him about hers. They are left to hear each other's inner lives through third parties – he when he reads her latest column in the paper (which she knows he still does, even though he no longer tells her what he thinks of it), she by listening in on a conversation he is having with someone else.

'You're being very quiet, Eva. Is the enormity of your situation finally dawning on you?'

'What? Oh. God, no. I'd completely forgotten we were here, actually. I was just listening to you.'

'Sorry, Eve, I didn't mean to monopolize the conversation . . .'

'You're not monopolizing anything, it was fascinating! All you'd told me about was getting the grant – you get all the philosophical musings, Jonathan.'

'Well, of course, Eva, you must never forget that mundanity is the province of the good wife. You should hear what Adam and I discuss in the smoking room.'

'Hi guys! What are you lot talking about?'

'Oh, the usual – the metaphysics of diabetes, Adam and Eva's marital breakdown in communication. Tom, verily, you grow handsomer every time I see you. Where did you get that gorgeous bronze sheen from?'

'Oh – I'm just back from Baghdad . . . I miraculously managed to escape being embedded and actually got out into the sunlight.'

'You valiant warrior, you.'

Jonathan grasps him at the waist and plants a kiss on both his cheeks. Tom, infuriatingly assured of his own sexual magnetism and unwavering heterosexuality, manages to enjoy the attention without in any way being shaken by it. His eyes drift to Eva's. They always do.

'Hi, Eva. Adam.'

'Hi.'

'Hi.'

He kisses Eva, extends a dark, heavy paw to Adam, whose skin looks so pale in comparison.

'So. Congratulations.'

'Thanks.'

'I'm keeping my fingers crossed. Gave you my vote, of course.'

'I should think so.'

Jonathan has his hand on Tom's biceps, which even

underneath a dinner jacket still manages to show off how substantial and defined it is. Or perhaps it is just that Eva has seen it so often in perfect outline through skin-tight T-shirts that she is seeing the memory of it right now. At any rate, Jonathan is just as beguiled by it: he can't seem to let go.

'And where will your travels take you next, our valiant warrior?'

'Well. Hopefully the DRC in a couple of weeks' time, together with our award-winning journalist here, right?'

'I haven't won the award yet.'

'Yet! So you do recognize you're going to win it?'

'No! I don't know. Not award-winning, anyway.'

'Yet.'

'The Congo, eh. Thank God I'm too old for fieldwork.'

'It'll be a doddle after having to deal with the bloody American military.'

'That's what you think, Captain Kurtz.'

'People get the wrong idea about the Congo.'

'Well. That's true. But you can't deny that the mosquitoes are punishing.'

'Do you know, they don't really go for me, it's weird.'

'Young man. Is there any aspect of your life in which the gods have not smiled upon you?'

'Oh come on, Jonathan – I'm a war photographer. We're as fucked up as they come.'

'I'm glad to hear you've had some price to pay. Anyway, can I introduce you to my young protégé, Patrick? He's trying to make his way in the world of journalism, and I think he'd probably be interested in speaking to you.'

'Sure. Is he a photographer?'

'Yes, he went to art school. Don't look like that. I doubt he's made for conflict zones, but you can probably tell him a thing or two about pitching to editors.'

'Where is he?'

Jonathan beckons at Patrick who, it turns out, has been

hovering within view of them all along. Eva has never seen any-body be at once so striking and unobtrusive; he will probably make a good journalist. She strains to hear him speak once he is standing between Jonathan and Tom, but he is just out of ear-shot. What can his voice be like?

'I didn't realize you'd said yes to the Congo trip after all.'

'Well, I haven't. I'm still thinking about it.'

'I thought we'd agreed on this . . .'

'No, I said I'd think about it. I know you're worried, but really, Tom's right, people just have this completely overblown idea of how dangerous it is.'

'How do you know? You've never been there.'

'Tom has. I trust his judgement.'

'Well, I don't. He's a bloody war reporter – he probably can't even feel the most basic of emotions unless he's got three bombs going off around him.'

'I know he looks like a hothead, but he knows what he's doing. He's very careful, really.'

This isn't, strictly speaking, true – Tom does know what he's doing, but he also can put himself into some fairly hairy situa-tions, and though he would never encourage Eva to take the same risks he does, she has often felt tempted to. It's one of the things she finds attractive about him – he is so fearless he makes you forget that anything might happen to you. Whereas Adam always worries about her so much that she starts to feel unnerved.

'Adam, this is my job. It's what I do.'

'It's not! You don't have to go to the DRC! You could write a feature about that beekeeper down the road from us and you'd be paid just as much money!'

'He's a really good photographer. The war there has claimed over four million lives so far, way more than Iraq and Afghani-stan put together – I mean, come on, that's getting to Holocaust levels. And yet hardly anyone talks about it. I just know we'd come back with an amazing piece.'

'You always come back with amazing pieces! You're up for the fucking Holden Prize!'

'Can you keep calm, please? I'm feeling enough at the centre of attention as it is.'

'Yes. OK. Sorry.'

'Adam, I've done this sort of thing before. I've been to Iraq, for Christ's sake.'

'I know. And I've always been terrified for you every second you've been out there.'

'But it wasn't that bad! Really. I've got more chance of dying riding my bike down the Holloway Road than in either Iraq or the DRC.'

'They're still dangerous places. People die in them every day.'

'People die every day everywhere. Why can't you just accept that it's really important for me to go on this trip?'

'Why can't you accept that it's really important for me that you don't go?'

'. . .'

'. . .'

'Look. Let's talk about this tomorrow. As I said, I haven't decided yet. I don't think this is a very good forum for this discussion.'

'Sure. Yes.'

'. . .'

'Eva, it's only because I love you that I—'

'Oh fuck! Sorry.'

A passing tray has been nudged into Eva, spraying champagne down her front.

'Great.'

'Shit. Sorry.'

'Don't worry. At least it wasn't red wine.'

'Shall I – um. I could get—'

'It's fine. I've got a tissue. It's fine, really.'

'OK. Sorry. Well done on the nomination, by the way – I'm a great fan of yours.'

'Right. Thanks.'

Tom seizes the opportunity to disengage from Patrick.

'Hey. What happened to you?'

'I know. The perils of cocktail parties. I'd better not win now, I'd look like a right tit having to get up on stage like this . . .'

'Hm. Yes. "Tit" being the operative word.'

Eva looks down to see her left breast moulded by diaphanous white, her nipple red and perky, seeming to want to push through both bra and shirt into the cloying air of the party. She lifts the fabric off it; it detaches reluctantly, like a limpet.

'Fuck.'

She blushes – standing there like that, wafting her champagne-drenched front away from her nipples. Tom has an uncanny ability to make the blood run to her cheeks even in quite innocent situations; this level of embarrassment she simply has no defence against.

Adam runs a hand down her shoulder in an awkward gesture that is either proprietorial or consoling.

'Don't worry, it's rather fetching. Maybe they should add a wet T-shirt category to the Holden Awards . . . Anyway. How are you doing, Adam?'

'Oh, er – good, yeah, thanks. Fine.'

'Good.'

'How are you?'

'Great, man, great.'

'Great.'

'So. Eva. What are you going to spend the prize money on?'

'I don't even know if I've got the prize, Tom.'

'No. You don't know, that's true.'

He looks at her, the faintest of smirks at the corner of his lips.

'What?'

'Nothing.'

He won't let go of her gaze, and his eyes mock her gently. She narrows hers at him.

'Do you realize what a talented woman you've married, Adam?'

'Believe me, it's not easy to forget.'

'No, seriously, though – I've been wanting to say this to you, Eva, before everyone else comes and sucks up to you. There aren't that many journalists who are as committed to their job as you are. You should see her out there, man, she's fierce. I mean – have you ever been to Russia?'

'Oh bullshit. I wouldn't have done half of it if you hadn't been there.'

'What happened in Russia?'

'Where do I begin?'

A tinkle on the opposite side of the room signals the start of the evening's proceedings. Allegra Brookes is on the stage, reeling off a long list of thank-yous. Can Tom really have any inside information? He does have a vote, after all – but she thought they always kept the results quiet. And Tom is definitely the kind of person who would pretend that he knows something just to get a rise out of her – a rise of red to her bashful cheeks . . .

She can feel how the eyes in the room are all centred on her and the handful of other people who are also up for the prize – they are each like a little sun, attracting attention with a gravitational pull: darted glances, sideways monitoring, unabashed stares. Even the looks that avoid them are doing it in reaction to their glow, and cannot escape their orbit: they are merely turning their backs on the focus of their attention, like the hidden side of the Moon looking outwards into infinity while it floats around the Earth. Eva has covered her fair share of celebs in her time, and she's starting to understand what makes them so nervy: the energy in this room, it is, well, pretty intense. Occasionally, she steals a glance at Adam, who responds with warm, supportive eyes. Occasionally, she steals a glance at Tom, who leaves her with a cryptic look.

And when they say her name and the eyes in the room all turn towards her, her sun eclipsing all the others, it's pure instinct: she leaps into Tom's arms, those magnificent arms which clench around her joyfully, and they both laugh, because he knows how hard she works, and he understands what it took to get here, and they've been through the wars together, and when she opens her eyes and meets Adam's he's doing his best to give her a congratulatory smile, but oh – how sad he looks, how sad.

HE IS THERE, with you, always.
Even though he is increasingly not there.

In spite of the strength of the novelty of this place, which has made your mind able to focus on other things, the stimulation of a new sight, a new experience, these things that carry you forward and away from him, so that sometimes you can go for several minutes without thinking of him, half an hour even.

Even when he is not there he is there, like background chatter in a café, shut out but not unheard.

Adam is present in his absence.

And on some days you can even convince yourself that there is something gentle and comforting about it, having this ghostly companion always a few inches behind you, with you always, now that he does not have a body to be his own man in – but no sooner have you felt that than you rebel against it, because you do not want him to be reduced to a shackled existence as the product of your mind, you do not want yourself to be condemned to always missing him, you do not want both of you to remain the prisoners of his death.

You would like to see him screaming for joy as he runs through the long grass of a field in springtime, you would like to smell the sweat on him afterwards, you would like to feel the heat of blood pumping through his body again.

But he remains unseen, unsmelled, unfelt, not there, never there, always not there.

'MAYBE I EXPLAIN to you how me and Adam met? Probably that is the best thing, I think, no?'

'I don't – well, I mean, I don't know. I don't know what it is you have to tell me.'

'I have nothing to tell you – this is the point. We found out nothing.'

'Found out?'

'This is why I maybe should start at the beginning.'

'Right. Sure.'

'When Adam first started coming to Berlin, I am finishing my PhD at Humboldt. Adam was very interested in history, he came to some of my classes, and also sometimes I would see him in other seminars. Then some few years ago he asked me if I could help him find out about your grandfather.'

'About *my* grandfather?'

'Your grandfather was called Jochen Krantz, yes?'

'Yes, but . . .'

'Adam wanted to find information about him. For you.'

'But – why?'

'He wanted to surprise you, I think – like a gift. He thought you should find out about your family, and maybe if he helped you it will be easier. I think also he hoped maybe he could find some people from your family who were still alive, who you could talk to. He never has told you about this?'

'No. Never. What did he tell you he wanted to find out?'

'He told me his wife is the granddaughter of Jochen Krantz, a pastor in the Evangelische Kirche. He told me that your mother fled to the UK in the seventies, and that she never saw her parents again. This is correct?'

'Yes – but I'm surprised . . . I mean – I never even talked about my grandfather, my mother's family, that much . . . My mother barely talks about it.'

'Yes, he told me this. He found it strange, I think. Maybe also he was doing it because he thought you should be doing it.'

'Well, I mean – it's kind of complicated – my mother's parents died when she was still quite young, it was quite traumatic for her. I guess I always worried about hurting her with that stuff. Besides, it's my right to choose whether or not to look into my family history, isn't it?'

'Absolutely. This is what I told him. Since the *Wende*, a lot of families have had this choice: to look into their family history, or not. Many prefer not to: maybe you find out your neighbour was writing reports about you for the Stasi, maybe your wife, your husband, your child. Not everyone wants to know, and I respect this choice for an individual, even though being a historian I think it is important for a society to examine the past.'

'But you helped him?'

'I told him I would try. When Adam discovered I am looking at the Stasi archive for my research, he asked me if I can find out about Jochen Krantz. I did not know the name Jochen Krantz – you know, there were a lot of evangelical pastors, and a lot who said after the *Wende*, yes, I was involved in the resistance, blah blah . . . So I was thinking this English guy does not know nothing, probably this Jochen Krantz is nobody.'

'But my grandfather died way before the *Wende*.'

'Yes, I know – but still, often people want to believe their family was involved in something special, you know.'

'Hm. I can imagine.'

'But I liked this Adam, and that he was interested in doing

more than going out to Berlin nightclubs. That he was trying to understand this city a little bit.'

Eva felt a smile curl up a corner of her lips.

'Adam always liked to understand everything.'

Lena smiled too.

'Yes, he had a nice mind. A curious mind.'

'But so – you did look into what my grandfather had done?'

'I thought, why not, after all? I can try the few obvious places, and then tell him there is nothing to find out. But then, well – there was nothing, but this was strange.'

'Strange? How?'

'There was too much nothing, so to say. Nothing in the Stasi files, but OK, they did not have files on everybody, so maybe this could mean that your grandfather was not as important as your mother thought, or was not even a dissident at all. But then, I looked through the records of the Evangelische Kirche, and here too, nothing. There was not your grandfather's name, anywhere.'

' . . . '

'I checked the city register, also, and I could not find any trace of your mother or your grandparents.'

'But . . .'

Her grandfather. Opa. Oma. They had just been an absence in her life, an absence with faint contours made out of a handful of stories repeated enough times to be remembered, and some bare facts. A pastor. A schoolteacher. East Berlin. The Wall. Childhood summers swimming in the lakes, earning Pioneer badges, being taught that you shouldn't repeat the conversations that you heard at home, gatherings in the living room with music turned up loud to confound anyone listening in. Letters sent on cigarette-thin paper, wondering if there was a code, a hidden meaning, how much the censors were taking out. And now, it seemed, Eva was being told that her grandparents were even more evanescent than that, that there was no trace of them anywhere.

'Maybe I get us some more coffee, oder?'

'Oh – er – yes, why not? Thank you.'

Lena picked up the mugs and disappeared.

Adam. Adam trying to find out about her grandfather, a man who had always been a ghost to her. And Adam a ghost too, now. Faces on the edge of her vision: a young man with golden hair who loved her so much, a man in starchy 1950s clothing who would never get to know her, his only granddaughter on the other side of the Iron Curtain. Jochen. A man she would never get to know, because there was nothing left of him.

'Everything is OK?'

'Oh – yes. I was just. I mean . . . this is all very strange.'

'Yes, I think so too.'

'What – I mean, what do you think happened?'

'Honestly? I don't know. I said to Adam, of course, we cannot be sure, a lot of documents were destroyed just after the *Wende*, so maybe these papers are just missing.'

'But – why would they destroy them? Some sort of cover-up or something?'

Lena Bachmann smiled wryly. 'This is what Adam thought, also. I think he somehow liked the idea that there was some big scandal being hidden, that your grandparents had been murdered by the Stasi . . . But honestly, I think it is very unlikely. Maybe if it was just a Stasi file missing, that could be the case. But I think no, if it is something like this, then maybe it is just chance.'

'But that doesn't seem very likely either, does it?'

'Well . . . I'm sorry to say this, but maybe your mother has not told you her true story. Maybe she is not from Berlin, or her father was not a pastor.'

' . . .'

'I'm sorry. I am just making conjectures, of course.'

'What . . . what did Adam say about all this?'

'He seemed troubled. As I said, at first he very much insisted that there must be some scandal to uncover. We continued looking – then at some point, Adam called me and said that he had found out that the pastor of Sankt-Michaelis-Kirche, in Pankow, had been arrested with his wife at around the time of your mother's story, with a daughter who had died trying to escape to the West in the 1970s. I think he has seen this in an exhibition. He asked me to find out if there were still members of the family we could contact. And it did seem like this could be your mother's family. We thought maybe she has changed her name, and her parents mistakenly thought she was dead – Adam was very convinced, he said he had a photo of your mother and her parents, that he was sure they were the same people.'

'He – did he have a copy of the photo?'

'He said he would get one, that he would show it to me – but then he went to visit the family, and they had nothing to do with you. He saw he has made a mistake.'

'Who in the family did he visit? They were still alive?'

'No, the pastor and his wife had died, although not in prison like your mother says. But their son still lives in Pankow.'

'Well, my mother doesn't have a brother.'

' . . . '

'As far as I know.'

' . . . '

'So what's your theory on all of this?'

'I think maybe it could be that your mother did go to that church, and used their story for herself. It is not that unusual for people to reinvent themselves when they start a new life somewhere. And it can be a good way, if you want to hide, to take on the identity of someone who people think is dead.'

'But – why would she do that?'

Lena Bachmann shrugged. 'You would have to ask her that. If you want to.'

'And did Adam agree with this interpretation?'

'I think he did, yes. He seemed to lose interest in looking any further after we had come to this dead end. I was surprised, in a way, because he has been so insistent. But it seemed like maybe he felt it was not the right thing to do, after all. After that, he was not contacting me again.'

'And you didn't try to get in touch with him?'

'I just thought, probably he is busy, or not in Berlin so often now, or he has accepted that there is nothing to find out. I did send him an email some time ago, to ask how he was, as we had not been in contact for so long.'

'Yes – I think I saw that email. He died shortly after you sent it.'

'Oh.'

'Yes.'

'. . .'

'. . .'

'I think Adam was very in love with you, Eva. You should not worry.'

'I don't – Well, I don't worry he didn't love me, I know that, I just – I don't know. Sometimes I worry I didn't know him enough – I feel now, I wish I had paid more attention to him. That must sound so crazy. I mean, of course I knew him so well, and we talked about so much, but . . . But now sometimes I'll be thinking about him and I'm like, who was this guy? Who was he really? Do I even know that?'

'Maybe you are suffering because we cannot always know people completely. You do not know Adam like he was when he was with me, or with his mother, or with another of his friends. But he did not know those other parts of you either.'

'No, but – I'm still alive to have all those different parts.'

'It is very sad that Adam is dead. It is terrible.'

'. . .'

'Eva, I'm very sorry, but I will have to leave – I have to go and pick up my son from his school.'

'Yes, of course.'

'But I am happy to meet again, if you like – I can show you the documents that I collected for Adam, maybe there is something there that will make sense to you? I don't have the file here, but I can bring it in.'

'Yes, that would be fantastic – I'd like to see what he found out, at least. What you found out.'

'Good.'

'. . .'

'I think Adam wanted to give this gift to you – to tell you more about your family, about who you are.'

'Yes.'

'But you must decide for yourself if you want this gift or not.'

THEY HAVE TO rush for the train because they're late as usual, because Adam insisted on stopping to buy a paper even though it was already clear they were cutting it fine, and they only just make it, air hacking through Eva and an unpleasant film of sweat coating her body. Adam bumps into her as he pounces on a free pair of seats.

'Ow!'

'Oh, sorry . . . You OK?'

'Yeah, yeah, I'm fine.'

It didn't actually hurt at all, but Eva is so *annoyed* with Adam at the moment. He's been in such a weird mood for the past couple of weeks – ever since he got back from his last trip to Berlin, really – and she can't seem to do anything to draw him out of it, and now they have just got to the point where she's irritated too and their respective moodinesses feed into each other in a bilious, vicious circle.

Adam fumbles around in his seat, heaps of paper and paraphernalia everywhere, while Eva takes the one opposite him. He doesn't even pay any attention to her, just stares out of the window and thinks about whatever it is that has been so playing on his mind. London zips past outside, terraced houses and terraced houses and terraced houses, miles and miles of people and city and lives, and Eva wishes it could all just pause for a moment, this constant activity and movement, this constant sharing your life with someone, day after day after day, whatever mood they are in. She looks at Adam and she still feels the pull of her love for him, the physical need she has to be close to him, but there is a force field of stress around him right now that is too much effort to break through, and she wishes she could just take some time out from her whole life, not have to deal with these constant negotiations any more.

Her dad picks them up from the station, as always. Eva feels a surge of tenderness when she sees him standing by the car: age has started its slow work on him in recent years, pushing out his bald patch, turning brown hairs grey, weighing down on his shoulders so that, if you know him well, you notice that he stoops ever so slightly now. Small marks of time that hint at a terrifying future of weakness and decay – Eva wants to protect him against it, like he protected her from the world when she was a little girl. Eva feels the thickness of blood. And into this wades Adam, glum and monosyllabic in response to her father's nervous cheeriness, and as they sit in the car driving down familiar suburban lanes, the way home that Eva has known by heart since childhood, her father happily giving her the news on the latest small developments in their town, and Adam far away, mute on the back seat, she thinks this is my family. I love you but this is my blood, and you are behaving like an intruder right now.

'Oh, we've finished redoing your room, by the way, did Mum tell you?'

'Yes, she did – she seemed to think the colours all work well together?'

'Looks good to me, anyway. You can judge for yourself shortly . . .'

Kurt Cobain is gone. The horses are gone. The desk covered in doodles and Panini stickers is gone; the poster her friends made her for her eighteenth birthday is gone. Her room is hers and not hers. It is simple, clean, the new paint on the walls elegant and immaculately applied. One wall is a light blue, the other three are white.

'It works OK, doesn't it? Having the one wall in colour.'

'Uh-huh. Yeah, it's nice.'

There is a new bed, a double, purchased to give her and Adam more room when they come to stay. Her childhood and adolescence have been picked up, filed away: they no longer hang on the walls in exuberant tastelessness, but sit in ring binders on her bookshelves and in boxes under the bed. The bed, which Adam sprawls himself out on.

'Aaah. It's going to be so nice to have enough space to sleep in at night . . .'

Eva lies down next to him, cuddles into his side.

'I don't know – there was something I quite liked about sharing a single bed . . .'

'Well, yes, it had a certain romanticness to it, but, you know, it'll be all right to not have you whacking my funny bone in the middle of the night, too.'

'I've never whacked your funny bone in the middle of the night!'

'You so definitely have.'

'Hmph.'

Adam strokes her hair, kisses her forehead. Eva thinks of the cocoons of intimacy created by walls: the walls of this bedroom around her and Adam, the intimacy of a husband and wife; and the walls of this house around her and her parents, the intimacy of a family. And once upon a time, how this room was hers and hers alone, the intimacy of a child with dreams and stories and anxieties and ever-expanding thoughts about the world; the intimacy of a teenager with a melodramatically exploding self. She has let Adam in, through all the walls.

'Are you sure you're OK, Ad? You're very quiet today. You're very quiet generally, these days, in fact.'

'Yeah, I'm fine – just got a lot on at work at the moment, with this new funding application. Sorry.'

'You're sure that's all it is?'

'Yeah, honestly.'

It's not, of course – Eva can tell it's not. But sometimes you have to let the other person keep things to themselves. And Adam has closed up again now anyway, after this brief moment of softening – his body tense against hers, his hand paused mid-stroke, and now falling limp on to the new duvet.

'Top-up?'

'Oh, yes, lovely.'

They are all four agreeably merry, having started drinking an aperitif earlier than is strictly reasonable. Eva's dad is flushed from the wine and his excited monologue about the upcoming by-election; her mum is relaxed, refilling the bowls of nibbles and laughing at everyone's jokes. Adam has relaxed too, although there's a certain hint of hysteria to some of his interjections, and he is drinking very fast. Eva leans back against the Aga and feels its comforting warmth grow around her. When she was small she used to try and hug it, as though it were a family pet, and she would make up stories about the adventures it had been on before ending up in their house. It still feels like a living being, the pulsing heart of her family home. She watches Adam as he helps her mum set the table. He knows where everything is, the plates, the cutlery; he knows the ways of their house.

'Hanna, I've been meaning to ask you: what church did your father work for, again?'

'The Evangelische Kirche. It is like the German version of the Anglican Church.'

'It must have been strange, growing up as the daughter of a pastor in an atheist country.'

'Yes.'

'Did it feel like a big deal, when you were growing up?'

'Hard to say. I mean, yes, of course, it had a huge effect on my life later – but as a child, you do not always notice these things.

Definitely, we knew that we should not say the same things out-side our house as at home – but that is something many people who grew up in the DDR would say.'

'And which church was it that he ran? It was in Pankow, right?'

'Why do you ask?'

'Oh, I was just there on my last trip to Berlin – in Pankow, I mean – and I wandered into a church and it occurred to me it might be the one you grew up in. Sankt-Michaelis, I think it was.'

'No, it was not this church.'

'Oh. Which one was it, then?'

'Actually, it was not a church at all. He used a room, in a nor-mal building. The church that used to be in our part of town had been destroyed during the War, and there was not enough money to rebuild it. I remember we would play in the ruins. Sometimes, you could find strange objects in there: some burnt pages of a Bible, a piece of a crucifix. Some few things that were left, that had not been taken away by people. The bells, for example, had all been melted down for the metal.'

Eva's mother has a faraway look, as though she's staring down a wormhole through time at those singed pages of the Holy Book. She looks sad, monumentally sad, filled with all the grief of her unfortunate home city.

'What was the church called? The one that was in ruins?'

Then she tenses, throws Adam a look that is a brick wall.

'I do not remember. We just used to call it "the Church". "Die Kirche".'

'Oh. Where was it, exactly?'

'Adam, if you do not mind, I would rather we change the sub-ject. It is not easy for me, remembering this time. I'm sorry.'

'But, just – I'd just like to know where the ruin was, it sounds like it might be something worth seeing . . .'

Eva feels herself be propelled forward, and sees her father move in too, both of them driven by an instinct to surround her mother, protect her from these questions she doesn't want to answer.

'Come on, guys, enough of the chit-chat, we've got a roast to carve . . .'

'Yes, Mum and I wanted to try out a new recipe for the marinade today, we need you all to get stuck in and tell us what you think . . .'

But Eva's mother doesn't want anybody to step in and defend her – she stays there, looking Adam straight in the eye.

'Another time, Adam. If you really want, we can talk about this another time. Yes?'

And Adam stares at her squarely too, a flintiness in his voice that Eva has never heard before.

'Yes, Hanna. Let's do that.'

'What on Earth was all that about?'

'What on Earth was all what about?'

'With my mum. In the kitchen. You had a kind of weird moment when you were facing off against each other . . . Have you had an argument with her or something?'

They are tucked up in Eva's new double bed. On the side table is the heap of books that Eva used to have just lying around on the floor. It's like seeing someone you know out of context: your physics teacher at the beach, swimming trunks and knobbly knees. It doesn't look right.

'No, I just – I was just interested in knowing where your granddad's church was. Don't you think it's weird she wouldn't tell me?'

'Look, you know what she's like – she just clams up about that sort of stuff.'

'But doesn't it bother you? That she's told you so little about her childhood?'

'She's told me lots of things – She always used to tell me about what things were like in Germany when I was a kid – like, what food people ate, what games they would play. She's told me about the ruined church. She's told me loads of stories about my grandparents, too – she just doesn't like talking about the political stuff they were involved in.'

'I wasn't asking her about their political activities, Eva – I was just asking for an address.'

'Well exactly, you were probably bringing back memories of the Stasi with that inquisition . . .'

'You don't think it's weird she wouldn't tell me what her dad's church was called?'

'I think she doesn't like talking about that stuff, and she just wanted to change the subject.'

' . . .'

'Look, I mean, what are you even insinuating here?'

'Don't you wish she would tell you more about where she's come from?'

'I mean – sure. If she wanted to tell me, I'd love to hear it. But it's her choice how much she tells me. What she tells me.'

'Don't you have a right to know?'

'I have a right to ask. I probably will, one day.'

'But what if there's things she hasn't told you? Important things?'

'I think if there are things she finds it difficult to talk about, then it should be up to her to decide when she wants to bring them up.'

'And what if she never does?'

'Well. Everyone has a right to their secrets, don't they?'

Eva, who has been lying with her eyes closed, opens them to find Adam is looking at her. He seems about to say something, then stops, then seems about to say something again, then stops again, then thoughts left unsaid flit across his face like a thousand butterflies. She is about to ask him what he's thinking about, but suddenly he draws her to him in a desperate, tight embrace, and they lie there squeezing their bodies into each other as closely as possible, as though Adam is trying to comfort her for some loss that she is not aware of.

THERE WAS NOTHING different about Mühlenstraße for most of the walk from the S-Bahn, except that there was no traffic: the wide street stretched out, grey and quiet, in front of the Wall, like an echo of the death strip. Eva had been expecting throngs – she remembered the Iraq War demonstration, how all the Tube stations had heaved with people, how you had to fight to get a few metres further down the street. How exhilarating it had been, how pointless.

They walked along the so-called East Side Gallery: one of the last few remaining stretches of the Wall, now covered, on its eastern side, with graffiti of varying degrees of quality, where once the watchful eyes of the *Grenzpolizei* would have kept it a pristine white. On a normal day it would have been lined with a steady flow of tourists, but somehow word about the demo must have got out, or else the various strategically positioned police vans were off-putting, because there was hardly anybody around.

'I still don't get it, why the city council would be prepared to knock it down. I mean, even leaving history aside, even if you're looking at it purely from a self-interested economic perspective, surely this is one of the main tourist attractions in Berlin?'

'I think they would say they only want to knock down a small part of it.'

'But isn't that the beginning of the end, if you let that happen?'

'That is why we are here, no?'

Ulrich smiled at Eva. She smiled back. They smiled at each other a lot, these days.

Now they were approaching the demo: in front of them, a small group of people were busy unfurling a banner which read

MAUER RETTEN. Other than them, it was mainly policemen that you saw dotted at various points along the street – until they came to a small huddle of demonstrators in front of the offending section of the Wall. On the other side of it loomed a crane, poised to start its demolition work. A few cops clustered near to where Ulrich and Eva were standing; but the bulk of the police force was across from them, on the other side of the crowd, lined up already, riot helmets hanging ominously at their sides.

Standing in front of the Wall, the huddle of demonstrators looked small and unlikely to achieve much.

Ulrich touched a hand to Eva's shoulder, lightly, and led her into the huddle.

'There aren't very many people here.'

'Yes. I am surprised.'

Up against the Wall, a sign read: MR OBAMA, TEAR DOWN WALL STREET. Their fellow demonstrators were a mixture of faintly threatening young men clad entirely in black, many of them with scarves and hoods covering most of their faces, and placid thirty-somethings. Here and there, a toddler perched on someone's shoulders. Everyone was looking around in a sort of ill-defined bewilderment.

'I would have expected there to be more people here.'

'Me also. A lot of people signed the petition.'

'I guess – maybe it doesn't feel like a burning enough issue. Protecting a piece of wall that everyone used to want to knock down, when there are so many other problems in the world.'

'Maybe. Maybe it seems like it is not a big problem. But getting rid of history, just so some investor can make more money on luxury flats – I think it is a big problem, actually.'

'No sure, I agree – I'm just saying I can see how other people might feel there are more pressing issues, you know: people dying in Afghanistan, the financial crisis, climate change . . .'

'It is all part of the same problem: we let money ruin everything that is important.'

The crowd around them started to shift nervously. The lines of police were taking form, spreading out and stretching so that they were almost completely encircling the demonstration. Eva felt her heart rate leap upwards. One of the cops was talking into a megaphone.

'Achtung, hier spricht die Polizei. Wir weisen Sie darauf hin, dass Sie sich strafbar machen, wenn Sie den Platz nicht verlassen . . .'

'What's he saying? I can't make it all out.'

'That starting from now it is an offence to be here. It's bullshit, don't worry.'

A voice was shouting competing instructions at the crowd:

'Hinsetzen! Hinsetzen!'

Little by little, the demonstrators sat down on the ground. The police now formed a solid, towering circle around them. The officer with the megaphone put it down – he didn't really seem to care that no one had done as he said. For a while, a vigorous young woman led the crowd in a chant:

'KRAN WEG! KRAN WEG!'

'Kran weg! Kran weg!'

'KRAN WEG! KRAN WEG! KRAN WEG!'

Then eventually it died down, and people resumed chatting to each other. Eva kept the police line in the corner of her eye. They weren't so tight yet. You'd still be able to get out if you wanted to – but it wouldn't take them long to solidify into an impenetrable barrier. She found herself wishing that Adam were there, that she could seek refuge in the crook of his arm, solace against the firmness of his chest. Ulrich gave her arm a reassuring squeeze, and it felt strange, the touch wasn't quite right, the pressure of it, and Eva felt that she was on her own in a strange land, with a strange man, fighting a strange battle which was nothing to do with her, and now this ring of policemen around them, telling them that if they wanted to leave they should leave NOW, and was she really just going to stay here, waiting to be beaten up for a piece of concrete in a foreign land? She felt her chest tighten. But still, she didn't move.

Instead, Eva looked at the other people in the crowd. Two young men with dreadlocks, smoking a spliff. A cluster of people in animated conversation. A few nervous faces that reflected Eva's emotions back at her.

Behind the police line, a squat little man in a high-vis jacket was leaning against the Wall, a cigarette drooping out of his mouth, texting: the crane driver, his day's work interrupted by this small attempt to hold on to the past. He was beyond the border, in contact with the outside world, an integral part of it. And they were here, cut off by the barrier of the Law.

Just next to them was a young family, the parents about Eva's age and a little girl of about three, warmly wrapped up against the grey day. Eva worried about the girl: would the police take care not to harm her if they did close in on them all? Could kids that age cope with tear gas? Her parents didn't seem too anxious, anyway. They were keeping her entertained by teaching her political chants, clapping along to them. Eva looked at the mother and wondered what it would be like to be this German woman in functional rainwear teaching her child anticapitalist chants under the nose of riot police, and wouldn't it be wonderful to be that woman, rather than me, Eva, without my Adam.

And maybe her mother had been like that woman. But maybe not. Since meeting Lena Bachmann, she had imagined all sorts of fanciful explanations for why there might be no trace of her here. Sometimes the uncertainty made her reel: her mother could be *anybody*, which meant of course that she, Eva, could be anybody. Sometimes she thought it was all nonsense, didn't prove anything, probably just a file put back on the wrong shelf and hey presto everyone thinks the Krantz family never existed.

Sometimes she thought of telling Ulrich about it, but something held her back – she didn't want to let him get that close. This was still an affair for Adam and her.

Suddenly, there was a scuffle behind them, and the crowd

pulsated like a flock of starlings changing direction, some people half rising to their feet, others ducking instinctively or shouting warnings. Ulrich put his arm around her and pulled her into him, and she buried her face in the warmth of his chest, inhaled the comforting scent of him. Out of the corner of her eye, she saw one of the young black-clad men slip through the crowd, pursued by two officers, until he was forced into the police line and swiftly packed away into the back of a van.

The crowd relaxed, and Ulrich's hold grew softer around her, but he kept her against him, his hand sketching the faintest of strokes down her arm.

Eva felt both an urge to let herself sink into the tenderness that Ulrich was offering her and to push him off her, run away from him, even if this meant ending up in the back of a police van.

She gently disengaged from under his arm, turned her back to him slightly.

'Achtung, hier spricht die Polizei . . .'

The announcement-making policeman had picked up his megaphone again.

Ulrich leaned into Eva's ear.

'He's saying we can leave. The owner has agreed to stop all building works for today.'

The police line loosened, but stayed in place. The demonstrators looked at each other in some confusion.

'What – that was it?'

'Yes.'

'I thought demonstrations in Germany were meant to be really hardcore.'

'They can be.'

'This is really weird.'

Little by little, the people in the crowd rose to their feet. They chattered excitedly. The squat little man in the high-vis clambered up into the crane on the other side of the Wall.

'KRAN WEG, KRAN WEG, KRAN WEG!'

He gave them a wry wave and pulled some levers. The crane started to edge away slowly.

The crowd erupted into a triumphant cheer, then returned to standing around uncertainly. The cops had all dropped back now; some were standing lined up against the Wall, others had assembled into more amorphous configurations that echoed those of the protesters. The guys in black stood mutely on the sidelines, watching them with wary eyes.

'So – what – really? They're just going to stop?'

'At least for today. That's what he said, and I think they can't do anything if they have made this public announcement.'

'So we've won?'

'For now.'

It felt too easy. Eva watched the crowd dissipate like bacteria seeping out of an exploded cell. On the other side of the Wall the crane had stopped at a safe distance, and its rotund operator was climbing out of the cabin.

How could it be this easy? They should have had to put up a fight. They should have something to show for their struggle: bruises on their bodies, broken bones. She thought of Adam's bloodlust and let it well up inside her, the rage, let herself feel the need to hurl herself against the police, feel the crack of their batons against her shins. She thought of her grandparents and how their lives had been circumscribed by this Wall, how her mother's life had been divided by it, how this trauma had been handed to her, Eva, before she was even born, and now she didn't even know what the trauma was exactly, just that it was there, and she looked at all these people who were going back to their daily lives, who were from here, and yet they were treating it like it wasn't that big a deal – Oh OK, well that's done then, let's get out of the cold – and she thought, do you realize what this Wall used to mean, the impact it had on so many people, do you realize how important this is?

Ulrich stretched, yawned, looked up at the sky.

'So, maybe we go get some breakfast? There is a nice place not far from here.'

The police were piling into their vans, the crowd was almost gone, the squat crane operator was packing up. The sun was coming out, and the air smelt like spring. What else was there to do?

'Sure. Let's go get some breakfast.'

ADAM IS RECEDING. He puts his hands forward to try and grab hold of yours, but when you close your fingers they only meet thin air, and of course you should have expected this: he has no body any more. And he looks at you, his arms outstretched, and it's not clear whether his look is telling you to hold on to him or let him go, and the world shoots forward around him as he is catapulted far, far away from you.

And yet – simultaneously he stays right where he is, just beyond the clasp of your hand.

'**H**RMPH.'

'Mm.'

'Hng.'

Warm. Smooth. Arms. One under her head, hers over a smooth chest. A lot of arms. Another one of hers is underneath him. The world is dark, she hasn't opened her eyes yet, and she is not quite on the right side of consciousness. She isn't sure where she is – she could be anywhere.

'Gnrnhmph.'

She isn't sure who he is – but he is warm and smooth and smells of hot sand.

'Hello there.'

'Hm.'

He laughs. He shifts his body so that he can fold his arms more fully around her.

'Hmm.'

'Is there anybody in there?'

She lets the light in, and finds a pair of wide blue eyes looking into hers, an amused, cocked eyebrow, their noses almost touching . . .

'Adam.'

'Eva.'

They smile at each other. It could be weird, them being here like this, when they have been such good friends for so long – well, only a couple of terms, but it feels like much longer – but it feels fine. It feels good. Simple. Like they've known all along that this is where they'd end up. They kiss.

'D'you think you could move your arm a bit?'

He raises his body slightly and she tries to pull her arm out from underneath him, but it's gone to sleep.

'I think it's gone to sleep.'

'Oh.'

He picks it up and moves it for her.

'Gah!'

'Sorry.'

'Ow ow ow!'

She writhes and shakes her hand out, while Adam laughs and holds on tightly to her; they are in a single bed, so there's not much room for manoeuvre.

'Watch it, you're going to push me off the bed!'

'Yow! I can't believe you did that.'

'Well, at least it seems to have woken you up a bit.'

'Hmph.'

She turns into him, nestles her face into the curve of his neck; strange, how familiar this seems. How another person's body can be so distant, untouchable, and suddenly become something that is yours to touch and taste and bury yourself into, not really an extension of your own because it is so much more than that – so much more interesting than your own, for a start. She strokes Adam's back; he groans contentedly. She thinks about that night in Henry's house – so that was what he wanted, after all. It's amazing, really, that it took her so long to work out that it was what she wanted, too. How can she not always have wanted this beautiful, slender body, those beautiful blue eyes?

'I think there's someone knocking on your door.'

'Really?'

'Mm-hm.'

Indeed there is. Because Eva has preposterously big rooms – a bedroom and a giant study – it isn't always easy to hear what's happening at the other end of them. But there is, indeed, a knocking on the far door. She clambers over Adam, who harrumphs a bit as her weight passes over him, lets her feet slip on to the floor, stands. Whoa.

'Whoa.'

'You OK?'

'Yeah, just – shouldn't have stood up so quickly.'

She closes her eyes to collect herself, and hears another knock. She's enjoying being naked – it's so fun, especially when you have someone knocking on your door, like being on the phone while you're in the bath – until she opens her eyes and sees Adam is looking at her, which makes her grab for her dressing gown.

'Oi, I was enjoying that.'

'Hmph.'

She snatches the duvet and pulls it off him; in the brief instant it is uncovered, his bare body looks fragile, like a creature that is supposed to have a shell. Adam gives a girly shriek and pulls the duvet back over himself. Eva raises an eyebrow at him and bends down to kiss him before flouncing out to answer the door.

'Bloody hell, you took your time.'

Carmen is wearing enormous shades and an optimistically light dress, and holds a bottle of something bubbly by its sturdy neck.

'Get some clothes on, we're meeting the boys in, like, ten minutes. Champagne breakfast. Well, Freixenet. Henry's gone to Sainsbo's to pick up some food.'

'Huh?'

'Summer's here! We need to get to the river before everyone else does.'

'Oh. Right.'

Eva casts a dubious glance out of her study window, but Carmen's right: it's glorious out there.

'Cool, give me five minutes . . .'

Carmen is staring beyond her, wide-eyed, gawpy.

'Noooooo waaaaaaaaaay!'

'Hi Carm.'

Adam is in his boxer shorts and T-shirt, leaning nonchalantly against the doorframe to her bedroom. His hair is all flat on one side of his head and stands in erratic spikes on the other. He looks

315

very much like he has spent the night here. Eva's eyes meet his, and she feels a thrill at the understanding that passes between them, the delicate, wry smiles they exchange, their memories of the night before: partners in crime.

Carmen looks from Eva to Adam, Adam to Eva, her face passing through varying, complex shades of incredulity and delight.

'Well, well, well. Well done.'

'Thanks. Anyway. Um. I guess we'd better, er – get dressed.'

'Yeah, you bet you had. I can't wait for Henry to see this.'

'Well, aren't you going to come in, then?'

'Oh. Er. I don't want to . . .'

'Don't be ridiculous. You can just wait in here. We're not going to drag you into some kind of sex game or anything.'

'OK. As long as there aren't any sex games involved.'

Carmen comes in, and the door clicks shut behind her. Eva and Adam go into the bedroom and the door clicks shut behind them. Eva is very aware of these two clicking doors, of Carmen sitting between them, like in the air lock of a spaceship. Just yesterday there wouldn't have been this: they would either all three of them have been in the same room, or if any one of them needed privacy, that person would be alone. This is new, this privacy of two people. While she's rooting around in her drawer for a clean pair of knickers, Adam comes up behind her and encircles her in his arms, and they can feel the warmth of each other's skin through the thin dressing gown and boxer shorts. He kisses her, nuzzles her cheek. Adam whispers,

'You smell good.'

Eva whispers,

'I can't find any clean knickers.'

'Ah.'

'Will you judge me if I wear the same knickers as yesterday?'

'Not at all, I have very fond memories of them.'

'OK. Just don't judge me.'

'Tramp.'

'You haven't changed your boxer shorts, as far as I can tell.'

'Hm. Fair point.'

Then they are dressed, and they pick up Carmen, and they are out into a glorious day, the first day of summer, with the genteel sun beaming down on them, cyclists weaving lazily up to the university library, grass so lush you could kiss it, and the smell, the sound, the sight of life, life, life all around them.

Two swans have built a nest in the ditch by the side of the Avenue, and the cygnets hatched last week. It seems an unlikely venue for these noble creatures to set up house in, so muddy and shallow. The male in particular looks cramped, floating in the tight space between the nest and the bank, his head moving too slowly on the end of his long neck to keep up with his progeny, who are paddling off in all directions around him. Ugly ducklings, feathers all stubby and brown, looking half ungainly in the water and half made for it: you can see the frantic paddling that keeps them afloat – they haven't yet developed the skill to glide seamlessly above it.

'Blimey, it can't be easy to keep tabs on that lot, can it?'

'No, look: they never go too far.'

Sure enough, the mayhem is actually more circumscribed than it looks at first. The cygnets launch out, avid for the world, but as soon as they get to a certain distance from their parents, they turn back. Most of them have a range of about three feet; a couple don't dare to go much further than one and a half or two. And then there is one cygnet with a bald patch on one side of its head and an Iroquois-like plume of white on the other, who ventures to four, maybe even five feet, followed by the beady eye of its father.

Then, with a soft hiss, the female swan moves off down the water, and the cygnets fall into line behind her at neatly spaced intervals – except for the little Iroquois, who had further to swim back and now lags behind, its small body rocking from side to side with the effort of catching up. The father brings up the rear, massive, imperious.

'It's hard to believe those tiny things will turn into that, isn't it?'

'Yeah.'

'You know we're some of the few people in the country who are allowed to eat those?'

'Oh. Hello, Henry.'

'Special royal dispensation. It's only us and maybe a bishop or two who are given the privilege. They belong to the Queen, you see.'

Henry went to Harrow, and is full of such arcane knowledge. How to truss a pheasant. Who owns the land you're walking on as you clamber over a stile in Dorset. When to toast Prince Charles if you're having him over for dinner. How the country really works, its secret etiquette, centuries of rules that you wouldn't think still apply, but then you meet someone like Henry and you realize they do.

'Roast swan.'

'Pretty similar to goose, I imagine.'

'Right, come on, chaps.'

Henry strides off down the Avenue, his hulking form weighed down by two heavy Sainsbury's bags. Adam is lightly running his hand down Eva's shoulder blade in an unconscious gesture of affection. Now he and Eva and Carmen exchange glances, and the pressure of his touch takes on the firmness of awareness before he lets his hand fall. Henry turns round and hollers,

'Oi! Come on, you lot!'

Miraculously, they find an unoccupied spot on the riverbank: the gods are smiling on them today.

'You got the bubbly then, Carmen?'

'Yep. Did you remember to buy plastic cups?'

'I nicked some wine glasses from hall.'

'Oh, how refined of you.'

'For you, my dear, only the very best.'

Henry pulls an improbable selection of foodstuffs out of his Sainsbury's bags and hands them over to Carmen. She eyes them with the full suspicion of her Mediterranean heritage.

'Jesus, Henry, these look disgusting.'

'What's wrong with them?'

'No kind of food should ever be that colour.'

'I've had them before, they're delicious.'

'Spicy Peking Duck, *and* guacamole, *and* brie? Could you have chosen anything that went less well together?'

'I was thinking, you know, we could do a sort of tapas-y thing. Right up your street, surely.'

'Please don't debase the word "tapas" in my presence.'

'I'm only a poor English boy, Carm.'

'Next holiday, we're going to Madrid. I'll show you what tapas means.'

They're such an unlikely pair. Henry has the fleshy features of a man who has spent his youth playing rugby and will spend his adulthood drinking port; his physiology does not exist outside the English public-school system. Carmen combines the willowy form of her English father with her Spanish mother's olive skin; she is graceful and wild, whereas Henry has all the oafishness of his class. And yet anyone can tell they love each other.

'Right, who's up for some of this delicious nectar, then?'

Henry hands out the glasses of Freixenet, and is holding his own up in preparation for a toast when a loud squawking and splashing erupts behind him. He jumps, spilling fizz on to his chinos, and they all turn towards the noise. On the river next to them, three ducks are attacking a fourth in a flurry of beaks and wings. They rise briefly out of the water, each in turn, to give it a brutal peck before splashing down again. The bullied duck tries to retaliate, its slender neck twisting like a hose, but none of its blows ever quite hit home.

'Blimey. Talk about henpecking.'

'Yeah. I wonder what the duck's done wrong?'

'Guys. I mean – shouldn't we . . . ?'

Adam is on his feet, looking helpless.

'I mean, you know . . .'

He steps down to the edge of the water and stands there hesitantly for a while. Eva worries he might jump in. He tries to kick at the duck closest to him as it flies by on one of its pecks.

'Bugger.'

'Adam, mate, I wouldn't get involved.'

'But they're going to kill it!'

He turns towards them, scanning the things they have strewn over the grass in search of a weapon. Eva thinks how handsome he looks, with his body tensed for action and his eyes as focused as a hunter's. And how cute, how like a little boy, too, so distressed at seeing the ducks pick on each other.

He grabs Carmen's handbag, an elegant little leather number on the end of a long strap.

'Hey!'

'Hang on.'

He takes out its contents and sets them down next to the Spicy Peking Duck: a wallet, a tampon, a copy of Wordsworth's *Selected Poems*.

Henry picks up the book.

'You enjoying these?'

'Meh. Not sure. He's a bit namby-pamby, isn't he?'

'Really?'

Henry sounds disappointed.

'I quite like Wordsworth, actually . . .'

Adam swings Carmen's bag at one of the attacking ducks and lands a square blow to its side, which sends it flapping into the water. Its acolytes move away and regroup by the other bank of the river. They still look conspiratorial, though. The victimized duck has stayed put. Adam squats down and reaches out to it – 'Come on, ducky' – at which point it takes fright and flies a short distance away, landing again on the water at the foot of the bridge.

'Right. Can I have my bloody lunch now?'

Henry removes the wrappers from his luridly pigmented items. Just as Adam sits back down next to Eva, the racket starts again: the ducks have flown back to their victim once more, and now that they are under the bridge, their cries are amplified and distorted into harrowing sounds. Adam starts, but Eva lays a hand on his.

'You won't be able to get down to them there, Ad. And I don't think you're going to be able to stop it, anyway.'

'Goodness. I think they might be gang-banging it.'

'Shut up, Henry.'

Adam looks so downcast, so innocent with his golden hair in the summer sunlight, that Eva wishes it were possible to wrap herself around him entirely, smother him in her tenderness.

'Oh, Adam.'

She kisses him, takes his head between her hands and holds it to her chest. Adam wraps his arms around her waist.

'Bugger me.'

Henry looks at them in disbelief.

'Have I missed something here?'

'Er. Yeah. Kind of.'

'When did this happen?'

Adam and Eva roll into each other, giggling against the onslaught of questions and wisecracks from their two friends, so that none of them notice the sound of the carnage dying down as the fourth duck loses strength and lets herself sink underwater.

They have finished – well, Henry has finished – the Spicy Peking Duck. They have finished the guacamole, the brie, the Freixenet. They have explained what happened last night, how it all came to be, they have laughed at the innuendo, evaded the more indiscreet questions. Adam and Eva are out in the open, the wave of gossip about them has rippled around the college garden and is starting to die down now, and they do not know it but there is a handful of people whose hearts have been broken by that wave, distant admirers with crushed hopes that will never be revealed, and now Adam and Eva can recline on the banks of the river with her head on his chest or his head on her belly, and enjoy the warmth of the sun, of each other's bodies, of this new entity which is the two of them, together. Henry and Carmen are also reclining, in their separate spheres, but maybe they will be pulled together too, eventually, who knows? Right now Eva is propped up on one arm, and Adam is propped up on the other and sort of curled around her, and they are, as often happens, listening to Henry hold forth to the increasing infuriation of Carmen.

'I just don't really see how anyone with half a brain could possibly vote anything other than Conservative.'

'I don't see how anyone under the age of sixty-five can possibly vote Conservative! What's happened to your youthful idealism, Henry?'

'I'm very happy to say I've never had any.'

'Gah! I can't deal with talking to you about this.'

Eva nestles into Adam's arms, enjoys a warmth that feels familiar already, laughs at the sound of her bickering friends. They are quiet for a moment. They are all glowing in the sun, young, happy, lightly clothed. The college is beautiful; from where they sit, they cannot see a single building that has changed in the past four hundred years. Only the plants, the ducks, the people have changed. There will be nothing today but food, and drink, and conversation.

'This is perfect, isn't it?'

'Yeah.'

'I can't believe we're almost at the end of our first year already. It feels like we've only just started, but also like we've been here for ever.'

'Yeah.'

'It feels like this will last for ever.'

'**N**A DANN, WO war das . . .'

Lena – she was 'Lena' to Eva now, and despite the absurdity of her situation – a widow following the traces of her husband following the traces of her mother – she could see the funny side of it, how her imaginary love rival had turned into an accomplice sleuth who served her terrible cups of coffee – Lena handed over an open book, a wide spread of photographs.

'Here. This is the family who ran Sankt-Michaelis-Kirche.'

Eva gasps: inside the book is a photo of her, in black and white, looking very young. She's gazing straight into the camera, and her eyes are defiant and magnificent.

But Eva can't place this photo: she can't remember it being taken, and she can't remember the clothes she is wearing.

And then she realizes her face isn't quite right, the nose is a little too thin and the lips are a little too full, and the arch of the eyebrows is wrong too, and actually none of these features are quite hers although they look very much like hers, and suddenly Eva sees it's her mother she's looking at, her mother aged maybe seventeen or eighteen, she's never seen a photo of her this young before, but it is her, it's definitely her, staring into the camera with passionate splendour.

Next to this is a reproduction of *Disputatio* – though it is a different edition to the samizdat that hangs on her bedroom wall. But it also shows an article written by LUTHER.

Underneath the photo was the caption 'Hanna Stein, die Tochter der Steins, auf der Flucht in den Westen ums Leben gekommen' – 'Hanna Stein, the Steins' daughter, who lost her life trying to flee to the West.' Either the copy of the newspaper article was bad, or the photo was overexposed from the start, because she was covered in a hazy sheen that made her look evanescent, as though she had always been destined to disappear.

Eva's own gaze falls on to the next page of the book: a man and a woman, in their fifties, grinning on a church porch, surrounded by a small group of younger men and women. 'Johann und Maria Stein, Pastor der Sankt-Michaelis-Kirche und seine Frau, kurz nach ihrer Entlassung' – 'Johann and Maria Stein, the pastor of Saint Michael's Church and his wife, shortly after their release.'

They were the familiar faces she had looked at so often since her childhood, always set into a single expression in the only photo she had; but here they were different, proud, defiant, but also the same, definitely the same, definitely her mother's parents, definitely her grandparents, definitely recognized by Adam and handed over to her from beyond his grave.

'You know them?'

Eva looks up at Lena, dazed, words failing to come out of her mouth.

'Adam said this is not your mother's family, but it seems like you know them?'

'No – I mean yes – no . . .'

She looks again at the photographs. Perhaps she is mistaken? The faces stare back at her, their contours growing in and out of familiarity, shifting between strangers and blood relations, and for a while she thinks perhaps she is mistaken, it is just a passing resemblance and these faces are nothing to her, but no, it surely must be, the young woman is almost her and she can't believe Lena can't see it, but she doesn't seem to, and she can't believe Adam can't have seen it, so why did he lie to Lena?

He must have had his reasons.

'No. It's not my mother.'

She and Adam, lying to Lena, conspirators again. They have always been on the same side.

'But . . . the samizdat. I have a similar one at home. My mother, she wrote articles for them. Under the pseudonym "Luther".'

She points at the book, somewhat superfluously.

Lena smiles.

' "Luther" was the pseudonym of Thorsten Stein – the son of Johann and Maria.'

Reaching across the desk, she turns over the page to reveal a large portrait of a young man with eyes just like Eva's.

'He was very involved in the resistance. He still lives in Pankow.'

'And – how did Adam come across these people?'

'He saw these photos in an exhibition and thought they are your family. I can understand why, this woman looks very much like you. But after he went to visit them, he said he had been mistaken. He brought them a photo of your mother and her parents, and it seems he had been wrong.'

' . . . '

'Maybe he had wanted too much to believe that he had found your mother.'

' . . . '

' . . . '

'And – this Stein family – what's their story, then?'

'As I said, Thorsten and his parents were very involved in the resistance movement – this is why the parents went to prison. They were apparently planning on hosting a journalist from West Germany who the regime thought might be a spy, and Johann and Maria were caught when they met him. Someone informed on them. Their daughter, Hanna, did not seem to be involved in the work they did, though – actually, she was a very enthusiastic member of the FDJ, the Freie Deutsche Jugend, the Communist youth movement. But it seems she was not so happy with the regime either, or she got scared when her parents were taken to prison, because that is when she tried to escape.'

'And – what happened to her?'

'She died. She drowned in the Ostsee.'

'. . .'

'So, I think it is possible your mother knew her, and took on her identity. Especially now you say your mother claims to have written as "Luther". She must have known the Stein family.'

'. . .'

'If you want, I can give you Thorsten Stein's contact details. Maybe he will be able to help you understand what really happened.'

THESE ARMS ARE monumental – each one as thick as one of her thighs, almost. She's never been so close to such a strong man. But he kisses softly. Eva strokes the curve of a prodigious biceps. Ulrich spreads his hands on the small of her back, presses her gently into him. She thinks how many of Adam's slender arms could fit into this massive one: two, maybe even three. She thinks that Adam kissed differently, tenderly as well, sensually, but differently. Their kisses were sort of on the same wavelength, whereas this kiss is new; it surprises her.

'Are you OK?'

'Yes, of course. Why?'

'I don't know, I just . . . You must tell me if I go too fast, Eva.'

'It's fine, really.'

'I understand if this feels strange for you.'

'Honestly. It's fine. I like the way you kiss me.'

Ulrich smiles. It is a smile that lights up the world. He looks so serious most of the time, earnest, brows furrowed, dark brown eyes watching the world. And then this smile, a flash of Colgate teeth, mischievous crows' feet.

'I like the way you kiss too.'

He leans in again, and she tries to lose herself in the kiss, to not compare it to Adam's.

Ulrich pulls away, looks at her, traces the curve of her cheek with his hand.

'You are very beautiful.'

She laughs it off nervously.

'Don't be ridiculous.'

'Why do you say I am being ridiculous? You are very beautiful.'

Adam wouldn't have put it so earnestly. They had a way of communicating these sentiments to each other, through quips and innuendo and subtext, saving the earnest stuff for really special occasions. Though, she supposes, this is a special occasion. She needs to learn how to take a compliment.

'Thank you.'

'Would you like something? A drink, maybe?'

'No, I'm fine, thanks.'

'I fetch a glass of water.'

He gives her another kiss and stands up. Towering. And walks out of the bedroom like a panther, dark and muscular. She is hit by the force of him, and a sudden fear: how much stronger than her he is, and of course he won't, he wouldn't, but if he wanted to he could completely overpower her, she wouldn't stand a chance, and she tries not to think about how little she knows him, how strong he is. She tries instead to look at his bedroom, which she hasn't really had a chance to register since they tumbled into it snogging, eyes closed. It's weird – she's been sleeping in the room right next to this one all this time, and yet all she's seen of Ulrich's bedroom have been brief glimpses through a half-open door. And now here she is right inside it. Not where she should be, in her room. Adam's room. Adam in the room next door. She focuses on Ulrich's room. A lot of history books. A cluttered desk with an expensive computer screen angled towards the bed. The mattress she is sitting on – does no one have a bed here? – a dark-blue duvet cover, clean but crumpled. This man does not iron his sheets.

Ulrich comes back in, and again the image flashes into her head of his arms holding her down, and she has to look into his eyes, to remember she has seen them and they are kind eyes, but when she does she can't read them: they are too busy trying to decipher her. He stands there, she sits there, they try to read each other's eyes.

'You are sure you are OK?'

'Yes, really. Honestly.'

Ulrich sits down next to her, and the only way to escape this feeling of how strong he is, is to move into his body. She puts her head on his chest, her arms around his waist, and he enfolds her in his arms, kisses the crown of her head, so strong around her, but now it feels comforting and the fear is gone. She can hear the beating of his heart, his breathing, and she thinks how until Adam died she'd never realized how precious these sounds are.

'I can hear your heart beat.'

'Ah yes? Does it sound OK?'

'It sounds nice.'

She turns her face up towards his. His eyes have a striking green ring around his pupil that bursts into the soft brown of his iris; they are exceptionally beautiful when you look at them up close like this, a movie star's eyes. It was the opposite with Adam: the blue of his appeared weaker the closer you got to them, whereas from afar they looked like two dreamy little lagoons against his blond hair. Ulrich kisses her.

They kiss for a long time, and eventually they fall back on to the bed, trying to pull each other's bodies as close as possible. Eva is still wearing her jumper, thick and woolly, and she can feel what a distance it is putting between them, how its chunkiness is preventing Ulrich from being able to properly feel the contours of her breasts, but she's not sure how to get out of their current embrace to pull it off. She's not sure what the protocol is, really – she and Adam were so young when they got together. She puts her hand under Ulrich's shirt and feels the small of his back, the muscles that stretch majestically out from it. She wonders what it would feel like to have him on top of her. She turns on to her back, and pulls him over. She lets out a breath of surprise at the full weight of him.

Ulrich lifts himself off, makes to roll back on to his side.

'Sorry, I am quite heavy.'

'No, stay, I like it.'

She pulls him back towards her, and he lets himself down

slowly, so that she has the time to exhale gently, and somehow she finds a way to breathe under him. She can feel his erection pressing into her through both their pairs of jeans, and how her hips are arching towards him with a will of their own. Ulrich takes hold of her jumper and pulls it over her head, together with her T-shirt, and she undoes the buttons on his shirt, enjoying the feel of their smallness slipping out of the fabric, his warm skin underneath, the black hairs on his chest. Adam had almost no hairs on his chest at all, was only starting, in later years, to develop a few odd, straggly ones. She loved his smooth skin, and always thought that she would find a hairy chest unattractive; but she likes it on Ulrich, this light scattering around his pecs, and the line that leads down to his belly button.

She fumbles with his belt buckle, and this is just like it was with Adam: the fabric stretched so taut that it's difficult to get enough give to undo the flies. Ulrich undoes her trousers too, and then they pull them off each other, and the socks as well, and at last here they are, naked, warm skin against warm skin. She breathes him in. Ulrich kisses her mouth, her neck, her breasts, then looks up at her.

'So, what would you like me to do?'

Eva laughs.

'What?!'

'What would you like me to do?'

'Um. Well. Er . . .'

'What's so funny?'

'Um. I mean. You're just sounding a bit – you know – transactional.'

'I am sounding what?'

'I mean – it just seems a bit weird to be – um – giving you, like, instructions . . .'

'Why? I just want to know what you like.'

'I know. I guess – I'm just used to things being, I don't know, more instinctive . . .'

She bends towards him and kisses him, to put an end to the conversation – and so she doesn't have to see the confused look on his face. When she thinks about what she might say – well, the words, they're just so *technical* . . .

Mid-kiss, Ulrich pulls back, puts his hand on her cheek, stays put there. She can feel his face just an inch away from hers, hear him breathing – seriously, through his nose. It's like the breath of a thoroughbred. He stays like that for so long that she has to open her eyes, meet his gaze. He strokes her face – so lovingly. So earnestly. Lets his eyes rove over her features, then come back to her eyes. It's the same look Adam gave her sometimes – on the night he asked her to marry him, and then again on their wedding night, on the day she came back from the Congo and they both understood they weren't going to split up after all – a look that does not try to hide its feelings. It's extraordinary that Ulrich should have this look on their first night together. He must – he might – she thinks with some surprise – be in love with her. This is a terrifying thought.

Ulrich kisses her again, so she closes her eyes, and then feels him kiss his way down her body until his tongue is inside her, and she feels an absurd thrill of pleasure at the fact that this would have been exactly what she'd asked for if she'd answered his question but she's still glad she didn't actually have to say it, and some curiosity as well because this too Adam did differently, and then she's just lost in the moment.

Ulrich kisses his way back up her.

'Did you like that?'

'Can't you tell?'

' . . . '

'Yes, I did – I liked it very much.'

'It was OK? How I—'

'Yes! Can we – let's – can we not discuss it?'

'But why? I just want to—'

'I tell you what . . .'

331

She clambers on top of him, even though she could do with a bit more time to get her energy back. Anything to stop him dissecting his sexual technique with her. Ulrich seems to get the message, or at least to be sufficiently distracted by what she's doing to shut up. They tryst. He reaches for his bedside table, opens a drawer, produces a condom.

A condom. The last time she used one of those was, what? Five years ago? That time they were away for the weekend and she'd forgotten to pack her pills. And before that, well – not since the first few months of her relationship with Adam. Now, seeing Ulrich unroll the thing, she feels like such a novice: this is the world of adult sex, of mature partners in pleasure – responsible, guarded. She and Adam were children, really, all along. She wonders how many women Ulrich has slept with, what acrobatics. With the condom on, he tries to push into her, but it's not working: she can't open up, or he softens, or both. He tries, she tries, they fail.

'I'm sorry.'

Ulrich is lying next to her now, curling a strand of her hair around his finger.

'No need to apologize. I guess we are both a little nervous, no?'

He squeezes his arms around her.

'I am glad you're here, Eva.'

'Thank you. I'm glad to be here.'

He falls asleep so quickly, drifting away from her into heavy snores. She tosses and turns, kept awake by the closeness of him. Sometimes a change in his breathing will register one of her movements, but she never seems to be disturbing his sleep; he is either so oblivious to her presence, or so comforted by it, that nothing can shake him. Eventually she gives in to her sleeplessness and opens her eyes: and she looks at Ulrich, this sleeping man – this story that is about to begin.

'HAVE YOU GOT your video on?'
'Oh, er . . . Yeah . . . Hang on . . .'

Adam's voice pixelates into electronic noise, while Skype tries to heave an image on to the screen. It blips into being, blips out again, then Adam's face is there, frozen with his mouth half open while Eva tries to parse words from the ongoing crackle.

'Ad, on second thoughts I think video was a bit over-ambitious . . .'

'W . . . h . . . a – a . . . a . . . t – t – t?'

'Can you hear me?'

Parts of the picture start to shift, trying to follow his movements, while the rest of him remains stuck in the previous instant of time, so that he looks like he is dissolving into himself. Behind him, in contrast, their bedroom is in perfect focus: the slightly blue-tinged white of the walls they spent so many hours deciding on when they had just bought the flat, the print they brought back from Paris, a corner of the bedstead. Her home seems unreal to her after today.

'I . . . c – c – c . . . a . . . n't . . . ####'

'Adam, switch off your video.'

'####'

The Adam image is now frozen with eyes lowered to the keyboard, forehead leaning into the camera. He pings an instant message over.

You're breaking up.

Try switching your video off.

Adam's face disappears from the screen.

'#### . . . C . . . #### . . . y . . . o – o . . . u . . . h . . . ####'

'Hm. It's still pretty crappy. Can you hear me?'

'I . . . ####'

'I can't really hear you, if you can hear me.'

'I – I – I . . .'

'Adam, let's try both restarting Skype.'

'I – I – I . . .'

Let's try restarting Skype.

Yep.

He blips offline. She closes down on her side, waits a beat, then restarts the program. It takes ages to load, struggling to find a decent pathway to the internet. The light in the ceiling flickers menacingly – oh Christ, don't let it go out again. They've been battling electricity cuts ever since they got to this hotel, which normally wouldn't particularly bother Eva, but in this cloying heat, a night without air conditioning would be unbearable. It was out all this afternoon, apparently, so she returned to find her room solid with warmth; it's only just returned to a vaguely acceptable temperature. Although a power cut would give her a good excuse not to have to speak to Adam. Not that she doesn't want to, but these conversations really take it out of her when she's on assignment, the reminder of her normal, Western life too sharp a contrast to the new realities she's exploring, and plus she and Tom still have a couple of things they need to go over this evening. Her laptop starts ringing at her.

'Hi. Can you hear me?'

'Ah, yes. Can you hear me?'

'Yes. Great.'

'It's weird, it often helps to just restart.'

'Yes, I think it must set itself on a different channel or something.'

'There's kind of a weird hissing noise in the background, though.'

'Oh – that's probably the air conditioning. I will literally die if I turn it off, I'm afraid.'

'Don't worry, I can hear you fine. So, ####'

'So, how are things? Oh. You just broke up there.'

'Sorry, what was that?'

'You just broke up. Can you hear me?'

'Yes, I can now. Can you hear me?'

'Yes, but I didn't hear what you asked me just then.'

'I was saying how's Congo?'

'Hot. Like, you have no idea how hot it is here.'

'Make sure you drink loads of water. And that it's boiled.'

'Yes. Thank you.'

'But the job's going OK?'

'Yes, it's great. I mean – we're seeing some pretty rough stuff. But I think it's going to be a really good piece. Today was tough, though.'

'Really? What happened?'

Images, feelings flash through Eva. The anxiety about travelling down those roads, which can still be quite dangerous, especially if you're a high-added-value white journalist; Tom somehow sensing that, and putting a reassuring hand on the small of her back. His hand on the small of her back. The face of that girl, only twelve but already looking defeated by life, like she has seen more horrors than any form of happiness could make up for. The paradisiacal colours of the Congolese countryside, all luscious green and rich ochre and vibrant blue skies, the closest to Eden Eva has ever seen. Grace, who runs the crisis centre, her incredible vitality, the long black scar that runs down her arm, and the other scars she showed Eva when they were in the privacy of her small, stifling office. The children playing outside, laughing at Tom as he magicked sweets and rollerball pens out of various pockets. The stories that those women told. My God, the stories.

'We went to this village today, a couple of hours' drive away . . .'

'Really? Are you sure it was safe?'

'Yes, it was fine.'

'Are you sure? Because I was looking at the Foreign Office's website, and it recommends not leaving the cities at all at the moment . . .'

'Honestly, it's fine. The Foreign Office is always over-cautious . . .'

'Still, you know. It says there are still armed rebels out there, that hijacks are pretty common . . .'

'Well, I mean . . . yes, but we're careful, you know? We made sure to avoid the really dodgy areas.'

'Sorry, what was that? You broke up there.'

'Can you hear me now?'

'Yes. Can you hear me?'

'Yes. I was saying we're very careful. Plus Tom's been here before. He knows what he's doing.'

'Hm. Well. Just don't do anything stupid, you know.'

'No.'

'It's not worth it, Eva.'

'No. I know.'

' . . .'

' . . .'

'But, so, anyway, you were saying you went to this village?'

'Yes. It's this place where these women have set up a rape crisis centre—'

'####'

'Oh. Ad, can you hear me?'

'I . . . ####'

Ad, I can't hear you.

'I . . . c – c . . . aaaa . . .'

'Oh, hang on, maybe it's coming back.'

I can hear you, more or less.

'Ah, OK. Well, I can sort of hear you better, maybe let's wait and see if it gets better.'

OK.

'Keep talking, though, otherwise I won't be able to hear whether I can hear you or not.'

'O – o – o – o – h . . . Y . . . e – e – e – a – a – a . . . h – h – h'

Oh yeah.

This is so annoying.

'Yeah.'

'Oh. I think it's back. Say something?'

'Can you hear me now?'

'Yes. Great.'

'Great. So you were saying: some women set something up?'

'A rape crisis centre.'

'Oh wow.'

'Yes. It was a huge problem during the civil war – a lot of systematic rape.'

'Sorry, what was that? I didn't catch the end of your sentence.'

'A lot of soldiers would systematically rape the women in the villages they captured. There's basically a whole generation of women – well, several generations, in fact – who are collectively traumatized in this region.'

'Right. Wow.'

'Yeah. It was really intense. Some of the stuff they were telling me, Adam, it was just . . .'

'####'

'. . . it was just so shocking.'

'Sorry, what was that?'

'No, I was just saying, some of these women have some really shocking stories. I haven't really been able to process them yet, I don't think.'

'Wow.'

'Like, this one girl . . .'

'####'

'Oh. Can you hear me?'

'Y – y – y . . . e – a – h . . . N – n – no – o – o – o . . .'

'Um.'

'####'

'Adam?'

'Yeah.'

'Oh. Can you hear me now?'

'Yeah. Sorry, the line keeps breaking up.'

'Yeah, I know.'

'You were saying.'

'No, I – well. There was this one girl who was, I don't know, maybe fourteen or fifteen . . . And she was telling me she was gang-raped by this group of soldiers, they took her to this back room somewhere and just raped her, over and over again.'

' . . . '

'Hey – can you hear me?'

'Yes, I'm listening. It's horrible.'

'Yes. And so then she overheard them saying they should kill her, she didn't really know why. This was after they'd raped her, she was alone in the room and they'd all gone outside. And they were having this debate about whether they should take her with them or just kill her.'

'Jesus.'

'But then they came back in, and she must have been in shock because one of them took her hand and it was so cold that he thought she was dead.'

'####'

'Sorry, what was that?'

'No, nothing, I was just saying, wow.'

'Oh. And so anyway, they thought she was dead, and she just continued to play dead, and let herself be completely limp, and they chucked her into this other room of the house where there were the bodies of her father and two of her brothers – they'd all been killed when the soldiers arrived.'

'Christ Almighty.'

'Yeah. So then she had to lie there pretending she was dead for, like, hours, because she could hear the soldiers were still coming and going in the village, and she was worried they could probably see in to where she was. They'd thrown her across her brothers' bodies, and she said she could feel them grow colder, she could feel the blood on them drying, she could hear them making these weird sounds, emptying themselves, the stench. And the hardest was she had to be completely still, even when there were, like, flies crawling over her, she said it was almost impossible to resist the tickling of these tiny flies. And then even after the soldiers had gone, she said she lay still for a few more hours, just in case. Then when she got up at last – this is, like, in the middle of the night now – she realized she was the only person left alive in the village.'

'Wow.'

'Yeah.'

'Shit.'

'Yeah. It was – God, Adam, I mean, that's just one of the stories. It was so intense.'

'####'

'Oh. Adam?'

'####'

'Ad?'

'Ah, there you are.'

'Oh, yeah, I can hear you now.'

'I missed that last part, what were you saying?'

'No, I was just – I was just, you know, I was just saying it was all pretty intense.'

'Yes, it sounds like it.'

'But anyway. How are you?'

'Well – nothing as dramatic as that to report. Obviously.'

'Well, that's a good thing.'

'Yes. Although there is one thing I need to talk to you about – sorry to go from the sublime to the ridiculous, here . . . b – b – b . . . u . . . t – t – t . . . ####'

'Oh, hey, Adam, you're breaking up.'

'####'

'I can't hear you, Ad . . .'

Adam's voice and intonations pour forth in a garble, sound waves sliced up and broken down into their elemental ones and zeros and blasted halfway across the globe at her, but all in the wrong order. All in a muddle.

Adam, I can't hear you.

Oh.

'Can you hear me?'

I can't hear you either.

Maybe we should try another restart.

Yes, OK.

It's almost ten already. Tom will be back in the bar by now. She feels an urgent sense of every minute she is not seeing him while she is up here, and fights back an impulse to rush out of her room right there and then. His hand on the small of her back.

She is online again. She rings Adam.

'Hi there. Can you hear me?'

'Yep. Can you hear me?'

'Yes. Great.'

'Great.'

'So, yes, I was saying, I'm afraid the washing machine has died the death.'

'Oh. Fuck.'

'Yeah. Really annoying.'

'What happened?'

'Well, it stopped spinning the other day. I put in a load of clothes and th – e – e . . . y . . . c – c – c . . . a – a – aaa . . . m . . . e . . . ####'

'Er . . .'

' . . . soaking, and then—'

'Adam, sorry, I didn't catch that bit. What happened to the clothes?'

'Sorry, what was that?'

'Can you hear me?'

'I can now – just lost you for a few seconds there.'

'No, I was just saying I didn't hear the bit about what happened to the clothes.'

'Oh. Yeah, so I put in a load and it came out half dry and half soaking wet, basically. So then I tried putting it on again and the machine wasn't spinning.'

'Shit.'

'Yeah.'

'That's so annoying.'

'Yeah. And that's not the end of it. It's started pissing water now, too.'

'Oh you're joking.'

'I'm afraid I'm not. OK, I mean, pissing is maybe a bit of an exaggeration. But it's leaking.'

'Oh fucking hell.'

'Yeah. So I think . . . ####'

'Oh fucking hell. Adam, I can't hear you.'

' . . . two days or so.'

'Sorry, Ad, I didn't catch that last bit.'

'Oh. No, I was saying we kind of need to replace it pretty quickly, otherwise it's just going to leak everywhere and fuck up the basement flat.'

'Fuck. Yeah. This is so annoying.'

'Yeah.'

'I'm sorry I'm not around to help sort this out . . .'

'Well, you know, it's not your fault. But don't worry, I've arranged for a guy to come over next week – the only thing is we need to have the new washing machine to install by then.'

'Right.'

'Which pretty much means . . . ####'

'Say that again?'

'It means ordering it in the next couple of days, otherwise we'll never get it delivered in time.'

'Right.'

'Yeah.'

'How much does a washing machine cost?'

'Well, so, yeah, this is what we need to discuss – how much we want to put into it, and what model we want.'

'Hm.'

'I've looked into a few options already, I'll send them over to you and maybe we can talk through them . . .'

It's ten now. She told Tom she would be down in the bar by ten. She accepts the file transfer from Adam.

'Adam, I don't think I've got time to do this right now, I told Tom I'd meet him and I'm already late . . .'

'What – now?'

'Yes.'

'But it must be, like, ten your time right now.'

'It is, but we've got some stuff to prep for our trip tomorrow.'

'What, you're going off again?'

'Yes.'

'Where to?'

'To this place called Nkanwa.'

She hears the clatter of Adam googling Nkanwa.

'Where's that?'

'It's about a five-hour drive. Well, it's closer than that really, but we're going to stop off in a couple of places on the way.'

'You're sure it's safe?'

'Adam, we're being really careful, I promise.'

'I mean, Eva – look at the woman you met today.'

'I know. Believe me, I wouldn't be going if I thought anything like that was going to happen to me.'

'You're always sticking with Tom, right?'

'Yes, and we've got the fixer there, too. Honestly, Adam, it's much safer than whatever you're imagining.'

'Hm.'

'. . .'

'Well. Just make sure you're careful.'

'Yes.'

'What shall we do about the washing machine, then? Can we Skype tomorrow evening?'

'Hm. I'm not sure I'll have a great internet connection in Nkanwa.'

'I really need to order it on Friday, otherwise it won't get here on time.'

'Well, maybe you should just decide.'

'. . .'

'Adam?'

'Yeah . . .'

'Is that OK?'

'I mean – yeah, obviously, I can do that, but . . .'

'But what?'

'Well, you know, I mean, this is really a decision we should be making together.'

'It's only a washing machine.'

'####'

'Adam?'

'What was that? I didn't hear that last thing you said.'

'I said it's only a washing machine.'

'Well – yeah, but . . . It's a fair chunk of money, you know. And we want to get the right one.'

'We just need one that washes clothes properly.'

'Look, take a look at this list I've made and you'll see that's not as easy a call to make as it sounds.'

'Right, well . . .'

'How about you just email me what you think once you've had a look at it, and call me with the satellite phone tomorrow evening?'

'Those calls cost a fortune!'

'We won't need to talk for long, you can just tell me what you've decided.'

'I'm just not sure I'll have time to take a proper look at it before we leave . . .'

'Oh come on, Eva. It'll take you five minutes.'

'Well – OK. Fine. I'll try and email you before we go.'

'I don't want to be annoying, it's just . . .'

'Yeah, no, look, it's fine.'

'It's just . . .'

'Adam, honestly. You're right, it's just five minutes. I'll email you tomorrow morning at the latest.'

'OK.'

'I really need to get going now.'

'OK.'

'And I'll call you on the satellite phone tomorrow.'

'Yes.'

'Right. Well, have a good evening, then.'

'####'

'Say that again?'

'Oh. Can you hear me?'

'Yes, I can hear you now. Can you hear me?'

'Yes. I was saying be careful tomorrow.'

'Yeah. I will be.'

'I love you.'

'Yeah. Me too.'

'So. Bye.'

'Bye. Talk to you tomorrow.'

'Yeah. Bye.'

'Bye.'

She shuts Skype down. Quarter past ten. Eva grabs her room key and hurries out.

There is no air conditioning in the corridor. The air is so humid it sticks to your skin immediately, coating it in a veil of moisture that is indistinguishable from your own sweat. She tries not to rush too much down the stairs – she's going to be drenched enough as it is by the time she gets to Tom. She hopes the air conditioning is working in the bar. His hand on the small of her back.

The air conditioning isn't working in the bar. Eva can feel a red flush spreading over her face. Tom is sitting at the counter, chattering amiably to the barman – though she notices him clock her as she walks in, and puff up ever so slightly, even though he doesn't turn towards her until she is just a few feet away. He is glistening in the heat, too, but with his tanned skin it just makes him look even more sexy.

'Hey. Sorry I'm a bit late.'

Tom stands up and kisses her in greeting, perfectly unnecessarily. God, she must feel so sticky.

'Don't worry – I've been having a fine time chatting to Godfrey here.'

He pulls out a bar stool for her, and somehow manages to gracefully help her into it, taking her hand in his, his other on the small of her back.

'All well in Blighty?'

'Oh – yeah. Well. Actually, our washing machine just broke.'

'Ah. Annoying.'

'Yeah. I mean. It seems kind of surreal to be discussing something so trivial after what we've seen today, but you know . . .'

'Yeah. I know . . .'

He gives her one of those looks of his that seem to delve deep into her very soul, to blast through her eyes, her skin, the thin veil of consciousness that separates her self from his.

'Christ. It's sweltering down here.'

'Yeah. Godfrey was saying they've decided to cut the air conditioning everywhere except for the rooms, to make sure it doesn't overload the system.'

'Right. Well, I guess better that than it cutting out in the middle of the night.'

'Yep. It's working in your room, right?'

'Yeah.'

'Mine too. So actually, I was thinking, maybe we should just get a couple of drinks and go to my room – it's going to drive us crazy if we stay down here.'

'Yes, I don't think I can bear this much longer. I must look disgusting, I'm sorry.'

'You look gorgeous. G&T?'

'G&T.'

He smiles at her while Godfrey mixes the drinks, which look as crisp and cool as a Schweppes advert.

'Are you OK?'

'Yeah – sure – why d'you ask?'

'It's just – I know that days like today can take it out of you, you know?'

'Yeah – I mean, it has. Or, to be honest, I think I haven't quite come to terms with everything we heard yet. This drink is definitely more than welcome . . .'

'Cheers to that.'

'Cheers.'

'Come on, let's go up to my room.'

He guides her up the stairs and along the corridor, his hand on the small of her back again, his voice rich and warm in her ear, telling her to watch her step there, making jokes about the poor, harassed, antiquated air-con units.

His room is typical of the seasoned traveller, his suitcase open in a corner revealing neatly folded T-shirts and boxer shorts, his shirts hung up, his camera and computer recharging on the desk – only essential items unpacked, everything ready to be rebundled and carried off again in about five minutes. Eva looks at him, his perfect body, as he puts their G&Ts down on the table. Adam seems so far away. It occurs to her that she hasn't been thinking that it would actually come to this, which is perhaps a little naïve. That she hasn't properly thought about whether this is what she really wants.

She moves to the window and looks out at the dusty streets, weirdly clear because the pedlars and lepers and down-and-outs are discouraged from coming too close to the places Westerners stay. Tom comes up behind her, snakes a hand behind her waist and starts gently kissing her neck. Those hands, those forearms, brown and strong and manly. She turns towards him and he kisses her on the mouth, a gentle kiss, and pulls her in closer to him. She feels she could melt into him right now, she wants so desperately to extinguish any space between them. But then he kisses her harder. His mouth becomes foreign to her, his lips too wide around her own so that she can feel saliva beginning to trickle on to her cheek. His tongue barrels around hers like the drum in a washing machine.

'I – er . . .'

Tom twirls a strand of her hair around his finger, looks at her tenderly.

'Everything OK, babe?'

'I – Tom. I don't think I can do this.'

'Oh.'

'I'm sorry. I – I do want this. Kind of. But, you know . . .'

He takes her left hand in his, plays wistfully with her wedding ring.

'Yes. Precisely. I'm sorry. I shouldn't have come up here.'

'No, it's fine. I understand.'

'I'm sorry.'

'You're missing out, though.'

'I'm sure I am.'

He still has his arms around her, their pelvises touching. He lowers his forehead so that it is touching hers.

'You're sure about this?'

'Yes. Really. It's not right. I'm sorry.'

'Right.'

'I'll see you tomorrow.'

'Sleep well, gorgeous.'

He pulls her in and kisses her again, a gentler kiss that makes her reconsider her decision somewhat, and they must be standing there kissing for about five minutes before he thankfully starts barrelling his tongue around again and it is frankly disgusting, and she finds the strength to break away.

'I really have to go.'

'See you tomorrow.'

'Good night.'

She looks at him again as she closes the door to his room behind her: silhouetted against the clear moonlit night, his broad shoulders as taut and smooth as a soldier's, his wistful gaze. He is definitely the best-looking man who has ever wanted to kiss her.

Eva hurries back to her room through the fug of heat, her heart racing, her mind firing wild and incoherent thoughts. In the safety of the cool air, she switches on her computer and looks through Adam's list of washing machines. She ends up selecting a choice of two, at the more expensive end of the price range, which have the best environmental efficiency grades, and also a specific silks wash. Sleep eludes her for hours, and when her alarm goes off the next morning, it takes her a considerable amount of time to pull herself out of the incredibly graphic dream she is having about Tom, and what she might have missed.

SOMETIMES, YOU THINK you have forgotten him entirely: you close your eyes but cannot see him, you open up your ears but cannot hear the familiar voice.

But then you remember how his hand would run over the curve at the base of your spine, how his lips would deposit a kiss on your shoulder blade.

Despite death, you still know the truth of a touch.

IT TOOK A FEW moments for Eva to remember where she was, so that at first she thought the arm lying heavily across her stomach was Adam's, until she noticed its unfamiliar weight, and also recalled that Adam was dead, and that she and Ulrich had kissed yesterday evening, that they'd tried to have sex without success, then fallen asleep, or rather he'd fallen asleep and she'd lain there for ages without being able to fall asleep, except she must have done because then at some point in the morning they'd both woken up and had shagged with mind-bending intensity, fallen asleep again, and now here she was with this enormous arm lying across her. She pulled herself out from underneath it, thankfully without waking him. She looked at him. Up close, you could see the thick stubble pushing through his skin, his crow's feet, the other lines time had drawn over his face. The weather-beaten details that were part of what made him so attractive. Then she thought of how Adam was no longer growing older, how he would never get to feel the growing weight of years on him, and why was Ulrich allowed to? What made him so special?

She looked at him and thought how little she knew about him, and how strange it was to be lying naked next to a complete stranger, or at least a virtually complete stranger. She got up, stole his bathrobe and left the bedroom.

How strange, too, to be walking through a virtual stranger's flat, wearing their bathrobe, and helping yourself to a glass of water in their kitchen. These were gestures you did in your own home, in the home you shared with the man you had been married to for years and years, not in a flat you were temporarily renting a spare room in.

But then again, how much had she and Adam really shared? Why hadn't he told her about what he had found out here? Why had he lied to Lena about the Stein family? Was Adam really any more known to her than Ulrich?

She unscrewed the coffee jar.

'Hey. Hallo.'

Ulrich wandered into the kitchen, bleary-eyed in his boxer shorts.

'Oh. Hi.'

Eva hadn't seen his naked body in daylight yet; she resisted an urge to pounce on him.

He came up to her and folded her gently into his arms, nuzzled her neck.

'Have you slept well?'

'Mm. OK. It took me a while to get to sleep.'

' . . . '

' . . . '

'Is – are you OK, about what happened? I know that . . .'

'I – I don't know. I feel a bit weird about it, to be honest.'

'Me also.'

He stroked her hair. It was such a tender gesture. Too tender. Eva wriggled away from him.

'Anyway, I was going to make some coffee.'

'I will do it.'

He gave her a peck on the lips. Eva wiped away the dab of moisture he had left on her mouth.

Ulrich had his back turned towards her now. His pants were tight around two perfect buttocks; she followed the line of his spine as it curved down towards them, first with her eyes and then with the lightest touch of a finger. He shivered. Adam would have turned round immediately to kiss her, press her into him – but Ulrich continued to pile coffee grounds into the espresso maker. With every second his back stayed facing her, she felt more urgently the need to see him turn round, to be able to kiss him, touch him. Adam stands behind me, but I can't turn round to look at him; Ulrich stands before me, but won't turn round to look at me. She wanted to scream at the heavens, tear them down in fistfuls – she wanted to turn round and for Adam to be there and to be able to hold him, melt into him – she wanted to make love to this beautiful man in front of her, lose herself in sweat and skin and inarticulate noise. She dragged Ulrich back to the bedroom, kissing him quiet whenever he tried to talk, running her hands over the strands of hair on his chest, the curves of his muscular arms, and felt for once as though she was the one getting the upper hand over death, as though death couldn't touch her where she had got to now.

'SO, RIGHT ALONG HERE . . . There's something I want to show you just along this road.'

They turned on to Schlesische Straße. A phone pinged: Henry's, of course.

'Uh. Sorry ladies.'

They had to stop while he consulted the text message and composed a reply. Henry, bent over his tiny phone like a bear who had just befriended a sparrow. Eva and Carmen exchanged a 'What is it Georgie wants now?' look.

'All good?'

'Er. Yeah. Just – turns out that the museum isn't open today so she's gone to KaDeWe instead – I said to just text when she's back on her way over here.'

'OK, cool.'

'So what was it you wanted to show us?'

'Oh. It's just a bit further along here.'

They started walking again. Schlesische Straße was still covered in post-First of May detritus: shreds of flyers and banners in various forms of disintegration, countless empty beer bottles. Henry picked his way through them gingerly: he was wearing rather nice shoes.

'Sorry, Henry, I should have told you to wear more sensible shoes.'

'These are the most sensible I have with me, unfortunately.'

Carmen bent down to peer at them.

'They're very nice.'

'Yes. Present from Georgie. She recently discovered this guy who imports loads of handcrafted stuff from Italy, so there's been something of a revolution in my footwear.'

'Blimey. Can you still afford handcrafted stuff from Italy?'

'Ha! Not really. But Georgie's been difficult to rein in since she discovered that her credit card wasn't going to be taken away from her after all. Plus I kind of figure she's been really good about us having to sell the house, and this is a small luxury in comparison.'

'Plus you get a nice pair of shoes out of it.'

'Carmen's right, they're gorgeous. I just hope Berlin doesn't destroy them.'

'Yep, me too. It's funny, I was just thinking – it seems like a funny place for Adam to have fallen in love with the way he did, don't you think? I mean, he was so tidy, and this is – so *dirty* . . .'

'Maybe that was what he liked about it.'

'Yes, I think it might have been – well, I mean, you guys shouldn't assume it's always quite this bad. It's particularly dirty right now because of the First of May – but I think he liked that Berlin has this chaotic edge to it.'

'Despite being so unchaotic himself.'

'Hm.'

They cross over the canal, Eva, Henry and Carmen, the three old friends. It's good to have them here. Even though they are missing the fourth member of their company. They are missing him, but at the same time he is there, and not lagging behind them out of reach, but in and around them, in their minds, their conversation, in the coat that Henry is wearing.

'It looks really good on you, Henry, you know, Adam's coat.'

'Thanks. It has served me well. Though I have to say it's a little too warm for the weather today.'

'Yes, it almost feels like summer is on its way, doesn't it?'

'You're wearing all the wrong clothes, Henry.'

'I am. Always have. Now I mainly let Georgie decide for me, but she gets it wrong most of the time too.'

'Ah well. It's part of your charm, old banana.'

'Thanks, Eve. Good to know I can still rely on my old friends to take the piss out of me.'

She has not told them about Ulrich. She will not tell them about Ulrich, about his living, breathing body. She has made sure they won't meet. 'He's too busy,' she has lied. A small lie, to preserve the greater truth of her and Carmen and Henry and Adam, of her and Adam.

She scans the tarmac for where the Wall once stood.

'OK, so anyway, here we are . . .'

They had now reached the trace of the Wall. The line ran right across the street, between a petrol station and an unkempt park.

'So OK – these bricks are where the Wall used to be, so if you imagine, the street we just walked up was a dead end.'

'And this was West Berlin, right?'

'Where we've just walked up was, yes. And where we're standing now would have been East Berlin – or, to be more precise, the death strip.'

Now it's just cars whizzing by, and the petrol station, and, on the side of the road they're on, a sort of park with patchy bushes and thin trees sprouting into the spring.

In the park, unnoticeable at first because it was covered in a camouflage of graffiti, stood the ominous form of a *Wachturm*: a small concrete tower with a flat roof terrace. Eva, Henry and Carmen wandered up to it. People lay in the grass and drank beer.

'And this here would have been a watchtower. They were dotted along the death strip every few dozen metres.'

'It must have been quite boring to spend your days sitting up there waiting for something to happen.'

'Yes – boring and terrifying. If anyone escaped, the guards on duty were held responsible. You would basically be suspected of being an accomplice – unless you shot them.'

They stood in silence, watching the *Wachturm*.

'It's hard to imagine – that there was this impenetrable barrier here, so recently.'

'Yes – and actually, when you do see the bits of it that are still standing, they look really flimsy, like it's hard to believe they could divide a country so effectively – though of course, well, there was the death strip too . . .'

'There are still some bits left, then? Of the Wall?'

'Yes – though maybe not for much longer. I went on this demonstration, to try and save this one section from being knocked down so some investors could build some flats behind it – and they fobbed us off by stopping the work for that day, then just coming back a couple of days later and bulldozing through it before anyone could organize getting the protesters back out . . .'

' . . .'

'The city is changing so fast – even in the short time I've been here, I've seen whole new buildings appear out of nowhere.'

'Yes, I remember Adam telling me about that.'

'Have you guys – did Adam ever tell you about him trying to track down my mum's family when he was here?'

Carmen shakes her head.

'Nope.'

'Oh, he did mention something like that to me, actually – that he was thinking of trying to find them.'

'What did he say exactly?'

'Not very much – I mean, this was ages ago – just after I'd got together with Georgie, in fact. I remember because we'd met up so I could tell him about it. He was about to make one of his trips here, and he was thinking of trying to find out whether your mum might have any relatives that were still alive. I think he felt it might be a way of making you feel more connected to the place – of helping you get over your mental block about coming here.'

'He said I had a mental block about coming here?'

'Yes. Well, I mean – you did, didn't you?'

'What did Adam say about it?'

'He said he thought your mother put you off it – maybe not consciously or deliberately, but that she'd sort of passed on her trauma about the place to you.'

356

'Well. I suppose that's not an entirely bad analysis.'

'. . .'

'He stopped asking me, you know. To come to Berlin. He'd ask me all the time at first, and then he just didn't any more.'

'Well yeah, I think he got tired of hearing you say no.'

'And I think he was hoping you'd come round to it on your own – that one day you would be the one to suggest it.'

'. . .'

'But I think that's also why he started to look for your relatives. I think he hoped that if he could find some great-uncle or something, someone who would actually be able to tell you about your family, that that might make you curious enough to come over.'

'And did he tell you whether he ever found anyone?'

'No. We only ever talked about it that one time, when he was thinking about looking into it. Actually, I think I asked him, years later, whether he'd ever had any luck, but he just said it hadn't come to anything, and that he'd changed his mind about it being such a good idea anyway.'

'. . .'

'Why do you ask?'

'No, I just – I found . . . some notes he'd made. Nothing very substantial, but I was wondering whether he'd talked to you guys about it.'

She had been trying, repeatedly, to call Thorsten Stein, but he never answered. It was driving her crazy, and yet she couldn't tell her friends about it – the story still felt like something private to her and Adam, something she had to decipher before opening up to the world. Their last adventure together.

They started walking again. On a decrepit billboard, rising out of the May Day mulch, was a glossy poster for a new luxury apartment block.

'See, this is what I mean – there's stuff like this being built on every street corner.'

Henry was wrestling himself out of Adam's coat, sweat beading on his ruddy face.

'Blimey, it really has got boiling all of a sudden.'

'I wonder what it's like, for people who've lived here their whole lives – having their city be so radically transformed.'

'The ones I've spoken to don't seem that perturbed by it, weirdly. It's as though the Berlin they lived in as kids, say, is just a different place from the Berlin they live in now.'

'Like time is the space that divides you from it.'

'Time, politics. History.'

'And they don't feel the need to go back to that time, ever? That place?'

'I suppose only in the way we all do – we all have moments when we wish we could go back to when we were kids, don't we? Staying at our grandparents' or something. Or wishing we were back at university. And you get this pang that it's not possible, but you just have to accept it.'

'Yes. Wanting to turn the clocks back.'

Carmen's face has sharper angles, even compared to how it was when Eva left London – but apparently she hasn't been having too hard a time, all things considered. It's just they're all losing their puppy fat – even Henry, whose bulk has solidified into something more dense and streamlined – more substantial, somehow. Already, they are different from the people Adam knew – they are starting to outgrow him. Eva winces at the unfairness of it.

'I'm glad you guys are here.'

'I'm glad we're here.'

'Yeah, me too.'

Somehow, they had started slowly circling the watchtower again. On its far side, the slightly elevated surface of a steel door was barely perceptible underneath thick layers of graffiti, like a wound half healed under mottled skin.

'So, Eve – do you think you're going to stay here, then?'

Eva looks at her friends – the years they have known each other, the life they have shared, its peaks and troughs. Adam still alive in their minds.

'You make it sound as though you think that's what I'm planning on doing?'

'I don't know – you seem . . . You seem well. I mean, maybe it's just that time has passed . . .'

'No, it's . . . Well, yes. Time has passed. But it's more – I feel I have things to do here. With all this family stuff. I want to come home, though. I've been thinking – I don't know, maybe I could pitch Bill some sort of series about East Berlin. Or just do it for myself. I was thinking I could come back to London but still spend a lot of time here – sort of commute.'

'The Adam Lorvener system, in short.'

'A fitting tribute, no?'

'He'd certainly be excited that you're trying to find out about all this after all.'

'Yes.'

'It'll be good to have you back, anyway.'

'It certainly will.'

'Thanks, guys – it'll be good to be back.'

'Oh.'

Henry's phone again. It was in the pocket of Adam's coat, which he had draped over his arm, so it took him a while to wrestle it out into the open air. He walked away from them.

'Do you think Henry's OK?'

'How do you mean?'

'Well, you know, with losing his job and everything . . .'

'Oh, he's fine. I think in a way he welcomes it – it gives him an excuse to do something more interesting. I think it's been hard for Georgie, though.'

'Not the life she'd imagined.'

'No. But then which of us has the life they'd imagined?'

Carmen smiled ruefully.

359

'You're OK, though, Carmen – right?'

'I'm managing.'

'You'll be OK.'

'. . .'

Eva looks at her friend, and thinks: there is so much I don't know about you. What is it actually like, to have your own mind betray you? I don't know what you're really thinking, most of the time – I used to think I did, but I was wrong.

'Do you wonder, sometimes, what it would have been like if you and Henry had ended up together?'

'What? No!'

'. . .'

'Honestly, Eva . . .'

'I just think he'd be happier with you. And maybe you'd be happier with him.'

'What, you mean I wouldn't have gone mental?'

'. . .'

'That was always going to happen, Eva.'

'. . .'

'Better for Henry to be lumbered with a prissy posh girl than with a psycho, don't you think?'

'. . .'

'Besides. We don't know what goes on between them, behind closed doors. Georgie may seem dreadful to us, but do we really know her well enough to judge that? Henry must have chosen her for some reason.'

'Hm.'

'I think you and Adam just liked the idea of the four of us being able to double-date.'

'Ha! Maybe you're right.'

Henry was walking back towards them.

'It's Georgie. She's on her way.'

'Right, let's head back then – you've kind of seen all there is to see here anyway.'

They walked away, and crossed back over the scar of the Wall, leaving the mournful eye of the *Wachturm* to watch over them, Adam's coat swinging heavily from Henry's arm as the sun continued its warm rise.

DEATH IS THE only certainty, the great divider, the ultimate boundary of the self.

That you can die, and I not die.

That I can die, and you not die.

You wonder what this thing is, love, that hurls itself against this boundary like a sparrow flying at a pane of glass, not understanding its transparency, mistaking it for non-existence, wings flapping frantically in an attempt to gain the necessary momentum to burst through, hurtling at it again and again until glass cracks skull.

The dead hide behind their panes of glass, with their secrets, their closed books. What do they know about themselves that you do not know? What do they know about you that you do not know?

You fly into the glass again, it cannot be, it cannot be there, your thin, thin bones spread your feathers once more and you slice through the air, head down, determined this time that you will break through to the other side.

EVA LOOKS THROUGH the window of the S-Bahn as the landscape flutters between Plattenbau, shopping centres and the quiet façades of older residential streets. She still hasn't managed to get an answer from Thorsten Stein's phone number, but with Carmen and Henry now returned to London, there is nothing to stop her from simply going to the address Lena gave her.

They've had time to sink in now, the absurdities she has found out.

They thought she, Hanna, was dead. She, Eva, thought that they were dead, and they, her grandparents, thought that their daughter, her mother, was dead. Why did everyone think everyone else had died?

And how could Eva's mother have brought herself, with her fratricidal retelling of the family story, to rob Eva of an uncle? How could she have deprived Eva of her true name?

She gets out at Wollankstraße, and just after passing underneath the dark arch of the railtracks on her way out, crosses over the line of the Wall, the familiar double thread of bricks in the ground. Bloody hell. The bloody thing is everywhere. Stop it, she wants to scream, disappear, I do not need to be reminded of the carving up of this city, I do not want to see yet again the hurt it caused, the hurt it caused my family, and what is going on, why has my mother not told me the truth, why did Adam not tell me the truth?

Did Adam walk down this street? Did he step over this line of bricks on his way to see my uncle, as though they were nothing more than marks in the ground?

She presses the buzzer next to the name 'Stein', then when a crackly voice asks her who she is, is not sure how to explain, and stammers. She hears the sound of a door opening inside, steps coming towards her.

'Ja?'

The door swings open, and the man pushing it recoils when he sees her, gasps, as though she is a ghost.

'Und Sie sind?'

'Ich – um. Ich heiße Eva. Ich . . . Sind Sie Thorsten Stein?'

He nods, slowly. He is a tall man, with the heavy density that age confers on those who were muscular in their youth.

'Um. Er. I think – sorry. Ich glaube . . . Sie kennen meine Mutter? Vielleicht.'

'Ja. Das glaube ich auch. So. You better come in.'

Eva follows him in, through the dark hall of the building. She feels slightly irritated with Thorsten for having switched to English, irritated with herself for having fumbled words she is perfectly capable of speaking. But perhaps it is better this way. The world is feeling unsteady enough as it is – at least she has the solidity, the familiarity of English to hold on to.

They walk up a short flight of stairs, into the mezzanine flat. Its entrance is filled with a riot of shoes, coats, a pushchair and various toys: a small football, a chunky plastic digger. A voice comes from the next door down the corridor.

'Papa? Hey, was meinst du, wenn wir . . .'

A young woman appears at the door, and stops short when she sees Eva. Eva stops short too. The woman is blonde to Eva's brunette, but the curve of their eyebrows, the angle of their cheekbones, echo each other. They stare, as though they are recognizing something.

Then the young woman turns to Thorsten.

'Das hier ist Eva. Eva, this is my daughter, Johanna.'

'Hello.'

'Hallo, Eva.'

'Könntet ihr uns kurz alleine lassen? Wir müssen reden.'

'Ja klar.'

Johanna disappears back into the room briefly, then returns with a little boy and girl in tow. They totter out into the corridor, holding on to their mother's hands, and stare at Eva with curiosity. Eva stares back, and thinks that they are something to her, cousins removed in some way.

'So Eva, please, come and sit down.'

Johanna bends down to pick up a small jacket from the floor. 'Nice to meet you, Eva – maybe see you later?'

'Er. Yes. Maybe.'

They leave her to wrestle small arms into small coat sleeves – Thorsten closes the living-room door, gestures Eva to a sofa.

'So. Eva. You really are Hanna's daughter?'

'I – er – well . . .'

'You look just like her.'

' . . .'

'Did she ask you to come here?'

'No, she – she doesn't know I'm here. She doesn't even know I've found you. I – She never told me about you. That she had a brother.'

'So it is Adam who sent you?'

'So you did meet Adam?'

'Yes, he came here, maybe – I am not sure – some years ago. But you do not know this? It is not him who told you to come here?'

'No, I – well. Not exactly. He . . .'

' . . .'

'He died, you see. And . . .'

' . . .'

' . . .'

'I am very sorry.'

'Yes, no – thank you. And so – well, he'd never told me anything. About – about you, about my mother. But – looking through his papers, I found out . . . It's a long story, it doesn't matter. I'm sorry to just turn up like this. I did try to call your phone but I couldn't get through . . .'

'Ah. Yes – the number has changed.'

' . . .'

'Here.'

Thorsten hands Eva a tissue.

'And – you're my uncle. I never knew I had an uncle.'

'I never knew I had a niece – well, until Adam came here. Actually, we thought Hanna had died, trying to cross the Ostsee to get to West Germany.'

'Yes, I know.'

' . . .'

'So he's the one who told you? That my mother was alive, after all?'

Thorsten nods slowly. He does not say anything, and so Eva stays silent also.

Her eyes wander around the room. There is a dark mahogany cabinet next to her that reminds her of the furniture on display in the Stasi Museum in Lichtenberg. Behind its glass panels sit plates and dishes of various sizes, the family porcelain, gifted at weddings and passed down through the generations for everybody to spoon their soup out of. And then she notices a familiar twist of ivy and violets on paper-thin bone china, and there it is, the rest of the tea set, there are tea cups and a pot as well, and she wonders what Adam thought when he saw them, the precious heirlooms, the siblings of the one he smashed.

'I – my mother always told me that she was an only child. And that her parents had died very soon after she left East Germany, in prison, both of them . . .'

'Yes, Adam told me. This is . . . well. A quite fanciful story, let us say.'

'But – why would she make something like that up?'

'For this, you should ask her – I cannot answer in her place. This is what I told Adam, also. But I can tell you, of course, what happened here. I do not know exactly how Hanna told you the story?'

'She said that your parents were betrayed – that they were meant to be helping a journalist from the West, who was barred from entering East Germany, to come to the GDR incognito. And that someone had tipped the Stasi off about it so that as soon as he arrived, they were all arrested.'

'Yes. This is all true.'

'And then, she said, she was worried that things could get dangerous for her too, because she'd been writing these samizdats that were distributed throughout the church groups, and so she had to escape. And soon after that, her parents died in prison – her mother from a heart attack, and then her father committed suicide when he found out.'

A half-smile has budded on Thorsten's lips, dances over them like a shadow. The crinkle at the corner of his eyes suggests he is struggling not to let it grow, unfold into mirth.

'Actually, I wrote those samizdats.'

'Yes, I found out recently.'

'I'm sorry. For you, of course, this is difficult – this story, it must have been hard to hear. But I find it funny to hear that Hanna pretended to have written my articles. She was very opposed to them, back then.'

'. . .'

'But yes, I must explain to you. Though first I have to say this: you must understand, these were complicated times. For people like us, our family, people who were opposed to the regime or were connected to the resistance movement – it made your life difficult. Not always in a very dramatic way – of course, some people were put in prison, some were killed, even – but your life could also be made difficult in small ways. People would find they couldn't get a job, or they would come home and discover they had no – how you say, in the kitchen, Geschirrtücher . . .'

'Tea towels?'

367

'Maybe? Tea towels? To dry plates and things, yes? So, someone would come home and find suddenly all the tea towels have vanished from the kitchen. And so you would know: the Stasi were here. They are watching me. We were not suffering like Russians in the Gulags, but it was a strange time. You often could not know who to trust. And I must say for Hanna, also, she believed in the GDR. In the Socialist project. It was maybe a way of rebelling against the family – In a family of dissidents, the only possible rebellion is to be for the regime, oder? But she believed in it for good reasons. She wanted a just world. And we knew about suffering, even if we were born after the war ended: this city was in ruins, everyone we knew had family who had been displaced or killed. In school, we were taught that Socialism was the way to avoid this happening again, and she believed it.'

'But – then why did she leave?'

Thorsten looks away from Eva, ponders, ponders. She feels like a child, not understanding, waiting for the grown-up to make sense of information that she isn't old enough to grasp yet. She looks at him, and thinks, my *uncle*. I should have memories of being bounced on those knees as a child, a gallopy-gallopy-gallopy-gallopy into a ditch!

'I was the one who was supposed to leave. The plan, over the Ostsee – it was arranged for me. But when my parents were taken away, I decided not to go. I would not have been able to help them from outside the GDR, and of course then we did not know if they would be released soon or not. But the plan was arranged, and then Hanna said she will go instead. It surprised me, because as I said, she loved the GDR, she believed in it being the way to build a better society. But she suffered from her family connections: she could not get a place at university, she was being punished as a way to try and get my parents and me to stop our political activities. And so, I thought this was why she decided to leave: because in the West at least she would be able to study.'

Again, the faraway gaze: Thorsten remembering things that little Eva is not privy to.

'You say you "thought" this was why she left, though?'

'After the *Wende*, we – me, my parents – decided to look at our Akten – the files the Stasi kept on us. And there we realized that she had been the one who told them about the journalist. Where they were going to meet him, what their plan was for him to travel around the country without being noticed. It was the first time my parents were involved in something so obviously illegal – up until then, they had mainly just been running discussion groups at the church. And it was Hanna who told the Stasi. It was because of her that my parents were arrested.'

Thorsten pauses and looks up at her. His eyes are dark, almost black, just like hers, just like her mother's. The family eyes.

'She had done a deal: she would get a place at university, if she became an IM – you know? Inoffizielle Mitarbeiterin, an "unofficial employee" – the people who watched other people for the Stasi. This was not so unusual. A lot of people did it, and sometimes it was difficult to say no. But still. Hanna was spying on her own parents.'

ADAM IS IN the sunshine. She is not sure where. He is laughing, and gold flecks his hair.

His eyes reflect the blue of the never-ending sky.

She walks up to him, and he puts an arm around her shoulder, and she feels the weight of his bone and muscle, the warmth of his blood.

She's not sure where they are or when, but it is a sunny day and they are in love, and Adam is there, by her side, pulling her into him and smiling enigmatically.

EVA WAS FROZEN, unable to react to what Thorsten had just said – this demotion of her mother from freedom fighter to informant. The pettiness of it, double-crossing your family for the sake of a place at university.

Despite her lack of reaction, Thorsten seemed to read her thoughts.

'You must understand, Eva, these were not easy times – and your mother was young, still a teenager. She felt her family was ruining her life, she felt it was unfair. And probably she was not expecting that our parents would get arrested.'

'. . .'

'I think that when our parents were taken away, she panicked – realized that what she had done was very serious. Or maybe she thought this GDR project is not so great after all. Or she felt too guilty. Maybe all of these things. And maybe it was easier to leave.'

'But – why did you think she'd died? And why did she lie to me about her parents dying? Why lie about you? Why change her name? Why – why break off all contact?'

'I asked myself this question a lot, especially after Adam came here. You need to ask her, of course – but I think probably she was ashamed. At that age, things can seem black and white. I imagine she paid the smugglers to tell us she was drowned. That she was worried we would find out she was the one who had informed on us.'

'. . .'

'We didn't find out, actually – not until after the *Wende*, as I said. So, in a way, she was worrying for nothing.'

'. . .'

'But I was very angry when I found out that she had pretended to be dead. When Adam told me this. To disappear . . . This was very painful for my parents. Much more painful than finding out she had reported on us for the Stasi. This, I think, we could all understand, in a way. She felt she had no options – and also, she thought she was fighting on the right side. Just like we did. But for my parents, to lose their daughter – this was terrible. Until they died, they suffered from this.'

Eva feels the pain that has been hers since losing Adam. Imagine giving this pain to your own parents, letting them think you were dead. Imagine poisoning their lives with this grief.

'When did they die? Were they still alive when Adam came to see you?'

'Yes.'

' . . . '

'Yes. But they were both very ill, they were not strong. I was worried it would be too much of a shock for them, to find out that Hanna was alive, had always been alive. That she had abandoned us.'

' . . . '

' . . . '

'So you didn't tell them?'

'No. I'm sorry, no. I was angry, also. That she could have done this.'

' . . . '

'Probably I was wrong not to tell them. But anyway, my parents died quite soon after Adam came here, maybe a few months or so. They died quite close to each other.'

' . . . '

'Sometimes I think what Hanna did not realize was how much my parents loved her. How much we all loved her. She thought these politics were dividing us, but they weren't. We still loved her. I think if she had realized that, she would not have disappeared like she did.'

'You know – she told me a lot about your parents. In a modified version of the story, it seems – but she loved you all too. She loved you so much she pretended to have done what you did. Maybe she was trying to rewrite the story, to make it into what she would have liked it to be.'

'Yes.'

'And . . . Did you tell Adam not to talk about what he had found out?'

'I told him he should decide, of course, what to tell you, what to tell Hanna. But that for me, I did not need to see my sister again. I was so angry.'

'. . .'

'I'm sorry.'

'. . .'

'But I see things differently, now. Time has passed, you cannot be angry for ever. Or I cannot, at least. I am glad now that he has led you here.'

'. . .'

'Welcome back to your family, Eva Stein.'

W HEN SHE GOT back, Ulrich was having a nap.
And it was at precisely this moment that her mother chose
to call her back. Eva stared at the display flashing on her phone,
felt it vibrate heavily, urgently in her hand. 'Mama.' 'Mama.'

Eva had tried to call her as soon as she'd walked out of Thorsten's front door, fired up with anger at everything she had
discovered, brimming with questions she wanted to fire at her
mother like bullets. But the journey back had numbed her. She
felt overwhelmed, now, by her new history, not ready to receive
yet more new answers to new questions.

And besides, she didn't want to have to keep her voice down
for fear of waking Ulrich next door, afraid of him overhearing
what should be a private matter, strictly between her mother and
herself.

She rejected the call. They would have this conversation soon
enough.

For now, she walked softly into the bedroom. Ulrich was in his
jeans and T-shirt, half under the covers. His hair was fluffed into
dissonant angles, and his face, smoothed by sleep, seemed age-
less. And looking at him, a thought occurred to Eva: did he know
about what Adam had found out?

And anger rose inside her again.

Her new family history was like a crack that had opened up
under her feet, just wide enough for a body to plummet through,
and unfathomably deep. She couldn't let herself fall into it, not
yet. It turned out she had not been told the true story. It turned
out Eva had an uncle, and cousins. It turned out her mother, far
from being a refugee dissident, had betrayed her own parents to

the secret services of her country. It turned out her mother had lied to everybody, in guilt and shame. It turned out her mother had let her own family, her own parents, her own brother, her own flesh and blood, believe she was dead. It turned out she had murdered them, in turn, in her mind.

All the way back from Pankow, she had thought of how Adam would have had these thoughts – poor Adam, not knowing what to do with them. Wanting to surprise her with good news – a distant relative, some family heirloom to replace the tea cup he had broken – and finding himself uncovering an uncomfortable truth, a story that was meant to remain untold. Being told by Thorsten to leave it alone. Thinking he needed to think about it. Thinking he had more time.

But not having that time. Poor Adam, who had been robbed of time.

Ulrich shifted in the bed, turned towards her.

'Hey.'

And she felt herself suspect him of having hidden the truth from her, felt herself ready to hate him.

Although Adam was the one who had been snooping around. Adam was the one who had decided not to tell her.

But she and Adam – they had a history. They knew each other as well as two individuals can, perhaps. Adam had made a call that had been his to make.

And Adam was dead, and she loved him. It is hard to stay angry with the dead for too long, when you love them.

Whereas Ulrich.

'Did you know about my mother?'

'Huh?'

'I've just been to see Thorsten Stein.'

'. . .'

'My uncle.'

Ulrich's body dropped ever so slightly, as though the air had been let out of it.

'You knew.'

She felt her hands tense into claws that could rip his eyes out, a boiling rage in her belly.

'Why didn't you tell me?'

'Eva . . .'

'You knew . . .'

'I didn't know what to do.'

' . . .'

'I didn't know, what is the right thing to do.'

Ulrich doesn't know her. Ulrich is a stranger. He has no right to have known these things about her, to have withheld them from her.

'I talked about it a lot, with Adam. When he found out. He really did not know, should he tell you or not. What it will be like for your mother. What it will be like for you. He wished he had never found out all this.'

'And so the pair of you decided it was better to keep little Eva in the dark, not upset her too much?'

'Eva. I am not even knowing you then. And actually, I thought he should tell you. I do not think hiding the truth is a good thing.'

' . . .'

'But this was Adam's decision. This was his discovery. And when you came here . . . I felt it is not my place to go against this decision.'

'But all this time . . . We've been talking about things, I've been telling you things, and you knew they weren't true.'

'Yes, I hated that. But tell me, what I should have done?'

'You talked to Adam about all this. The conversations you had with him – he should have been having them with me.'

'I'm sorry. But it was his decision.'

'I need to get some air.'

Eva bolts out of the flat, and out into the city. The day is waning, returning Berlin to what seems its natural state: dark, shadowy, hard to decipher.

An energetic charge down the street is enough for her body to rid itself of the anger she feels for Ulrich. He has, after all, only been caught in the crossfire. He is, after all, in the grander scheme of her life, not necessarily that relevant, a blip over the past few months that may not settle into anything permanent, that may not be here to stay.

Whereas Adam.

Eva wishes she could talk to Adam about what she has just found out – what he found out. She wishes she could hear the tale of his gradual discoveries, what he thought when he first saw the photo in the exhibition and recognized her mother, whether the world seemed to collapse around him like it has around her. She wishes she could tell him that he knew her so well, better than she knew herself, better than anyone will ever know her again. She wishes she could tell him that he loved her so well.

She pauses for a moment and looks up at the buildings around her, the warm glow of lights being switched on in kitchens and living rooms, all of these lives, these families, and she wonders how many of them are like hers, broken, riven by history, by secrets and lies and untimely deaths.

Quite a few, probably. This is Berlin, after all.

She starts when she looks down again and sees, about twenty metres ahead, Adam crossing the road towards her. Her reaction is so electric that he pauses and meets her eye, and in that moment assumes the form of a man whose height and body shape look vaguely, from a distance, like Adam's. They hold each other's gaze for a moment. Then the man walks on, and away. From behind, he really does look exactly like Adam, so much so that Eva has to stop herself from calling over to him. But she doesn't. Instead, she says to herself, maybe if he turns around, he will really be Adam. If he turns around. Maybe. If he turns around. And he can take her with him.

But Adam doesn't turn around. He doesn't take her with him.

EVA FUMBLES IN her pocket for the change she's just been given at the newsagent's. Puts in 50p, since when you call a mobile the money bleeds away at haemophilic speed anyway, punches in Adam's number.

'Hello?'

'Where the hell are you?!'

'Ah. Yes. I'm running late. Sorry.'

He doesn't sound like he's even outside.

'Are you still at home?'

'Um. Yes.'

'Oh fucking hell, Adam. Couldn't you have called me or something?'

'I tried, but you'd gone already. Now see, if you had a mobile . . .'

'Oh, so I should get a mobile just so you can flake out on me at the last minute?'

'I'm not flaking out on you, I was literally just leaving – now. I'm leaving now.'

A closing door bang, and the whoosh of street air in the background.

'Well, it's going to take you at least half an hour to get here, though, isn't it?'

'Um. Yeah. I might not get there in time for the start of the film, actually.'

'No, you clearly won't.'

'Hm. Sorry – it's just I suddenly realized I had to send off an email today about my summer placement and—'

'Yeah, whatever. Listen, I'll just go to the cinema and see if there's anything on a bit later – just come and meet me there.'

'Yes, great, good idea. OK, I'm going down to the Tube now. I'll be as quick as I can.'

'Yeah. Great.'

What a twat. Eva gets the hell out of Embankment, cursing the ditherers blocking the entrance to the station, and walks up the steps on to the Hungerford Bridge. She sneaks a peak at the Houses of Parliament through criss-crosses of steel before a train clatters past, blocking them from view. Then she turns to the skyline of the City, unreal in its cleanliness, cranes sprouting all over it like a fungal infection. It's a beautiful evening, still light despite the time, and she has to struggle a bit against the atmosphere of springtime good cheer spilling over from the South Bank: the tinkle of buskers, the wafts of caramelized nuts. Bloody Adam. Does he just take her for granted now or something?

She usually loves this part of her trip back to uni from her parents': getting off the train at Waterloo and wandering up to the river to kill a few hours – she has resolved to always leave herself a few hours – before catching the Tube to King's Cross. She loves the South Bank, with its bare concrete and promise of music, art, theatre, the refinements of world-class cultural events. She loves the hours she has spent here on her own, watching a show or whiling away the time with a book in one of the cafés.

But to Adam, who lives just a short Tube ride away, this probably seems like a shamefully obvious place to have suggested as a meeting point. And what possessed her anyway to stick her neck out like this and suggest they go on basically a romantic date, thinly disguised as a hey why don't we make the trip back up to Cambridge together, we can share a taxi from the station that way?

It is all so unbelievably embarrassing.

And it's been weird, really, since they got back from Henry's ridiculously extravagant holiday pad. She replays all the elements in her mind, as she has done already so many times. Those two weeks in the South of France, so perfect, how well they were getting on, a bond forming between them without her even noticing it. That last evening in his room, the feel of his hand as he tended to hers, the look in his eyes that was already asking her if she wanted him to kiss her, and she comically oblivious to it, the penny dropping only when she got back to her own room, and it would just have seemed too weird to go back at that point . . .

Except maybe she should have. Maybe she's blown it now. Since they returned, they've been unable to recapture the magical complicity that united them during the holiday, and while her desire for Adam has kept on growing, he seems to take another step back from her every time they meet. Maybe she wounded his pride by not kissing him that evening. Maybe he wasn't really that interested anyway, just thought it would be fun to have a bit of a fling over the holiday. Or maybe she misread the situation completely and he actually didn't want to pull her at all. Oh, who knows? Who knows what goes on in other people's minds?

'Hi. So. Hi. Sorry – I'm really sorry.'

Eva lifts her eyes from her book to find Adam towering over her in the dusky sunlight, looking breathtakingly sexy.

'Oh. Hi.'

'Are you still angry with me?'

'Well, now that you've reminded me . . .'

'OK, so, look, tickets and drinks and everything on me, and for the record it really wasn't my fault, I just suddenly realized today was the deadline for sending off my form for this place- ment, you know . . .'

'Well, not tickets – the other screenings are all too late for us to make our train.'

'Oh. Oh well. Why don't I get us dinner then?'

'I guess we could do that.'

Eva necks the last of her wine and gets up; Adam gives her an awkward hug which fires through her body like quicksilver. She feels herself blush and hurries ahead of him; a friendly hug, he obviously doesn't expect anything to happen between them, she just needs to calm down about the whole thing.

They walk off towards Gabriel's Wharf, and somehow the mildness of the evening, the hand-in-hand couples that pass them by, dissipate Eva's anger, relax the air, break down the invisible barrier between them. They walk in silence, but it's a relaxed silence. Every now and again, they look at each other and smile, and Eva wonders if Adam feels it too.

'I'll have the Pizza Napoli, please.'

'And I'll have the Quattro Stagioni.'

'Certainly, sir.'

'God. I can't eat Quattro Stagioni.'

'Really? I love it.'

'I mean, I know, I can see how in theory it should be nice, but we always used to get them frozen when I was a kid and they were kind of disgusting, I can't really escape from the taste-memory of it.'

'What was it like, when you were a kid? You never really talk about it.'

'Huh? What do you mean I never talk about it?'

'Well – just that. You've never told me much about your family life.'

'Well – has anyone? I mean, I don't know much about your family life.'

'No, but yours is really interesting. I mean, what was it like, with your mother? What was it like not being able to go and see your family and all that stuff?'

'Well, I mean – it was just the way things were, you know? And anyway, we didn't have any family left in Berlin. It was just my grandparents, and they died way before I was born.'

'What – and your mum really had no other family?'

'No. Well – I don't think so. Definitely no one she was in touch with.'

'And she's never wanted to go back?'

'No. I think the whole thing was quite traumatic for her, to be honest. I mean, imagine leaving home when you're that young – pretty much the age we are now. And then her parents dying in prison . . .'

'How did they die, though, exactly? I mean, it's kind of weird they *both* died in prison, isn't it?'

'Yeah, tell me about it. Apparently my grandmother died of a heart attack – from the stress, I guess. And then, well – when my grandfather heard, he committed suicide.'

'Jesus.'

'Yeah.'

'. . .'

'. . .'

'And – I mean. OK. Don't take this the wrong way, but – you're sure that *is* what happened?'

'What do you mean?'

'Didn't you say your grandparents were, like, dissidents?'

'Are you suggesting my grandparents were bumped off by the Stasi or something?'

'Well, I mean – isn't it a bit fishy? That they both died in prison? And, I mean – it's not like your mother was there to check that it was true . . .'

'Jesus! We're not living in a John Le Carré novel, Adam.'

'Well, no, I know, but—'

'No, but actually, in all seriousness, I know what you mean. I have wondered that myself – but to be honest, my mum has never suggested there was any foul play involved, and I think she would if she did think that. I mean, she left East Germany because she was a dissident herself . . .'

'Oh really? What had she done?'

'Oh, she like, wrote these pamphlets. Stirring up trouble, I guess.'

'Wow. That's pretty cool.'

382

'. . .'

'Sorry, I mean, obviously "cool" is a silly word to use. I mean, clearly she was taking huge risks, and paid a big price.'

'Yes – it's something I'm proud of, I guess. That I come from a line of people who really fought for what they believed in, who put their lives on the line. It makes me feel like – like I should honour that. Try and find something worthwhile to do with myself, you know. God, does that sound really pompous?'

'No, not at all! It's an admirable goal. I'd like to find something worthwhile to do with my life, too.'

'Well yes, I mean, of course, everybody does. And, I mean, I'm not trying to big myself up here – I'm talking about all this crazy East German stuff now because we're on the topic, but it mainly feels quite remote from my life, to be honest. At the end of the day, I had a pretty average middle-class English upbringing.'

'Well – with a family that was pretty different from other people's . . .'

'I guess so . . .'

'Don't you ever – I mean, don't you wonder?'

'Wonder what?'

'What your grandparents were like – what your family's story really is. I mean, for all you know they might have been involved in the craziest stuff, fighting against the East German government . . .'

'I don't think they were really fighting as such – just, you know, dissenting.'

'But still, don't you wonder what that means? What they did?'

'I guess, yes, it would be interesting to know. It's just – it doesn't seem that urgent somehow. It feels more urgent to . . .'

To be here with you. There is nothing more urgent than that right now.

' . . . to – to – you know. To study, hang out with you guys, work out what I want to do with my life.'

'But mightn't it have something to do with that? You've just said it's knowing about what your grandparents and your mother did that makes you want to do something meaningful. Isn't it all a part of who you are? The language, for example. Isn't there a part of you that feels weird, not speaking your own mother's language?'

'I think you're kind of idealizing this foreign part of me – I'm very English, really, Adam.'

'But that's what I'm saying – maybe you're not. Maybe if you looked into it . . .'

'Well, how would I look into it, as you put it?'

'Go there – to Berlin. I'll come with you, if you like.'

'Um. Right.'

'We could go there for a year, even – after we've graduated.'

'Aren't you meant to still be studying medicine for, like, the next gazillion years?'

'I'm sure I could spend one of them in Berlin. My German's pretty good, I could study medicine there.'

'Where on Earth has this idea come from?'

'I guess – I've just always wanted to do something like that. To live abroad for a while. And I love Berlin – it's, like, such an exciting place to be at the moment.'

'Hm.'

'You're not tempted?'

'I don't know. I'd need to think about it.'

'Well – do. It would be a cool adventure to go on together.'

They leave the restaurant, woozy from the house red. It's a balmy evening, and the South Bank is bathed in warm, nocturnal colours, hushed voices drifting around them as the evening draws to a close. They stand for a while, undecided, looking at each other. Adam is a head taller than her, slender but strong, his gentle blue eyes twinkling with a hint of mischief, his blond hair ruffled and sexy. There couldn't be anyone else.

'Shall we go and sit down?'

They walk over to a bench facing the river; Adam puts his arm around Eva as they sit. She lays her head on his shoulder. Before them, the Thames, inky blue under the moonlit sky, creeps towards the sea with the habit of centuries.

And then they kiss.

Acknowledgements

Thank you, thank you, a thousand times thank you, to:

My wonderful agent, Laura Macdougall, for believing in this book when it was still a baby and coaxing it and me along the long road to publication.

My equally wonderful editor, Suzanne Bridson, for believing in this book once it was a surly teenager, and helping me turn it into a presentable adult; and everyone else at Doubleday and Transworld.

Charlotte Maddox and the whole team at Tibor Jones for their enthusiasm and support.

My comrades-in-arms, Jeremy Tiang, Sarah Day and Angela Clarke, for feedback and pep talks and general sharing of the highs and lows of the writing life.

Jim Crace, for words of encouragement uttered at exactly the right time.

Alison Flood née Bone, Johann Hari, Kerry Hudson and Nick Harrop, for help in navigating the publishing industry; Tim Moore, for providing a roof over my head on countless 'business trips' to London; and my many other friends who have had their ears chewed off with book-related anxieties, and without whose reassurance and support I would not be able to function.

My family, and above all Mum and Dad, for more than can adequately be expressed in a page of acknowledgements; Rich, for being incorrigible; Tes, for keeping him in line; and James, for giving him a taste of his own medicine.

And of course, of course, with all my love, Stefan, thank you for everything – and Aloys, for being such a good sleeper and generally extraordinary little human being.

Kate McNaughton was born and raised in Paris, and now lives in Berlin. She read English and European Literature at Cambridge and filmmaking at the European Film College in Denmark. She is also a documentary filmmaker and translator. This is her first novel.